HIDDEN FIRES

A "Holmes Before Baker Street" Adventure

By

Jane Rubino

Hardcover ISBN 978-1-80424-091-5
Paperback ISBN 978-1-80424-092-2
ePub ISBN 978-1-80424-093-9
PDF ISBN 978-1-80424-094-6

Published by MX Publishing 335 Princess Park Manor,
Royal Drive, London, N11 3GX
www.mxpublishing.com

Cover design by Brian Belanger

"I assure you that the most winning woman I ever knew was hanged for poisoning three little children for their insurance-money."
Sherlock Holmes to Dr. Watson, in *The Sign of Four*

"Could this be my stern, self-contained friend? These were hidden fires, indeed!"
Dr. Watson, in *The Hound of the Baskervilles*

PROLOGUE

Whenever I wade through the pedestrian sea that flows 'round Charing Cross Road, I smile at the indifferent stragglers who pass the façade of Cox and Co without so much as a sidelong glance. For behind that façade is a room, and within that room is vault, and inside that vault is a battered tin box, my own name, *John H. Watson, MD Late Indian Army* yet discernable upon the lid, (though the years have worn away the gloss of those painted letters and laid a film of tarnish upon the tin.) Hidden away in this humble box are tales of such adventure, corruption and yes, even romance, that would 'rouse all but the most hardened passer-by from his ennui. These are the untold adventures of Sherlock Holmes.

No thread can be traced that binds this patch-work canon into a harmonious whole, for woven among the unpublished triumphs are the unsolved puzzles destined to remain half-told tales, the outright failures, some daring exploits and several diabolical histories whose publication awaits the passing of some noble name before I may be liberated from a vow of secrecy.

And one that is all of them together.

This remarkable tale has lain upon my desk for a week, a week of sleeplessness and indecision, while I ponder its destiny. To keep it would risk its discovery – for I must always assume that the day may come when the contents of this tin box will find their way to light. To destroy the

4

document would be to destroy one of the most extraordinary narratives of my friend's career – indeed, one which may have shaped what he was to become. We all have some chapter of our lives that we would not wish opened to the eye of the public. In this, Sherlock Holmes is no different from any man. And yet, Sherlock Holmes is unlike any man I have ever known.

What ought I to do? I cannot leave it where it lies. I cannot toss it in the fire.

ELIMINATE THE IMPOSSIBLE

CHAPTER ONE

To be a friend of Sherlock Holmes was no easy task. For nearly two decades, I had been subjected to his fits of ill temper, his untidiness, his noxious chemical experiments, the frequent disdain he had expressed for my literary endeavors, his aversion to society, his contempt for anything akin to love or sentimentality. Yet, for every provocation and eccentricity I endured, there were a thousand rewards, not least among them was the singular honor of being the confidante of a great man, and the chosen partner in his extraordinary adventures.

So many years' worth of adventures will take its toll, however, and it was in the particularly vile January of '02 that a spell of wet and miserable weather, and the aggravation of my old injury, brought on a severe bout of rheumatism. My incapacity was such that it should not have escaped Holmes' notice, yet it did escape him, so deeply preoccupied was he with some private matter of his own. For the first fortnight of the year, I do not believe he addressed more than a dozen words to me, while his mood shifted from sober reflection to restless agitation. At last, I did venture to ask, "Is it a case, Holmes?" but his "No" was uttered in a brusque tone that it put an end to all further enquiry on the subject.

I was too hardened to such conduct to be offended by it, and resolved to suffer in silence until whatever cloud bore down upon him had lifted. And yet, it was not two days later that I sat down to breakfast to find an envelope beside my tray. "I think that London will not do for your latest rheumatic spell," Holmes observed, as he sat before his untasted breakfast, smoking a cigarette.

I opened the envelope and found that arrangements had been made for a first class passage to Aix-les-Bains, and six weeks' lodging at the Grand Hotel de l'Europe.

"But, Holmes – !"

Holmes cut short my astonishment and protests with a wave of his hand. "Go and restore yourself to health and usefulness. I am lost without the old Horatio."

And so, I left London for that celebrated spa, where I found that Holmes had arranged the very best of accommodations. For more than three weeks, I enjoyed the benefits of the therapeutic regimen, and if the weather were no more fair than that of London, the society provided a considerable compensation.

And yet, as my health was restored, I could not help reflecting upon how neatly Holmes had got me away from London. His weeks of anxiety and unrest suggested that a matter of some importance had preoccupied him, a matter that he had no wish for me to share, and this led me to recall the one other occasion in our long relationship when he had contrived to remove me from the scene of danger because he had anticipated an encounter that might mean the forfeit of his life – and mine, perhaps, if I were at his side. I remember standing upon the path above the falls at Reichenbach as if it were yesterday, sick with the knowledge that my friend had not survived his final engagement with Professor Moriarty. Had I once more allowed myself to be lured from the scene of danger while my friend confronted some deadly antagonist alone? No – I did not believe that I could be duped twice in such a fashion, and yet I could not be easy in my mind until I knew for certain. Better to return to London and be proved wrong than to have my fears confirmed by a dire newspaper announcement in France.

I arrived in the middle of a bitter afternoon, and found our sitting room deserted, but with marked signs of having been occupied that day. I confess to feeling equally foolish and relieved, and summoned the page to ask after the whereabouts of my friend.

"I don't know, Doctor. Since you've been gone, he's been odd, very odd. And then, just this morning, that note there," he nodded to an envelope upon my friend's desk, "was handed up and he ran his eyes over it and tossed it aside and charged me to fetch him a cab. I heard him call out, 'Newgate Prison, cabby!' and he has been gone ever since."

"Newgate? Surely you are mistaken."

"Clear as bells," he repeated, with an emphatic nod.

I thanked the page and dismissed him, and settled into a chair to ponder what sort of summons may have drawn my old friend to Newgate. I devised a number of scenarios, each one more elaborate and dangerous than the one before, until the curiosity to know what he was about overcame the fatigues of my journey. I looked at the envelope upon the desk. It would be wrong, of course, to open my friend's private correspondence, and yet, I could not help but think of Reichenbach, and told myself that, by committing a small transgression, I might forestall a greater tragedy, and that it was, therefore, morally justifiable.

The address had been penned in a very simple hand, and what the envelope contained was neither a summons nor a threat – it bore today's date and a list - a very peculiar list, at that.

Oaken doors, iron-cased, half-latticed
Washing basins, copper
Kitchen utensils, various
Blankets
Flag-staff
Oaken pulpit
Wooden stools and benches
Surplus scaffolding lumber
Death masks, various.
Rope

To anyone but a Londoner, this curious inventory would have no significance, but there had been talk for some time, that Newgate would soon be closed down – indeed be torn down – and this inventory would seem to confirm it. It appeared to be a list of prison paraphernalia to be offered for public sale.

Yet, what interest could my friend have in any of this grim detritus? He had, over the course of many years, assembled a respectable library on the subject of criminals and sensational crime, and collected a number of singular relics, but nothing so common as a prison's copper basins and wooden stools.

I set the note aside and went down to summon a cab, and directed the cabby to Newgate. There, I asked him to wait across the street from the principal entrance, and there I sat for a quarter of an hour, feeling more foolish with the passing of each minute. I had just made up my mind to return to Baker Street when I saw Sherlock Holmes emerge from a side passage not thirty feet from where I sat. He was carrying a bundle wrapped in a white cloth under one arm, and upon the other rested the gloved hand of a very striking young lady.

At the pavement, the lady detached herself from my friend and strode to the curb, whistling sharply to a four-wheeler. This provoked a laugh from my friend, and when the vehicle drew up, he handed her in and climbed in after.

Had *this* been the reason I had been hurried off to Aix-les-Bains? Had Holmes wanted me away from Baker Street and out of London because there was a private relationship of his own that he wished to pursue? No, such a thing was impossible. It argued against everything I knew – or believed that I knew – about Sherlock Holmes. Yet, had I not more than once seen a suggestion of hidden fires, a current of deep emotion which coursed beneath his self-command? I confess that my curiosity was so great that I sank to playing the spy, and calling up to my impatient cabby, I directed him to follow my friend's vehicle.

Their four-wheeler drew up at the Savoy Hotel. Holmes alighted and ordered it to wait while he handed down his companion, and they stood for some minutes upon the pavement in animated discourse. While they were thus engaged, I was able to get a better look at the lady. She was tall and slender, with a countenance that was an interesting study in opposites. There was an almost medieval asceticism in her scholarly forehead and delicately pointed chin that presented a striking contrast to the sensual mouth, dark, animated eyes and abundance of copper-colored hair.

It appeared to me that my friend was attempting to press upon this lady the parcel that he had carried from Newgate, while she, with equal determination, was insisting that he keep it.

At last, it was the lady who prevailed and – to my astonishment – stood on tiptoe to kiss him upon the cheek before she disappeared into the hotel.

The exchange brought home to me all of the awkwardness of my situation. What business had I in shadowing my friend? Was he not entitled to a private acquaintance? I had spied upon him shamelessly.

The cabby called down to me impatiently and I looked up and realized that my friend's four-wheeler had departed. I paid my fare and dismissed the fellow, and then took a long ramble from the Strand and up Regent Street almost to the park, until, no wiser and much wearier than when I had set out, I returned to Baker Street.

There, I found Sherlock Holmes seated before a fresh fire, his long legs stretched out from beneath an open newspaper. The object that he had carried out of Newgate lay upon the settee, still shrouded in white cloth.

"Watson!" he tossed his paper aside his paper and rose to shake my hand. "The page told me of your arrival! Nothing wrong, I trust? You were to be in France another fortnight at least."

"No, Holmes, I'm quite well."

"The spa has done its work, then! It must have, if you are spry enough to hurry back to town, pass half the day rattling off to Newgate and then, I surmise from the state of your boots, ramble 'round London for another hour or two."

I expected his expression to be one of rebuke, or perhaps amusement that I had been such a clumsy spy. But his gaze was very solemn, with a hint of melancholy. Holmes could be sulky and brooding, or grave and reflective, but I had never before seen anything approaching sentimentality. Now I saw a trace of it; more than a trace, perhaps.

"I beg your pardon, Holmes."

"There is nothing to pardon, Watson. You saw my companion, I presume?"

"Yes."

"A striking young lady, is she not?"

"Yes, quite striking."

"Nature has put her together by combining the best features of her father and mother, while discarding their imperfections." His gaze softened once more. "Beauty and brilliance are a formidable combination, Watson."

"How did you come to be – what I mean is," I stammered, "- is she a recent acquaintance?"

"I have known the lady longer than I have known you." He regarded my expression with a faint smile. "I suppose," he added, in a tone of resignation, "that you want to know the particulars."

"Not if you don't wish to make them known to me."

"Prevarication doesn't suit you, Watson."

"All right, Holmes. Who is she?"

"Her name is Eden Henrietta Holmes."

Holmes regarded my astonished expression with a chuckle. "No, she is not my flesh and blood. But it became necessary for her to adopt a name, and I flatter myself that mine is as good as the next man's. Have you ever speculated, Watson, that if we could choose the members of our family, how much more congenial the relations with them would be?"

I thought of the sad history of my brother, and the estrangement that had resulted from his intemperance and degeneracy.

"We all have secrets, Watson. We all have some territory of the soul that we guard against the scrutiny of the world. But I suppose," he added, "it is a rare secret that is hidden forever. If you will give me a few hours, I promise you a tale that will compensate for the forfeit of two more pleasant weeks on the Continent."

CHAPTER TWO

Holmes reclined in his chair, one leg crossed over the other, his hands resting on his knee. "Do you recall our first meeting, Watson?"

"As though it were yesterday. Stamford brought me 'round to Bart's. You were in one of the chemical laboratories."

"Yes. I had come to London in late spring of '77 and taken a room at Montague Street. Close quarters, but I didn't much care where I hung my hat, as I spent most of my time at the British Museum or the book stalls, or the laboratories at King's College and Bart's.

"It was to the latter that I made my way one Monday in late December of the following year. It is not the season when chemicals and cadavers are uppermost in one's mind, but I liked having the laboratory and, more particularly, the dissecting rooms to myself whenever possible. Access to the cadavers had become particularly difficult. They were in short supply and the best ones were reserved for the students of surgery and anatomy. It was said that the more enterprising of them would often bribe grave-diggers at the pauper burial grounds to notify them when any particularly desirable remains had been interred.

"'Anything interesting?' I asked of the porter.

"'A young girl's brought in, the sort of odd 'un that the students of surgery have a taste for, but my orders are to admit no on but the carrion hunter, so she's locked away and

14

only until the mother comes by funds for a box. I'm sorry, lad, for it's the kind of fantastic thing that you'd like to have at. If we were alone, I might risk it, but...' He gave a nod toward the laboratory, and I heard a hushed exchange from within.

"'It's the Lord Craden and an elder gentleman,' he said, lowering his voice. 'I heard mention of the Earl of Granville, but the older fellow looks an ordinary tradesman to me. Some of your titled folk are getting a bit common, in my opinion.'

"I thanked the man and approached the laboratory.

"I will, Watson, briefly describe the *dramatis personae* as they appear in the narrative. Lord Henry Craden was the only child of Lord Warrington, 'Craden' being the family name. Lord Craden was, at this time, twenty-six or twenty-seven years of age and in possession of all that nature, birth and good fortune can bestow upon a man, with a first-rate brain in the bargain. Yet, for some unfathomable reason, he seemed determined to squander it all, drifting from the lecture halls, to his clubs, to the dens where he indulged in the sort of depravity that will undo even the best of good looks and good fortune – and, indeed, he appeared somewhat worse for wear that morning. He sat in his shirt-sleeves, perched upon a stool, with a silver flask and a couple of phials of blood before him. His sleeves were rolled up and a handkerchief had been knotted above one elbow. I saw that his arm was dotted with needle marks, some of them quite fresh, and as he and the elder gentlemen spoke, Craden plunged a syringe into his flesh.

15

"His companion viewed this performance with disapproval, but he made no attempt at a reprimand, inhibited, perhaps, by a sense of his inferiority. Though he was many years Craden's senior – I put his age at sixty or thereabouts – he was clearly no earl, unless the rank had got quite common indeed. His speech had the studied formality of a modestly educated fellow who wishes to emulate his superior, but the callosities upon his thumbs and index fingers were suggestive of manual labor.

"'The apparatus has been fitted up and should be ready within a week – no more than two – but there are some small adjustments which cannot be made until the last,' said the elder. 'Nothing will go awry because I have not done *my* part – and I will keep Knowles in check as far as I can.'

"'Knowles can drink himself into remorse afterward. Or into the grave. It's all the same to me,' was Lord Craden's reply.

"'If I may be so forward, sir, mind that *you* do not do so beforehand. Everything depends – ' Here, he spied me standing in the doorway, and said, 'We are keeping this young man from his work.'

"'I am the intruder,' I said. 'Craden.'

"'Holmes,' he greeted in return. 'Mr. Holmes, Mr. MacInnes,' he introduced, casually.

"The gentleman and I shook hands. 'I see that you are a cobbler, sir,' I remarked.

"His heavy eyelids raised in surprise.

"'Your boots are hand-tooled, and of superior fit and quality which are considerably more fine than either your frock coat or your cravat. The peculiar callosities of your hands, and the staining upon your fingers is suggestive of one who works in leather.'

"'You are very astute, young man,' he said, and handed me his card. 'I see that you are not a medical student.'

"'From my appearance?' I asked.

"'From your sobriety,' Craden interjected, with a wry laugh. 'Holmes is a mystery,' he added. 'Nobody ever knows quite what he is about.'

"MacInnes donned his overcoat and hat and bade us good-day, and Craden returned to his occupation in earnest, drawing another phial of blood from his vein.

"'So, what mystery brings you here today, Holmes?' he asked, with his eyes upon his task.

"'I hoped I might get at one of the cadavers.'

"'No such luck! Resurrection Reade keeps them under lock and key!'

"'What are you doing there, Craden?'

"'I am curious to know how long after consumption alcohol can be measured in the blood. I'm in a fair way to exhausting my supply.'

"'Of whiskey?' I said, with a nod toward his flask.

"'Or blood!' he replied, with a laugh, and took a long draught.

"'You will be too drunk to produce creditable results.'

"'Perhaps. Or perhaps drunkenness brings out the pluck that is essential to experimentation.'

"'I have never found you to be wanting in pluck, Craden.'

"Here we were interrupted by the appearance of a ragged little street urchin, who tugged off his cap and said, 'Got somethin' wot needs done, Guv?'

"Craden nodded, and attempted to get up from his stool. The measure of his pluck became evident, for he stumbled, sending a couple of books upon the stool beside him skidding across the floor.

"I bent down to retrieve them and got a look at the titles – Christison's *Treatise on Poisons* and a very rare volume of Nicholas Culpeper's *The English Physitian* – and saw that an envelope had slipped from between the pages of one of them. Craden snatched the items from my grasp, then took a ball of twine and, tucking the envelope back into one of the books, he bound the volumes together tightly and handed them to the boy along with a sovereign – a handsome fee for delivering a pair of books, rare though they were. 'You know the address?'

"'Old Compton Street, sir.'

"'Off with you, then.'

"The lad took up the bundle, and setting his cap back upon his head, he hurried away.

"'You are very trusting, Craden,' I observed. 'What is to keep the little fellow from taking your sovereign and purloining a pair of valuable books?'

"Craden seemed amused by the question. 'Do you know Scripture, Holmes?'

"'Somewhat.'

"'The story of the Roman officer who does not need to see his commands carried out. "Do it," he says, and it's done, and that's the end of it.'

"'I only know one man in London who has that sort of authority.'

"Craden became very grave and reached for his flask once more. 'Then he's the very devil,' he muttered, and returned to his curious experimentation, while I decided to abandon the laboratory for Brodie's."

"Brodie's?"

Holmes nodded. "Even if I had not heard the lad mention his destination – Old Compton Street – I knew that two such rare volumes as the Christison and Culpeper could have no destination but Brodie's.

"In those days, I hadn't the income to support my avarice for books, and the Reading Room was only useful so far as their hours suited my irregular schedule. I had not been many months in town when I discovered that I could get my hands on all the books I wanted and keep hold of my purse strings as well by patronizing a subscription library in Old Compton Street, run by an old bookseller named Brodie. His collection numbered some thirty thousand, and for the modest sum of a guinea a year, one might have access to the lot. His common stock were popular novels, for the most part, but he kept a fine store of histories and scientific works, some of considerable value, though I don't believe that any patron of Brodie's would risk banishment from his shop by purloining one of them.

"Brodie has been gone these twenty years. I have always been a man of few friends, Watson, even when I was younger, but I counted Aiden Brodie among them. He was a peculiar old gnome who knew everything and everybody, not just the bookish set. If you wanted to know where to hire a groom or a locksmith, or what had been paid for the recovery of some compromising letters, or who had discreetly replaced the family jewels with paste, or where to buy fresh oranges or penny herring, Brodie was your man. I had spent many interesting hours at his establishment, not only going through his stock, but also listening to his endless and entertaining stores of gossip.

"I hailed a cab and on the way to Old Compton Street, an uneventful ride save for one singular episode. As I muddled over the encounter at Bart's, I recalled MacInnes' card and drew it from my pocket. Wait – I have it still."

Holmes rose and went to the desk, pushing through the disorganized papers in one of his drawers and came up with a yellowed square of cardboard which bore the following:

Marwood Laird MacInnes
Crafting in Fine Leather Goods
Oxford Street
Below this, was his other trade: *Executioner.*

CHAPTER THREE

Holmes beheld my astonished countenance with a grin. "Did I not tell you that the *dramatis personae* were interesting, Watson? They shall become more interesting still. As for Marwood MacInnes, cobbler and executioner, we shall meet him again at a later point in my narrative, although his place in the annals of crime would not continue long beyond this meeting. In the summer of '79, he was to resign his grim post and depart from London.

"Brodie's shop was kept as quiet as the Diogenes Club, and the old gentleman himself was usually to be found at his desk or dozing before the fire. I was surprised, therefore, to find the front of the premises vacant and to hear Brodie's bark of a laugh emerge from the rear of the shop and to hear that laugh echoed by the merry retort of a woman.

"I made my way through a maze of shelves to a small clearing where Brodie kept his chessboard. Four pieces remained upon the squares, the only white one being the old gentleman's king, toppled over in defeat. It was evident that he had just been beaten in a match, and that he was highly amused by the rout. 'Excellent!' Brodie declared. 'Brilliant! Your mastery of the game will serve you well. I daresay *someone* will come to regret what a shrewd and daunting antagonist he has fashioned!'

"His companion raised her head and replied, 'I hope you do not underestimate *my* contribution to the process.

One cannot make bricks without clay. But I think,' she added, looking up at me, 'we keep this patron waiting.'

"'Sherlock!' cried Brodie. 'I did not hear the shop's bell. How long have you been standing there?'

"'No more than a minute.'

"'In time to witness my humiliating defeat!'

"He turned from me to address the lady. 'Sherlock here needs to be beaten by a woman, for that might shame him into mastery of the game. He has perfected the craft, but is too lazy to apply himself to the art.'

"'Or too gallant, perhaps, to acquire the artifice?' The girl favored me with a most winning smile.

"She was – and I say this with complete impartiality, Watson – the most beautiful woman I have ever beheld, before or since. She was slender, and a bit above average height, with auburn hair and large violet eyes that conveyed an otherworldly penetration as though she meditated upon subjects far too advanced for her years. Do you know the painting *Lady Lilith*?"

"Rossetti," I nodded. "Oil painting of a girl in a white dress, holding a mirror, combing her hair."

"Rossetti used this lady for his model."

I readily admit that my knowledge of art was far beneath that of my friend, but I protested at this. "That cannot be, Holmes. Rossetti's model for the work was a seamstress he found on the street."

"Alexa Wilding," Holmes smiled. "Yes, Rossetti laid Miss Wilding's face on the oil, but there was a watercolor rendering which preceded it, the subject every bit as striking, though clearly younger in face and figure, for Miss Turner could not have been more than ten or eleven at the time. I was told this by the artist himself at the opening of the Grosvenor in '77.

"But it was not solely that exquisite face which I found so intriguing. It was the fact that young ladies who visited Brodie's confined themselves to his stock of modern novels at the front of the shop. Few ever ventured into the cluttered maze of academic tomes, and none were so audacious as to challenge the old man to a game of chess.

"'What will you take for your victory?' Brodie asked her. 'I have twenty volumes of *The Maid of Cremona*, not yet out of the box.'

"'I prefer my *Stradivari di Cremona*,' she returned. 'It's much more lyrical. Or as lyrical as these poor fingers can manage. But will you not introduce me to your friend?'

"'Miss Violet Turner, may I introduce Mr. Sherlock Holmes?'

"The lady offered her hand, and I shook it. To my surprise, she did not release it but held it in hers, while perusing my expression as if she were reading one of Brodie's scientific tomes. When she had finished examining my countenance, she turned her gaze on my hand and studied it with the same grave and unsentimental scrutiny. 'What luck to have such long fingers. It is a decided advantage in a musician. But you must take more care in the chemical laboratories, acid burns upon the fingertips can impair the precision of your fingering. And you should put some sticking plaster on those excoriations, sir, if you dabble in poisons.'

"'I see how you conclude that I am a chemist,' I replied, with a smile. 'But the music? *That*, I presume, was a guess.'

"'You should never guess,' she replied. 'If your observations and your memory are sound, you never need to. I saw you, Mr. Holmes at the Wagner Festival last year. You attended every concert that Wagner conducted himself. All of the true musicians in the crowd were unconsciously conducting along with the composer. There was quite enough flapping to stir up a refreshing breeze. I expected one or two of them to take flight.'

"Brodie's mirthful bark was echoed by the gong of his old mantle clock. The young lady drew on her cloak, and took a pair of volumes from a chair, the very same books that Craden had consigned to the lad.

"'I must go. If I have my liberty next week, I will stop after the lecture and give you a chance to redeem yourself,' she promised Brodie. 'If you are here, sir, I will engage you as well.'

"'Is a week sufficient to prepare for inevitable defeat?'

"I spoke in jest, but the lady's reply was quite grave. 'Methodical preparation may eliminate the possibility of defeat,' she said. 'Mitigate it, at very least.'

"The three of us made our way to the front of the shop. The lady threw a broad fringed shawl over her hair, and as she did so, I saw the flames in the grate billow upward, and caught a brief glimpse of an envelope before it was consumed. She had she tossed Craden's note into the fire.

"I watched through the door-glass as she dashed to the curb and hailed a vacant cab by springing at its head so heedlessly that she was nearly trampled.

"'She might have fallen to her death!' I exclaimed.

"Brodie only shrugged. 'It's how she plays the game. Heedless and bold, and always prepared to improvise when she must, and yet never a misstep.'

"'I would not let a sister of mine tear about the streets in such a fashion.'

"'Well, she is not a sister of yours, is she? Tell me, young man, the eternal debate over nature versus rearing, where do you stand on that?'

"'I believe that there are natural tendencies as well as natural talents and natural intellect.'

"'Art in the blood, eh?'

"'As the lady herself observed, one cannot make bricks without clay.'

"'Ah, so you overheard that, did you? Well, clay is to be found everywhere,' Brodie replied. 'But bricks? The best of those do not come from material alone – credit must also be given to the mason. There is in nature, after all, the diamond in the rough, those rude stones in the river bed that only wait upon someone with the shrewdness to distinguish them from pebbles and the skill to bring forth their brilliance. I have rarely come across a better faceted mind than hers, certainly not one from cruder raw material.'

"'And to whose faceting is she indebted?' I enquired, with studied indifference.

"'To that of a simple army tutor. Though there is little in nature that is truly simple, either, would you not agree? Professor James Moriarty. I know that you know the name.'"

CHAPTER FOUR

"Professor Moriarty!" I ejaculated. "What was the girl's connection to that monster!"

"Suffice to say," replied Holmes, "that she was no more his sister than she was mine. He took possession of her when she was not yet fifteen years of age, and at the time of this tale, had owned her for six years."

"She was his ward, you mean?" I asked, puzzled.

"No, Watson. He bought her. Paid five pounds for her, and I daresay a better bargain was never struck."

I was offended, and made a move to rise. "I apologize," I said, somewhat coldly. "If you do not wish to discuss a personal matter, I would never force a confidence. You need not put forth such a detestable fabrication."

"Why, Doctor," he protested, mildly. "One would think you never ventured to the east of London Bridge."

I said nothing for a moment. A physician in general practice sees a great deal, and, indeed, my profession had exposed me to aspects of humanity that were equally wretched and vile.

"Well, well. It poses one of those questions that tests the fabric of honor, does it not? You have seen the Rossetti. You recall the tale of Pygmalion? If, for a mere five pounds, you could purchase that artist's model, Miss Violet Rose Turner, beautiful, promising, clever and whose youth and dependence would allow you to sculpt her to your liking, would you not be tempted?"

Violet Rose. My gaze turned involuntarily to the mantle, pockmarked with the *V.R.* from one of Holmes's bouts of indoor target practice. I had thought, at the time, that it was an expression of patriotism. Now, I was not certain.

"No," I said, but I confess that there was a moment's hesitation before I gave my reply. "Would you?"

"Not for five shillings," he said. "Nor five pence. My curiosity was 'roused, Watson, as yours is now – how could it not be? I pressed Brodie for an account of the girl's history until, persuaded that I would seek it out on my own if he refused me, he consented to tell her tale.

"Her father, it seems, had been an art forger named Victor Turner, a handsome rogue with the sort of cunning and charm that even the most well-bred lady will find irresistible. The lady, in this case, was the governess in an aristocratic household in Oxfordshire. According to Brodie, she was a woman of extraordinary beauty and sound education, but possessed a headstrong and passionate nature, which was her undoing. Her fate was a familiar one: seduction, dismissal from her post and the inevitable course to the gutter. Turner averted the course by offering her marriage, and, as her family had thrown her off and she had no friends, she accepted him, though the gutter would have been a kinder fate. A daughter was the only issue of this wretched union, and she was christened Violet Rose, after her mother.

"Turner led his wife and child an itinerant existence, moving them from here to there, or abandoning them for weeks and months at a time, only to wheedle his way back again. When the girl was three or four years of age, Turner was tried and convicted for forgery and sentenced to seven years' imprisonment. Mrs. Turner, long estranged her from her kin, would not humble herself by appealing to them, but she had attracted the notice of Rossetti and his set when they had been in Oxfordshire, and so she sought them out and offered them herself and, in time, her daughter, as models. The occupation gave the two some little independence until Turner was released from prison.

"For a year or two, he allowed his wife and daughter to earn their keep, and his, while he applied himself to reviving those talents which had lain fallow in prison, and then he took it into his head to return to Oxfordshire. There, he produced some passable reproductions in the Pre-Raphaelite vein, one in which his daughter had been the subject, and he decided to pass this one off as the genuine article to a gentleman who had some small reputation as a connoisseur. When he called on this gentleman, he had his daughter with him."

"And that gentleman was Professor Moriarty," I said.

Holmes nodded. "Moriarty interviewed both of them for some time, before he sent them on their way. The next day, however, he summoned Turner and offered him five pounds. Turner promised to deliver his handiwork that afternoon, but Moriarty informed him that if all he wanted was a canvas to hang upon his wall, he could have the original, and that it was the subject he wanted. Turner understood, with the instinct which allows one dark mind to recognize its superior, that Moriarty was not a man to be crossed. The mother, when she was informed of this devil's bargain, protested with all of her might, but with neither family nor friends to take her part or offer her refuge, she was powerless to oppose him, and so, she saw but one avenue left to go down. She poisoned herself and her child.

"You look horrified, Watson. Well, the world can be a horrifying place. Mother and daughter were both denied a merciful end. Their lives were saved, but while the girl's health was restored, the poison had a ruinous effect upon the mother. She was placed in an institution, and lived only another year or two. Turner delivered his daughter to Moriarty, pocketed his five pounds, and submerged once more into the criminal mire.

"Rumors of the manner in which Moriarty acquired the girl, and the atmosphere of scandal that will hang about when a scholar just under thirty lives with a girl of fourteen made it uncomfortable for him to remain in Oxfordshire, and so he gave up his post and moved to London. He took up residence on a quiet street, ostensibly making a living as an army tutor. With his cerebral air and his brilliant conversation, he was soon coveted in illustrious circles, even as he applied his dark and vicious talents toward fixing his place in the criminal ones. In town, of course, a beautiful companion who was not his wife was no impediment to favor. He was not the first distinguished man – or woman –

to live so without the benefit of marriage, nor would he be the last.

"'But why did Moriarty not simply answer the rumors by passing the girl off as his ward?' I asked, when the old man had finished his recital. 'He might have remained in Oxfordshire.'

"'It would have been difficult to pass Miss Violet off as his ward after she gave birth to their child.'

"'She has a child?'

"'Children,' Brodie replied. 'A daughter born in Oxfordshire and twin sons who arrived not long after they installed themselves in town. The Professor has always taken a vain pride in Violet's intellect and accomplishments – they reflect upon him, you see. And his pride – his ambitions – toward his offspring are even greater. He looks upon their rearing as his great experiment in that subject of nature and nurture. He does, indeed, think himself quite the Pygmalion – though where Violet is concerned, he may come to find one day that he has been her Frankenstein all the while,' Brodie added, with a grim laugh. 'You know the sensational novel?'

"'She is no monster,' I protested.

"'But she is that mixture of odd parts that makes for a force to be reckoned with! May she be his undoing in the end! You smile, Sherlock. 'That mere slip of a girl,' you think. But you have not yet faced her across a chessboard. She thinks moves ahead and maneuvers for advantage with such deftness that you don't see the checkmate – and then you're done for!'"

CHAPTER FIVE

"I left Brodie's with a copy of Winwood Reade's *The Martyrdom of Man* and returned to Montague Street prepared to enjoy a quiet evening with the book. My scheme was overthrown, however, somewhere around seven o'clock when I heard the sound of a thunderous vibration that could only portend an earthquake or the approach of brother Mycroft. A resounding knock pointed to the latter and I threw open the door to find my brother standing upon the threshold in his evening dress. I let out a groan.

"'You devil!' he cried, surveying my disheveled state. 'You've forgotten!'

"'Forgotten what?' I parried.

"'Hamlet! Henry Irving! A box!' He strode into the room and considered which of my frail chairs would best bear his weight, then sat with a wheeze. 'Make yourself presentable and don't sneak off before the final curtain, we've been invited to supper afterward and you know I can only be sociable for so long.'

"'Then why be sociable at all?' I replied.

"'I do this for *your* good, Sherlock. What you cull from Bart's and Brodie's is wasted if you won't cultivate those who might pay for your talents someday.'

"Clearly, he had deduced where I had spent my afternoon. 'Invited where?'

"'Southampton Street. Stoker and his bride have managed to get a nice set of rooms. She's one of Lieutenant Colonel James Balcombe's daughters, one of the middle ones, I quite forget her name. The one who had a flirtation with that fellow Wilde some time ago. You must come, for I count upon you to recall some urgent matter of business after an hour or so. If I go alone, I shall be obliged to simulate a fit to make my escape, and you know I'm not the actor you are, Sherlock.'

"'I'm not certain that I can stand Stoker for an hour.'

"'There's nothing wrong with the man. We could use a few of his kind in government service. He's got a head for numbers and his talent for organization is remarkable.'

"'Who else will be there?'

"'The sort of menagerie that theatre folk attract. A few of the Lyceum set, Whistler, Alfred Kempe, a couple of the bride's marriageable sisters. The Hunts and their daughter, who is quite clever. Francis Buckland, who is said to be an interesting fellow.'

"'Until the household pets disappear.'

"'Sherlock. Manners. Lord Craden will be there, and his conversation is usually lively.'

"'When he's sober,' I replied, coolly.

"'Stoker cannot afford to be so particular. The earl contributes generously to art and science, and Stoker knows the importance of courting money. Perhaps he entertains the hope of getting Lord Craden to take one of his sisters-in-law off Balcombe's hands. Professor James Moriarty is invited, too, and it is said that he will bring his companion. Whistler declares that she is the most beautiful woman in London, and Hunt maintains that she plays with the deftness of Sarasate and sings like the Swedish Nightingale. Stoker tells me that she and her children are the professor's most coveted possessions. You know what that suggests? That Moriarty has a point of vulnerability. I find that interesting.'

"'Mr. Brodie said that Moriarty bought her.'

"'Moriarty thinks like an American,' Mycroft shrugged. 'If you see something you want, set your price from the outset. It saves time. Get dressed, and be quick about it, or our cab will not get within two streets of the theatre.'

"I dressed and followed Mycroft down to the four-wheeler. We did not occupy it long, for Mycroft had been correct. Wellington Street overflowed with vehicles and we were forced to quit ours some streets from the Lyceum.

"I do not believe you were in London at the time, Watson, so you will not remember that night, although I am sure you have some fond remembrance of the place. This was not long after Henry Irving had taken over the property, but it was Stoker's administration that gave it the sort of cachet. A box was a coveted thing. I have no idea how Mycroft came by his, and I daresay there were one or two titled names who looked up from below and wondered how it was that the portly Mr. Holmes and his younger brother had been placed among the privileged.

"Under the new administration, many refurbishments had been made to the interior. There was color everywhere. The carpets were red, the ceiling was gold and blue and the women dragged trains of green, saffron, primrose and purple up and down that broad double staircase.

"My brother was not the only commoner to secure a box. The privilege had also been extended to the estranged Mrs. Irving (though one wonders why she had any inclination to accept it) and just before the first act curtain, Moriarty and Miss Turner took their seats in a box opposite the one occupied by Mycroft and myself.

"The lady's gown was not a patchwork of two or three incompatible fabrics, nor was it weighted down with flowers and furbelows. Her simple white satin made the other women look gaudy and vulgar. 'Round her throat, she wore a thread of black velvet from which hung a remarkable teardrop pearl, and there were pearls nestled in her russet hair.

"I confess that not even Miss Terry's superlative turn as Ophelia could keep me from occasionally glancing at the Professor's perch, and I observed that I was not the only one whose attention was drawn from the stage. Lord Craden, sitting in the box directly above, did not once take his eyes from her immobile form.

"The curtain did not fall until midnight and Mycroft and I stopped at the portico to don our overcoats and mufflers. Cabs were in short supply, and it happened that Sir Charles and Lady Hardy offered us a place in their brougham. Mycroft readily agreed, but I wanted the backing of some fresh air and a cigarette before I answered the call of the tiresome social summons, and, promising my brother that I would not decamp to Montague Street, I headed toward the Embankment.

"I had just lighted my cigarette when I saw a woman's silhouette gliding along the path. There were few motives for an unescorted woman to haunt such a place at such an hour, yet her brooding and melancholy bearing did not suggest an assignation. Again and again, she looked down upon the black surface of the water, and for a few tense moments, I believed that she meant to throw herself into the Thames. Then she took a step back and shook her head as if to dispel her dark musings and hurried in the direction of Wellington Street, toward the Lyceum. As she passed under a street lamp, a trick of the wind swept the hood from her face, and I saw that the solitary rambler was Miss Turner.

"You may have heard the rumor, Watson, that Miss Terry, overwhelmed by the passionate adulation of the audience, suffered a fit of nerves and fled to the solitude of the Embankment. I have often wondered whether Miss Turner was mistaken for the actress by the gossips, for their coloring and figures were not dissimilar.

"I extinguished my cigarette and followed her as she returned to the throng spilling from the theatre. Then she disappeared among them, and I fell in with a small party making their way to the Stokers', whose apartments were an easy walk from the Lyceum.

"I was relieved to find that the Stokers' guests were not as tiresome as the usual parade of ambition and worn-out fashion. I kept my distance from Moriarty, which prevented me from approaching Miss Turner, who was rarely far from his side.

"After supper had been served, the gentlemen collected around some excellent port, and the ladies drew by the fire to admire each other's finery. I sought out Stoker's library, for Brodie had once told me that it was a superior collection, a few of the volumes quite rare and valuable.

"As I approached the doorway, I heard Miss Turner whisper urgently, 'You have been drinking again, Henry – and heaven knows what else! How can I trust in you when all may be thwarted in the end by your weakness? We have too little time as it is – he goes to the Continent in a matter of months! If you do not have the resolve – if you no longer wish to back me, say so at once, and we will get free of him the only way left to us – my mother's way.'

"'Say that again and I swear I will strike you, Violet!' he hissed in return.

"'You would not be the first.'

"'I could kill him for you.'

"'Do not be a fool, Henry. You would only be signing your own death warrant.'

"'Ah, Violet!' he sighed, his voice choking. 'I am signing it now.'

"I saw him take her hand and press it to his lips. A burst of laughter from the salon caused them to start; the lady pulled her hand away, and Craden saw me upon the threshold.

"'Sherlock Holmes – you spy upon me again!' he greeted with an insouciant grin. 'You are a connoisseur of the theatre, are you not? Where do you find more intriguing melodrama, the stage of the Lyceum or the Stoker's salon?'

"'I find one no more intriguing than the other.'

"'Very diplomatically spoken.' He turned and bowed to the lady and left us alone.

"Miss Turner studied me with the same quizzical concentration with which she had studied the configuration of my hand. 'I don't think that you find the company particularly intriguing, Mr. Holmes or you would not have come here so unwillingly.'

"'How do you deduce that?'

"'From your boots. The heels are worn where you dug in as you were dragged from your den.'

"'It does not follow that the wear is recent.'

"She conceded the point with a smile. 'They have been rather hastily blacked, and there is a suspicious smudge on one of your brother's – it is your brother, correct? On one of his gloves. I suspect he blacked your boots while you dressed. Did he do the dragging as well?'

"'He did.'

"'Well,' she advised, 'you must do as I do – learn to find some diversion in studying the people around you. It makes the evening bearable and can be very instructive.'

"'And what have you learned this evening?'

"'Sir Charles and his wife are at low water. She has had her gown remade. You can see needle tracks where the seams have been cut open and resewn. The fabric is at least three years out of date. And she has an odd button on her left glove. That's why she carries them instead of wearing them.

I detect a suspicion of talc applied to the knees of her husband's trousers, just enough to conceal the gloss that betrays wear. As for Mrs. Stoker,' she continued. 'She was too beautiful for a convent and too poor for a count, and there are the four other sisters to be put on the market, as well. I think Mr. Stoker promises well, but in the meantime, her petticoats tell me that they must economize.'

"'Indeed?'

"'When she lifts her skirt, you can see washing silk beneath, which is the fashionable fabric for petticoats. But her petticoat is ordinary muslin, with only a border of silk at the bottom. It is one of the devices whereby one may appear fashionable yet practice economy.'

"'I cannot disprove your theory, as the garment is not visible save for that occasional inch of hem.'

"'But it is audible,' she replied, with an enchanting smile. 'Her skirts are silk gros grain. The sound of silk against silk is quite different from the sound of muslin against silk, and I hear muslin when she walks. That is my method. Start with the shoes, then the gloves, then the trouser knees on a gentleman, or the petticoats on a lady.'

"'Is your method the result of natural talent or education?'

"The lady shrugged. 'Is one of any use without the other? Particularly for women. We must live by our wits, or die for lack of them.'

"At that moment, she looked beyond me and the light in her eyes faded. I turned and saw Moriarty standing in the archway. He was at this time but in his mid-thirties, yet with his receding hairline and high-domed forehead, he looked somewhat older. He had the unconscious habit of moving his head from side to side, a behavior that called up the sinister vacillation of a serpent. He did not acknowledge me at all, simply spoke one word: 'Rose.' I learned afterward that he preferred her middle name to the Christian name that had also been her mother's.

"'Yes, James?'

"'Miss Hunt has brought her Amati. I told the company that you would play.'

"There was no protest, nothing more than a simple current that vibrated the fabric of her gown, the slightest quiver of rebellion. 'Of course,' she said and passed before him into the salon.

"He followed, turning his back upon me with the disregard one might have shown for the most menial of servants. I remained in the room, and after a moment I heard the first notes of an unfamiliar and haunting composition. Never had I heard an instrument played with such power, emotion and precise technique.

"I moved to the doorway and saw her standing before the company, her bow hand gliding with such delicacy that it did not seem to be playing upon the strings so much as conjuring the melody from them. The company was mesmerized by her skill, but none more so than Lord Craden, who stood at the back of the room, half hidden, his gaze so fervent that I believed she must have felt its heat.

"When she finished, her hands dropped to her sides, the instrument and bow dangling loosely from her slender fingers. There was a moment of awed silence before the host began the applause that swelled as the company took up the praise. Only the Professor did not join in, but looked upon his protégé with the quiet self-confidence of possession.

"Then, at last, she did blush with what appeared to be shame, though I suspect the company took it for the flush of pleasure. She did not look my way again that evening, and soon after, she and the Professor departed."

CHAPTER SIX

"I am certain that at this time, the world looked upon me as a strange, nomadic creature who migrated from the dissecting rooms to the Reading Room, from Bart's to Brodie's, from lectures halls to concert halls and, in the days after that strange evening, I added to my pursuits a futile attempt to reproduce that haunting melody on my battered violin, with such poor results that my long-suffering landlady finally hammered upon my door and begged me not to drive her other boarders away.

"A week to the day after I had first met Miss Turner, I attended a lecture at King's College, on the subject of Post-Mortem Examination and the Forensic Dissection presented by Sir Joshua Reade. This, of course, was many decades after those dark episodes that had driven him from Edinburgh to London.

"His monographs and books on anatomy, and his reputation as a lecturer on the subject, as well as his campaigns to have professionally appointed coroners' courts and mortuaries to replace the less formal if more colorful custom of the public house inquest, had got him a knighthood, and an appointment to the post of coroner. As for rumors of his early life, and tales of Resurrection Reade, they were not entirely forgotten, as the laboratory porter's epithet – carrion hunter – attested.

"I sat in the second row of a crowded lecture hall taking rapid notes as Reade stood behind a large desk upon which were assembled his collection of the skulls of murder victims. He used these to make several observations on comparative anatomy, and the relationship between various weapons and the pattern of fractures to the skull. 'A dead man may be a more reliable a witness than a live one, if we approach the post-mortem dissection as a matter of science rather than guess-work, which has no place in the art or the business of the scientist. A true scientist should always adhere to the following pattern.' Here, Sir Joshua took up a nub of chalk in his long fingers and turned to the chalkboard behind him. He wrote the word 'ORDER' in large letters, and struck the 'O' with the knuckle of his long forefinger. '*Observe*,' he intoned. 'not only the deceased, but his surroundings. *Remove* the deceased to the mortuary with as little contamination as possible,' he continued, with a rap upon the letter 'R.' '*Dissect* with the precision of a skilled surgeon.' Letter 'D.' '*Examination* and *experimentation,* should be applied to all organs and bodily fluids.' Letter 'E.' 'And?' He pressed his right forefinger to the final 'R' while his left roamed the hall, seeking out a volunteer.

"Lord Craden rose to his feet.

"'Sir?' the lecturer frowned.

"'*Resurrect* your dead theories,' Craden replied. This insolent remark drew snickers from a few of the cruder fellows. Craden dropped back into his chair with a smile.

"Another student rose, a young fellow named Ernest.

"'Sir?'

"'*Record* one's conclusions,' the young man offered.

"'Precisely. Record one's conclusions,' Sir Joshua repeated as he knuckled the final 'R.' He faced forward, his eyes studiously avoiding Craden's. '*Theories* are as cheap as they are plentiful, and often worth no more than the breath expelled when expressing them.' It was as close as he dared come to a reproof, for Lord Warrington had contributed generously to the rebuilding of the hospital.

"Craden spoke no more, but I observed that several times, he turned in his chair to glance toward the two rows at the back of the room where the ladies sat. Medical education had only just become available to women, and so it was not uncommon to see several young ladies in attendance at the lectures on anatomy and biology. It was Sir Joshua's custom to relegate them to the back of the room. I did not know whether this was a mark of his disapproval of female medical students, or to allow them to make a discreet departure should the frankness of science become too candid for their sex.

"Courtesy dictated that the gentlemen allow the ladies to exit before we made our way to the doors. As I gathered up my coat and gloves, I saw that it was Miss Turner who had been the object of Craden's glances, and I observed a discreet look and gesture pass between them before she left the room.

"When I stepped outside, I saw the two of them at the pavement in earnest conversation, he addressing her with great urgency, while Miss Turner was all steadiness and composure. When he had done, Miss Turner extended her hand and Craden shook it, and as he did so, I saw him slip a square of folded paper inside her glove. Then he withdrew his hand and tipped his hat and walked quickly toward his waiting carriage.

"As the lady turned away toward the Strand, she was approached by another gentleman. It was the fellow, Ernest, the one who had responded to Sir Joshua's question.

"I must interject a word about this person, Watson, since he was to figure in a later case – a none too distant one, and one in which you played no small part. His full name was Rayleigh John Ernest."

"What! I cried. "Not the young doctor, Ray Ernest, who seduced the wife of that miserable fellow Josiah Amberley!"

"The very same," said Holmes with a grim nod. "'Young,' of course, is relative. He was certainly much younger than Amberley, who was, you will recall, in his early sixties. Ernest was closer in age to Mrs. Amberley who was more than twenty years her husband's junior. You have not yet published an account of that matter, and I ask that should you ever do so, you will omit any suggestion of my prior acquaintance with the scoundrel."

"Of course."

"Ernest was a year or two younger than myself. His family hailed from Durham, and they were humble folk, but ambitious to have him rise up in the world, and he was no less determined to cast off his working class origins. About the laboratories and the lecture halls, he was better known by his epithets – one of them was 'Deadly Ernest,' for the tenacity with which he applied himself to study. It is neither exaggeration nor false modesty, Watson, when I say that so far as chemistry was concerned, only Ernest was my superior. His other epithet was 'Heep,' for an unctuousness and insincere humility that he paraded before anyone of influence. He was considered to be Sir Joshua's *protégé*.

"Ernest laid his hand upon Miss Turner's sleeve and she flinched as if he were a loathsome object. I could not hear their exchange, but their bearing was more eloquent than words, for he was all oily supplication and she was as cold as the snow beneath her feet. He made a second attempt to detain her, which met with a more forceful repudiation and his toadying veneer cracked, even as his grip tightened on her arm.

"I approached the pair and bade the lady good-morning. 'I trust you remember me, Miss Turner. We were introduced at Mr. Brodie's. You and Mr. Brodie had just concluded a game of chess. You were the victor, if I am not mistaken.'

"'Hello, Holmes,' Ernest greeted in his high, nasal tone. 'So you play at chess? My studies have left me little time to apply myself. I am certain that your game is superior to mine, or I would offer a challenge.'

"'Whenever you like. But, Miss Turner, we mustn't detain you. May I fetch you a cab?'

"Ernest understood that he had been thwarted for the present, and offering an icy 'Good-day' to us, he turned on his heel and stalked off.

"'Odious creature.' She favored me with a grateful smile. 'Why do you suppose he was blessed with so excellent a brain? It is such an irony. The people one ought to know, one never meets except by chance. And the people one cannot avoid meeting are never worth knowing.'

"'And which is Lord Craden?' I was surprised at my own bluntness. 'The unintentional, or the unavoidable?'

"'Lord Henry Craden,' the lady replied, 'is someone people believe they want to know, but for the wrong reasons. And who is worth knowing for reasons he does his utmost to conceal.'

"'I cannot think that a gentleman as willfully indiscreet as Craden conceals anything.'

"'Perhaps you should make an effort to know him better.'

"'Perhaps *you* should keep him at a distance.'

"She smiled and shook her head, as though I were a hopeless naïf. 'We will never agree upon such a conundrum as Henry Craden.' She wrapped her muffler more tightly around her throat. 'A warning about taking up Heep on his challenge, for I have seen him play. His game lacks imagination, but there is an underhandedness to it and a great deal of stealth, that makes him the victor more often than not. And if you should be triumphant, beware – he does not forget a slight or a defeat. As for our match, I have not forgotten. Until this afternoon, Mr. Holmes.'

"With that, she struck out toward the Strand at a brisk pace. She had the curious habit of pausing to lean into a doorway as she made her way, and I observed that these recesses were makeshift havens for those poor wretches who sought a few minutes' shelter from the bitter weather. There they huddled, with outstretched hands ignored more often than not. Miss Turner did not pass, however, without reaching into the pocket of her Ulster and pressing something into the upturned palms.

"These pauses served to expose a spy, for a slinking figure followed some paces behind her and dashed for cover whenever she stopped to dispense a few shillings. It was almost comical to watch Ernest's clumsy surveillance, and I would have stepped forward and put a stop to it, but Miss Turner was too swift for us both. She slipped into the crowd and disappeared, leaving Ernest standing, frustrated and befuddled in the middle of the busy street."

CHAPTER SEVEN

"Miss Turner's 'Until this afternoon, Mr. Holmes' told me that she had not forgotten our appointed match, yet when I arrived at Brodie's just before four o'clock, I found the old gentleman alone, shuffling around in his slippered feet as he poked through cartons and assembled a stack of books upon his desk.

"'Halloa, Sherlock! Is it not a bitter day? How did you like *The Martyrdom of Man*? "Men should be virtuous without the fear of punishment, and without the hope of reward and that such virtue alone is of any worth!" Is that not a provoking sentiment? Take that chair by the fire. I fear I must disappoint you – Violet cannot come – she just now sent word that she squandered this afternoon's liberty on some errand or other, and must be home at the hour dictated by the Professor, so that she can give him an account of her day before he leaves. Tonight is his night to tutor those sons of Admiral Sinclair – for all the good it may do them! – but at least Violet will have the evening to herself. She was to take these home with her,' he said as he tallied the books upon his desk, 'but now I must have them delivered. Ah, here is the last of them!' He unearthed a volume from the bottom of a box. 'Claude Bernard's *Lecons sur les Effets des Substances Toxiques*.' He laid it upon the stack and began to bind them up with string. 'But wait – I believe there is one more that goes with this lot – if you will just reach under your chair, Sherlock.'

"I reached under the chair and came up with a flat parcel wrapped in blue paper.

"'Indeed, no, I was wrong – I believe that is yours.' The old man's eyes twinkled. 'It is an occasion for some good wishes, if I have my dates right.'

"The item was Joshua Reade's *The Practical Post-Mortem: A Guide to Medical Jurisprudence*. A first edition and in such excellent condition that it might have been issued twenty days ago instead of twenty years. 'Mr. Brodie, this is too valuable. I cannot accept it.'

"He waved off my protests with a laugh. 'Nonsense, lad – I am sure that you will find it to be very entertaining reading! Medical jurisprudence, indeed! The business has got too nice!' He waved a spindly index finger and sang out:

'Once you've breathed your last
Your soul ascends to God
But Resurrection Reade will raise
What lays beneath the sod.'

'Ha, ha, ha, crude poetry! Resurrection Reade! Ah, me – those were the days when four shillings would get you your pick of cadavers, and an inquest played out in the public house with the anti-dissection harpies pounding at the door! *Those* were lively times! But lively times and the memory of them are short-lived. I daresay Reade is grateful for that. I'll wager nobody thinks to call him Resurrection Reade anymore.'

"'Not to his face.'

50

"'Hah! Well, the battle for subjects back then was fierce, and men like Reade did not always play fair. Not entirely a bad thing, mind you. I'll wager a great deal of what we know about disease and cure is owed to men who are not hobbled by law or religion. Though a century or two ago, I would have been burned at the stake for saying so. There may be a few who would do it today, what do you think?'

"'I think it would be a shame for you to be burnt to a cinder, when your corpse might bring in four shillings.'

"'Hah! Good boy! I will bequeath you my cadaver, what do you say to that?'

"'I would rather have your books than your bones, Mr. Brodie.'

"'My bones, you may have exclusively, but Violet must have her share of the books. It is no more than she deserves, for I have never seen a more inexhaustible appetite for knowledge, nor wits better suited to its practical application. I am not certain that I would exempt even Moriarty – nor present company, for that matter. Now Sherlock,' Brodie chuckled, 'I haven't offended you? Or perhaps it is that you do not find Miss Violet here which puts that frown upon your face? Ah, well,' he sighted, 'the Professor is a miser when it comes to dispensing her freedom. She cannot take liberties that he is not inclined to give. You ought to be glad that she could not make good on her challenge. You are spared a humiliating defeat, and by a woman, too.'

"'I may have been the victor, sir.'

"'Hah!' was the terse reply.

"'Perhaps Moriarty is miserly with her freedom because he suspects that he may have a rival. It is only natural that he should feel some jealousy. She is a very beautiful woman.'

"'No emotion is so unnatural as jealousy, my boy.'

"'Why does she stay with him?'

"'She stays with her children, Sherlock.'

"'Why does she not leave with them? Moriarty is not her husband.'

"'Do you know nothing of Moriarty? The Professor would never let her take them away – take away his flesh and blood?' The old man shook his head, grimly. 'And she would never leave without them.'

"'She might marry someone with the influence and rank to stand up to Moriarty.'

"'Gentlemen of influence and rank are all on the hunt for American heiresses. Violet has not a penny but for what the Professor gives her.'

"'I was speaking of Lord Craden.'

"'Craden!' the old man looked at me keenly. 'What a curious notion! If Craden knows her at all, it is only because he is acquainted with the Professor.'

"'Perhaps Craden made Moriarty's acquaintance with no other purpose than to know Miss Turner. He is clearly smitten with her.'

"'He is not alone in that. It is part of the settled order of nature that a girl such as Miss Violet should have admirers, Sherlock.'

"'He more than admires her, he pursues her. In the past week, I have observed them *tête-à-tête,* once at the Stokers' and today, after Sir Joshua's lecture. Before they parted, he slipped a note into her hand. And now, when you tell me that Moriarty is away for the evening, I must wonder if Craden means to take advantage of his absence.'

"'A tryst? Unless she accompanies the Professor, Violet never goes out in the evening, and Craden would not be admitted. No visitors are, when the Professor is not at home. And Craden would not risk,' Brodie paused, and his frown expressed a conviction that there was little Craden would not risk.

"'Let me have those books, sir,' I suggested, with a nod toward the bundle. 'I will deliver them for you.'

"'To intercept Craden if he is hanging about?'

"'To spare you the expense of hiring a messenger.'

"Brodie gave a grim chuckle. 'Very well. Here is the address – Paradise Walk,' he said, as he scribbled upon a slip of paper. 'Now, you will not go to the front door, but 'round to the kitchen area. But you must stay for some tea first. You will not want to go until Moriarty leaves at six o'clock. The servants do not leave until after seven.'

"'Leave? Where do they go?'

"'To their own lodgings. Moriarty keeps four servants: his man, a woman who is cook and housekeeper, a nurse for the children, and a girl of all work, yet only the girl lives under his roof. I suppose that he wishes to thwart any opportunity Violet may have to cultivate a household friend or confidante. Come – it is not yet five. Let me see what I can find for our tea. And mind you, Sherlock, if you see nothing of Craden, then just hand over the books and depart. Don't go lurking about Paradise Walk.'

"'It is a public street, and a pleasant one for a stroll.'

"'I recall that someone else once took a similar view,' said the old man. 'A young police detective, an inquisitive upstart of a lad, not unlike yourself. He was pursuing a criminal case against the Professor, and took to hanging about Paradise Walk. It was even rumored that he made his way into Moriarty's house. Winters was his name, I believe. Yes, yes, the late Mr. Winters. They didn't find all of him, just bits and pieces. Just enough for a proper identification. Enough to have it get 'round what had been done to him. Ah, look what I have got saved, a nice pâté, smooth as cream.'"

CHAPTER EIGHT

"Moriarty lived on Paradise Walk, not far from Chelsea Embankment," Holmes continued. "It was, at the time, the sort of genteel, out-of-the way address that was particularly attractive to one who desires privacy.

"Moriarty's residence was a handsome brick dwelling, set well behind a high wrought iron fence. On either side of the gate were slender columns upon which perched stone lions, their snow-covered manes giving them the appearance of somber, wigged magistrates prepared to ward off trespassers. I had my cabbie leave me at Queen's Road, and, drawing my hat brim down to my eyes, and my muffler up to my chin, I would have been taken for one of the bundled pedestrians making for Chelsea Hospital or the Shelley Theatre. For nearly half an hour, I made a cautious survey of the area, but I saw nothing of Craden.

"Promptly at six o'clock, a handsome carriage, the Sinclair crest upon its door, rumbled to a halt in front of Moriarty's address. A liveried footman hopped to the pavement, and a moment later, Moriarty emerged from the house and stepped into the carriage. An extraordinary courtesy for a common army tutor, do you not agree, Watson?

"I hung back in the shadows until the carriage was out of sight, and then made my way 'round to the kitchen area and pulled the bell.

"It was the manservant who came to the door. He was a tall, brutish-looking fellow, who smelled of drink; the sort of fellow whose value to a master such as Moriarty was not intellect, but the unswerving allegiance of a brute beast.

"'Books for a Miss Turner, sir, from Brodie's on Old Compton Street,' I said. The man took the books and handed me a shilling and closed the door in my face.

"And there, Watson, might have ended my night's adventure but for one barely discernable sound – or the absence of it, I should say, for when the door was closed, it was not followed up by the snap of a bolt being thrown, or the snick of a lock. Drink had dulled his vigilance, I daresay. I peered through the door pane and saw the man walk down a passage that ended at the stairway, ascend the stair with the books and, in a few moments, return without them. He then turned through an arch at the center of the passage which led, I supposed, to the kitchen. I waited another moment or two, but no one else appeared.

"Now for the inquisitive upstart of a lad that I was at the time, a bolt that is not thrown is as inviting as a watch-dog that does not bark, and so I turned the knob. The drunken fellow had indeed left the door unlocked. Silently, I stepped into the passage, and closed the door behind me. Now, Watson, there is no need to give me such a look, for you yourself have been my partner in such transgressions more than once."

"But the risk could have been fatal, Holmes!"

"And yet, here you see me," he said with a grin. "I heard the murmur of a woman's voice reciting a blessing, and tiptoed toward the arch which did, indeed, open into the kitchen. I glanced into the room and saw the manservant and two ladies, one middle-aged, one barely out of her teens – the housekeeper and the servant girl – at the table, their heads bowed as the housekeeper recited the blessing. Piety has its rewards, you see. Those bowed heads allowed me to pass to the staircase undetected.

"I crept upward to a hallway that ran from the back passage to the front door. There were two rooms on each side, and, I tried the nearest door, which, to my surprise, was the Professor's study."

"Unlocked? I cannot believe that Moriarty would be so reckless."

"In my experience there are but three explanations for a man to leave his private room unlocked." Holmes leaned back in his chair and ticked off the reasons on his fingers. "He is careless. Now, a careless man is careless in all things, and Moriarty was not a careless man. He has nothing to hide, nor anything of value and so he has nothing to fear from intrusion. Or he is a man so monstrous, so feared, a man who has already answered such a violation with an unspeakable consequence, that no one would dare trespass in the future."

"As he did with that fellow Winters."

Holmes nodded, grimly. "The room itself appeared modest; only the most learned observer would see that the books upon the shelves and the paintings upon the walls had been chosen by a true connoisseur, and had been paid for by one whose income exceeded that of an ordinary tutor.

"Upon his desk was a great deal of correspondence ready to be posted, and the large blueprint of some building, with notations made in the vicinity of several of the passages. I dared not risk lighting a lamp nor striking a match, and I had not the materials to copy the document, nor could I carry anything away without exciting Moriarty's suspicion and perhaps bringing down his wrath upon the innocent members of his household.

"Had poor Winters got this far before he was apprehended? The thought should have made me fearful, and yet I was only angry, Watson – angry that I had come so ill-prepared to take advantage of such an exceptional opportunity. I resolved that I could do nothing more than to commit the arrangement of the rooms to my head, while my head was still upon my shoulders, and retreat until such time as I might plot out a more fruitful surveillance.

"I withdrew and made my way to the next chamber, a sitting room, the door ajar. The lamps had been lit, but I heard no voices within.

"Clearly, this was Miss Turner's retreat. It was a handsome room, larger than my humble quarters in Montague Street, elegantly appointed in shades of violet and green, yet with a decided air of informality. Books and music were heaped upon the chairs and atop the piano. A porcelain vase, crammed with stalks of common heliotrope, lay upon a cluttered desk beside an open volume, and next to it were a row of mortars containing some dried heliotrope blossoms, stems and seeds, as though the flowers had been obtained not for ornamentation, but for study.

"An embroidered shawl had been tossed on a velvet settee, an exquisite Cremona and bow lying upon it, the case lay open upon the carpet. I could not resist a desire to examine the instrument, and I had just lifted it when I heard the sound of footsteps descending the stair, and then a brief exchange; Miss Turner stating that she meant to collect a few of her books and retire early as the Professor was dining at his club, and the nurse, I presume – as she had not been in the kitchen – replied that she was going down to her tea, and would bring the children's tray up in half an hour.

"The only concealment the room offered was a high, ornamental screen, and so I darted behind it, just as the door handle turned. Through the narrow gap above the hinge, I saw Miss Turner enter, and begin to pace nervously. After a minute or two, there came a footfall outside the door so light as to be nearly inaudible, and then the door opened and three children entered the room, identical boys no more than three years of age, and a girl who appeared to be five or six. Upon seeing their mother, the children sprang upon her with expressions of pleasure that were quickly hushed.

"Then Miss Turner knelt on the floor beside the boys, while their older sister tied a blindfold over her mother's eyes. There ensued a brief game of Blind Man's Buff, played out with energy yet in complete silence, as though they knew to be mindful not to 'rouse the attention of any of the household.

"When they had exhausted the game, they settled upon the carpet and the lady took the little boys onto her lap and began to spin a tale full of gallant knights and resourceful maids, a perilous escape from a vicious fiend and a sea voyage filled with mystery and adventure. I did not recall this particular fable from my own childhood, and I suspected that the lady drew only upon a colorful imagination. When it had finished, the children implored her for some music, and the lady took up her violin and, with a caution that they must keep absolutely still, and played three or four lively airs.

"A mantle clock struck the half hour and the lady stopped playing immediately. 'You must go up now!' she whispered, urgently to the children.

"'One more song!' the little girl begged.

"'Just *one* more!' the little boys echoed.

"'I'm sorry – my poor lambs. Go up, now! Hurry – we would not want your father to learn of this or we shall not be able to do it again.'

"Invoking their father's name silenced them, immediately. 'Good night, Mama,' said the little girl, and taking each boy by the hand she led them toward the door. Miss Turner suddenly sprang forward and seized them into a fierce embrace and murmured, 'I love you so much! I would die for you, you know that!'

"'What is the matter, Mama?' the little girl asked. 'We're not going to die.'

"'Of course not. Mothers are silly sometimes,' said she, and wiping away her tears, she forced a smile. 'Go, now. I will come in to kiss you good-night after the servants have gone.'

"The children left the room, and I heard the faint patter of three pairs of feet on the carpeted stair. After a moment, Miss Turner took up her violin, and plucked a few chords in a desultory fashion and then laid the bow to the strings in earnest and began a variation of that same melody she had played at the Stokers'. It was in a minor key now, and once or twice she hit a false note as her bow hand trembled. She broke off playing and allowed both bow and instrument to slip to the floor. Then she fell into an armchair and began to weep.

"Watson, I have never heard such a heart-rending outburst from any human being. So despondent was she that I was tempted to reveal myself and ask what I might do to relieve her misery. But after a few moments, she regained her composure, cast a searching glance 'round the room as if to determine whether any trace of the children's' visit was evident, and satisfied that it was not, she gathered up the paraphernalia of her study – a few books and some of the seeds and flora. As she passed the mirror, she took one last, searching look at her reflection, pushed her loose hair away from her face, wiped her eyes, and then she left the room.

"I was ashamed, Watson, of having witnessed a despair that was meant to be expressed in private. When I heard her footsteps fade upon the staircase, I slipped from my hiding place, and picked up her instrument and bow from the carpet. I laid them back into their case and placed it on the sofa. Then, I made my way out as I had come, like a thief."

CHAPTER NINE

"And you did not see Craden at all?"

Holmes shook his head. "Whatever had been contained in that note he had passed to her after the lecture, it was evidently not to beg for a rendezvous that night.

"The next morning, I took myself to Bart's to spend a few hours in the chemical laboratories, and there was Craden, perched on a stool before an assortment of beakers and phials.

"'Halloa, Holmes,' he greeted, indifferently.

"I sat down to my own task, and we worked in silence for nearly an hour when he said, apropos of nothing, 'Women medical students, what is your opinion, Holmes?'

"'I haven't sufficient data to form one.'

"'Sir Joshua thinks that it is not a respectable vocation for a lady. It is what makes his lectures so entertaining – the dread that his veneer of respectability will crack and crumble as he lectures respectable young ladies on subjects we are taught not to discuss before them in a drawing room, while he endeavors to hold the attention of respectable young lads who cannot keep their minds off the ladies.'

"'You don't have a good opinion of Sir Joshua?'

"'I think,' Craden replied, with a grave candor, 'that nature ferries us down the Styx while the spirit labors to drag us toward Elysium. Most men – men like Sir Joshua – end up torn apart.'

"'And you?'

"'I let my nature take its course.' He laughed, as if to drive off his gravity, and returned to his task, and was absorbed in it still when I left him to meet Mycroft for luncheon.

"We had a pleasant meal, much of it involving Mycroft's good-natured interrogation into how I got on with my studies. I mentioned Sir Joshua's lecture, and Lord Craden's insubordination, and observed, 'Craden will often spend hours at the laboratories, but I cannot think what he is studying. Nor why he studies at all.'

"'Dear boy, I imagine people say the same about you.'

"'There is a method to my madness. I see none in his.'

"'Perhaps you see, but you do not observe, Sherlock.'

"'I see that he has gifts and might observe that it is worse to squander one's gifts than to have none at all.'

"'How many heirs squander hours in fetid laboratories and dreary lecture halls? How many have his command of the sciences?'

"'Not many,' I conceded.

"'Not any, I should think.'

"'You say that I must not judge a book by its cover.'

"'Or by the literary critics. Read it for yourself, if you want to determine its merit.'

"When we finished our meal, Mycroft attempted to discreetly slip an envelope into my palm. I protested of course, but Mycroft would hear none of it. 'Dear boy, some day, I may have to enlist your aid on a matter of national consequence. Think of this as a retainer.'

"'My dear Mycroft, I don't foresee that.'

"'Stranger things have happened.'

"We shook hands on that note and parted at the door of the restaurant.

"When I returned to Montague Street, my landlady, a somewhat addled creature, greeted me at the door. 'I took the liberty to keep up your fire, Mr. Holmes, so your sister wouldna be cold.'

"'My sister?'

"'Yes, she *would* wait, so I let her go up. I didna know you had such a pretty lass of a sister.'

"Nor did I, though I did not say so. I simply thanked the lady and hurried up to my room. I supposed that the lady in question was some troubled friend or relation of one of my former university chums, for they had made much of my ability to solve puzzles, and had got into the habit of sending the occasional problem my way. I was wrong, however. My visitor was Miss Turner, who sat in my seedy armchair, with one of my volumes of anatomy on her lap.

"'Please close the door,' she said, for I had left it ajar.

"I hesitated, but I did as she asked. 'Perhaps you would tell me, Miss Turner, how I have got through a quarter of a century without knowing that I had a sister.'

"'You should have been more observant, sir,' she replied with a grave smile.

"'Since this is not a family visit, I can only conclude that you have come for your match. Alas, I have no chessboard.'

"She laid the book aside and rose. 'I come to extract a promise, Mr. Holmes. You must give me your word that you will never enter the Professor's home again.'

"'Ah. Was it the violin?'

"She nodded. 'Only a musician would have given it such consideration. And,' she added, gravely, 'only a fool would enter James's study. Not even I am permitted there unless he is present.'

"'There is an expression about where fools will go.'

"'Such heedlessness may make an angel of you before your time, Mr. Holmes. I beg you not to act in a way that will take others with you. We may not be in such a hurry to get to heaven.'

"'Has there been some repercussion?'

"'Not yet, but that does not mean that he is oblivious. James always chooses the proper moment to exact vengeance. He likes for his victims to enjoy the full measure of agonized suspense. I have said what I came to say. Heed it, Mr. Holmes, for your own sake. I do not doubt that you and James will cross paths one day. Do not anticipate *that* match, sir,' she said, as she advanced toward the door. 'You will not be the victor. Good day.'

"I stepped in front of her to block her path. 'You can leave him, you know. He is not your husband. He cannot keep your children, if you choose to take them away.'

"She looked at me with a sorrow in those changeable eyes that was well beyond what twenty-one years of living gives you, Watson. 'Take his little human laboratories? He once called me that, and now it is what he calls the children. They offer a more fresh slate than I did, you see, so his research has a – purity? – that I could not bring to his experimentation. James has been very candid about what he will do if I attempt to take them away.'

"'And what is that?'

"'He will sell my daughter for five pounds, as I was sold to him,' she said, quietly. 'And to someone far less – benevolent – than James has been to me. And then he will kill one of the boys in front of me, and then kill me in front of the one he allows to survive.'"

"My God – that is monstrous, Holmes!" I cried.

Holmes nodded, grimly. "'Is there no one you can turn to for assistance?' I asked her.

"'In exchange for what?'

"'No gentleman would be so base as to set a price when a lady is in need of his help.'

"'Ah. Virtue without hope of a reward? Goodness for its own sake?' She stepped 'round me and laid her hand upon the doorknob. 'I don't know whether to honor the credo, Mr. Holmes, or to scorn your credulity for embracing it.'

"'The violin could only have told you that I was in your room, Madam. How could you know that I had been in the Professor's study?'

"She smiled up at me. She had the most winning smile, Watson! 'Because I know that it was a temptation you could not resist.'

"She left, and from my window, I saw her cross the street and hurry away on foot, passing shillings as she went to the crawlers in the cold."

CHAPTER TEN

"Miss Turner was quite correct. The temptation was irresistible. It lured me to Paradise Walk again and again in that early part of '79, in the hope that I might make my way into Moriarty's lair once more. Those were bitter vigils, Watson, for the weather was not my friend, yet I believed that if I could slip into Moriarty's home and turn up one secret file, one incriminating letter, one purloined *object d'art* that might give proof of his criminal conduct, I might set the law upon him and free Miss Turner and her children from his grasp.

"'Virtue without hope of reward?'" I said, with a smile. "I take it you were not successful."

"I was not. I discovered which afternoons Moriarty lunched at his club, what evenings he dined there, what days the grocer's boy made his deliveries, and when letters were taken to the post, and how often the constable made his pass down the street – but I was not able to gain access to Moriarty's house again.

"As for Miss Turner, I saw nothing of her for a fortnight; yet, in that time, I was witness to clandestine meetings of another sort which persuaded me that she and Craden continued to correspond.

"In spying upon Paradise Walk, I observed that nearly every morning, the children walked out with their nurse, a woman named Mrs. Stewart. Apparently, Moriarty's regimen for them included regular exercise, though the days were often bitterly cold. At times, these excursions took them no more than a few streets from Paradise Walk, but when the weather was less severe, they walked much farther.

"One morning, while they strolled toward one of the more crowded thoroughfares, a gentleman approached and greeted Mrs. Stewart, and when he tipped his hat, I saw that it was Lord Craden.

"The nurse did not appear to be surprised at his address, and her manner of returning his greeting suggested that they were acquainted. The lady directed the children to a near-by window display, and when they were out of earshot, she and Craden engaged in an earnest *tête-à-tête*. They spoke for five minutes or so, and then Mrs. Stewart summoned her charges and walked on.

"These meetings were repeated with a regularity that suggested they were no chance encounters, but that the nurse acted as liaison between Craden and Miss Turner. I saw no exchange of written correspondence, though their discourse suggested passion and urgency – on Craden's part, at least. The lady was more inscrutable.

"When these meetings concluded and the conspirators parted, Mrs. Stewart would purchase a mug of cocoa for the children at one of the stalls – a bribe for their silence, perhaps. She was very careful to wipe all traces of the treat from their lips with her handkerchief before they turned back toward Paradise Walk, and I wondered whether this indulgence opposed some dietary command of Moriarty's.

"It was on the first Monday in February, a rough, snowy night, when matters took a very dramatic turn. It commenced as it had two months earlier, with the sound of Mycroft's heavy tread upon the stair, and a summons to another disagreeable engagement.

"'The reception for Sir Joshua's great-niece,' Mycroft said. 'Mary Reade from New York City. She comes with a clear half million dollars, and Sir Joshua has agreed to help her to a title. I think Falkland will take her, he is said to have no money at all. I told you of the invitation, Sherlock, and accepted it on your behalf. You must come. You may meet a pretty American heiress yourself.'

"'What use would I have for an American heiress?'

"'Sherlock. You know that I am not a marrying man. You are far more eligible, provided you can find a wife who will put up with your detestable habits. Think what a sad fate it would be if we were the last of our line.'

"'Fate has played stranger tricks. There seems to be no shortage of pretty American girls with money. If I miss this week's mating dance, there will be another to come. I cannot be expected to attend them all.'

"'I thought you enjoyed that gathering at the Stokers in spite of yourself. Many of the same people will be there. The Hardys and the Hunts and Professor Moriarty with that extraordinary Miss Turner. Perhaps she may be encouraged to play again – you must admit that she plays superbly.'

"'She will sing or play or juggle oranges or do whatever Moriarty tells her to do. I do not need to go to Sir Joshua's to see that. There is a puppet show on every street corner.'

"'Why so bitter, Sherlock? That is not like you.'

"'I have been preoccupied, that's all. Offer my regrets, Mycroft. You will know what to say. I am not fit company tonight.'

"Mycroft's retort was that I was not fit company on any night, and he departed, grumbling his rehearsed excuses for my absence as he lumbered down the stairs.

"I waited only for the splash and clatter of Mycroft's departing four-wheeler before I threw aside my book and sprang to my feet. Moriarty and Miss Turner gone for the evening, and no obstacle before me but the one servant girl and three sleeping children! My opportunity had come at last! I pulled on my old dark pea coat, pocketed what tools I should need to contend with locks, and set out for Paradise Walk.

"It was nearly seven thirty when I arrived at Paradise Walk. I concluded that the three elder servants had gone, and waited only upon the departure of Moriarty and Miss Turner before I approached the house. I was frozen nearly to the bone when I heard the clatter of carriage wheels, and saw a hired coach draw up. A moment passed and Moriarty emerged with Miss Turner on his arm. She was wrapped in furs, with diamonds glistening upon her throat and in her hair. I do not believe I have ever beheld a more exquisite creature, Watson!

"The carriage set off in a whirl of snow, and I waited only until it was out of sight before I dashed across the street toward Moriarty's gate. My swaddled state, and the anticipation of the mission before me must excuse some inattention to my surroundings, for I never heard the drumming of hoof-beats until the carriage was almost upon me, and only by a combination of supreme effort and very good luck was I able to leap from its path."

CHAPTER ELEVEN

"I sprang for the pavement and plunged into a pool of slush as an icy spray, thrown up by the carriage wheels showered upon me. To my surprise, the vehicle did not race by, but lurched to a halt.

"'You, there! Why the devil don't you look where you're going!' roared the driver.

"'Why the devil don't you keep a better grip on your pair?' I retorted.

"'What? Sherlock Holmes – is that you, man?'

"I looked up at the bundled figure in the driver's perch. It was Lord Craden.

"He sprang to the pavement and hurried to my side. 'Not hurt, are you?'

"I got to my feet, my trousers and pea coat soaked through. 'No, just wet.'

"'Thank God for that! An accident would have been a damned inconvenience.' He scrutinized me, and looked up and down the street. 'You've strayed off course, haven't you? What are you doing in Paradise Walk?'

"I looked at his vehicle, an out-moded Clarence, one of those re-fit for growlers. 'You've abandoned your usual conveyance, haven't you? What are you doing in that rattletrap?'

"He chuckled. 'Let me give you a lift, you're wet to the bone. It's the least I can do for nearly running you down.'

"'I don't believe we are going in the same direction.'

"'One must always be prepared to change course,' he replied, with an inscrutable smile.

"'All right,' I said. It was rough night, Watson, and as my plans had been disrupted, I decided to spare myself the discomfort of making my own way back to Montague Street.

"'Hold the reins for me, will you? I've got a message to be delivered to this address.'

"I climbed onto the seat and watched as he ran up to Moriarty's front door and pulled the bell. After a moment, the door opened and a woman's silhouette appeared in the entry-way. From her height and carriage, I knew to be the nurse, though she ought to have been gone a half hour before. I counted myself fortunate that my plans had gone awry – I believed that I could have slipped past the girl, but Mrs. Stewart might have proven a more formidable opponent.

"I watched as Craden and Mrs. Stewart exchanged a few words, and I believe I saw her glance past Craden toward me, and then their exchange resumed in a more urgent fashion. At last, she gave a nod and closed the door.

"Craden hopped up beside me and took the reins. 'You have digs in Montague Street, correct?'

"'That's right.'

"He was silent for several minutes as he guided the horse through handsome, middle-class neighborhoods. 'Homey, isn't it?' he said at last. 'You look up at the lamp light glowing behind those curtained windows and you think of a comfortable berth, and a brisk fire, a pretty wife to greet you at the door. Smiling children and slippers upon the hearth. Do you know what I see? *I* see that these stone façades and velvet curtains can muffle a scream as effectively as if it rang out in the middle of a desert. Give me the thin walls and the common facilities of the Shoreditch or Shadwell or Bethnal Green – anywhere east of civilization. There, you know where you stand.'

"'What would you know of that part of the world, Craden?'

"'More than you think. I've got a flat there. In Rotherhithe.'

"I took this in jest, as I knew that the family estate was in Oxfordshire and the town residence on Belgrave Square.

"'You don't believe me, Holmes?'

"'No, I don't believe you.'

"'Let's go, then. I'll show it to you. You'll find me much better company than the company I keep.'

"I confess that my curiosity was piqued, Watson. Craden was something of a mystery, and mysteries were to be my trade after all. 'All right.'

"He slapped the reins and altered his course, taking a quite circuitous route, first upward toward Whitehall, and then across Waterloo Bridge. 'The Bridge of Sighs,' Craden muttered as we clattered across it. 'The poem – you know it, Holmes?

"*Sisterly, brotherly,*
Fatherly, motherly
Feelings had changed,"

'Damn!' he slapped the reins in frustration. 'What is the rest?

"*Mad from life's history,*
Glad to death's mystery,
Swift to be hurl'd—
Anywhere, anywhere
Out of the world!"

"'Such drivel they drum into you at university!' He said with a cynical laugh and then fell silent, and I turned my attention to the surroundings in which I now found myself. My knowledge of London was not as thorough as it is now, and as we passed below the river, we strayed far from those scenes of middle-class comfort and into a region where, despite the noble intentions of Barnett and Barnado, we were surrounded by wretched poverty. For some minutes, we rambled along Rotherhithe Street, a hodgepodge of flat-fronted tenements, crumbling dock houses, warehouses, ale houses and tobacco shops. And yet, for the bitter cold, all the foulness and gloom, it was neither deserted nor quiet. Humanity of every age and race, spilled from public houses, loitered in doorways, staggered in and out of alleys, bellowing, laughing, swearing, in a half dozen tongues. Men wore garments that were no more than an assembly of patches, women wore the welts and bruises that were their compromise for survival, children wore layers of dirt and outsized boots, when they had boots at all.

"'Prince's Street,' Craden announced as he reined in the pair beside a clean-swept patch of cobblestone. 'Though I daresay no prince but the Prince of Darkness ever set foot upon it.' He sprang down and gave a sharp whistle. Two disheveled boys, one who was eight or nine, perhaps, one some years younger, emerged from the shadows. The elder was the lad who had delivered Craden's stock of books to Brodie weeks before.

"Craden handed the reins to the elder. 'There you go, Wiggins.'"

"'Wiggins!'" I cried.

Holmes nodded and smiled. "And even then, sharp beyond his years. Craden shrugged off his overcoat and held it out for the boy to don, took off his hat and set it upon the boy's head, pulling it down by the brim.

"The boy laughed. 'Take me f'r a reg'lar toff, they will!'

"'There's a paper in the left pocket with an address where you're to go. Do what you're told when you get there.'

"'Yessir, Guv.' The lad hopped up and took the reins, smartly.

"Craden opened the carriage door and allowed the little one to scramble inside. 'Back here when you're done. See to the horses, and not one scratch upon the coach – I must get it back in the morning.'

"'Yessir, Guv.' The lad slapped the reins.

"'Come, Holmes.'

"I followed Craden through a sort of courtyard, past a common well and outhouse to a door that sank on the hinges when Craden opened it. We entered a dank, unlit corridor and mounted three flights of uneven wooden stairs, passing flats from which cries and oaths and pleadings emerged in a chorus of misery.

"Craden ignored the noise. He stopped on a landing where there were doors on either side with a narrow window between. All but one pane had been shattered and patched with old newspaper and rags; still, the wind found its way through.

"The door opened into a small, but surprisingly clean flat. It was a single room, with a bit of an alcove behind a curtain where there was a cot and washstand. The main room was square, with shelves laid against most of the walls, filled top to bottom with books and pamphlets. Between two high, paned windows was a wooden table that served as a sort of desk, with a tray of pens and pencils and an inkwell upon it. The bare planks of the floor had been covered with a rug that had seen some wear. There was a small secretary in the corner upon which many bottles of wine and spirits as well as chemical paraphernalia; a mismatched assortment of upholstered sofas and chairs lay about the room, and someone had seen to it that there was a brisk fire in the grate.

"'Toss your coat over the back of that chair behind you and push it up to the fire.'

"I did as he asked, and Craden shed his jacket and his cuffs as well, and rolled up one of his sleeves. He yanked his four-in-hand loose and knotted it around his arm above the elbow, then reached for a pouch on the bookshelf and drew out a syringe and a couple phials. He poured a bit of clear liquid from a bottle onto a patch of gauze, and swabbed the inside of his arm.

"'Here! What have you got there?'

"'Morphia,' he replied. 'Five percent solution. Care to sample it?'

"'No.'

"'Are you quite certain? I would think a man with your lust for fresh knowledge would want to give it a try.'

"'Do you ever consider the cost of such a vice, Craden?'

"'The price for a bit of oblivion? That's nothing. It's the alternative that is too dear.' He tapped the protruding vein and drew the liquid into the syringe. 'I've never heard rumors of you taking to the usual vices, Holmes. Opium, drink, women. Never trust a man who appears to have no vices.'

"Craden plunged the needle into his arm, slowly releasing the tourniquet with his teeth. 'Ah, better.' He turned his gaze on me. 'How about a whiskey and soda, Holmes?'

"'Yes, all right.'

"'Take a seat.' He prepared the drink and one for himself, then took a wooden chair by the table and raised his glass in a casual toast.

"There was a knock on the door. Craden set down his glass with a frown and called a brisk, 'Come!'

"A sturdy fellow entered, wearing a dark pea coat and a battered wide-awake pulled rudely over his ears. Wisps of gray hair were visible and his nose was bright red, not from drink, as I had first supposed, but from exertion and cold.

"Craden introduced me to the man as an associate. The man nodded to me and tugged on the brim of his shabby headgear.

"'Habout y'r- '

"'Packages,' Craden interjected, hastily.

"'Yessir, your packages. It's set.'

"Craden treated himself to a large draught from his glass, drew a pair of sovereigns from his waistcoat pocket that he handed to the fellow. 'Very well. I may want your services again tonight, so make certain Wiggins knows where to find you.'

"The creature tugged upon his hat brim again and exited.

"I was about to enquire of Craden the nature of this exchange when another knock sounded on the door. This time it was a woman, a slim, pretty thing, Watson, yet when she pushed back the hood of her mantle, I could see that her features were marred by a scar that ran from her left ear to her jawbone.

"The girl looked up at me, a bit apprehensively.

"'Don't worry, Laurel, he's a friend,' Craden told her. 'You didn't come here on your own, did you?'

"'No, sir, George is on the landing.' Her glance darted to me once more, and then she drew a small packet of papers from her cloak and handed them to Craden. He examined them under the lamp, then folded them and slipped them into a drawer, and then, this person, too, was given a few sovereigns. 'For you and George. Coming up the stair, I believe I heard Wiggins getting a bit rough with the wife.

Ask George to have a word with him on your way out, or I shall have to remedy it myself.'

"'Yes, sir.' The girl tucked the coins into her glove and drew the hood up over her hair, covering the scarred half of her face. With a silent nod to both of us, she turned to go.

"As she opened the door, I spied another woman upon the threshold. She was of middle age, wearing a man's heavy, thick-soled boots, her stout figure bundled in shawls. The two women nodded to each other, and the stout one stepped into the room. 'Beg pardon, sir, I meant no inconvenience,' she apologized. 'We can settle another time.'

"'I never allow myself to be inconvenienced.' Craden drew out four five-pound notes, and handed them to the woman. 'One's for Knowles. He will get the rest when it's finished. I expect you will find some use for the rest.'

"The notes were tucked into the recesses of the woman's shawls. 'It's been a bad winter, true enough. Influenza. And those worst off take up the most of my time.'

"'And are least likely to pay, is that it?'

"'They are the least able, sir.'

"Craden sat back and crossed his arms over his chest. 'An interesting irony, don't you think? Those who are ill cannot work and so cannot earn the money for doctoring, yet they require doctoring because they are ill.'

"'Yes, sir, true enough.' She offered him an awkward curtsey and withdrew.

"'You will forgive the intrusions, Holmes,' Craden said when the woman had left us. 'But there are some matters of business that must be concluded tonight.'

"'Who are those people, Craden?'

"He took my nearly empty glass and turned away to refill it. 'They are people who need a bit of help from time to time, and who are willing to work off a debt.'

"'You are a philanthropist?'

"Craden laughed. 'Never trust a philanthropist, Holmes! Their benevolence is all for show. My father is a philanthropist. I am a common trader. I trade in talent. Pay for it when I have to. You have no idea how many really clever people are to be found in the unlikeliest places.'

"'How do you find them? Or do they find you?'

"'How does an animal find food and shelter, Holmes? Instinct drags us toward survival, even when common sense tells us we would do better to die and have done with it.'

"'And what talents do they possess? That ruffianly-looking sort of fellow, for example?'

"'Drink up and I'll tell you. His name's Evans, or at least it's the name he goes by. Lost his berth. He said if he could only get enough for a donkey and a cart and a shed to shelter them, he could earn his way, hauling goods. So, I staked him and he pays me out of his earnings, and believe me, Holmes, if you ever want some unwieldy thing carted from here to Herefordshire, he's your man.'

"'The young girl. The one with the scar?'

"'Laurel? She is one of those thousands of women who are poor and genteel, women who must take what they're given or starve. She is fluent in five languages – what, you look surprised – and she is something of an artist with pen and ink.'

"'A forger.'

"Craden shrugged. 'She'd found honest work translating correspondence for men of business, but that took her into some low parts of the city, and she walked into bit of trouble. The sort that plagues young women who have neither father nor brother to stand up for them. She found her way to me. It is known in these parts that I am always ready to barter. She asked if she might be of use to me, and as it happened, I had some documents that needed her particular touch, which she was willing to produce in exchange for...reprisal against those who injured her.'

"'Vengeance, you mean?'

"'I leave it to the law to make such nice distinctions. One man's vengeance is another man's justice.'

"I had begun to feel the effects of the whiskey and the warm fire. 'And the other woman?' I asked, suppressing a yawn.

"'Mrs. Skinner? She was a nurse. Crimea. After the war, she worked in an asylum, where she was charged with helping the young women out of their difficulties, and the older ones out of their pain. The charges broke down, but she was dismissed, so now she makes her way, tending to the poor, going where the medical men will not set foot. She is a fair chemist as well, though she does not while away her time in a dull laboratory as do we – she puts her skill to more practical use.'

"'Helping people out of their difficulties and pain,' I muttered. My head had begun to feel quite heavy, and I noted a dreamy and faraway look in Craden's eyes.

"'Ever visited the asylums, Holmes?' he asked.

"I shook my head.

"'The indigent wards? No? No matter. Walk these streets and you hear the same as you do in their corridors, that symphony of pain that never stops. And all they're crying out is for someone to make it stop. The physicians and the apothecaries, they'll tell you what is wrong with you, as though you cared. All you want is for the pain to stop. Just make it stop. I hear their cries in my dreams, Holmes. Ironic, isn't it? My father can hear those same cries and sleep like a stone. So that's what I try to do, Holmes, what any man should do when a fellow creature is suffering beyond all endurance – I make the pain stop.'

"'Yours or theirs?'

"'There is a decisive thrust to your questioning, Holmes.'

"'And as deft a parry to your responses.'

"'Nonsense, Holmes, I'm as clear as glass – ask me any question and you will get an answer.'

"'A truthful one?'

"'Perhaps better,' he chuckled.

"'You must have been invited to the reception this evening for Miss Reade. Why didn't you go?' I was curious to know what reason he would give for declining an occasion that would bring him together with Miss Turner.

"'I despise Sir Joshua.'

"'So I've observed.'

"'I cannot tolerate a fraud. A man who loves the bubble reputation so much that he will deny his very nature to keep it from bursting. Ah, well, we all do strange things for that which we love.' Craden emitted a bitter laugh and reached for his drink once more. 'You're better off without it.'

"'Without love or a reputation?' I asked. My voice sounded quite distant to my own ears, and I have no recollection whether he responded, or of anything else, for that matter, until morning."

CHAPTER TWELVE

"I woke in my own bed, 'roused to consciousness by the sound of a loud and persistent knocking on my door.

"'Mr. Holmes!' called a familiar voice. 'Mr. Holmes are you awake!'

"I struggled to my feet and cast my eye 'round the room. My boots had been set beside the grate, my pea coat and muffler draped over a chair to dry, and my pouch of lock picks and instruments were on the table next to the bed. Not an item, not a shilling was missing and I had not the faintest notion of how I had got from Craden's room to my own.

"I threw open the door and found our old friend Tobias Gregson upon my threshold.

"Another odd habit of mine – I do seem to have had more than my share – was to hang about the public inquests, which is where I had met Gregson. He had been appointed to the post of coroner's officer. Whenever the coroner received a notification that warranted some scrutiny, it was Gregson who was dispatched to the scene, and his investigations would often determine whether or not there would be an inquest.

"I had found Gregson to be a clever and energetic fellow, if somewhat lacking in intuition and imagination. Perhaps that is why Sir Joshua chose him for the post. Given a reasonable degree of independence, Gregson would not exceed his authority, nor would he overshadow his superior with any demonstration of brilliance. I had, on occasion, made one or two small observations which Gregson had reckoned somewhat clever, and he had fallen into the habit of seeking out my opinion whenever he came upon a situation that was particularly troublesome, or presented some unusual feature of interest.

"'What time is it?' I asked as I waved him into a chair.

"Gregson sat. 'Just past seven. Can you come out, Mr. Holmes?' The thrill of the hunt had pinched some color into his pale features, and I knew that the game was afoot.

"'Something good?'

"'Bad. A very bad business. I have just come from the scene. A house fire, and a deadly one at that. The nursery was ravaged and three children are dead.'

"'When did this tragedy occur?'

"'I only stopped to have a look and to have a word with the constables on the scene. I must go back directly. But the blaze could not have begun before one or two this morning, perhaps later.'

"'And it is now just past seven? The coroner's office was notified rather quickly.'

"'The children's father is acquainted with Sir Joshua – in fact, both parents were at a reception given by Sir Joshua earlier in the evening. At midnight or shortly thereafter, the lady returned home and the gentleman went to his club. He was not at home at the time of the tragedy and it was not until the fire was brought under control and the bodies removed, that anyone could be spared to notify him. It is my understanding that it was he who dispatched a request – a command – that the matter be investigated without delay.'

"Gregson passed a shaking hand over his forehead in agitation.

"'What is it, Gregson?' I demanded.

"'Stevens – one of the constables who was inside the house when the father arrived – says that he overheard the gentleman claim that the fire was deliberately set, and that it was the mother who was the culprit.'

"'Indeed! What motive did a husband give for making such an appalling accusation against his wife?'

"'I cannot say. But Stevens declares that the gentleman was in a violent fury, and that he overheard the accusation made in the course of a bitter exchange between the couple, and that it was followed by the sound of a blow. It is a very delicate business, and I would consider it the greatest of favors if you would come back to the scene with me and give me your opinion of the matter. Oh, and Mr. Holmes, the couple are not husband and wife – the children's parents are Professor James Moriarty and his mistress.'"

CHAPTER THIRTEEN

"Moriarty! Miss Turner! Their children!" I cried, now thoroughly engrossed by the tale. "What did you do?"

"What could I do? I threw on a fresh shirt, pulled on my boots, took up my pea coat, and accompanied him.

"We were at the scene within fifteen minutes. A constable was directing foot traffic away from the pavement in front of the site, but there was no stopping the curious pedestrians from collecting across the street to survey the scene. It was a sad sight, Watson. Soot-covered brickwork surrounded the first floor nursery window. The panes had blown outward in the blaze and glass shards lay upon snow that had turned black with smoke and ash.

"Gregson and I approached the constable who stood shivering at his post on the pavement. Gregson introduced me as 'My assistant, Mr. Holmes' and asked for a report.

"'The housekeeper and manservant have just got here, but I have seen nothing of the nurse.'

"'All but one of the servants board elsewhere,' Gregson informed me in a low voice as we entered the house. 'When the tragedy took place, only a servant girl was at home.'

"'And the mother.'

"'Yes, and Miss Turner.'

"A second constable, the man, Stevens, stood in the hallway between the lady's room and the Professor's study. The smell of smoke was perceptible, and the circulating soot had given the area a semblance of fog.

"'The servants have all been kept to the kitchen,' he told Gregson. 'The Professor has not left his study, nor has the lady left her sitting room since they had words. I have not heard so much as a peep from either one of them.'

"'We will examine the first floor before we interview anyone,' said Gregson. 'Everyone is to remain in the house until I give them leave to go.'

"We mounted the staircase to a landing that divided the first floor corridor. Acrid smoke clouded the air. Black and peeling wall coverings and the stamp of boot prints upon the carpet directed us toward the children's quarters.

"The suite consisted of three rooms. There was a sitting room, which had been fitted for a classroom with two bedchambers adjacent, a small, windowless one to the side, and the larger nursery with windows facing the street.

"The classroom had been furnished with tables and chairs, a chalkboard and a large globe upon a pedestal, several shelves of books. All reeked with smoke and were covered with a fine layer of soot, but I was able to examine a few of the volumes, texts of history, science, mathematics and languages, most of which seemed far too advanced for the children that I had seen in the company of Miss Turner and the nurse.

"I was also able to detect a trace of another odor underlying the smoke. It seemed to be particularly concentrated at the corner of the braided rug nearest the threshold. I got down on all fours and examined the rug around the table and detected the irregular pattern of a dried stain on the rug, as though something had spilled and evaporated upon it.

"'What is it?' Gregson asked.

"'Do you not smell it?'

"'I smell nothing but smoke.'

"'Oil of peppermint if I am not mistaken,' I said, tracing the stain with the tip of my finger.

"'A tonic for the children?' Gregson suggested. 'Peppermint is sometimes used to soften a bitter or disagreeable flavor.'

"'Perhaps. Let us have a look at the nursery.'

"Clearly, the blaze had been concentrated in this chamber, and we were forced to put our handkerchiefs over our faces, for the smell of the smoke and the scorched furnishings was overpowering. The air was a gray film that stirred about us as we moved, and a layer of cinder covered every surface. Black remnants that had been curtains twisted in the wind that whipped through the shattered windows, and the wall coverings were all mottled and blistered from the heat.

"The three narrow beds were arranged in a row beneath the windows. They were nothing but charred frames now, but I spied something wedged between the mattress and the frame of the middle one. I bent down and plucked free a scrap of pale blue wool.

"'What have you got there?' Gregson asked.

"'It appears to be the remains of a blanket,' I replied. 'It was probably wedged so securely beneath the mattress that it was insulated from the flame.'

"'Well, give it here.' Gregson drew a second handkerchief from his pocket and laid the scrap of fabric on it, then folded this and put it back into his pocket. 'Sir Joshua will want anything in the way of evidence. This room will yield up little else, I think.'

"'Not so hasty, Gregson. The fire seems to have been concentrated in the vicinity of these cots. The bodies were very badly burnt, I gather.'

"'It is said that they were little more than charred skeletons.' Gregson shook his head and blinked his eyes at the stinging smoke. 'The fire made quick work of them.'

"'They did not awaken? Did they not cry out?'

"'They were likely asleep and rendered unconscious by the smoke before the worst befell them. It would have been the greatest of mercies if that were the case.'

"'This chamber,' I pointed to the spare room adjoining the nursery. It does not appear to have been occupied.'

"'No – I understand that it is kept for Mrs. Stewart, the nurse, when she is asked to stay the night.'

"'And the apartment across the hallway is the mother's chamber?'

"'No, that is the Professor's room, not Miss Turner's. Her chamber is at the far end of the corridor.'

"'That is singular. Do you not think it odd that the mother should not be nearer to her children?'

"'Yes, now that you mention it, it does seem out of the ordinary, and a great misfortune, too, for she might have heard the children if she had been closer. I suppose we ought to have a look at both of their rooms?'

"'It is always best to be thorough,' I replied, careful not to betray my eagerness to have a look at Moriarty's chamber.

"I was not rewarded for my cunning, however. Moriarty's room was as spare as my own. Other than the bed, the only furnishings were a bookcase, a wardrobe, a plain washstand with a basin and pitcher, and a night table and lamp.

"There was one dramatic touch, however. A large portrait of Miss Turner had been hung on the wall opposite the bed. It had all of the markings of a Rossetti, but it was one that I had never seen. She reclined before a mirror, wearing a dress of violet blue. There was a long rope of pearls around her throat, and she held a loop of it over one hand as she studied her reflection, one pearl pressed against her lower lip.

"'She is a stunner,' Gregson muttered. 'I cannot fault his taste. Let us get a look at her room.'

"Miss Turner's apartment could not have been a greater contrast to the Spartan chamber in which the Professor slept. It was as richly furnished as a seraglio, with a large canopied bed and some sort of brocade covering on the walls. An ornate fire screen stood in front of the hearth, and I put my hand to the ashy coals and felt the faint heat of the fire that must still have been alight at the time of the blaze.

"'The lady did not retire immediately when she returned last night, or the hearth would be cold.'

"I turned my attention to a little lace-covered, bow-legged table upon which had been set a tray bearing a china teapot, a cup and saucer as well as a tumbler and a teaspoon.

"I lifted the lid of the teapot. It was about a quarter filled with some sort of brownish liquid, and some of this same liquid, as well as traces of a sort of sediment, were in the cup and tumbler. This liquid bore the same pronounced aroma of peppermint oil, which did not entirely mask a less agreeable scent beneath, which I could not identify.

"'Is there an empty jar of some sort upon the dressing table?'

"'A small glass jar for hairpins.'

"'Hand it to me, if you will.' I poured the residue from the cup and teapot into the jar and capped it carefully. 'You are likely correct, Gregson – this appears to be the residue of some tonic prepared for the children. May I take it to Bart's? I would like to try to analyze it further.'

"'I will have to report it to Sir Joshua.'

"'I will provide him with a report myself.'

"'Wait – what is this?' Gregson swept something from the dressing table into his palm and showed it to me. He had found several brown-gray seeds of a peculiar heart-shape.

"'There are no flowers or plants in the room.'

"Gregson took a sheet from his notebook and swept the seeds into it, then folded the paper and placed it into his pocket. 'Perhaps Miss Turner or one of the children tracked them in on their shoes.

"'And walked about on the lady's dressing table? Well, well. I can think of nothing more to be discovered here. Perhaps we should begin the unhappy task of speaking to the household.'"

CHAPTER FOURTEEN

"We descended to the kitchen and found that the nurse, Mrs. Stewart, had just arrived, nearly an hour beyond her usual time and who stood, white-faced, as she listened to the housekeeper's account of the tragedy. The housekeeper paused in her recital to invite us to warm ourselves by the kitchen fire, and to introduce the staff. I am certain that you will be surprised when I tell you, Watson, that this lady was our own Mrs. Hudson."

"What! Impossible!"

Holmes smiled. "I am certain that she would have regarded the notion that Gregson's rather disheveled colleague was to be her future boarder with the same expression of incredulity. The sottish manservant, whose drunken inattention first allowed me entrée into Moriarty's lair was Frederick Hudson, her late husband's brother.

"The girl of all work was Miss Serenity Moran. I had put her age at twenty or thereabouts, but it was her cool self-possession which gave her that air of maturity for I was to learn afterward that she was barely sixteen. It was she who stepped forward to offer us the use of her apartment that adjoined the kitchen for our interviews.

"Gregson thanked her, and we entered a comfortable pair of rooms, somewhat larger than the usual servant's quarters. In the sitting area were two worn upholstered chairs, a stove in which the fire had been lit, and a braided rug upon the floor. The bedroom was beyond, and I observed that there was little in the way of feminine adornment or occupation, no trinkets, nor pictures, no handiwork of any kind, though there was a small store of books, neatly stacked in the corner.

"Gregson took one of the chairs and summoned Mrs. Hudson. I remained standing and gestured for the lady to take the other chair, which she declined.

"Gregson began at once. 'Why do you not board at your master's house?' he began.

"'I do not board with my *employer*,' she stressed the distinction, 'because he does not wish it. I have a comfortable berth at Edgeware Road. Professor Moriarty is a very private man and likes to have his house and family to himself as much as possible.'

"'And how did you come to be employed here?'

"'Frederick had an acquaintance in service who told him of the Professor's desire for a manservant. When the Professor interviewed him, he enquired whether Frederick knew of a respectable and discreet lady who could keep his household during the day. I had not sought employment after my husband's death, as I had enough to get by on, but I had often thought that I would like to purchase a property of my own one day, and the income would allow me to do it. And one must do something. One cannot be idle.'

"'And yet I would not think that you could support such a hope on what salary an army tutor could offer,' I observed.

"To her credit, Mrs. Hudson was direct. "'Frederick and I each are paid a hundred twenty pounds a year.'

"You are surprised, Watson. You will be more surprised still to learn that the Professor paid above five hundred pounds per annum in salaries to his household staff. Well beyond the means of an army tutor, wouldn't you agree?

"Gregson next asked Mrs. Hudson how the household duties were divided.

"'Moran resides here, so she will sweep the grates and start the' Here she had to stop for a moment. '… the fires in the morning. She will prepare tea for the Professor, Miss Turner the children. Mrs. Stewart, Frederick and I arrive at seven. Frederick goes immediately to the Professor, while I prepare breakfast for the family. Mrs. Stewart bathes and dresses the children and breakfasts with them and then takes them for their morning exercise. The Professor sends down the menus for the day in time for me to make out the list for the butcher and the grocer.'

"'A moment,' I interrupted. 'These orders are not given by the lady of the house? The children's mother?'

"'No, sir. The Professor is very particular about the children's diet.'

"'Pray, continue.'

"'When Mrs. Stewart returns, the Professor will give the children their lessons and then spend the rest of the morning in his study. He frequently lunches at his club and occasionally dines there when he is not engaged with one of his pupils.'

"'And at what hour do you leave for the night?'

"'Frederick and I always leave at seven.'

"'And how does Miss Turner pass the day?'

"'Miss Turner is a scholar, and she spends a great deal of time with her reading and music. When she does go out, it is to the book stalls or to the lecture halls or museums.'

"'It seems a very quiet routine,' I observed. 'Did anything occur yesterday, before their evening engagement, which you found to be out of the ordinary?'

"The lady hesitated.

"'Speak up, Mrs. Hudson,' Gregson commanded.

"'It is barely worth mentioning. Miss Turner went out to perform some errands and as a result of it, I believe there were words exchanged.'

"'What sort of words?'

"'The Professor always insisted upon knowing where Miss Turner went and when she was to return. Yesterday, she went out without the Professor's leave – without his knowledge,' she amended, 'and he seemed annoyed and spoke to her harshly when she returned.'

"'Do you know where she went?'

"'She told me that she had gone to take some of the children's cast-off clothing to a Ladies' Aid in Rotherhithe and to leave her violin for new strings somewhere near Oxford Street, I believe.'

"'It seems a slight provocation for a quarrel,' I remarked. "Could there not have been some other source of irritation? The Professor suspected that Miss Turner had gone to call on a friend at Rotherhithe or Oxford Street, perhaps? Someone of whom the Professor did not approve?'

"'I do not believe that Miss Turner has any friends.'

"'What, none at all?' cried Gregson. 'Who were her callers?'

"'Miss Turner never received visitors. Mr. Hudson was instructed to turn them away, if anyone should happen to call for her.'

"'That is rather singular,' I remarked.

"'As I said, sir, this has been my first engagement as a housekeeper. I do not know what is considered out of the ordinary, but it has been my experience of the world that studious folk like the Professor are often of a solitary and even eccentric nature.'

"'Still, it seems a lonely life for a woman.'

"'I would not choose it for myself,' she admitted.

"'Thank you, Mrs. Hudson.' Gregson rose to dismiss her. 'Would you ask Mrs. Stewart to come in?'

"The lady withdrew, and in a moment, Mrs. Stewart entered. I had previously seen her only at a distance. Now, at close quarters, I was surprised to find her appearance quite striking. Indeed, she might have been beautiful had her life been an easy one, but toil and adversity had drained the bloom from her complexion and streaked her russet hair with premature gray.

"Despite this, she carried herself with extraordinary poise; indeed, considering the shocking news she had just received, her composure was disquieting, to say the least.

"'You have arrived only in time to hear the terrible news. I expect you are out of a place now,' Gregson began, somewhat clumsily.

"'I will make myself available if the Professor should need my help until matters are settled,' the woman replied, gravely.

"'Mrs. Stewart, were you here last night at the time the Professor and Miss Turner left for their engagement?'

"'Yes. After the Hudsons had gone, Moran and I had a cup of tea and then I went up to tidy up the classroom and to look in on the children once more before I departed.'

"'So you were the last one to see the children alive?'

"'Unless Moran looked in on them, or Miss Turner did when she came home. I was told that she and the Professor did not return together.'

"'Before you departed,' I said, with some caution, 'did anything out of the ordinary occur?'

"'Out of the ordinary"?' she enquired, calmly.

"'Any callers, or carriages that were unfamiliar, or people lurking about?'

"'No, not at all.'

"She was a cool liar, Watson. Perhaps Craden had not told her that it had been I who waited in his carriage during their clandestine exchange, but I could not challenge her without revealing to Gregson that I had, indeed, been lurking about.

"'Do you leave the house and return in the morning at the same time?' I continued.

"'Yes.'

101

"'And yet, today you were more than an hour late.'

"'My cabbie's horse fell lame and I had to summon another.'

"'Were there any matches or candles left in the nursery?' Gregson asked her.

"'Never. The nursery lamps were never lit in the evening. Either Moran or I would bring in a single candle for light, so that the children might undress and put their clothing away properly, but this candle was always removed once the children were in bed. The Professor inspected the children's rooms daily. I am certain that if a match or candle stub had been left behind, or made its way into the children's possession, I would have heard of it.'

"'Been sacked for it, you mean?'

"'Yes.'

"'No problems with the gas that you are aware of?'

"'None.'

"'Then what would you say was the start of the blaze?' Gregson looked at her, keenly.

"'I cannot say. I was not here.'

"'You have heard what the Professor says, no doubt,' Gregson persisted. 'He accuses Miss Turner of starting the blaze. Why would he do that?'

"'I have no opinion.'

"He tried another tack. 'The Professor and Miss Turner – relations between them were easy, would you say?'

"The woman hesitated. 'The Professor was a man who made it very clear what he expected of both staff and family. To my knowledge, Miss Turner never contradicted him.'

"'What about the staff?'

"'I don't understand you, sir.'

"'Did any of the staff ever contradict him? Deviate from his stipulated routine, or have any associations the Professor would not approve?'

"'The fact that we are still in his employ, sir, is proof that we did not.'

"'It may only be proof that such encounters escaped the Professor's notice,' I replied.

"'Little escapes the Professor's notice.'

"'Very good, Mrs. Stewart,' Gregson said. 'We will see Miss Moran now.'

"The girl entered and faced us with an equanimity that was not many degrees from disdain. It is a daunting thing, Watson, to see such hardened self-possession in one so young.

"'It is our understanding,' Gregson began, 'that there was some small dispute between Professor Moriarty and Miss Turner yesterday afternoon.'

"There was the slightest hesitation and a narrowing of the gray eyes before she replied. 'I believe the Professor was only concerned that Miss Turner had forgotten about their engagement, and would not return in time to dress.'

"'After Miss Stewart departed, did you immediately retire?'

"'No – I felt uncommonly tired and, in fact, fell asleep in a chair in the kitchen. It was Miss Turner's bell that woke me.'

"'You did not hear her when she entered, then?'

"'No.'

"'What time was this?'

"'It was not half past midnight. Miss Turner asked me to fetch her some hot water so that she might prepare a pot of tea, and mentioned that the Professor would likely be quite late at his club. She said that I need not wait up for him, and so I went to bed.'

"'Did she mean to wait up for the Professor?'

"'I do not know.'

"'And she ordered the fire lit in her room?'

"'Yes, she did.'

"'She asked only for some hot water – why did she not simply ask you to prepare her a pot of tea?'

"'It is not my habit to question Miss Turner's whims.'

"The trace of animosity in her voice was not lost upon either of us.

"Gregson bade her continue with her account.

"'I went to bed, and had fallen asleep when I heard Miss Turner crying out for help. I hurried up the stairs and saw Miss Turner running from the nursery, smoke pouring after her. She ordered me to raise the alarum for the fire brigade and I threw on a shawl and ran out into the street. I could see the flames from the upper window-'

"'One moment,' I interrupted. 'You say you were awakened by Miss Turner's cries – did you hear the children cry out at any time?

"'No.'

"'Please continue.'

"'I summoned the brigade and when I returned, the hallway had filled with smoke. Miss Turner had got a blanket and I suppose she meant to beat down the blaze, though she only seemed to be fanning the flames higher. The firemen conducted her down the stairs, but she her refused to leave the house, and as the first floor rooms were untouched, she was allowed to remain in her sitting room. I opened the windows in the sitting room and dining room, and went down to open the kitchen door. The firemen made quick work of the blaze, but there was nothing to be done for the children. The coroner's van was sent for and the constables arrived. I sent one of them to summon the Professor and went down to dress.'

"'And what did Miss Turner do when she was told that her children were dead?'

"'Nothing. She was as cold as marble.'

"'She did not attempt to go to them, to see for herself whether they had perished before they were taken away?' Gregson persisted.

"'No. I expect that they were in no state to be seen, yet if she had asked, I do not think they would have denied her.'

"'When the Professor arrived, I understand that he and Miss Turner had words – it is said that he accused her of deliberately causing the blaze. What do you make of that?'

"'I cannot know. But the Professor is not the sort of man to make an idle observation. Will there be anything more?

"'One or two more questions,' I said. 'I understand the Professor engaged the staff. Mrs. Hudson was recommended by her brother-in-law. May I ask how you came to his notice?'

"'My uncle is a friend of the Professor's. He has always tried to assist my sisters and me, as our father has been able to do very little for us.'

"'Quite so. And what of Nurse Stewart? Was she also recommended by a friend of the Professor?"

""I do not know that I would call him a friend, only a casual acquaintance, a gentleman who was a member of the Professor's club.'

"'Would you happen to know the name of this friend?'

"'Yes. Lord Craden.'"

CHAPTER FIFTEEN

Holmes reached for an old briar-root pipe. "I was astonished, of course, but also somewhat relieved," he said, as he struck a match. "This established a link between the nurse and Craden and I was spared, for the present, from disclosing my own knowledge of their acquaintance."

He leaned back in his chair once more. "We meant to send for Hudson next, but we were informed by Mrs. Hudson that he had just been summoned by the Professor. 'You must sit and take some breakfast,' she invited, 'for you cannot have had time to eat before you arrived.'

"'Thank you, no, we will speak to Mr. Hudson, and then interrupt you no further,' I said, for which I received a sharp nudge in the ribs from Gregson.

"At this moment, the manservant clambered down the stairs, his haggard face taut with shock and bewilderment.

"'What is the matter?' demanded Gregson.

"'The Professor has ordered Miss Turner out of the house immediately. He has left the house and said that he will return within the hour and expects to find her gone.'

"'Left the house?' Gregson cried. 'I instructed Stevens that no one was to leave!" and beckoning me to follow, he hurried up the stairs.

"We found Constable Stevens standing sheepishly in the hallway. 'I'm sorry, sir – I could do nothing to prevent it,' he stammered. 'Professor Moriarty rang for his man and it seems he gave orders that the woman was to be gone within the hour, and then he stormed out, his face black as thunder.'

"Gregson peered beyond the flustered man into the room. Miss Turner was slumped in a chair, her eyes dazed, her face as white as alabaster save for the dark red mark upon her jaw where the brute had struck her during their earlier altercation. 'What is to be done?' Gregson said in a low voice.

"'It is his house. He can order her out if he likes.'

"'But where is she to go? She cannot leave London – she must be at hand if there is an inquest. Is there anyone who will take her in? The housekeeper says that she has no friends.'

"'Sergeant, I must be frank. When you came to me this morning and asked for my help, I might have refused if I had known from the outset that this was the family involved. You see, I have met both Professor Moriarty and Miss Turner on one or two occasions. I would not want you to think that any opinion I rendered was tainted by partiality.'

"'I do not think that your judgment would be biased by a casual acquaintance.'

"'I did not mean to say that it would affect my judgment,' I corrected him. 'I only say that I would not want to be accused of it.'

"'Well, I cannot say that I would blame you if you had allowed reason to give way. She is a stunner.'

"'As to the immediate problem,' I said, 'it happens that Miss Turner and I have a mutual acquaintance, Mr.

Aiden Brodie, a book dealer in Old Compton Street. He is a respectable old gentleman and I am certain he would offer her shelter until a better plan can be devised.'

"Gregson gave a reluctant nod, and stepped into the sitting room. 'Miss Turner, my colleague, Mr. Holmes suggests that we prevail upon the hospitality of your friend, Mr. Brodie. If one of the servants will help you gather a few things, I will have Mr. Holmes escort you to Old Compton Street.'

"The lady seemed to notice my presence for the first time. Her gaze met mine, and I thought that I saw a flicker of something like irritation in it.

"'I will not trouble your *colleague*, sir. Mrs. Stewart will do as well. There is nothing to occupy her here.'

"She had suffered a tremendous blow and some concession must be made for a state of shock, and yet it seemed a very cold reply. Nonetheless, I stepped into the passage and summoned Mrs. Stewart.

"She listened to our proposal and replied with some reluctance, 'I must not leave the house without permission from Professor Moriarty.'

"'I will take full responsibility,' Gregson assured her. 'He will know that it was done on my authority.'

"'Very well,' she said, resignedly. 'Come, Miss Turner, you will need one or two warm dresses and a cloak, for it is very cold.'

"Gregson waited until they were well out of earshot, then turned to me. 'She may have the nurse for a chaperone if she likes, but I want you to escort them. I do not like this at all – the nurse is a cool one, and Miss Turner colder still. How can they behave so when three little children have been burned in their beds?'

"'She has suffered a terrible blow,' I said. 'We must allow for that.'

"'The Professor does not allow for it. He puts the blame on Miss Turner. I see nothing to support such a charge, and yet...' Gregson shook his head. 'She is a stunner. And she is not bound to the Professor by marriage. There must have been admirers. Perhaps one of them became enraged when Miss Turner rejected him – lost his wits, perhaps, and set the fire in a fit of madness.'

"'To discover the hour when neither the Professor nor most of his servants were at home, to avoid 'rousing Miss Turner or the girl, shows a premeditation and stealth that one does not find in a lunatic. I would like to have a look around the property, and then I will wait for the ladies on the pavement.'

"It would have been difficult to detect the sign of an intruder in the wet snow which had been trodden to a gray slush by the constables and the fire brigade. I walked around the little slate path to the kitchen area and saw that the ground was likewise trampled all the way to the mews, so that no impression of any kind could be distinguished.

"Something caught my eye, a blue scrap that had snagged upon the wrought iron railing. I plucked it free and saw that it was a bit of blue plaid wool, the remnant of a shawl or blanket, but clearly not the same fabric as the scrap that had turned up in the nursery.

"I pocketed it and walked back around to the street and summoned a four-wheeler, then waited for the ladies.

"It was a sad journey, Watson, for Miss Turner did not speak one word, merely sat with her head bowed, the dark veil of her hat covering her face. Mrs. Stewart broke the silence only once to say, 'It was not necessary for you to accompany us, sir.'

"'In such unhappy circumstances, a gentleman ought to do more than what is simply necessary,' I replied.

"It was now after nine in the morning, and I was surprised to see that the shades of Brodie's shop were still drawn, for the neighborhood was a busy, bohemian sort of street with many shops and cafes that bustled from dawn until long past sunset.

"I bade the ladies wait in the cab while I got down and rapped on the door. I heard the shuffle of a footstep inside and called out, 'Mr. Brodie! It is Sherlock Holmes!'

"I saw Brodie's grizzled features peer from behind the shade, then the sound of the bolts drawn aside.

"'Are you ill, sir?' I asked, when he opened the door.

"'Sherlock Holmes!' cried he, quite evidently astonished to find me upon his doorstep. 'What can bring you here?' And then, recovering himself, he said, 'Oh, bless you, I am not ill. The advantage of being in business for oneself, you see. I may open early or late or not at all. Who is in that carriage yonder?'

"'Miss Turner, sir, and her children's nurse.'

"'Where are the children?'

"I laid a hand on the old man's shoulder. 'Mr. Brodie, the children are dead. There was a fire in the nursery last night and none of them survived. The household is in disarray, and Miss Turner is in need of shelter, for the present.'

"The old man let out a cry and ran out to the pavement in his slippered feet. Mrs. Stewart got down from the cab and spoke a few words in his ear and then turned to help Miss Turner alight.

"'Come in, come in, my poor girl.' Brodie paid the cabman before I could protest. 'Sherlock, you take the valise.'

"We followed Brodie to the narrow staircase at the back of his shop and up to his apartments above. These consisted of a large, comfortable room that served as sitting room and dining area. There were many bookshelves, more books stacked in the corners. Adjacent to this was a small area fitted out for a kitchen, and an alcove beyond which contained a bed and night table.

"'It is humble but quiet, and you won't be bothered by my patrons, I will keep my doors shut today. My pantry is in fine shape for an old widower. You ladies prepare whatever you like. Violet dear, you must rest. You must preserve your strength. Come downstairs, Sherlock, I want to talk to you.'

"We settled in chairs before the fire, and Brodie propped his feet up on an ottoman and gazed into the flames for several minutes, his grizzled face haggard and grave.

'Now, lad,' he said at last. 'How do you come to be mixed up in the business?'

"'The coroner's officer came to me this morning, and asked me to offer my opinion.'

"'The coroner's officer – a fellow named Gregson, is it not? Tall fellow? Pale pinched face? So, you know him, do you?'

"'Yes.'

"'Is he sharp?'

"'Sharp enough. Somewhat lacking in imagination, perhaps.'

"'And why is poor Violet in need of shelter?'

"'Moriarty accused Miss Turner of setting the fire and ordered her out of the house.'

"Brodie's brows shot up. 'What does your friend Gregson make of that?'

"'He does not know what to make of it. He does not know what Moriarty is.'

"'I doubt that you do, either, lad. Not completely. You only know what a man is when you know what he *will not do* – and Moriarty is a man who will stop at nothing.' He sighed. 'And what do the household say? I'll wager they back the Professor.'

"'Well, save for the housekeeper, perhaps, they did not seem to take Miss Turner's part. Nice, amiable people the Professor collects around him. What do you know of them?'

"'The household? Only gossip.'

"'Yet even gossip may have a foundation in truth,' I reminded him. 'The Moran girl, for example. How does a lowly girl of all work come to be in such favor that she lives under her master's roof while the others must shift for themselves?'

"'Because Moriarty determines who stays and who goes and it suits him to keep the girl close at hand.'

"'I see.'

"'Not for *that* purpose, young man.' He tapped his forehead. 'It is brains. All of the Moran girls are sharp and Moriarty knows the value of a clever mind. Does the name 'Moran' not mean anything to you?'

"'No.'

"'Well, I will tell you a bit of the girl's history. In the first place, she is not lowly by birth. Her grandfather was Augustus Moran, British Minister to Persia. Her father, Selden Moran, was the elder of two sons. He was raised to great prospects, but given to drink and dissipation, and he produced nothing in life but five daughters for whom he could ill provide. His younger brother, Sebastian, fared better. He inherited his father's brains, you see, and that, combined with a cold heart and iron nerves, made his reputation in the military. You will hear Colonel Moran spoken of with the sort of awe one reserves for killers and kings. After his military career concluded, he placed his wits and mettle on the open market. There has only been one purchaser, but that one has allowed the Colonel to take some heavy losses at cards, and be none the worse for it.'

"'And that patron is Moriarty.'

"Brodie replied with a lift of his bushy brows. 'Moran has assisted his brother's children, and those with no expectations understand that such backing comes with a price. He has got them placed in some excellent households. The eldest has just been taken on as governess to the Merryweather girls. Their father is the chairman of directors of one of the principal London banks.'

"'What of the Hudsons? She seems a respectable sort.'

"'So she is. It is the brother-in-law that bears watching. It is said that he got into a bit of trouble that would have found him on the wrong side of the prison door if he had not fled to Australia. He laid low until matters cooled a bit and then made his way back to England.'

"'And Mrs. Stewart?'

"'Ah, Mrs. Stewart,' he sighed. 'She is the younger daughter of a tradesman who could give his girls no dowry but education. She took a post as headmistress of St. Andrew's Collegiate School, where she married Stewart, the school's founder. After his death, the office became too difficult for his widow to manage and so she yielded the post and returned to London where she applied to a few of St. Andrew's benefactors for assistance in finding a situation.'

"'The Moran girl said that it was Craden who recommended Mrs. Stewart to Moriarty. And, as Craden is no philanthropist, I can only surmise that it was done to install a go-between in a household where visitors were discouraged.'

"'His hopes alone would not have done the trick. Moriarty would not have engaged her had her character and reputation not been excellent. A maid of all work is one thing – but the Professor is very particular when it comes to the supervision of his children.'

"'I think that Craden's cunning is equal to Moriarty's caution,' I said as I rose.

"'Where are you going?'

"'Bart's. I will return later. There are a few questions I would like to put to Mrs. Stewart, but I want to speak to Craden first, and there is a bit of chemical analysis I want to try.'

"'Ah, lad,' he sighed, as he ushered me to the door. 'The only chemistry at the root of tragedy is the chemistry of the human heart, and not all of your scientific analysis can explain it.'"

CHAPTER SIXTEEN

"Sir Joshua Reade had been given the courtesy of an office at most of the city's hospitals. At St. Bart's it was a small room and antechamber in the same wing as were given over to the chemical laboratories, and it was outside these chambers that I came upon a group of the students and dressers huddled in conspiratorial silence.

"Upon spying me, young Stamford, who has a fixed place in both of our memories, put a finger to his lips, exhorting me to be silent. A moment later the opening and closing of an inner door anteroom sent them fleeing in all directions.

"Stamford grabbed my sleeve and pulled me into a corner just as a disheveled Lord Craden emerged from the room, his handsome face dark with passionate anger. He charged past me without any sign of recognition and stormed out of the building.

"'You have come too late for the excitement, Holmes!' Stamford whispered. 'It will take all of Lord Warrington's influence to buy the son out of this scrape. Are you going to the chemical laboratory?'

"'Yes.'

"'I will walk with you, then.' He waited until we were out of earshot and then resumed his normal tone. 'Craden and Heep got into a fight, and it took five of us to separate them,' he announced.

"'A physical altercation? Surely not!'

"Stamford nodded, gleefully. 'Craden is such an odd fellow. He staggered into Professor Paget's first lecture looking as if he'd had a bad night of it, and fifteen minutes late, too. Paget threw him out, and a few of us found him slumped over his stool in the lab. He ignored us until the gossip started going 'round the room.'

"'What sort of gossip?'

"'Good God, you haven't heard? You know the girl who comes to so many of the anatomy and botany lectures? Miss Turner? You must know who I mean, Holmes, none of the lads can concentrate when she is in the room. A genuine beauty, though why a girl that pretty needs to fill her head with the anatomy of the primate and the distilling of vegetable extracts is beyond my comprehension.'

"'I know who you mean.'

"'Did you know that she is the mistress of Professor James Moriarty? And the mother of his children?'

"'I know that as well.'

"'Well last night, there was a fire at their home. All of the children perished. Burned in their beds. Beastly business, and it is said that there has been a call for an inquiry, and that it is to be held tomorrow.'

"'So soon? The investigation and the post-mortem will not be complete.'

"'I know nothing about the investigation, but it is said that there is little enough left of the children to drag out a post-mortem and that it will be finished this afternoon. It was all that was talked about in the laboratory, and at last,

Craden raised his head and shouted, "Keep quiet, you insufferable peahens!" Well, not two minutes later, Heep came into the room and started up the gossip once more. He expressed not one bit of pity for the little ones, only speculated aloud 'pon which of us might be chosen to assist Sir Joshua, knowing full well that *he* is Sir Joshua's favorite, though his anatomy is nowhere near as precise as Craden's. Craden turned upon him and enquired in a scathing tone whether Heep ever got tired of being Sir Joshua's spaniel, whereupon Heep lost all pretense of humility and made a rather foul reply.'

"'What did he say?'

"'He said that he had gotten more satisfaction as Sir Joshua's spaniel than Miss Turner must have gotten as Professor Moriarty's – well, he said something quite crude. *I* think it is because she would not look at him, and there were rumors that Craden and the lady – well, it would not be fair to repeat what was said, though Craden's response would seem to confirm the rumors for he went all white in the face and said that he would be damned if he heard a lady spoken of so in his hearing and demanded that Heep retract his remark, and Heep said that they were not talking of a *lady* and refused to take it back. Well, Craden went for him and it took five of us to pull them apart.'

"We entered the laboratory and saw one of the attendants sweeping some broken glass into a little pile.

"Stamford lowered his voice. 'Craden was summoned to Sir Joshua's office to account for his conduct and Heep was taken to the surgery with a dislocation of the wrist and a black eye. What good luck for you, for if Heep is crimped, Sir Joshua will *have* to choose you to assist with the post mortem, as your anatomy is quite good, and you are just about as well up in chemistry as Heep. I wish I might have the opportunity. You don't know what I would do to get my hands on a fresh cadaver now and then, Holmes! It's enough to make a fellow take to burking!'

"The two of us sat down to our work, then. I drew from my coat pocket the jar of brownish liquid that I had brought from Miss Turner's bedchamber. When I removed the lid, I detected the immediate sharpness of peppermint and the pungency of an underlying odor, not unlike stale cheese. I wondered whether the liquid might have been brewed from some sort of dried fungus, rather than tea leaf. That, of course, suggested poison, but, as it was in such a diluted state, I did not believe that it would do me any harm to take a pinch. If the worst came of it, at least Bart's' the meager store of cadavers would increase by one.

"The brew, however, had no adverse effect upon me other than leaving a somewhat stale taste upon my tongue. I concluded that it must be no more than an herbal tea that had been flavored with peppermint oil, though why this fetid brew should be preferred over the conventional British beverage was a mystery.

"I next decided to see if I could extract some precipitate from the solution, but I had no sooner assembled my instruments than Sir Joshua's little page appeared at my shoulder and informed me that Sir Joshua requested me to come to his office immediately.

"Stamford looked up from his work and gave me a knowing wink. I capped the liquid and put the jar on the table, then followed the boy to his master's office.

"The office was a small cubicle with barely room for a visitor's chair, for the desk was a large one with bookcases on either side and the walls were covered with charts of the anatomy of the brain. The hapless visitor was obliged to sit facing a row of gaping eye sockets from the collection of skulls upon the desk.

"Sir Joshua was a tall man with a complexion so pale, and black, deep-set eyes so lacking in animation, that he almost resembled one of those prized skulls. The scalp had a scant covering of ashen hair, combed back from his forehead, a few wisps tied into a sort of knot at the nape of his neck. He was the sort of fellow one could not imagine as a young man.

"'You wished to see me, Sir Joshua?'

"'Please take a chair, Mr. Holmes. I am sorry that you were not able to attend the reception last night.'

"'I apologize, Sir Joshua.'

"'I had a most interesting conversation with your brother. He spoke quite persuasively of your analytical skills.' Sir Joshua seated himself behind his desk. 'I understand that those talents were called upon this morning by Sergeant Gregson.'

"'Sergeant Gregson and I are acquainted, and he asked for my opinion of the Paradise Walk tragedy.'

"'And you also know Miss Violet Turner, is that not correct?'

"'Very slightly. I've seen her occasionally at the lecture halls. May I ask the purpose of these questions, Sir Joshua?'

"'I was told that you escorted the lady from her home.'

"'With the children's nurse, and at Sergeant Gregson's request.'

"'Did Miss Turner say anything which might suggest her state of mind?'

"'She said nothing at all.'

"'I ask because all possibilities must be considered, including that of foul play. Anything which was said by a possible suspect, may have to be repeated at an inquiry by those who overheard it.'

"'I saw nothing to suggest foul play, and certainly the mother would have no motive.'

"'I have often found that when it seems that there is no motive, it is more likely that there is simply no *obvious* motive,' Sir Joshua replied. 'It is not too difficult, for example, to imagine that such an ambitious young woman might tire of the demands of three children, and the quiet routine of a scholar's household and come to think that she might do better if she were free. Of course, all is speculation until I am able to review Sergeant Gregson's report. I have every confidence that I can rely entirely upon Sergeant Gregson's independent observations. I would not have taken him for the post if I had not thought him entirely capable of managing his responsibilities. Do we understand one another, Mr. Holmes?'

"'I am not to offer Sergeant Gregson any further assistance.'

"'I think that would be best. I think it would be best if you turn over to me the material you removed from Professor Moriarty's home.'

"'Yes, Sir Joshua.'

"'My page will accompany you to the laboratory to retrieve it, so as to save you the inconvenience of making a second trip. Thank you for coming in so promptly, Mr. Holmes.'

"I had my hand on the doorknob when Sir Joshua made one last remark. 'I will have to summon you to the inquest, Mr. Holmes. If this material should prove to be significant to the matter at hand, it will be necessary to attest to the sequence of possession.'

"As there was nothing further to occupy me at Bart's, I decided to go to the Reading Room. As I approached the Museum, however, a wave of fatigue passed over me. It was nearly noon, and I had had little sleep and no food and as I was but a few steps from Montague Street, I decided to return to my rooms. I had no sooner entered my apartments than I fell onto my bed in a deep slumber.

"I was 'roused by a rude and persistent shake of my shoulder and opened my eyes to see Gregson staring down at me. 'What time is it?' I said, groggily.

"'Nearly five o'clock. Are you ill, Mr. Holmes? You did not stir when I knocked! I was ready to call in the coroner for you!'

"I sat up, feeling the weight of fatigue clinging to me. 'No. Ring the bell, will you?'

"Gregson rang for the landlady and I asked for a pot of coffee. Two steaming cups sharpened my brain considerably.

"'Sir Joshua summoned me in this morning,' I told him. 'He would much rather you conducted your investigation without my assistance.'

"'I know. He called me into his office and gave the same orders. Still,' Gregson added. 'He cannot prevent the two of us from having a friendly chat, now, can he?'

"'You have learned something?' I asked, for there were spots of color about Gregson's wan face and his pale eyes glittered with excitement.

"'I have spent a most interesting day. You know that sediment which was found in Miss Turner's room?'

"'The seeds?'

"'Yes. What do you imagine they were?' Gregson beamed.

"'I have not put my imagination to the task. The lady had a great many flowers in her sitting room, I observed, and there were some nature albums which seemed to contain pressed plants and petals.'

"'In her sitting room, but not in her bedchamber. And these seeds were found in her bedchamber.'

"I sipped my coffee, patiently.

"'Come, Mr. Holmes, do not be a poor sport about it.'

"'All right, what were they?'

"'I recalled that the staff had mentioned Miss Turner's patronage of the Physic Gardens, which are but a short stroll from Paradise Walk. For one who takes an interest in botany, there is no finer place to look over specimens or to attend lectures, so I took myself there and made enquiries.'

"'And what did you discover?'

"'I sought out one of the men who was tending to some plants in the Wardian cases and showed him the bits I had collected in my handkerchief and asked whether he could identify them.'

"'And he did?'

"Gregson nodded. 'He did not even need to examine them under a lens. He said that because of the peculiar heart shape, they were likely,' here Gregson drew a notebook from his pocket and read from his notes, '*Valeriana officinalis*. It is the scientific name for garden heliotrope. It is a commonplace flower which only blooms for a few months in the summer, so naturally I was curious to know how the seeds for a summer bloom came to be Miss Turner's bedchamber in the middle of winter.'

"'She had a bouquet of them in a vase in her sitting room,' I replied.

"'What? I did not see them.'

"'Well, say rather that you did not *observe* them. You may have overlooked them because they *are* commonplace. But it is the commonplace that is often far more unusual than the extraordinary. Pray, why are they significant?'

"'The roots, stems and seeds are said to have soporific properties. They are often dried and ground and brewed into a sort of tea – valerian tea, he called it – which is said to induce sleep.'

"'And this tea, I gather, can be somewhat unpalatable and has an unpleasant aroma?'

"'Yes! Like moldy cheese! How could you know that?"

"'The peppermint oil. It was evidently used to make the concoction more pleasing.'

"'Yes, that's it. Apparently, the blossoms have a sweet enough scent, but the dried roots and stems are disagreeable to the taste. That pot of tea Miss Turner brewed – most likely she suffered from sleeplessness and prepared this as a remedy. That may be why she was not 'roused by the fire straight away. I have known men who take to drink or opium and are lost to everything for days. But why would she take the trouble to prepare a sedation which must be inferior to the laudanum or chloral hydrate that may be got from any chemist?'

"'Perhaps the Professor did not approve of such measures and this more easily escaped his notice than would a parcel from the chemist,' I said. "But if Miss Turner were sedated and the maid was asleep and Moriarty was at his club, there is still the matter of who or what caused the fire.'

"Gregson frowned. 'There is another puzzling matter, as well. Miss Turner told Mrs. Hudson that she was going to leave some old clothes at a Ladies' Aid in Rotherhithe. I've been to St. Bartholomew's, St. Mary's, St.

Philip's, St. Olave's, Saints Peter and Paul and James and Jude. I've all but run out of parishes in and about Rotherhithe and I could not find one which had a Ladies' Aid that Miss Turner may have visited yesterday. There are some vendors of second hand clothing, but they deny ever seeing the lady, and I don't believe they would forget a face like hers.'

"'You ought to have attempted to trace her steps through her other errand. There are any number of places to dispose of one's second-hand clothes, there are only three places any true musician would take a good violin for new strings: Lott and Sons on Coventry Street, Guivier on Regent Street or Atkinson on Tottenham Court Road.'

"Gregson made a note of the addresses. 'I understand from Mr. Ernest that Lord Craden got himself into a scrape at Bart's this morning.'

"'When did he tell you this?'

"'I went to the mortuary earlier and he had already begun the post mortem. He said you will be called to give testimony at the inquest.'

"'Sir Joshua spoke of it only as a possibility.'

"'Really? Ernest spoke of it as if it were a settled thing. Let us meet at the coroner's court, shall we, but mind you, be prompt. If you do not get there early, you will have to stand, for this is just the sort of case that draws out the public like flies.'"

CHAPTER SEVENTEEN

"Mr. Brodie had lamented the decline of those lively tavern inquests, but with advancements in sanitation, came an increasing reluctance to lay out the deceased in the presence of victuals and ale. It was at the time of these events that the public house inquest began to give way to established coroners' courts, where inquiries might be conducted in more dignified surroundings. It was in such a setting that the inquiry into the deaths of the Moriarty children was to be held.

"The bodies of the three young victims had been taken to a children's hospital infirmary, not far from the Moriarty residence. A coroner's court had been constructed as a wing of this institution, and the deceased had been laid out in the infirmary's post mortem room, where they might be viewed by the jurymen before the inquiry convened.

"When Gregson left me, I set out directly for the site and went 'round to the mortuary entrance. Two attendants stood outside, their backs to the wind, sharing a cigarette.

"'It's a cold evening,' I greeted them. 'Why are you not inside?'

"One held up the cigarette. 'Resurrection Reade's orders. No smokin' 'roun' the bones. Not that a bit of smoke would 'urt *those* three,' he added with a nod toward the door.

"'The children who died in a house fire.'

"'Aye.'

"'Is he at work – Doctor Reade?'

"The man shook his head. 'A'n't seen 'im all day. Rat-faced toady was by. Gave us a dressin' down for our *carelessness* and *neglect*.'

"'Indeed?' I offered a cigarette to each. 'What caused him to make such an accusation?'

"'Seems when 'e set to task, 'e saw a bit or two of the remains was missin'.'

"'Those little ones're so far gone, what difference does a few bits of bone make to the weasel?' snorted the other. 'Though the toff wouldn've offered two gold sovereigns for 'em if he hadn't been in his cups. Shame there wasn't a good lock of hair left – a nice, long plait brings in a tidy sum.'

"You look shocked, Watson. Well, well, I am afraid that you are one of those whom Brodie would have found to be too nice. There has always been a market for morbid mementos, as the Newgate auction will attest. Two gold sovereigns, however, was a considerable sum, and I knew of only one person who might have offered it. 'I think I know the fellow,' I said. 'Tall, dark-haired gentleman, fine-looking and well-dressed? About twenty-five or six?'

"'Drink will have its way with his fine looks in time,' the first one grunted.

"Craden. What purpose could he have in bribing his way into the morgue in order to make away with a few fragments of charred bone? A vengeful prank, perhaps, as any mark of carelessness or neglect would be charged to Ernest.

"'Of course,' added the other, 'if it was only a *look* he wanted, *that* might be got for a few coppers.'

"I dug into my pockets for a few coins and handed them one each.

"'Porter will want something as well. Tell him Bill says you might have a peek.'

"I thanked the man and entered the mortuary. There was a small anteroom, where a porter lay in a half-doze in front of the register. I saw that Ernest had signed out fifteen minutes before.

"'Bill said I might have a peek.' I laid a coin on top of the register.

"The man closed his hand over it and nodded toward a corridor that led to the mortuary.

"There was a small closet where I hung up my coat and hat. Beyond was the mortuary where the three cadavers had been laid out upon slate tables, ready to be viewed by the jurymen, and on the opposite side of the room was an adjoining chamber for the chemical analysis of fluids, organs, whatever had been removed in the post mortem.

"It is now my sad task to describe what I saw Watson, and I will do that as briefly as possible. The remains of the twin boys were arranged upon one table, the remains of the girl on a separate one. There was little more of them than blackened skeletons, with the merest covering of charred flesh, which had not been sufficient to hold the cadavers intact. Every effort had been made to lay out the bones in systematic arrangement, but I observed at once that one or two of the smaller bones, as well as many teeth, were missing from the remains, and the mutilation was so great that, in the case of the twin boys, was not possible to distinguish one from the other. The tags affixed to both of them read the same: James or Amon Moriarty.

"I went into the adjoining room. To the layman, this would be a grisly place, Watson, for it was here that organs were removed to be weighed, and their contents assessed for poisons or disease. I spied a jar that contained a scant quarter inch of brown fluid which appeared to be the tea I had removed from Miss Turner's chamber. Upon a table lay an open notebook, a page covered all over in Ernest's spindly hand. Several of the words had been underlined, and a quarter of the page was yet blank, as though Ernest had left off abruptly.

"A rap upon the outer door gave me the signal that my time was up, and after making a gift of a few more cigarettes to the attendants, I set out for Brodie's, as I was eager to know how Miss Turner and Mrs. Stewart fared, and – in the light of Henry Craden's bizarre conduct – especially eager to know the particulars of the nurse's relationship with the man.

"Dusk had set in by the time I reached Brodie's shop. As I approached the door, I saw that the lamplight behind the drawn shades illuminated a pair of silhouettes and I heard Miss Turner's voice raised in anger. 'Take your hand from my arm and take yourself out of Mr. Brodie's shop!'

"My immediate thought was that Moriarty had pursued her here, but it was Ernest's whining voice that replied, 'Come, Miss Turner, there is no call to be high and mighty with me. I can conceal what I discovered, or I can have it all come out at tomorrow's inquest. It is up to you.'

"I tried the handle, quite prepared to force it open if it had been locked, but the knob turned in my hand.

"Ernest stood between Miss Turner and the door, his back toward me. I swung the door open, rattling the bell and Ernest spun around, his expression shifting from a leer to a frown. 'I thought Sir Joshua had asked you not to involve yourself in this matter, Holmes. But perhaps your visit here is not of a professional nature.'

"'You will be of little use to Sir Joshua if I put your other wrist out of joint, Ernest.'

"'You are out of your depth, Holmes, and in some very rough water. Mind you don't sink.' He stormed past me and left the shop, slamming the door after him.

"I turned to the lady. 'Where is Mr. Brodie? Where is Mrs. Stewart? Why have they left you here alone?'

"Miss Turner's fingers clenched over her skirts as if to keep her hands from shaking. 'Mrs. Stewart went to her lodgings to collect a few belongings. She said that she would not be gone longer than an hour, but when she did not return by noon, Mr. Brodie became concerned and went to look for her. I should have lifted the shade before I opened the door, but I thought it was Mr. Brodie. I had no idea it was that creature.'

"I looked at the clock on a shelf above the desk. It was after six. 'Perhaps she returned to Paradise Walk to gather up some of your personal belongings as well?'

"The lady shook her head. 'I took all that I need for the present.'

"'But after the present? Even when the inquest has been concluded, you cannot go back there.'

"She sank into a chair. Her dark eyes had a look of resignation about them, a quiet fortitude that had neither grief nor apprehension. 'After their verdict, I may have no authority to determine where I will go.'

"'Is that what Ernest implied?'

"'Mr. Ernest implied nothing, he hasn't the subtlety. He told me outright that a verdict of unlawful killing is all but certain and that I will most likely be the suspect. Mr. Ernest suggested that he might be able to alter certain laboratory findings so as to divert suspicion from me if I were willing to be...grateful.'

"I was outraged. 'Ernest goes too far.'

"'Mr. Ernest is not particularly adventurous. He does not stray far from home ground. What he told me is no more than what is being said in other quarters.'

"'Did Ernest tell you what evidence they mean to bring forward in order to justify such a verdict?'

"'I don't need to be told, Mr. Holmes. Ernest takes his orders from Sir Joshua and Sir Joshua takes his from James, and James has been deprived of his little human laboratories. Someone must be held to account, and if James has decided that I am to be accused, nothing will be left but the unpleasant formalities.'

"Before I could protest this alarming sentiment, the clang of the shop bell rang out and Brodie entered, his step weary and dejected.

"'Where is Mrs. Stewart?' I asked him.

"Brodie looked up at us and tried to put on a good face. 'Has she not returned? Well, I am certain that she decided to take the opportunity to attend to a few errands. How pale you look, Violet! Go upstairs and lie down. I want to have a word with young Sherlock here, and then I shall fix us a bit of supper bye and bye.'

"I rose and waited for Miss Turner to leave the room. When she had gone, Brodie sank into a chair with a heavy sigh.

"'What is the matter?'

"'I went to St. Thomas Street, where Mrs. Stewart lodges, thinking I would find her there, but her landlady said that she had not seen her all morning. I then went to Paradise Walk to make enquiries – I did not go to the house, of course, but only intercepted the greengrocer who had been summoned by Mrs. Hudson so that she might settle his account. He told me that he saw Mrs. Stewart in the kitchen, helping Mrs. Hudson and the girl to box up some household goods.'

"'She returned to Moriarty's?'

"Brodie nodded, grimly.

"'And was Moriarty there?'

"'No, I was told he has quit the place and taken a suite at Claridge's.'

"'Do you think that Mrs. Stewart has thrown in her lot with Moriarty?'

"'If that is the case – well, he was her employer, after all. Some compassion is due him, villain that he is.'

"'Should she not also feel compassion for the children's mother? Moriarty has many allies to take his part, but whom does Miss Turner have?'

"'I trust,' Brodie replied, with a patient smile, 'that I am as worthy a friend to Violet as all of the Professor's grovelers and minions put together.'

"'Well, there is one groveler whose mischief should not be underestimated.' I told him about the encounter with Ernest.

"Brodie leaned over and patted my hand. 'Good lad! You ought to have blackened the other eye! Oh, I know all about that business at Bart's. I heard that Craden's conduct got him tossed out of the place.'

"'Gregson believes that the fire could have been the work of a frenzied lover, and Craden's conduct has certainly been suggestive of a passionate and unstable mind.' I told him of the incident related to me by the mortuary men.

"'He is a strange fellow, to be sure, but he did not start the fire.'

"'How can you know that?'

"'Because it has come to my attention that Craden has an alibi.'

"'An alibi?' My immediate thought was that Craden's motive for inviting me to his East End lair was so that I might vouch for him later.

"Brodie nodded. 'At what time do they say that the fire started?'

"'Sometime between one and two in the morning, I believe.'

"'And there goes Gregson's theory, and yours. For at that hour Craden and the Professor were together, at the card table, at their club, and were still at play when the Professor was called away to Paradise Walk.'"

CHAPTER EIGHTEEN

"The next morning dawned bright and sunny, though it was a deceitful winter sun that brings no warmth with it. Nonetheless, when I arrived at the coroner's court on the following morning, I saw that Gregson's forecast had been correct: the case had drawn a considerable crowd, and the stairway to the public entrance was already crammed with hopeful spectators. In fact, it had been necessary to allow the jurors use of a private passage from the mortuary up to the court chamber, so that they would not have to push and shove their way through the public after they had examined the deceased.

"I heard 'Mr. Holmes! Mr. Holmes!' booming above the din and saw Gregson at the top of the staircase waving an arm aloft. He made his way toward me and seized me by the coat-sleeve. 'Half of London has turned out,' he bellowed into my ear as he dragged me upward through the crush of bodies.

"The room was of a fair size, but much of it was taken up by the coroner's bench and the box which must billet as many as twenty-three jurymen and no fewer than a dozen – and so there were only five pews left to the public – or, four, rather, as the first of them was reserved for witnesses. Several of the latter – the Hudsons, Miss Moran, Ernest, Constable Stevens, and two members of the fire brigade –

had already taken these places, and Gregson and I seated ourselves behind them."

"Miss Turner was not among the witnesses?" I asked Holmes, somewhat taken aback. "And what of Moriarty, and the nurse?"

"I confess, Watson, I was as surprised as yourself by these omissions, particularly when Gregson informed me that none of them was to be called. Of course, Moriarty and Mrs. Stewart had not been inside the home at the time of the fire. As to the lady – we shall come to her presently.

"The jurymen entered and were ushered to the box. There were twelve in all, stout, middle-class fellows, the type who could stomach a good deal, and yet they were white-faced and shaken, having just come from viewing the remains of the three children.

"A hush fell upon the room as Sir Joshua entered and made his way to the coroner's bench, and then I heard a gasp from behind, followed by another and another; I turned 'round and saw that Miss Turner, followed by Brodie, had entered the room and sat at the end of the pew nearest the door.

"I suppose, Watson, that it would be as impossible an undertaking for her to appear plain as it would for a plain woman to make herself into a beauty, but I thought that, under the circumstances, she might at least have chosen a more subdued attire. Instead, she wore a plush, feathered hat, its webbed veil covering only her eyes, and a walking dress fashioned of some iridescent fabric, which appeared to be black until movement revealed an underlying scarlet. I cannot imagine a mode of dress more calculated to suggest a wanton indifference to the gravity of the occasion.

"As for Brodie, the old fellow spied me and regarded my astonished expression with a shrug and a shake of his head, as if to convey that his objections to the lady's attendance had been overruled by the lady herself.

"Sir Joshua opened the proceedings with a brief, orderly review of the matter at hand, and called the first witness. I had expected that to be Gregson or one of the firemen, but he began with the household, first questioning Miss Moran and then Mrs. Hudson, who said nothing to contradict what they had said to Gregson and me the day before.

"Sir Joshua then called up Mr. Hudson, whose responses took a more troublesome direction.

"'While Sergeant Gregson was concluding his questioning of the staff, Professor Moriarty summoned you, did he not?' enquired Sir Joshua.

"'He did, sir.'

"'And what was the nature of your conversation with the Professor?'

"'He told me that Miss Turner had declared she would stay in his house no longer, and that she intended to leave within the hour.'

"'To leave the family home?'

"'Well – to leave the Professor – or so I took it to mean.'

"I heard Gregson's gasp, and was, myself, open-mouthed in astonishment at testimony which contradicted what the fellow had declared on the morning after the fire.

"'Did the Professor give any explanation for her conduct?'

"'The Professor seemed quite taken aback, sir, but he believed that Miss Turner spoke out of her own torment and did not mean what she said.'

"'And what did he do then?'

"'He said that he wanted fresh air and left the house. He was quite out of his head.'

"'And what of Miss Turner?'

"'She left as well, not long after the Professor.'

"'To take some fresh air?'

"'No. She went to stay with a friend.'

"'A lady friend?'

"'No, a gentleman friend.'

"I heard a murmur pass through the crowd.

"'And she has not returned to the family home?'

"'No.'

"'Only a few questions more, Mr. Hudson. What sort of father would you say the Professor was to his children?'

"'Excessively devoted, sir. I have never seen a man so devoted to his children. He spent a great deal of time with them, even at the sacrifice of his own leisure.'

"'And Miss Turner, did she also sacrifice her interests to those of her children?'

"'Not as the Professor did. It seemed to me she gave herself over to her own pursuits.'

"'Would you say, then, that she neglected her children?'

"'I would say that the Professor took pains to see that they were not neglected, sir. That is all I can vouch to.'

"'I see. And what has been the Professor's demeanor since this terrible event?'

"'He is very low, sir. I have never seen a man brought so low.'

"'And Miss Turner's demeanor?'

"'I have not seen her from the time she left the house until this morning.' He gave a nod, as if directing the jury's attention toward the elegant and composed young lady at the back of the room.

"Hudson was dismissed and resumed his place at the pew beside his sister-in-law. I detected something in the straightening of her back and the lift of her chin, which hinted at indignation, as if she were not pleased with the testimony of her brother-in-law.

"The next witness to be called was Constable Stevens who must, I supposed, refute Hudson's account.

"'You were posted inside the home of Professor James Moriarty after the fire was extinguished?' Sir Joshua began.

"'Yes, sir.'

"'And you overheard an exchange between Professor Moriarty and Miss Turner?'

"'Yes, sir. It seems that the lady had made up her mind to straight away leave the house.'

"Gregson and I exchanged an astonished look.

"'And did she leave?' Sir Joshua asked.

"'Yes, sir.'

"'Alone?'

"'No, sir, she was escorted by Sergeant Gregson's colleague, and accompanied by the children's nurse – to act as chaperone, I took it. It seemed to me that the nurse did so unwillingly.'

"Nothing further was asked of the man; he was dismissed and I was called next.

"'Mr. Holmes, what is your profession?'

"'I have a small income and I'm pursuing a course of study.'

"'Toward what end?'

"'I hope toward increasing my income.'

"I did not intend to be impertinent, Watson, but I disliked and distrusted the fellow, and I was unsettled by the direction his inquiry seemed to have taken.

"'You accompanied Sergeant Gregson to the home of James Moriarty yesterday morning, is that not correct?'

"'I did – at his request.'

"I expected next to be asked about Miss Turner's removal from Paradise Walk, but Sir Joshua's next question was, 'And in the course of your investigation, you discovered a scrap of blanket fabric wedged beneath one of the mattresses in the children's nursery?'

"'Yes. I turned it over to Sergeant Gregson.'

"Sir Joshua went to the table where several large envelopes had been placed in a row. He picked up one of these and removed the remnant and showed it to me. 'Was this the item you found?'

"'It appears to be, yes.'

"Sir Joshua replaced the item. 'Did you also remove the contents of a teapot from the residence?'

"'Yes.'

'And where was this teapot?'

"'In Miss Turner's bedchamber.'

"'Did the contents have any particular qualities which you were able to discern?'

"'The liquid was transparent and brown in color and resembled common tea.'

"'And what did you intend to do with it?'

"'I took it to the laboratory at Bart's to analyze.'

"'And why did you believe that this liquid which resembled common tea was something that ought to be analyzed?'

"'Because of its peculiar scent. It had a pronounced odor of peppermint with a less distinguishable aroma, somewhat stale, underlying it.'

"'And also because you observed a dried stain upon a carpet in the room outside of the children's chamber, which had this same peculiar scent?'

"'Yes.'

"'Might it not be possible, then, that the source of this stain just outside the children's nursery might have been some spilled contents of that teapot?'

"'Yes, it is possible.'

"'Indeed, would you say that it is also probable?'

"'It is not improbable.'

"'Not improbable,' Sir Joshua echoed with a frown. 'What became of the fluid that you brought to Bart's?'

"'You summoned me and asked me to surrender it to you, Sir Joshua, which I did.'

"To my surprise, he questioned me no further, but only made the perfunctory enquiry whether any of the jurymen wished to ask a question (which no juryman who sat before Sir Joshua Reade would ever dare to do), and then dismissed me and called up Ernest.

"'Mr. Ernest, you are training to be a surgeon, is that correct?'

"'Yes, Sir Joshua.'

"'And in the course of your training, you have made a study of such subjects as anatomy, physiology, dissection and the like?'

"'Yes, sir. I am also interested in many of the branches of science which might be considered above my training, and so have attended many lectures on all of the sciences, including botany, chemistry, and physics.'

"'And in attending those lectures, did you happen to meet any person or persons concerned in this matter?'

"'Well, sir, I have had the pleasure of attending one or two lectures given by Professor James Moriarty. They are outside of my field, of course, but the Professor has always made the subject intelligible to even the most humble student.'

"'Anyone else?'

"'Well, it was not uncommon to see Miss Turner at some of the scientific lectures which I attended.'

"'Miss Violet Turner who is the mother whose children are the subject of this inquiry?'

"'Yes, sir.'

"'Were you acquainted with Miss Turner?'

"'Very casually, sir.'

"'Did you observe that she was on familiar footing with anyone else –any of the other ladies – who attended these lectures?'

"'Not the other ladies, no, sir. But I did, on several occasions, see her addressed by Lord Craden.'

"'Lord Craden is a student?'

'I have seen him about the lecture halls and laboratories, though I don't know if he might be called a student. I've seen no evidence that he is working toward any profession in particular.'

"'Was Lord Craden at Bart's the morning after the fire at the home of Professor Moriarty?'

"'Yes, sir, though I cannot imagine why. He was not fit to engage in any sort of study.'

"'Not fit, in what way?'

"'He had evidently been drinking and was in quite a foul humor. When I made some innocent observation regarding the tragedy, he lost his composure and struck me.' Ernest held up his bandaged wrist.

"'Now, Mr. Ernest, to the present. You have assisted me several times in performing a post-mortem and such tests as are deemed necessary to determine the cause of death.'

145

"'Yes, I have had that distinct pleasure, sir.'

"'Yesterday, I gave you a jar of a clear brown liquid and asked you to attempt to identify the substance, is that not correct?'

"'Yes, that is correct.'

"'Can you tell us what you discovered?'

"'Well, sir, upon uncapping the vessel, I immediately detected a pronounced odor of peppermint oil, with a less potent and less pleasant odor underlying it. It was not like any variety of tea with which I am familiar. I do know, however that peppermint oil is used to flavor certain medicinal preparations to make them more palatable.'

"'How did you proceed?'

"'I visited several of the chemists and apothecaries to ask for their opinions.'

"'And what were the consensus?'

"'Well, some were quite baffled by the substance. A few, however, did mention that there is said to be a certain compound of oil of valerian with peppermint and sugar that is known as the French preparation. It is mixed into tea or hot water.'

"'What is oil of valerian?'

"'It is an extract of *valeriana officinalis*. The common heliotrope. It is a sort of folk remedy that is meant to induce sleep. The peppermint and sugar are added to make the concoction more palatable as the smell and taste of this valerian extract are somewhat unpleasant, akin to stale or molding cheese.'

"'Why is this mixture called the French preparation, were you able to learn that, sir?'

"'As the story goes, it was a French midwife who devised a mixture of distilled valerian when she was tending an infant who was plagued with a painful and incurable illness.'

"'She employed it to lessen the child's pain?'

"'No, sir, to end its misery. The woman observed that a tea of dried valerian had certain soporific properties, and through experimentation, she was able to come up with the more potent extract that did not bring on the discomfort of strychnine or arsenic.'

"'You suggest that this was used in the place of strychnine or arsenic, Mr. Ernest. Does that mean that this French preparation could be characterized as a poison?'

"Ernest paused before answering, deliberately allowing the word 'poison' to hang before the jurymen. 'Well, if the term encompasses both those naturally occurring substances and the compounded mixtures which may cause – or be administered to induce – death? Then, yes, it would most certainly be a poison.'

"Sir Joshua dismissed Ernest who left the table with a smug humility, pointedly averting his gaze from Miss Turner.

"The next witness called was Captain Shaw of the Metropolitan Fire Brigade. He was a staid and respected professional, who was said to be a personal friend of the Prince of Wales. Even so, the association had elevated his standing without making him vain.

"'Captain Shaw," Sir Joshua began, 'you visited the scene of the fire at Paradise Walk?'

"'I did, sir.'

"'And would you briefly describe your observations?'

"'The fire seems to have been largely confined to the first floor nursery. The occupants of the three beds, which were in a row against the wall opposite the door, were quite consumed by the fire. The heat had ruptured the windows and the blaze had caused severe damage to the room. The smoke had infiltrated much of the floor, though the other rooms, as well as the hallway and the lower rooms were largely spared.'

"'You arrived on the scene, then, before the bodies were removed?'

"'I did, sir.'

"'And would you describe what you observed?'

"'It appeared that the blaze had been the most intense in the area of the beds, and so the bodies of the occupants were burnt almost to skeletons. From their position upon the beds, it did not appear that they had struggled nor made any attempt to flee.'

"'And did you find this to be unusual?'

"'Yes, sir, for in my experience, flames will 'rouse even a sound sleeper, unless...'

"'Unless, sir?'

"'Well, a drunken man, for example, is not easily 'roused, of course. And one who is paralyzed could not escape the flames.'

"'The occupants – three children – were not paralyzed, and it is unlikely that they would have been drunk. Is there any other explanation you can think of, sir, for the condition in which you found them?'

"'It may be that they were already dead,' Shaw replied.

"'Dead - before the fire had started?'

"'Yes, sir.'

"Sir Joshua went to the table and produced the scrap of blanket once more. 'You heard the testimony of Mr. Sherlock Holmes, Captain Shaw, when he stated that this fabric was found lodged beneath one of the children's beds?'

"'Yes, sir.'

"'I asked you to inspect it, did I not?'

"'Yes, sir, which I did in the presence of yourself and Mr. Ernest.'

"'And will you tell the jurymen what was the result of your examination?

"'I concluded that a great deal of finely pulverized coal dust had been worked into the fibers.'

"'Could this have been soot from the blaze?'

"'No, sir, it was examined and found to be finely powdered coal, rubbed deeply into the fabric. If the bed coverings had been steeped in pulverized coal, it might explain why the fire in the nursery was so concentrated in a single area. Powdered coal is highly flammable.'

"'And if a blanket had been steeped with coal dust and ignited, what would be the result?'

"'It would burst into flame immediately.'

149

"'And if this blanket had been tucked 'round a sleeping child?'

"'That child would be consumed in flames almost instantly, and would burn to death in his bed.'"

CHAPTER NINETEEN

"As it was near lunch-time, Sir Joshua suspended the proceedings, though on a note that was certain to rob the public of any appetite.

"The jury were ushered out first. Then the public rose and engaged in a good deal of shuffling with wraps and gloves and headgear, although I believe that this was less a preparation for the weather than a desire to hang back and observe how Miss Turner comported herself.

"Miss Turner behaved as though she were at a morning lecture rather than the inquest into the deaths of her own children. She rose and calmly drew on her fur-lined gloves, then shook out the folds of her skirt and adjusted her veil and her wrap and passed out of the room, followed by the hapless Mr. Brodie.

"Gregson and I were separated in the crush of the public's exodus and when I reached the pavement, I saw nothing of him.

"'Well, Holmes,' said a nasal whine in my ear, 'it does not look good for Miss Violet Turner now, does it?'

"I cannot think that anything would have given me more satisfaction, Watson, than blackening his other eye, but I contented myself with saying, 'It is an inquest, Ernest, not a trial.'

"'That will come, and soon.'

"I had opened my lips to reply when the cries of 'Murderess!' and 'Child killer!' diverted my attention. I looked across the street and saw Brodie attempting to extricate Miss Turner from a knot of angry folk that had surrounded them.

"I pushed my way through the crowd and, spying a four-wheeler that had just left off its fare, I whistled sharply for it to wait. I then seized Miss Turner by one arm and Mr. Brodie by the other and dragged the pair toward the waiting vehicle, urged them in and then sprang up after.

"'Whatever were you thinking, Miss Turner?' I demanded. 'Why show yourself, and in such a fashion, if you're not to testify? How can you have allowed it, Mr. Brodie?'

"'My permission was not sought,' the old man said, mildly.

"'You must not go back for the afternoon session,' I declared.

"Miss Turner removed her hatpin and lifted her hat away from her hair. 'I do not seek your permission, Mr. Holmes. But as it is, there will be no afternoon session, only Sir Joshua's declaration that the jurors have decided that they have heard sufficient testimony to come to make their ruling.'

"'They must hear Sergeant Gregson. Whatever motive Hudson and Constable Stevens had for lying – Gregson's testimony will refute it.'

"It was Brodie who answered me. 'Their motive is survival, Sherlock. Hudson and Constable Stevens know its rules. They have played the game wisely and advantageously, I daresay.'

"'This is no game, Mr. Brodie. Do you say they were bribed?'

"'I hope so,' said Miss Turner. 'I would be sorry to think that they would perjure themselves for nothing.'

"Her confounding composure tried my patience. 'Miss Turner, you must exert yourself! Surely you cannot be insensible to the gravity of your situation!'

"Brodie scowled at me and patted her hand. 'Young Sherlock here is too passionate. He only means to say that it is always wise to prepare for the worst possible outcome and to provide against it.'

"'Mr. Holmes is quite right,' she agreed.

"When the carriage drew up to Brodie's shop, I helped Miss Turner down and asked if I might have a word with her.

"'Sit here by the fire,' Brodie said. 'I will go up and see to a cup of tea and some sandwiches.'

"Miss Turner sat in Brodie's chair, which kept her face in the shadows.

"'Miss Turner.' I spoke with the liberty I would have taken with a sister. 'You must endeavor to be as rational as possible. Sir Joshua has done you a great deal of harm, this morning – to implicate you in an abomination of the worst kind. You must act to preserve yourself from a criminal charge.'

"'What would you advise that I do, Mr. Holmes?'

"'The testimony suggested that the fire had been deliberately set – if you are to defend yourself, you must think! Who may have had a motive to harm your children?'

"'Whom would you suspect, Mr. Holmes?'

"'Lord Craden.'

"'Mr. Brodie tells me that he was at the club with James at the time of the fire.'

"'But how far *before* the fire can his whereabouts be determined? And Craden has some strange associates, who will do his bidding in anything.'

"'And what would his motive have been, Mr. Holmes?'

"'The most powerful of all. Love. You were not free so long as the children bound you to Moriarty.'

"'And would he not consider the pain that such an act would inflict upon me, if, indeed, I were his object?'

"'You cannot deny that he is desperately in love with you.'

"The lady looked down at the hands in her lap. 'I do not deny it,' she said in a low voice. 'But Henry's love brings pain to no one except himself.'

"'I would feel more at ease if I believed that were true, Miss Turner, but love can be a dangerous emotion when it is thwarted.'

"'I did not realize that love was among your many areas of expertise, Mr. Holmes,' she replied, with a faint smile.

"'I speak only from what I have seen.'

"'Perhaps you see but you do not observe.'

"'What have I failed to observe?'

"'The one other possibility, which an objective person would have considered.' The lady looked up and confronted me directly. 'That I may have actually killed them.'

"'I have considered it and dismissed it as impossible.'

"She shook her head, as though I were a persistent child who was testing her patience. 'You confuse the impossible with the improbable, Mr. Holmes. James has an excellent maxim, which you may be familiar with – if you want the answer to a problem, you first eliminate what is absolutely impossible, and whatever remains, however improbable it may seem, must be the truth.'

"'And are the Professor's axioms never to be contradicted?'

"'One does not contradict James, not ever. One stands down, or one is annihilated. Stand down, Mr. Holmes.'

"'While you are annihilated?'

"'If it means that I will be free of James at last? In that case, yes, Mr. Holmes, I would even allow myself to be annihilated.'"

CHAPTER TWENTY

Holmes fell into a grave silence after this remark and sat so for some time.

"Holmes," I said. "You need not continue."

"It makes no difference, Watson. Spoken or silenced, the past is what it is."

"Clearly you had some feelings for the woman. I think that most people would call it love."

"I don't know what to call it, Watson. It does not speak well for love if that's what it was, for it seemed that no one who loved that woman was ennobled by it. Moriarty's love was the covetous pride that could shift to hatred in an instant. Craden's seemed a hopeless and unrequited obsession and Ernest felt only the base desire which is incapable of rising to the level of his idol, and so hopes to drag her down. It was more like self-love. Like meeting yourself in another form, and recognizing yourself, all of yourself, including some corners of your character you would rather not see."

"And was she correct? Had the inquest been concluded?"

Holmes nodded.

"What, then?"

"I decided to direct my efforts toward seeking out anyone who might come forward on Miss Turner's behalf. I began with a tour of the public grounds where Mrs. Stewart had, on occasion, taken the children for their daily exercise.

I found none among the other nursemaids and governesses whose acquaintance with her went beyond a nod and a 'Good morning,' for it seemed that the children in Mrs. Stewart's care were not permitted to play with others. 'She was a very fine-looking, well-spoken lady, and the children were very handsome to be sure,' one nursemaid said to me. 'But why they should not be permitted to join in a game with the children of Sir John and Lady Merton is beyond my understanding. I cannot think that they would have been the worse for it, as they were only the children of a tutor and his mistress.'

"And so went an afternoon of futile investigation. Weary, confounded and feeling the pangs of hunger – for I had not eaten anything since the night before – I made my way back to my rooms on foot, stopping to buy a sandwich at a stall on the way.

"As I entered, the landlady approached me with a stern look. 'I am used to the comings and goings of your odd set of friends, Mr. Holmes,' she added, 'I canna have that ragged little street urchin pulling at my bell every fifteen minutes. I asked him to leave his message, but he said that he would speak only to you.'

"Even in those days, Watson, I had acquired a few of those colorful associates who are so irksome to a respectable landlady, though I had no notion of who this particular intruder was. Nonetheless, I begged the good lady's indulgence and asked her to show the 'ragged little street urchin' up if he rang again, and had finished half of my sandwich when I heard the patter of nimble feet on my stair and a brisk rap at the door.

"It was Wiggins, the lad who had tended to Craden's carriage on the night Craden had brought me to his flat, with his young companion in tow.

"I bade them step into the room. Wiggins tugged off his cap and nudged his companion until he did the same.

"'What can I do for you. Wiggins, is it?'

"'Yessir.' His eye darted toward the half sandwich on my plate. 'I'm sent t' find th' Guv'nor. We gone hev'rywhere we can fink, an' you're th' honely friend of 'is what's left I know of.'

"'How did you know where to find me?'

"'Why, it's 'ere th' Guv'nor 'ad us cart you t'other night, me an' Mr. Hevans. Guv'nor said you 'ad to sleep it off an' we're to bring you 'ere an' put you t' bed. Took y'r key from y'r pocket an' let hourselves in nice as you please. We didn't pinch nothin',' he added.

"'Monday evening?'

"The lad nodded.

"'At what hour, do you recall?'

"'Not yet midnight.'

"So, it was Wiggins and Evans, the carter, who had carried me home from Craden's Rotherhithe flat the night of the Paradise Walk fire. And well before the fire, which Gregson said had started no earlier than one o'clock, and quite probably later.

"'Why are you looking for Lord Craden?'

"'A fine lady come to 'is flat lookin' for 'im. She said they'd 'rranged t' meet an' seemed quite cross that 'e forgot. I said I know most the lush cribs from when I'm sent to fetch Pa 'ome, an' she said if I'd be so kind as to fetch the Guv'nor, she'd gimme a shillin'.'

"'What did this woman look like?'

"'Tallish an' very 'andsome an' dressed plain but what fit 'er too fine t' be got from th' rag fair. She 'ad a kind, gentle way of speech 'as if she 'ad some heducation. So, I left 'er at the Guv'nors an' looked for 'im heverywhere, but..." The lad shrugged. "Honly place left t' look's Mother Sun's an' I cannot go there as I got t' tend to Bob 'ere, an' I cannot take 'im to Mother Sun's for Ma says little 'uns mus' keep clear of the place or they'll likely be snatched up an' sold. But,' he added with a flash of inspiration, 'if *you* go to Mother Sun's an' should turn up the Guv'nor, I'll give you 'alf what the lady gives me.'

"I could not but smile at the lad's enterprise, and I was quite willing to take him up on the bargain, for I might confront both Craden – if he were sober – and the 'fine lady' who, I concluded from Wiggins' description, was Mrs. Stewart. Whatever her reasons for allying herself with Moriarty, they had not kept her from continuing her clandestine relationship with Craden. I was determined to get to the bottom of it.

"'Very well,' I said. 'Let me fetch my coat and muffler. I expect I will not be able to finish that sandwich. I don't suppose you would like the other half?'

"'Don't mind if I do,' Wiggins replied.

"I watched as he carefully tore it into two pieces, giving the much larger portion to his little brother. The little one ate ravenously, though the elder tried to consume his with a degree of self-control.

"'If you're quite finished, we will be off. You shall have to give the cabbie directions to this Mother Sun's.'

"'Oh, no cabbie'll go near the place. When we get to Rother'ithe, I'll point you the way.'

"The three of us piled into a four-wheeler, the little one laying his head on his elder brother's sleeve.

"'A question, Wiggins,' I said, as we clattered off toward Rotherhithe. 'Why did you give your brother the larger portion of the sandwich? You're bigger than he, you must have a bigger appetite as well.'

"'But 'e needs the strength. We just 'ad the Little Un go on us. Mrs. Skinner said 'e 'adn't strength enough to fight the fever. There's two more b'sides me an' Bob, but Bob's th' baby now th' Little Un's gone.'

"I recalled the name Skinner. She was the stout woman who had come to Craden's flat the night he had brought me there. 'Mrs. Skinner nurses the sick, does she?'

"'Yes, sir.'

"'Is there no doctor?'

"'None but Doctor Knowles'll come to Rother'ithe, but 'e's no better'n a crocus. If your time's come, folks would rather go quick an' peaceful with Mrs. Skinner than 'ave it drag out with Dr. Knowles.'

"'What's wrong with him?'

"'Drink. Ma says it's the 'angin's what's got to 'im. 'E's the 'angin' doctor at Newgate an' 'e's got to watch 'em swing an' then see to it they're cold an' not took down before th' rope's done 'ts work. Pa says it's bad 'nough to be 'ung but worse to be put in the box if you still got breath in you. Ma'd 'ave none but Mrs. Skinner when th' Little Un went bad, an' when Ma sent me to fetch the Little Un's tonic, Mrs. Skinner'd gimme a sweet. She's a kind woman, Mrs. Skinner is. I know she's got a rough way 'bout 'er but Ma says that's just 'er way of not lettin' the misery drive 'er mad. Ma says Doctor Knowles is more like the Guv'nor, can't keep 'is guard up, so 'e takes to drink.'

"It was dark when our cab drew up at Rotherhithe Street, though a frigid mist permeated the air and laid down a sort of milky fog that gave off the illusion of daylight. The noise, too, conveyed the liveliness of an afternoon, for the street echoed with the caterwauling of those who check neither mirth nor wrath. Tinny music from disreputable-looking public houses accompanied this vulgar chorus, while a few vendors idled on the pavement, though I could not imagine what trade they hoped to transact on such a dismal evening in such a dismal place.

"A door slammed like the report of a gun and an inarticulate oath swelled over the noise. Wiggins grabbed his brother's hand and darted into the shadows, looking up at me with a finger to his lips. A gangly lout, who had Wiggins' high forehead and pallid complexion shouldered past me and lurched toward a pub at the corner. When he was out of sight, the boy emerged once more. 'Ta,' he said. 'When 'e's in a temper, Pa lights into th' first one 'e lays eyes on. It's why Ma don't care if I run herrands for folks, it keeps me an' Bob outta 'is way.'

"'I see. Well, there can be no harm in going home now. Point me toward Mother Sun's.'

"'Jus' keep the river on your right side,' he said. 'It's beside the dock just 'fore you come to the East Lane steps. Look for two blue lanterns.'

"I nodded to the lad and made my way along the river-side. A sharp wind blew straight off the river, with its reek of filth and mud and rust. I passed a succession of docks, offices, tenements, warehouses, half vacant and left to ruin, the other half unsavory-looking establishments. Even in the poor light, I was able to discern a great variety of complexions, and my ear picked up Mandarin, Hebrew, Swedish and Italian, mixed with the mother tongue.

"I approached a rambling structure, which could only be reached by passing through the gateposts, upon which hung a pair of blue lanterns. Descending the makeshift steps, I encountered a tall Oriental fellow leaning against a post smoking a long pipe. He looked up at me with languid eyes.

"'Mother Sun,' I said.

"The man grinned at the sound of the name, and bobbed his head, pointing to the door.

"I walked past the man to an open door and through a passage dark as pitch. I heard the murmur of voices beyond and smell the heavy sweetness of opium mingled with the stench that rose from the Thames.

"At the end of the passage was a sort of parlor, with a staircase beyond, which descended to regions below. This room's sole occupant was a woman, who rose as I entered. She had a tall, compact figure and hair as glossy and stiff as onyx. She appeared to have some Oriental blood, though her voice was English with no trace of an accent. 'It is sixpence for a pipe,' she said.

"'I am looking for a friend.'

"The lady smiled. 'A friend will cost more.'

"'Lord Craden.'

"The smile vanished, and she cast a quick glance toward the staircase. 'I do not ask my customers for names.'

"'Then I will find him myself.'

"As I crossed the room, the lady clapped her hands and two burly Lascars appeared and blocked my way. I was in no mood to brook interference, Watson, and I had the advantage of acquiring a knowledge of boxing and training in some of the Oriental forms of combat. I made quick work of the pair, laying them both out upon the floor and, walking over them, I descended the stair to a long, low-ceilinged chamber.

"Here, I came upon a study in degeneracy of the worst order. There were men and women mingled, in stages of undress, on cots and divans, or, in some cases, on the bare floor. An appalling sight, Watson, made all the more dissolute by the stifling odor of incense and opium.

"A stout man of indeterminate race stood at the center of the room, though what his role was, I could not determine. Perhaps he was there to keep the pockets from being picked, or perhaps to do the picking. He would not have had to deal with much resistance, as the occupants of the room had all been rendered lifeless by the effects of opium and drink.

"I made a slow circuit of the room under the dark gaze of this custodian, but he made no move to intervene. Evidently, he was of the opinion that if I had got past Madam Sun's minions, I had leave to do as I liked.

"Craden was not in the room, but there was another passage concealed behind a curtain. I pushed it aside and found myself in a sort of kitchen. There was a black iron stove and a grate with a coal fire. In the center of the wooden floor was an iron ring. I gripped this and lifted up a trap door. The river was three or four feet below me, and wondered how often an inconvenient demise had been concealed by dropping the remains into the water.

"On the opposite side of the room was another door. I pushed my way through this and it was there that I found Craden, lying upon a cot, quite unconscious. His overcoat and frock coat were on the floor, and his collar was unfastened, his shirtsleeves rolled above the elbow.

"'Craden!' I gripped him by the shoulders and shook him, and then pressed my fingers to his wrist and felt a slow, steady pulse, and saw that he was breathing in a shallow, but regular fashion.

"I could not leave him there, and yet he was in no condition to walk out on his own. I rolled and wrestled his dead weight into his frock coat and then his overcoat, and gripping him by the arm, I leaned into him and lifted him onto my shoulder.

"Carrying him thus, I mounted the stair and confronted Madam Sun and her Lascar minions. 'He owes for the two pipes and the bottle.'

"'Reach into his pocket then, and take what you like,' I said.

"The woman nodded to one of her attendants who rooted in Craden's pockets and came up with three gold coins. The lady smiled and nodded for me to pass.

"There was not a cab to be found, so, with Craden slung over my shoulder, I walked to his flat. In the dimly lit streets, the fog had now reduced all life to malevolent silhouettes, but I was not waylaid in my journey. Perhaps the sight of one man hauling another through these streets was not an unfamiliar spectacle, and it was likely that those I passed took me for a dangerous character who had accosted and robbed some poor fellow and who was now in the process of disposing of his body. In less desperate circumstances, the experience might have amused me; it amuses me now to think of it.

"I carried him up to his flat, and balancing him upon my shoulder, I pounded on the door. 'Mrs. Stewart!' I cried. 'Open the door, I have Craden here!'

"The knob was turned from the other side, but it was not Mrs. Stewart who appeared on the threshold, it was Miss Turner."

CHAPTER TWENTY-ONE

"I will leave my state of mind to your imagination, Watson. I cannot say which emotion was the greater: astonishment, dismay or disgust. How could she do away with what little reputation may have survived the inquest by coming to this place?

"'Let me pass,' I ordered. She took a step back, and I carried Craden's lifeless form into the room and lowered him onto his bed.

"Miss Turner knelt beside Craden and laid her forehead on his matted hair, then felt his wrists and his breast. 'He must be attended,' she said. 'Go below and send the boy to fetch a woman named Skinner. He will know who she is and where to find her. After you have given him the order, you may go. I can care for him until she arrives.'

"The urgency of Craden's situation compelled me to hold my tongue. I went down to the flat below and knocked on the door.

"A woman answered the knock, a woman with the saddest countenance I have ever beheld. Trial and adversity had aged her, and though she could not be more than four or five years older than myself, she looked like a woman of fifty. Four children were with her in the single room, Wiggins, a girl of six or seven, one a year or so younger and little Bob. The only furnishings were a small bed, a table, two wooden chairs, a stove and a chest of drawers. One of the drawers had been removed and lay next to the stove; evidently it had been the Little 'Un's cradle.

"I told her that the neighbor in the flat above was very ill and asked her if she might send her oldest boy for Mrs. Skinner.

"'Go,' the boy's mother urged. 'Do not bring Doctor Knowles, see that Mrs. Skinner comes herself. And come straight back.'

"The boy dashed out the door and Mrs. Wiggins turned to me. 'Is there something I can do for him, sir?' she asked in a gentle voice. 'He has been so kind to me and mine.'

"I told the lady that there was nothing anyone could do until Mrs. Skinner arrived, and then returned to Craden's flat. Miss Turner had pulled up a chair to the settee and sat with a basin of water on her lap, gently sponging Craden's forehead.

"'I told you not to come back.'

"'How can you defend your presence here?' I demanded. 'Why do you persist in acting in every way that is calculated to rob you of your reputation and perhaps your liberty? As soon as Mrs. Skinner arrives, I will take you back to Old Compton Street, and I would advise that you stay there.'

"For her reply, Miss Turner motioned toward a basin. 'Until then, take that down to the pump in the courtyard, empty it and bring me some fresh water.'

"I took the basin down to the pump. The handle was frozen and it took all of my strength to draw up the small amount of icy water it took to fill the basin. I had just finished when Wiggins and Mrs. Skinner appeared in the courtyard. I sent the lad home and followed the lady's waddling form, up to Craden's apartment.

"I allowed the lady to enter first, and believed that I saw a glance of recognition pass between the two women. Then Miss Turner yielded her seat to Mrs. Skinner, who settled herself beside Craden and placed her hand on his throat. 'What is it, opiate?' she enquired.

"'And drink,' I said.

"The woman pulled her leather bag onto her lab and drew out a phial of a viscous brown liquid. 'Lift his head,' she ordered.

"Miss Turner knelt beside Craden and lifted his head in the crook of her arm. Mrs. Skinner forced the liquid between Craden's lips and massaged his throat.

"He jerked his head to the left and right, then sputtered a bit and coughed.

"'There, he shall come 'round in a minute. He must take nothing but liquids for the next twelve hours, and as much of that as he can hold.'

"'What is it that you gave him?' I asked.

"'Most who know of it call it theobroma. A simple extract, but it does the trick.'

"She drew a second phial from her bag. 'If his breathing becomes shallow and scant, get this down his throat, and do not leave him unattended until he revives. Keep sponging him with cold water, and send the boy if there is a change for the worse.'

"With that, she left Miss Turner and me to watch over the unconscious prodigal.

"There was nothing to be done, Watson. The lady was determined to remain at Craden's side, and so I pulled up a chair and kept vigil with her while she sponged his forehead and chafed his wrists.

"She spoke only once. 'Men. It is as I have always said. Men are not to be trusted, not the best of them.'

"At last, the first signs of life appeared, for Craden's eyelids fluttered and he turned a groggy gaze upon Miss Turner.

"'Vi'let?' he murmured.

"'Hush. Don't speak. We're not alone.'

"'Who is that beside you?'

"'Sherlock Holmes. He dragged you out of Mother Sun's.'

"Craden turned his tormented gaze on me. 'Curse you for your interference, Holmes.'

"'I will interfere no further. Come, Miss Turner,' I urged her. 'Mrs. Wiggins will watch over him. You must return to the protection of Mr. Brodie.'

"'No, I cannot go back.'

"I was about to respond when I heard the sound of a woman's shriek from below. Evidently, the elder Wiggins had got back from his nightly bout of drinking.

"Craden jerked as though the cry sent a current through him and tried to sit up.

"'Keep him still,' I said and left the room, following the sounds of the altercation to the flat below. I heard the pleas and cries of Mrs. Wiggins as well as the shouts of her children mingled with a drunken bellow followed up by a blow.

"The door to their flat was ajar and I pushed it open. Wiggins had his wife by the hair, and with his other hand was attempting to wrest a scrap of cloth from her grip. Little Wiggins had been thrown to the floor and the other children huddled beside the bed in terror.

"The man looked up, his wife's hair still clutched in his fist. 'Who the devil are you?' he demanded, with several oaths and expressions that I will not repeat.

"'Take your hands off her.' I did not raise my voice or approach the man, but my mere words seemed to inflame him.

"'Take them off, you tell me!' he roared. 'She's my wife and I'll do what I like!'

"As if to defy me, he gave her hair another wrench.

"I stepped forward swiftly and seized his hand by the thumb, twisting it outward to break his grip. It is a pretty effective maneuver, and left him in considerable pain. The man staggered toward me and swung wildly with his other hand, a blow, which I had no trouble avoiding, and a straight right put him on the floor.

"I stood over the bully. 'Your boy knows my name and where I can be found if you think there is something more to be settled. If I should hear that you laid your hands upon your wife or your children again, *I* will think that there is something to be settled, and it will be settled once and for all, do you hear?'

"The lout glared at me from the floor and said nothing.

"I could hear the whispering of the neighbors in the corridor. As I turned to go, I heard their feet scurrying on the stairs and the slamming of doors.

"'Wiggins, come here,' I said, and the boy followed me into the hall. 'It won't be the worse for you, will it, because I interfered?'

"The boy shook his head. 'Ma grieves for the Little Un. She keeps a bit of 'is blanket an' when she starts to weep over it, Pa can't stand for it, an' it's all the worse when 'e's in liquor. 'E'll sleep it off an' we'll have a bit of quiet.'

"It was nearly dawn now, and the morning activity had begun, the rumbling of carts and the cries of the street vendors, the echoes of dozens of similar quarrels emanating from the thin walls and cracked windows. I doubt that the lad and his family had ever known a moment of quiet.

"I reached into my pocket and handed him some coins. 'Find some coffee or tea in the street, will you, and bring it up to the Guv'nor's rooms. And a few buns, for yourself and your brother and sisters.'

"'Yes, sir.'

"I returned to Craden's flat. He was sitting up, now, his head in his hands. When I entered, he looked up at me with red-rimmed eyes, and I believe he had been weeping.

"'So, you dragged me out of Mother Sun's,' he muttered. 'That must have taken some doing.'

"'I ought to have left you there.'

"'Yes. You ought to have left me there.'

"As I have mentioned, the noise from the street was unrelenting; neither the hour nor the ill climate brought silence. None of us distinguished the clatter of the van, nor the rumble of footsteps upon the stairs as anything out of the ordinary until the police inspector appeared at the open door. Behind him was a constable and the two dark-gowned matrons that told us clearly their purpose.

"'Miss Violet Turner?' said the inspector.

"She stepped forward. 'I am Violet Turner.'

"'Miss Turner, you are under arrest for the murder of Rose Moriarty, James Moriarty and Amon Moriarty.'

"'Wait!' cried Craden.

"The lady's reaction was shocking, for she spun toward him and struck him full in the face. Then she turned her back to him and extended her hands to the constable.

"The constable clapped the bracelets upon her wrists and the matrons stepped on either side of her to escort her out. As she passed me, she turned and hissed, '*Do not interfere*,' in a low voice, and then looked back no more.

"Craden lurched toward the door and I seized his sleeve. With a superhuman effort, he tore himself free and sprang down the stairs, pursuing the grim party into the street. People had gathered now, a ragged collection of derelicts who stood gawking on the pavement at Miss Turner was raised into the black van.

"Craden cried out her name and she turned her face away from him. He lunged for the small grille at the back of the van and grasped it as the driver cracked his whip. The vehicle drew away sharply, which broke Craden's grip upon the bars. He was left lying in the frozen street as the van pulled away.

"All of this I observed from the window on the landing outside of his flat. I fought a strong urge to leave him where he lay, but at last I descended the stairs to retrieve him.

"As I passed the door of Wiggins's domicile. Wiggins, Senior sat at the wooden table with his head in his hands, sobbing, 'I miss him, too, Sarah. I miss him, too.' And his wife stood behind him, her cheek laid against the top of his head, stroking his shoulder.

"Misery makes no distinction between the high born and the low."

CHAPTER TWENTY-TWO

Holmes laid aside his pipe and continued his narrative. "Death was everywhere. Abroad, there was the savagery of Isandlwana and Eshowe, and at home, there was the savagery of a winter that swept through London like a plague. The weary public was in sore need of the relief that domestic scandal provides, and this one had all of the elements: intrigue, romance, and murder. I have kept many of the articles, though not all. They would have filled this room many times over."

Holmes went to the bookshelf and reached high for a weighty volume. Newspaper clippings had been pressed into the pages, and though the one which he handed me was quite fragile and somewhat yellowed, it was as immaculate as though it had been taken from yesterday's paper instead of one nearly a quarter of a century old.

The article was from the *Daily Telegraph*, and bore the heading, *Arrest Made in Children's Murder; Mother Charged.*

Early yesterday morning, an arrest was made in the death of the three children of Professor James Moriarty, not twenty-four hours after the inquest brought in a verdict of unlawful killing. Professor Moriarty, age thirty-five, lived with his companion, Miss Violet Turner, age twenty-one, and their three children on Paradise Walk. A celebrated mathematician and scholar, Professor Moriarty has been welcomed into the highest social circles, where his beautiful protégé has likewise been admired for her brilliance and accomplishments, for which she is indebted to the Professor's patronage and education.

On the evening of February 3rd, Professor Moriarty and Miss Turner attended a reception at the home of Sir Joshua Reade, held in honor of Miss Mary Reade of New York City. Some time after eleven o'clock, Miss Turner returned to their Paradise Walk residence and Professor Moriarty and several of his companions went to their club.

Between one and two AM, a blaze of suspicious origin prompted an alert servant, Miss Serenity Moran, to summon the fire brigade. Despite the timely response of the fire brigade, the first floor nursery was consumed and its occupants, a girl, age six and twin boys, age three, perished in the blaze. While the areas affected by the fire were being inspected, the children's father was summoned from his club and informed of the tragic occurrence. Professor Moriarty asked for an immediate investigation by the coroner. Constable Robert Stevens states that while the coroner's officer was interviewing members of the household, and before he could question Miss Turner or the Professor, Miss Turner left the residence for that of a gentleman of her acquaintance.

At the inquest, testimony was brought forth which strongly suggested that the fire had been deliberately set in such a fashion as to concentrate the blaze in the area of the children's beds, thus ensuring that they could not escape the flames. Further testimony from Mr. Rayleigh Ernest, who assisted the coroner in the unhappy task of performing the post-mortem, suggested that a narcotic poison may have been administered to the children. Captain Shaw of the Fire Brigade stated that there was evidence that the children's blankets had been steeped in coal powder to accelerate the blaze. On the weight of the testimony from Mr. Ernest and Captain Shaw, the jurymen concluded that the children had been poisoned and immediately afterward, the fire had been set to conceal the poisoning and to make the fatalities appear to be the result of an accidental house fire. A verdict of unlawful killing was brought in an hour after the matter was placed with the jury and the following day a warrant was secured for the arrest of Miss Turner.

Miss Turner's arrest added a further intriguing complication to the tragedy as she was taken into custody at a flat in the East End, occupied by Lord Craden, the only child of noted philanthropist Lord Warrington. It has been reported that this was the site of many clandestine meetings and that an elopement may have been contemplated in order that Miss Turner might escape apprehension.

It is not known whether Miss Turner will appeal to her estranged companion, Professor James Moriarty, or to Lord Craden for assistance in securing counsel for her defense. In the direness of the situation, competent counsel may determine whether Miss Turner goes in the direction of Mary Ann Brough or Rebecca Smith.

I handed the paper back to Holmes. "I am not familiar with Mary Ann Brough, or Rebecca Smith."

"Ah, well, Watson, I have always said that you did not keep up on your criminal history. Rebecca Smith poisoned at least one child, and very likely more. The Brough matter was even more singular. Mary Ann Brough was a loving mother to her seven children, and, in fact, had been wet nurse to the Prince of Wales. Driven to distraction by her husband's ill treatment and his threat to take her children from her, this affectionate mother slit the throats of six of her children and made a show of slashing her own. She was saved, only to be tried for the murder. It was so sensational an event that tours were conducted through the blood-spattered chambers of her home."

Holmes returned the article to its place and resumed his chair. "As Craden had remarked, our spiritual nature may pull one way, but a baser nature will drag us down. Women murder children and mothers will kill their own. And yet, Rebecca Smith was sent to the gallows and Mary Ann Brough was not."

"But why?"

"Because Rebecca Smith was a poisoner. In many such cases, the more violent the crime, the more likely the jury will view it as an act of uncontrollable madness, and treat the accused with leniency. But poisoning is regarded as a cold and deliberate act, and juries have often taken the view that madness precludes premeditation, and *vice versa*.

"So began the melodrama. It was, of course, necessary to assign the roles of hero and villain, and Fleet Street did not waver. Moriarty was the patron who had generously bestowed time, talents and money upon a woman who returned his benevolence by rejecting his offers of marriage while encouraging the attentions of Craden, neglecting her maternal duties while indulging her own pursuits and finally committing a most heinous crime that deprived the Professor of his beloved children. If there had been any doubt as to where one's sympathies ought to lie, it was finished when the newspapers printed sketches of three little caskets being taken for burial, the father walking behind the mourners, his head bowed in sorrow.

"But I get ahead of myself. I could not leave Lord Craden lying upon the street, so I got him into a cab and deposited him with a manservant at the Belgrave Square residence and then took myself to Montague Street to decide what I might do on Miss Turner's behalf, for though Sir Joshua had ordered me away from the case, his authority extended no further than the inquest.

"I spent a fruitless couple of days attempting to pick up some useful gossip around the lecture halls where Miss Turner pursued her courses of study. I was hoping to turn up a few friends who would defend her, but it seems she had been quite solitary, and no one knew her well. Moreover, all sympathy was on Moriarty's side. Moriarty's staff, of course, would feel the same, or so I had first supposed, but then I recalled how Mrs. Hudson had stated, 'I should not like it for myself,' when describing the solitude that Moriarty had imposed upon his household, and her evident disapproval when her brother-in-law had lied at the inquest. She had impressed me as the sort of woman who would not allow herself to be bullied or bribed out of her conscience.

"Her address, I recalled, was on Edgeware Road, and it was no difficult task to find her lodgings.

"She received me in a sitting room that had all of the snugness and order of a middle-aged matron's apartment, with no masculine touches to suggest that it was shared with her brother-in-law. I enquired whether they were to remain in the Professor's employ.

"'The Professor has taken a suite at Claridge's, and he has kept Frederick on for the present, but he has no need of a housekeeper.'

"'And what of the others?'

"'I believe he has found a situation for Moran in the household of Lady Morcar, and Frederick told me that the Professor may keep Mrs. Stewart as a sort of secretary. She was a great help to him in making the arrangements for the funerals, and in sorting through the papers and documents he will need when he goes abroad.'

"'He means to leave the country?'

"'Yes. That was all planned some time ago – before Christmas, in fact. He was to go abroad in the spring, though I imagine now he will leave as soon as he is free to travel, for the newspapers and gossip have made London unbearable.'

"'Where does he go?'

"'I understand from Frederick that there were some matters of business on the Continent, and then the Professor spoke of North Africa afterward. He was to be gone for many months – perhaps as long as a year.' She hesitated for a moment and then added, 'He had made arrangement to take the children with him.'

"'And Miss Turner?'

"'Miss Turner was to be left behind.'

"'Indeed!'

"'I thought it strange, and even a bit cruel. Miss Turner has always tried to bear up, but one woman can often see through another woman's mask, and I knew that the prospect of a long separation – perhaps a permanent separation – from her children tore at her heart.' She drew a handkerchief from her sleeve and dabbed at her eyes.

"'And what will you do?'

"'I have enough put aside now toward the purchase of property. There is an address in Baker Street that may be within my means if I can find one or two respectable boarders.'

"'Mrs. Hudson, can you give me your frank appraisal of relations between Professor Moriarty and Miss Turner?'

"The lady hesitated. 'I had nothing to complain of so far as the Professor was concerned. He was always proper, if a little cold and distant. I never minded that. I am not put off by a few eccentricities of manner. It is far better than the waywardness and intemperance of so many young men. As for Miss Turner, she was like one of those exotic flowers – brilliant by nature and made even more so through careful cultivation. Only it seemed that the purpose of the cultivation was to raise up an even more splendid strain.'

"'The children,' I concluded.

"'Yes.'

"'You mentioned that there had been some disagreement the afternoon preceding the fire. Were disagreements common between the Professor and Miss Turner?'

"'It was always calm on the surface, but as for what went on beneath?' She gave a slight shrug. 'It was the Professor's desire to know where Miss Turner went when she left the house even on the slightest errand, and that day she went out without so much as a word to him. I recall thinking at the time how unnecessary it was for her to perform such trivial tasks, as Moran or I might have done them for her. Of course, I would not have known where to take her violin for new strings. I am not musical in the least. But I know any number of parish charities that would have been happy to take the cast-off clothing.'

"'Perhaps the Professor suspected that she lied about the errands?'

"'I know what you mean – the rumors that she was carrying on with Lord Craden. I cannot believe it, for if the Professor was suspicious of any goings-on, I don't think he would have trusted in Lord Craden's recommendation when Mrs. Allen gave notice last summer.'

"'Who was Mrs. Allen?'

"'She was nurse to the children before Mrs. Stewart. Mrs. Stewart has only been with the family for six months, and I thought afterward how fortunate it was that such an excellent replacement could be found so quickly.'

"'Why did Mrs. Allen give notice, do you know?'

"'Perhaps she was not equal to another charge.'

"'Another charge?'

"She hesitated. 'Miss Turner was to have another child. She did not carry beyond three or four months.'

"'If she lost the child, Mrs. Allen need not have left you after all.'

"'I believe that the Professor had great hopes of increasing his family.'

"'I will keep you no longer, Mrs. Hudson. I will leave my card, and hope that you will notify me if you should recall the name of the parish where Miss Turner took the second-hand clothes the day before the fire.'

"'I will. I daresay whoever received the children's clothing was not disappointed. It seemed to me that some of the items had only just been purchased. The Professor spared no expense when it came to how the children were clothed and shod.'

"'Where were the clothes purchased?'

"'The clothing was ordered from Whitby's, and the shoemaker was in Oxford Street. Oh, dear, what was the name? McKinley, perhaps.'

"'MacInnes?' I suggested.

"'Yes, that is it.'

"MacInnes, the hangman."

CHAPTER TWENTY-THREE

"I thanked the Mrs. Hudson for her time, never supposing that a few years hence we should establish a more permanent relationship, and decided to call at MacInnes' Oxford Street establishment.

"The gallows do not provide continuous employment, and so Marwood MacInnes was obliged to earn a living in trade. His shop's façade, and the simple plaque which read 'MacInnes – Crafting in Fine Leather Goods' were modest when compared to the large windows and elaborate displays of his neighbors. Inside the shop, however, the goods were as varied and unique as museum pieces. Many were arranged behind glass cases: gloves, coin purses, knife sheaths, hat bands, riding crops. Upon the wall behind the counter, were displayed larger items; butchers' aprons, harnesses, and a variety of instrument cases for the medical as well as the musical practitioner.

"The lady behind the counter had the gaunt face and spare, black-garbed figure of a mortuary attendant. 'May I help you, sir?' she asked.

"'I would like to speak with Mr. MacInnes.'

"'I am Miss MacInnes,' she said, coolly. 'I will give my father your message, sir, or your card if you will leave it.'

"I handed her my card and she examined it with a something like relief. 'You are not from the press?'

"I said, 'Oh, no' in a manner that suggested a contempt for the breed, which seemed to win her over.

"'They have brought us nothing but grief since the Paradise Walk fire,' she sighed. 'At times, people do not need much encouragement to be in the mood for a hanging, though I cannot believe that a woman as ladylike as Miss Turner can have done what the newspapers suggest. It is strange to think that she was here that very day.'

"'Indeed?'

"'I do not know why – her business was with my father. Perhaps it was about the boots she had ordered for the children a few weeks ago. Surely, she would not have done that, if she meant to kill them. They were very costly boots.'

"'Indeed, it does seem quite unlikely,' I said, and then made a show of admiring some of her father's handiwork. 'I am not familiar with some of these objects,' I remarked, pointing to certain items mounted on the wall. 'But even to an untrained eye, the artistry is unmistakable. Is that a butcher's apron? Quite ingenious that the skirt can be detached from the bib! And that?'

"'It is a dog's lead – the strap goes 'round the muzzle so that it is guided forward by the head rather than pulled at the neck.'

"'And what is that harness?'

"'It is for country use. It will support a lame or fallen animal as large as a horse, so that the heart and lungs do not become compressed.'

"'Superior workmanship. Well, I will not take up more of your time. I don't expect that your father will be back today?'

"'No, he has been at Newgate these last four days, and will not be discharged until tomorrow afternoon.'

"There were executions, then, to be carried out, for it was the custom to lodge the hangman for some days in advance of the business, to ensure that he would not fail to appear, nor come to the task in a state of drunkenness.

"It occurred to me that there was nothing to prevent me from going to Newgate myself. Visits were subject to restrictions once a sentence had been passed; before that, visitors were freely permitted three days of the week.

"I went to Newgate Street, where the straggling queue which had formed along one side of the stone exterior, told me that it was, indeed, a visiting day. I took my place in the line, behind an old woman who informed me, 'It's a 'angin' day, so we must bide for the hour, but it will move along brisk enough once they cut 'im down.'

"At last, the weary and frozen petitioners were admitted to the Keeper's Lodge. Despite the mundane arrangement of its desks and stools and book-lined shelves, it was an ominous place, for its windows faced the interior of the courts, leaving the room so dark that lamps had to be lit, though it was midday. The ancient stones reeked with mold and deterioration, and their odor mingled with some rancid scent, which I later learned was from prison beer, brewed and sold by the warders.

"From this chamber, we were ushered through a sort of rogue's gallery, where there were arranged upon the walls and shelves, a great number of paraphernalia – pinions, shackles, chains, death masks, as well as many grotesque photographs. I did not know whether these grim accoutrements were intended to fascinate or to caution the visitor.

"We were instructed to sign our names in the register, and to name the person we wished to visit and that person's relationship to ourselves. Assistance was given to those who could not write, which, I am sad to say, were most of them. From here we were conducted to separate rooms according to our sex, where a cursory search of our clothing, was made. We were then directed toward one of two corridors, depending upon whether we had come to visit a male or female prisoner.

"These corridors were narrow passages, one side of which was a grille of iron bars that overlooked the female exercise yard, a broad square of hard, gray earth, patrolled by a few wardresses. These ladies strolled to and fro, occasionally stopping to converse with one another or stepping forward to intervene if any attempt were made between visitor and inmate to exchange a kiss or a handshake, as physical contact was prohibited.

"It occurred to me that though these visits were a highlight for the prisoners, it was the most tedious part of the day for their keepers, as it obligated them to remain on their feet in a courtyard that was as cold and bleak as a dungeon.

"There were many more prisoners than there were visitors, and at first, I supposed that Miss Turner had remained in the common cell. At last, I spied her, not by any sign of recognition on her part, but by the brilliant hair which hung in a loose braid. She knelt on the ground, utterly oblivious to the prisoners milling about, jostling her and treading upon her skirts. She had traced some imaginary grid onto the dirt, and was pushing a few pebbles upon it with great concentration.

"I signaled to one of the matrons as she passed. 'That is my sister,' I said. 'Would you please tell her that I have come, I don't think she has seen me.'

"The lady, who appeared a bit more gentlewomanly than many of her fellow wardresses, looked at Miss Turner with a shake of her head. 'I will try to alert her, but she is not right in her mind. The shock of it affects some of them so. Many go quite mad well before...' She left the unsaid words to hang in the air, but I knew that she meant to say that they went mad before they were led to the gallows, and it disturbed me that Miss Turner's guilt already seemed a settled thing in the minds of those around her.

"'What is she doing?'

"'She will draw a chessboard on the ground and go through the moves again and again with bits of gravel or stone.'

"She walked over to Miss Turner and tapped her shoulder, nodding in my direction. Miss Turner looked up with no change in her vacant expression, save for a faint light of recognition in her eye. She turned back to her makeshift game and finished a set of moves, then rose and shook out her skirts.

"She approached the bars, and her gaze probed mine and at last something like a smile passed over her wan face. 'Perhaps you would tell me, sir, how I have got through twenty-one years without knowing that I had a brother?'

"'You should have been more observant, Miss,' I replied.

"She tried to smile again, but her lips fixed in place and I saw that she seemed to be holding herself unnaturally still, as if steeling herself against a blow. I realized that she wore only a simple serge dress without a cloak or shawl to cover her. Her hands were ungloved and the small fingers, which had flown so nimbly over the strings of her violin were red and chafed.

"'Is there something I can do to make you more comfortable?'

"'You are the second person who has asked that since I have been put in this place, though with considerably more philanthropy.'

"'And who was the first?'

"The matron made a pass between us. Miss Turner waited until the woman had moved out of earshot before she spoke.

"'Come now, use your reasoning powers, Mr. Holmes. Who would endure all of the discomfort and inconvenience of coming to such a place in order to see me in such a state?'

"'Ernest.'

"She nodded. 'What became of Henry after I was taken away?'

"'I got him to Belgrave Square.'

"A hush fell over the prisoners, as two men crossed the yard. One was the lean, somber figure of MacInnes, whose pace seemed deliberately slowed for his companion. The other man was unknown to me, but even at a distance, I could see the disheveled attire and shaking extremities of a drunkard. MacInnes had one arm around this man's shoulder, though I could not tell whether it was done to provide comfort or a prop.

"'It is the hangman,' Miss Turner said quietly, when the men passed from view.

"'And who was his companion?'

"'The medical officer.'

"'Is his name Knowles?'

"'We have not been introduced.' She spoke with the sort of coldness that is assumed by the condemned, who cannot allow themselves to hope for reprieve.

"'Who will represent you in the courtroom?'

"'There are always the sort of barristers about who hope to get famous by way of an infamous trial. They will first look for those who might pay for their services, and then look to those who will barter. There is quite a thriving open market that goes on inside these walls.'

"'What sort of market?'

"'Whatever you want. Tobacco, jam, blankets. Companionship. Ernest attempted to buy the latter in exchange for amending his testimony at my trial. Now, do not be naive, Mr. Holmes. Why do you think you were searched before you were permitted to pass?'

"'Because visitors might carry in weapons?'

"'Because visitors might carry in merchandise, and the warders have the monopoly on trade. As for Mr. Ernest, be patient, Mr. Holmes. He will be undone by his weaknesses in the end, and in the meantime, I am quite safe. As for the discomfort, there are others outside of these walls who are far hungrier and colder than I.'

"'You are not safe as long as there is the possibility that you will be convicted of a crime which you did not commit.'

"'I am safe from uncertainty, Mr. Holmes, for it is not only possible, it is inevitable.'

"One of the matrons rang a small bell, and those visitors who knew the meaning of this signal stepped back from the bars.

"Miss Turner arm shot between the bars and reached for my hand. Her frozen fingers closed over my glove. 'I see what you want to do, Mr. Holmes, but I implore you to curb your chivalry, or at least use it to some purpose by looking after dear Mr. Brodie. It is wasted on me – worse than wasted, it is dangerous. Stand down, I beg you – stand down!'

"'Back away now, Miss,' said the matron, who gripped Miss Turner's arm and drew her hand from mine.

"Miss Turner shook herself free and looked at me for a moment, in that keen, searching fashion. She inclined her head in a slight nod, and then turned and walked away.

Then she began to sing, her voice rising over the din of parting exchanges, and the wind sweeping over the stone walls. The prisoners and company who had cried out at the termination of the visit, or turned back in dull resignation stopped in their tracks to listen to her. I don't think I have ever heard anything so musical and so haunting and so very sad. The notes rose clearly above the ragged assembly, above the stone walls, above the bleak shadows that obscured the light from the sky.

"As I filed out, I saw that the turnkey's blunt features were softened by the sound of her singing.

"'Killed her children, she did,' he said to me. 'Poisoned them, and then burned them in their beds to make it look an accident, that's what they say. Left their father with a broken heart. Only a madwoman could sing like that at such a time.'"

CHAPTER TWENTY-FOUR

"Miss Turner's plea reminded me that I had not visited Mr. Brodie since the morning she had been arrested. I took myself to his shop, where I found the shutters drawn, and the shop closed up. I ventured to rap upon the glass. After a moment, Brodie peered from behind the shade and opened the door.

"He was in his shirt-sleeves with a dusty apron tied around his waist. I observed many empty spaces on his shelves where certain precious volumes had been; some of them lay upon his desk, tied into bundles.

"'I am glad you have come by, lad, for you may take your bequest away now, you will not have to wait until I am laid in the ground. Look what I have here,' he said as he lifted a slim volume wrapped in tissue paper. 'Robert Hooke's *Micrographia*, printed two centuries ago. Why it ought to be in a museum! And a volume of Kircher, here, just as old, and Lessing's *Laokoon*. Take them with you, lad, for I would far rather you had them, and there is more than enough left to raise money on. I have put out the word that some prize volumes are for sale, and the vultures have started to circle 'round. I closed the shop to give myself an hour's respite from their talons.'

"'Mr. Brodie, what are you talking about?'

"'I am raising money for Violet's defense. I have retained Leslie Cummings.'

"'Does Miss Turner know? I have just come from Newgate and she said nothing of this.'

"'What? You have gone to Newgate? What business have you going there?'

"'The business of any gentleman when a lady may be in need of his help.'

"'Has she asked for your help?'

"'No. She rebuffs every offer of assistance.'

"To my surprise, Brodie took her part. 'She is quite right - you must not interfere. It would only prolong matters and a swift trial is best. Heaven only knows what she might be susceptible to in such a place. Newgate is a stewpot for disease, and jail fever has taken stronger constitutions than hers.'

"'Surely she is at greater risk if something which might exonerate her is overlooked in haste.'

"Brodie shrugged. 'And if she is exonerated, what then?'

"'She would be free of Moriarty once and for all.'

"'And do you think Moriarty will allow her to go her way in peace? He would make her come to think that the gallows were far preferable to the illusion of liberty.'

"I was about to reply when the bell at the door clanged, and Ernest sidled into the shop.

"'Holmes,' he greeted, sneeringly. 'Mr. Brodie, I come on Sir Joshua Reade's behalf. He understands that you are selling some of your books? He is willing to offer a fair price for Sir Charles Bell's *System of Dissections*.'

"The old man shook a gnarled fist. 'You tell Resurrection Reade that there is no price he may offer that I will accept.'

"'I think you will change your mind when you reckon what it will take to keep Violet Turner from the rope.'

"Now, Watson, you know that I am usually able to govern my temper. Allowing Ernest to goad me bespeaks a weakness on my own part. But I was younger, then. 'Ernest, watch how you speak the lady's name. She may have no relations to defend her, but she is not without friends.'

"'Oh, I have never supposed that she was without *friends*,' he sneered in reply.

"Brodie grabbed my sleeve, but I pulled it free. 'There is an alley-way twenty paces down the street, where we may resolve this in a manner that won't inconvenience Mr. Brodie.'

"As with all cowards, once he was challenged, he immediately looked toward retreat. I have no doubt that he would have fled if he believed that I would not follow him, so he made a show of bravado by stating, 'Come on, then,' and turning upon his heel, he made for the street.

"He strode in the direction of the alley, then attempted to surprise me by abruptly spinning 'round and swinging at my chin. I parried the blow, and returned a glancing one to his jaw, which sent him reeling backward. He was able to regain his footing, scrambled to his feet and charged like a mad bull. I believe I might have held my ground had not the slush and ice sent me off balance and the two of us tumbled into the pavement, pummeling at each other wildly.

"You may well chuckle, Watson. I have often noted that even the grimmest of events has a bit of humor about it. This combat was waged in front of the L'Aiglon, a public house that catered to political and artistic expatriates, the sort who are inspired by a good row and don't much care which side is on the right. By the time the constables arrived on the scene, it was difficult to determine which of the twenty or so miscreants was the instigator of the brawl, and so we found ourselves making each other's acquaintance in the back of a police van.

"I spent an hour in a cell, waiting to be called to answer for my conduct. To my surprise, I was released without ever facing the magistrate. The sergeant at the desk handed me a slip of paper which explained all, for the note contained a brief sentence in Mycroft's hand: *Come to my quarters immediately.*

"I could hear Mycroft's lumbering and agitated pacing as I ascended the stair. I entered his rooms to find him wearing down the carpet, his half-finished tea not yet cleared. For Mycroft to be so distressed that he would forego a meal was serious indeed.

"'Sherlock! What are you thinking!' he demanded, before I had taken a chair. 'It was bad enough when you were found in some East End hovel with an accused murderess and now brawling in the street like a common ruffian! It cost me no amount of bartering in favors to keep your name out of the papers! Explain yourself!'

"'The hovel is Lord Craden's favorite rat hole. I was sent to retrieve him before Madam Sun and her Lascar minions could pick him clean and drop him into the Thames. When I got him back to his hovel, the lady was there.'

"'And today?'

"'I was avenging an insult.'

"'An insult to Miss Turner?'

"'I did not say so.'

"'No, but you have a chivalrous streak that often clouds your judgment. I fear for you Sherlock. You are developing an unfortunate tendency for choosing both the worst of friends and the worst of enemies.'

"'Nonsense, Mycroft. I always choose the best ones.'

"'Don't be glib, the matter is too grave for that. Tell me frankly, is your interest in this lady founded upon admiration for her or your antagonism toward Moriarty?'

"'Why do you not consider that it may be entirely professional? You talk of nothing but the necessity to make my reputation. What better way to do that than to vindicate a lady whom everyone has decided is guilty?'

"'You will do no such thing.'

"'What do you mean?'

"'Sherlock,' Mycroft frowned, impatiently. 'I am the custodian of other confidences than yours. There is talk, the sort that my particular situation has allowed me to overhear. The sort that is not spoken idly. There is no possibility of vindication.'

"I was too shocked by this declaration to respond.

"'I'll strike a bargain with you,'" he said, in a milder tone. "Stay away from those East End haunts, make whatever amends necessary to retain your laboratory privileges and continue your studies. Do that, and when she is convicted, I will personally appeal to the Home Secretary so that she will not be hanged.'"

CHAPTER TWENTY-FIVE

"'*When* she is convicted.' The certainty with which Mycroft spoke those words called to mind the many times when justice has gone awry, when the guilty are free and the innocent sent to the gallows. Mycroft's assurance that, if the worst came to pass, Miss Turner's life would not be forfeit was a powerful inducement for me to stand down.

"So, I gave my word, and for the three weeks until the trial, I kept it, after a fashion. I made no further attempt to seek out information, but that did not mean I couldn't put myself in its path. Brodie was determined to pay for Miss Turner's barrister by selling off some of his stock, an enterprise that often took him away from his shop. I suggested that he might want to find some sharp, honest lad who would work for a modest wage so that his shop might be kept open when he was away from it. Young Wiggins was perfectly suited to the role; he was a likeable, clever lad, which suited Brodie, and he possessed a keen ear and ready tongue, which suited me. Between Brodie's gossip and Wiggins' ready chatter, I was kept as well-informed as if I had continued to conduct my own investigation.

"The trial began on the first Monday in March of '79. It was a cold and sunless day, with icy brown slush pooling at the curbs and a cutting wind that sent debris tumbling along the gutters. Still, the public were not to be kept away from the grim theatre of the Criminal Court.

"No one who has sat in the Old Bailey during a sensational trial would remark upon the spaciousness and comfort of the place; such was only an illusion given by the courtroom's high ceilings and large windows. The bench took up nearly an entire wall, and when added to the dock, the barristers' tables, the boxes for the reporters and the jurymen, little room was left for spectators who sat crammed sleeve to elbow on the wooden benches in the lower court – the first of which was reserved for witnesses – or the gallery above. Such crowding provided some insulation from the cold, for the center window was left open. This was done, I learned, to admit fresh air to offset the effects of jail fever that might be carried in by the accused.

"I made my way to a place beside Gregson, I saw that six witnesses occupied the first row: the Hudsons and Miss Moran, Constable Stevens, Captain Shaw and Ernest. As with the coroner's court, waiting rooms had been set aside for those who did not wish to observe the proceedings or, I imagine, be observed by the impatient reporters who sat crammed into their box, notebooks open and ready.

"Gregson leaned toward me as I settled beside him. 'Sir Joshua has resigned his post!' he hissed in my ear.

"'What? When?'

"'Saturday afternoon. It was done very quietly so that it might slip past the reporters. I will be re-assigned, of course, for the new appointment may choose his own officer, and I have no desire to stay on at the coroner's office in any case. I am quite ready for a change.'

"'What reason did he give for his resignation?'"

"'The *official* reason is that he has accepted an invitation to give a series of lectures in America and that he would not be able to prepare for the trip and maintain the office of coroner as well.'

"'And is there an unofficial reason?'

"Gregson lifted his brows and was about to reply when a rustle and a hush settled over the crowded courtroom, and we were called to order. 'Let us lunch together and I will tell you what is being said.'

"Sir Hillary Baen was the prosecutor, a thick-set, unimpressive figure, but for his pale blue eyes that seemed all white save for the cold hard dot of a pupil. He had so piercing a stare that it was a rare witness who could look him in the eye.

"Leslie Cummings, Miss Turner's defending counsel, could not have been more unlike his opponent. He was yet under thirty with delicate, elongated fingers, a waxen face and melancholy dark eyes. Had he lived a few centuries earlier, he might have been painted by van Eyck or van der Goes.

"The remaining players took to the stage, and Miss Turner was ushered in last. The raised dock had the effect of putting her on display and those who had read about her for weeks scrutinized her greedily. There was a Puritan simplicity about her hair and dress, but the lack of adornment drew attention to her beauty, rather than diminishing it. She took her place, a matron at her flank, and gave a slight shake of her head when she was told that she might sit. I do not know whether this conveyed to the jury her fortitude or her obstinacy.

"The charges were read out, and then Sir Hillary presented for the Crown, driving home the atrocity of murder, particularly when the victims were innocent children, and the murderess was their own mother. Such a crime outraged nature and society, and when the viciousness of act, and the exclusion of all other possible perpetrators were laid before the jury, they could not do other than to find her guilty as charged.

"Witnesses were then called forward; Miss Moran, Captain Shaw, Constable Stevens and Hudson, one after the other, all gave very much the same testimony that they had given at the inquest.

"Then Mrs. Hudson was called.

"Sir Hillary began with her arrival at Paradise Walk the morning after the fire and proceeded to Miss Turner's departure. 'When Miss Turner left, she took her clothing, and some personal items, is that not correct?'

"'She took what few things she might need for a brief absence. The greater part of her belongings remained.'

"'They would more correctly be called the Professor's belongings, would they not? It was he who purchased them.'

"'They were gifts to Miss Turner. It is a poor gift that is given only to be taken back again.'

"Sir Hillary scowled. 'In her rooms were a great many flowers, and these were also left behind, is that not correct?'

"'Yes. I had them sent to the invalid hospital. Such things cheer people who cannot get out in the air.'

"'Would you happen to recall what sort of flowers?'

"'There were roses, as well as violets and some exotic ones that are unfamiliar to me. And a vase of heliotrope.'

"'Were these flowers all arranged in vases and urns? For ornamentation?'

"'Yes, but for those that had been cut up, or pressed into albums.'

"'Miss Turner had an interest in botany? Was she well-versed in the subject?'

"'I cannot say. I know little of science.'

"'Thank you, Mrs. Hudson.'

"'Mrs. Hudson,' Cummings began, 'How did you learn that Miss Turner was to leave her home?'

"'I was in the kitchen, preparing breakfast. The kitchen was, for the most part, untouched by the fire and I was able to make use of it. Mr. Hudson came down and said that the Professor had ordered Miss Turner to leave the house.'

"'Mrs. Hudson, is it possible that in the confusion of the morning, you misunderstood what Mr. Hudson said?'

"'No, sir. He was quite emphatic. He said that Professor Moriarty had ordered Miss Turner out of his house and that she was to be gone within an hour.'

"'And yet he has testified both at the inquest and today that it was Miss Turner who chose to leave.'

"'I cannot explain Mr. Hudson's testimony, I can only tell the truth.'

"Cummings nodded. 'And what arrangements were made for Miss Turner's accommodation?'

"'I believe it was Sergeant Gregson's assistant who suggested that a respectable elderly gentleman of Miss Turner's acquaintance might be prevailed upon to offer his protection. Sergeant Gregson gave his consent and asked Mrs. Stewart, the children's nurse, to accompany her.'

"'Very good. After Miss Turner left the house, did you see her again?'

"'On those few occasions when I visited her at Newgate.'

"A murmur of surprise rippled through the chamber.

"'And why did you do that, Mrs. Hudson?'

"'She had not been found guilty of anything, and I knew that her affliction must be great, particularly coming so hard upon the loss of her children. I brought her a few sweets and sundries that I thought would make her a bit more comfortable.'

"'It is prohibited for visitors to bring personal items to the inmates.'

"'I do not know what is prohibited. I can only say that they did not prohibit *me*,' the lady replied.

"'Very good. Now, Mrs. Hudson, you said that you disposed of the flowers, as there was no point in having them wilt, I suppose. What of her remaining possessions?'

"'The Professor ordered them to be boxed up and disposed of.'

"'Her personal possessions? Not her clothing, certainly, as she might have need of it.'

"'Yes, clothing, books, music, everything.'

"'And how many days after the unfortunate event were these instructions given?'

"'That very morning.'

"'The morning of the fire?'

"'Yes, sir.'

"'At what time were the orders given?'

"'I cannot fix the exact time; the Professor had gone out, and come back again, and then arranged to move to a hotel. But I know that it was before noon, for we were well into the task when the clock struck and I insisted that we pause for a bit of luncheon.'

"'Thank you, Mrs. Hudson.'

"The judge looked toward Baen. 'Are there any questions that you wish to redirect to this witness?'

"Sir Hillary rose. 'Yes. Mrs. Hudson, you did not hear the conversation which took place between Mr. Hudson and Professor Moriarty, you only know what was related by Mr. Hudson afterward, is that not correct?'

"'Yes, sir.'

"'And you testify that Mr. Hudson was quite agitated. Is it possible that in his agitation, Mr. Hudson did not accurately convey the situation, and that it was indeed Miss Turner who chose to leave, rather than the Professor who ordered her gone?'

"Cummings got to his feet, immediately. 'My Lord, Mrs. Hudson is being asked to speculate.'

"'My Lord,' countered Sir Hillary, "Mrs. Hudson is the sister-in-law of the gentleman, and has known him for many years. In this case, I believe that her opinion may be relied upon.'

"'I agree, Sir Hillary. I will allow the witness to answer the question.'

"Sir Hillary stood waiting, with a smug smile upon his face, but Mrs. Hudson lost no time in dispelling it.

"'In my thorough knowledge of my brother-in-law's character, then, I do not think that he misspoke when he said that it was the Professor who ordered Miss Turner to leave. Perhaps *some* might be persuaded to amend what they have said, but I am not one of them, and it is far too late for me to change my ways.'"

CHAPTER TWENTY-SIX

"Mrs. Hudson was dismissed and the judge declared that there should be a respite of one hour. As Gregson and I turned toward the exit, we encountered Brodie, who had found a place in the very last row. I introduced the two, and together we made our way to the street.

"'I expect that you will be looking for another post, young man,' Brodie said to Gregson. 'Well, you seem a clever enough sort, you do not need to court the likes of Sir Joshua Reade to make your way, not as *some* do,' he added, with a nod toward Ernest, who had donned his most unctuous smile, as he sidled toward a knot of reporters.

"'How can you have heard of Sir Joshua's resignation!' Gregson exclaimed.

"'I hear a great deal,' Brodie replied. 'And I know that he was promised a lecture tour if he could deliver a title to Miss Reade. I believe he got Falkland to take her. Half a million, and she will be nothing more than a viscountess, but it is of no great import to the Americans who wouldn't know a duke from a draper.'

"'We are going to get a bite of luncheon, will you join us, Mr. Brodie?' I invited.

"'Ah, where shall we go? What say you to The Cheese, for it is just a brisk walk, and we may catch a bit of gossip, as the reporters favor the place.'

"We three fell into step, and made our way to the Cheshire Cheese, where Brodie was hailed by the landlord who ushered us himself to a table in the back, an area that was reserved for lawyers and for the reporters who hung about the courts.

"'I am known here, you see,' Brodie remarked, and ran his gnarled hands over the wooden surface of the table. 'There was a time when they would lay the corpse out in a place like this for the inquest, with all the jurymen standing 'round, a pint in hand. Those were livelier times!'

"'Our times are lively enough,' Gregson replied.

"'What of Sir Joshua's resignation?' I asked after the waiter set down our meat pies and ale and departed. 'If it were only a matter of a lecture tour, he would take a few months leave from his post, not resign it.'

"'There has been some unpleasant gossip going 'round the East End. They are ignorant folk, but a sordid rumor can do as much harm as a sordid truth.' Gregson glanced over his shoulder and lowered his voice. 'They say he has gone back to his old ways.'

"Brodie's eyes glittered with interest, and he urged Gregson to continue.

"'It seems,' said Gregson, 'that there is a woman, a Mrs. Radley, who had an invalid daughter, ten years of age. The unfortunate girl was undersized, lame, subject to fits, and an imbecile as well. Over the years, she had been examined by many specialists, but you know how it is. Such examinations are conducted more to satisfy curiosity than in any hope of bringing on a cure. Last winter, the poor child was brought to Bart's in her mother's arms, where she died just after Christmas Day, and some days after that, she was laid in a pauper's grave at Tower Hamlets cemetery. For weeks, the hard weather kept the mother from visiting the site, but on a day that was more favorable, Mrs. Radley set out to lay flowers upon the girl's burial place, and not long after, she was brought before the magistrate a bit done over and in great agitation. She declared that her girl's grave site had been interfered with, and demanded that the coffin be brought up and opened to determine that all was as it should be. The magistrate refused, for Mrs. Radley was a drunkard and her word was not to be relied upon. If he gave the order and the coffin were unharmed, he would have violated the grave site on a rumor, and if he ordered it brought up and the body *had* been tampered with, the neighboring folk might work themselves into a frenzy and tear up the entire burial ground to determine the state of their own kin. When the Radley woman got no satisfaction from the magistrate, she took her grievances to the public houses, and it is said that two or three fellows there were moved to bring up the box.'

'"Hah!' Brodie slapped the table. 'They take a page from Rossetti's book. He put some fresh verses into his wife's coffin, and the last shovel of earth had not been thrown upon her before he began to feel the pangs of regret. That viper, Charles Howell, urged him to dig up the coffin and so one night, Rossetti and several companions, roaring drunk, the lot of them, brought up the coffin and took the poems back! Dear me! Those were livelier times. We are a sad, sorry lot nowadays.'

208

"'We cannot all be as lively as drunken poets, sir,' I replied. 'So how does the tale end, Gregson? Had the girl's body been tampered with?'

"'The fellows swore that the coffin was empty and it was whispered 'round what a prize the girl would be to some enthusiast of deformity, and that if such a person had no chance to study her while she was above the ground, he might pay to have her brought up once she was under it.'

"Brodie shook his head. 'As entertaining as it is to imagine Sir Joshua taking up his shovel and spade once more, I cannot think he would risk it, not after all he has done to put the legend of Resurrection Reade in its grave.'

"'Not even if it were something very particular?' Gregson persisted. 'It was said that the Radley girl was a singular object.'

"'I have no love for Sir Joshua,' replied Brodie, 'But tales of the girl's disappearance are likely nothing more than drunken gossip. And even if she were taken up, it does not follow that Reade was the culprit. There are others who might want the girl more even than he – those who entertain themselves in ways that are quite unspeakable and foreign to decent men. If that is the case, it is better to leave matters as they are and spare the mother any fresh pain. Have we time for another kidney pie? I do not believe there is a lighter crust for twenty miles!'"

CHAPTER TWENTY-SEVEN

"A drizzle of fine snow had begun to fall when we left the public house, and we made a slow route back to the court and fell into step with the crowd pressing toward the entrance. We found places near the front of the courtroom, between two stout ladies who had evidently not yielded their seats for the recess. Each possessed a large bag, which had been placed at their feet, and I was able to get a glimpse of cloth napkins, apple peelings, tin flasks, and coin purses crowded within.

"The first witness of the afternoon was Ernest, who marched forward, head held high, pointedly ignoring the lady in the dock. The quarrel with Lord Craden was not raised at all. Baen did elicit a great deal of testimony on the subject of the "French preparation"; however, and each time Ernest uttered a phrase, such as "valerian oil" or "common heliotrope," it was accompanied by a nod to the jury, as if to indicate that they must make note of the terms.

"When Sir Hillary was finished, Cummings rose. 'This French preparation, as you call it, is not known in common pharmacology, it is simply a sort of folk remedy, is that not correct?'

"'Yes, so far as I understand it.'

"'And household cures are not precise formulas, do you agree? The recipe for one practitioner's French preparation might not be in exact proportion to that of another, and therefore its effects and potency will also vary?'

"'Well...yes.'

"'So, as the expression goes, one man's balm is another man's bane.'

"The pun upon the prosecutor's name was not lost on the jury or the public. Several reporters scribbled it down and it seemed that the judge repressed a smile.

"'When one is speaking of folk remedies,' Cummings added, innocently.

"'Yes,' Ernest replied, shortly.

"Cummings turned back to his table as if he were finished with the witness, then turned 'round again and asked, almost as an afterthought, 'Mr. Ernest, one more question. Did you attempt to visit Miss Violet Turner at Newgate?'

"A flush of embarrassment colored Ernest's sallow features. 'I – yes – once or twice.'

"'For what purpose?'

"'I – had some slight acquaintance with the lady, as she had attended some of the same scientific lectures as I. She had no family, and I merely wished to inquire, in all good charity, whether I might do anything that would be of service or comfort.'

"'Yes, very charitable, to be sure,' Cummings replied. 'Did you also have some slight acquaintance with the father of the deceased children?'

"'I had attended some of his lectures. He is a very learned man.'

"'And did you also make an effort to extend your sympathy to him? Make him an offer of service or comfort?'

"'I – no. No. I did not think that I should be so bold as to...I did not wish to impose...'

"'Thank you, Mr. Ernest, I think we understand you. I have nothing further to ask this witness.'

"Ernest was dismissed and a few snickers were heard as he strode from the courtroom, looking neither right nor left.

"'Mrs. Catherine Skinner!' was called next, and the lady emerged from the waiting room, swaddled in her coat and shawls. Her bonnet was secured to her head with stiff black ribbon, tied in an enormous bow, and the loops rose like a bat's wings on either side of her round face.

"'Mrs. Skinner,' Sir Hillary began, 'Do you have an occupation?'

"'I nurse the poor.'

"'And do you not also possess some small reputation as a chemist?'

"'I cannot say if it is small or great.'

"'Have you ever met the accused?'

"Mrs. Skinner looked up at Miss Turner. 'I have.'

"'How did the introduction come about?'

"'She came to me in January, saying only that she had got my name from an acquaintance.'

"Of course, Watson, I immediately thought of the day I had seen Craden slip a note into her hand in the street.

"'And did she identify herself by name?'

"'No, she gave no name – but a face like hers you do not forget.'

"'And what was the object of her visit?'

"'She enquired after the French preparation.'

"'This French preparation has been described as a remedy made from a concentration of oil of valerian mixed with peppermint and sweetening.'

"'Yes.'

"'What is the source of oil of valerian?'

"'It is extracted from the seeds of garden heliotrope.'

"'Ah, *he-li-o-trope*,' Sir Hillary repeated with a significant glance at the jury. 'And what properties does this extract of garden heliotrope possess?

"'It is used as a remedy for pain and sleeplessness.'

"'Mr. Ernest stated that this French preparation is a folk cure of questionable efficacy.'

"The woman seemed to puzzle over the word 'efficacy' for a moment. 'Well,' she declared, 'sickness is the bread and butter of medical men. It would not benefit *them* to have a patient relieved too quickly or sent off too soon when their profit comes from drawing out the matter.'

"'Sent off?' echoed Baen. 'You made no mention of *that* property.'

"'When I am asked to prepare it, it is for some poor pet that must be put out of its misery. We are often kinder to a little dog than we are to its master.'

"'I see. And it was this the reason that the accused wished to obtain the concoction?'

213

"'Oh, she did not want it from me, she wished only to enquire about methods of preparing it, how best to extract the valerian oil from the heliotrope and how to make a tincture and how much to put into a tea for a sleeping draught. She asked a great many questions, and I answered as best I could and advised her to begin with only a few drops, for too stout a dose might cause one to fall into a stupor or to stop breathing entirely.'

"'It could be fatal?'

"'Yes.'

"'And would this be a more likely result if it were administered to a child?'

"'Oh, the preparation as I laid out would not be one you would give to a child, unless...'

"'Unless you meant to send it off?'

"'Yes.'

"'If one were a poisoner,' Baen cast a quick glance toward his opponent, as if anticipating an objection. 'does this preparation have some advantage over arsenic or cyanide?'

"'It is painless.'

"'Now, Mrs. Skinner, after this encounter in January, did you ever see the accused again?'

"'Yes, in a flat at Rotherhithe.'

"'Who resided in this flat?'

"'Lord Craden.'

"'And was Lord Craden present in the flat when you arrived?'

214

"'He was, both he and another gentleman, a Mr. Holmes.'

"I felt Gregson shift to look at me, and saw the reporters scribbling. Mycroft would not be able to keep my name out of the papers now.

"'So Miss Turner was alone with two men. And what was the occasion for your going there?'

"'I was sent for. It seems that Lord Craden had turned up quite the worse for wear and I was asked to bring him 'round.'

"'And were you able to revive Lord Craden?'

"'Yes. I gave him a dose of a tonic to relieve the effects of the opium and drink and left orders for his care and went my way.'

"'And when you left, Miss Turner remained?'

"'Yes.'

"'Alone with Lord Craden and his friend, Mr. Holmes.'

"'Yes.'

"'In a flat at Rotherhithe.'

"'Yes.'

"Cummings's questioning was brief. 'As a nurse, Mrs. Skinner. I imagine you are often asked for medical information and advice. Have you been asked about this French preparation before?'

"'Yes.'

"'So there was nothing particular or suspicious about Miss Turner's request?'

"'I have been asked questions a great deal stranger.'

"'And she asked how much to add to tea if one wished to prepare a sleeping draught?'

"'Yes, that is what she said.'

"'And you do not know what she may have done, or not done, afterward?'

"'No, I do not.'

"Cummings thanked her and the lady was dismissed.

"Sir Hillary's next witness was called, and to my amazement the name 'Mr. Aiden Brodie!' echoed through the room.

"Brodie laid a hand on my sleeve and whispered, 'It is not unexpected, lad.' Then, with some clambering across laps and 'Beg pardons,' Brodie made his way to the front.

"'Mr. Brodie,' Sir Hillary began, fixing the old man with his piercing gaze, 'you buy and sell books and have a subscription library, is that correct?'

"'Yes.'

"'And the defendant has been a patron of yours?'

"'Yes.'

"'And how long have you known the defendant?'

"Brodie's gaze softened. 'It will be three years this summer that Violet – Miss Turner – first came to my shop.'

"'And how frequent were her visits to your shop since that time? Once a week? Once a month?'

"'Whenever the Professor would let her out,' Brodie replied, crisply.

"'Mr. Brodie,' the judge cautioned, 'you must not render your opinions unasked, or engage in assumption.

Simply answer the questions that you are asked, if you please.'

"'The books that she purchased, they were expensive volumes, is that not correct?' the prosecutor continued.

"'They were.'

"'And these books were paid for by Professor Moriarty?'

"'I would not want to render an opinion or make an assumption,' the man replied, tartly. 'It was Miss Turner who handed me the money.'

"The spectators tittered and fell silent.

"'You have a large clientele, Mr. Brodie.'

"'I do.'

"'And many young ladies of Miss Turner's age among them?'

"'Yes.'

"'What sort of books would you say generally appeal to young ladies?'

"Brodie hesitated. 'Modern novels, for the most part. Books on household subjects and foreign travel.'

"'And was that also Miss Turner's taste? Novels and domesticity and so forth?'

"'I cannot know what was to her taste.'

"'I meant to ask what books she took from circulation?'

"'She borrowed a great variety of books.'

"'I would like for you to be more specific, Mr. Brodie. Please tell the judge and jury any titles you may recall. What did Miss Turner borrow in, say, the past two months?'

"'Whatever pleased her. Miss Turner was an avid reader.'

"'You will have to be more specific, Mr. Brodie.'

"The old man bridled, visibly, and said nothing.

"'Mr. Brodie, do you understand the question?'

"'I understand a great deal more than you, young man!'

"'Mr. Brodie, this is a court of law, and you must answer.'

"'My answer, then, is that what Miss Turner or any of my patrons borrow or buy or read is no one's business but their own! My ledgers are not fodder for the courts or the newspapers!' he declared with a jab of his knobby finger toward the reporters' box.

"Sir Hillary was clearly frustrated, but he continued doggedly. 'Were they books of science?'

"Brodie's lips pressed together, stubbornly.

"'Books on the subject of botany?'

"Brodie crossed his arms over his chest.

"'Were they books about poisons?'

"'I object, my Lord!' Cummings declared.

"Sir Hillary's pale eyes were ablaze with frustration. The jurors were all tradesmen like Brodie; the prosecutor did not want to alienate them by badgering the old man, but his pride would not allow him to retreat. 'Were not two of these books *Lectures on the Effects of Toxic Substances* and *Treatise on Poisons*? A simple yes or no.'

"'I have said that I will not answer.'

"The judge looked down, sternly. 'Mr. Brodie, I order you to answer the question.'

"'And I say that I will not! I will not compromise the trust of my patrons by announcing to the world what they read in private.'

"'Mr. Brodie,' the judge attempted to placate the old man. 'No one is asking you to divulge information about any patron save the accused.'

"'Perhaps not today. But what of tomorrow, or the next trial, or another witness. I will not be the one to set the pattern for such intrusion.'

"'Mr. Brodie,' the judge rejoined, more sternly. 'I warn you that if you do not answer, the court will hold you in contempt.'

"'If this court does not want to be the subject of contempt, it ought not behave in a contemptible fashion!' the old man replied, hotly.

"'Mr. Brodie, this court will give you one final opportunity to answer the question that has been put to you.'

"Brodie was silent.

"'My Lord,' Baen declared, 'I would suggest that a night's berth at Newgate might soften the witness's obduracy.'

"The judge concurred, and Brodie was conducted through the passage to Newgate. As he was being escorted from the room, he turned toward me and I believe I saw an impish wrinkle to his brow.

"I looked toward the jury and saw a note of sympathy in their glances. They did not like to see one of their own bullied by Sir Hillary Baen. I had thought that their antipathy toward the prosecutor might work in Miss Turner's favor, but Sir Hillary was a superior strategist. His next witness was one who would distract the jury from any sympathetic musings on Brodie's plight – Lord Craden."

CHAPTER TWENTY-EIGHT

"Craden entered the court from the waiting room, looking every inch the aristocratic reprobate. His costly greatcoat was draped over his shoulders like a cape. The frock coat was buttoned high, with the edge of a silver brocade waistcoat visible, below a ruby and pearl tie-pin. He carried a silver-knobbed walking stick in one hand, and he carefully removed kid gloves that were the shade and texture of cream and dropped them into his hat before he took the oath. He attempted to perform these acts with nonchalance, but I saw that his hands were shaking. I might have taken this for drunkenness, but the haggard and haunted face suggested nerves that were strained to the point of snapping, rather than a mind blunted by drink.

"'Lord Craden,' Sir Hillary commenced, 'do you know the accused, Miss Violet Turner?'

"'I know her.'

"'Intimately?'

"There was an audible gasp from the gallery.

"'I will be as specific as the court requires, but I am a gentleman,' replied Craden. 'I was introduced to Miss Turner at a dinner given by Sir Arthur Paget – this would have been in the winter of seventy-seven to the best of my recollection, though I had seen her for some time at lecture halls and concerts.'

"'Would it be fair to say that you accepted Sir Arthur's invitation on purpose to secure this introduction?

"'It would be more than fair. I am not a social creature by nature or inclination.'

"'And who made the introduction?'

"'Professor Moriarty.'

"'You are a friend of the Professor?'

"'We were acquainted. He is a member of the Marlborough and Brooks, as am I.'

"'And after the introduction was made, did you call on Miss Turner at her home?'

"'I attempted to, but I was told that she did not receive visitors.'

"'And so,' continued Sir Hillary, 'you became more of a social creature, did you not, out of a desire to pursue an acquaintance with Miss Turner?'

"Cummings had half-risen to his feet when Craden responded, 'I did.'

"'And you continued your acquaintance with Professor Moriarty as well, dining with him, or playing at cards at one of your clubs?'

"'Yes.'

"'And it was upon one such occasion, sometime last summer, was it not, that Professor Moriarty happened to mention that his children's nurse had given notice? And did you not promote an acquaintance of yours for the post? A Mrs. Stewart?'

"'She was not an acquaintance,' Craden corrected. 'She was a widow who had been the headmistress of a reputable school in Scotland. She had appealed to some of the school's patrons when she sought employment in London, and one of these appeals had found its way to my father's secretary. My father's secretary is an excellent man who makes it possible for my father to enjoy a reputation for philanthropy without ever having to exert himself. My father's secretary happened to mention Mrs. Stewart's situation to me and it occurred to me that her character and education were precisely what would suit the Professor.'

"'And it suited you as well, did it not, Lord Craden, to have a person who was indebted to you placed in a household to which you wanted to gain admission?'

"'She had excellent credentials,' Craden replied. 'Professor Moriarty would not have engaged her otherwise.'

"'That is not an answer, sir.'

"'I hoped that Mrs. Stewart would be grateful to me.'

"'And express her gratitude by promoting communication, and possibly liaisons, between Miss Turner and yourself.'

"'Yes.'

"'And did she?'

"Craden hesitated. 'At first she did, when it was the matter of carrying or receiving a note, or notifying me of the invitations the Professor meant to accept.'

"'Did Mrs. Stewart object to being used in this way?'

"'I didn't care. I wanted only to see Miss Turner. But soon Mrs. Stewart came to be troubled by the situation in which she found herself, for she had a very high regard for the Professor's abilities and she was genuinely devoted to the children. Her loyalties were in conflict, and it was all my doing.'

"'Yes,' Sir Hillary nodded, somberly. 'It was all your doing. Now, Lord Craden, on these occasions when you were able to speak privately with Miss Turner, what was substance of the conversations?'

"'I told her that I wanted to marry her.'

"'And what was her reply?'

"'She refused me.'

"'Did she give you a reason?'

"'She said that the Professor would never allow her to take his children away, and that she would not abandon them.'

"'And what was your response?'

"'I told her that she must think of herself. The more she rejected my proposals, the more persistent I became. I suppose I did not see – or perhaps I did see and did not care – that such urging on my part was driving her to desperation.'

"'Let us come to the evening of February third, Lord Craden. You were invited to a reception at the home of Sir Joshua Reade, yet, despite the fact that you might expect to see Miss Turner there, you did not attend. Why not?'

"'I had received a note from Mrs. Stewart earlier in the day. She said that the situation had become intolerable and that she intended to resign her post. I waited until after the Professor and Miss Turner had left their home and then confronted Mrs. Stewart. I begged her not to give up the situation until I had persuaded Miss Turner to leave Professor Moriarty.'

"'And what was her reply?'

"'She agreed to remain at her post, but only until the Professor left for the Continent in the spring.'

"'And did you go from there to Sir Joshua's?'

"'No. I met up with an acquaintance and we went to a flat I keep at Rotherhithe. We had a drink and chatted for a short time, and then he departed.'

"'At what hour?'

"'I don't know. Perhaps ten or eleven o'clock.'

"'And then what did you do?'

"'I drank. I smoked a cigar. I took morphia. Later, I went to my club.'

"'What time did you arrive at your club?'

"'Midnight or a bit later, perhaps.'

"'You played at cards?'

"'Yes.'

"'For how long?'

"'A few hours. Until...'

"'Until the party disbanded because of the tragedy.'

"'Yes. A note was sent up to Professor Moriarty and he departed in a great hurry. It did not take long for it to get 'round what had happened. I left the club and made my way to Paradise Walk, but there was no getting near the place.'

"'Where did you go then?'

"'To Bart's.'

"'Where you provoked a row with one of the previous witnesses, Mr. Ernest?'

"'Mr. Ernest was the antagonist. He made the sort of reference to Miss Turner that no gentleman would abide.'

"Sir Hillary shrugged. 'And after this altercation, where did you go?'

"'I went back to my flat. I drank.'

"'This was Tuesday, February fourth?'

"'Yes.'

"'Were you visited in your rooms by anyone that day?'

"Craden showed the first sign of genuine distress. One hand clutched the stick and hat and the other passed over his eyes. 'Mrs. Stewart,' he said, hoarsely.

"'Mrs. Stewart came to see you?'

"'Yes.'

"'And what did she tell you?'

"Craden half-glanced at Miss Turner and dropped his head into his hand. 'She said that she had been pressed into accompanying Miss Turner to Mr. Brodie's. At Mr. Brodie's, they happened to be left alone and Miss Turner broke down and confessed all.'

"'Confessed what?'

"Cummings got to his feet to raise an objection. 'There is the matter of hearsay, My Lord,' he appealed. 'Lord Craden cannot swear to what, if anything, was exchanged between Miss Turner and Mrs. Stewart.'

"'I will allow Lord Craden to relate what Mrs. Stewart told him. Lord Craden, you are not to draw any conclusions or venture into opinion, do you understand?'

"'Yes.'

"It was clear that Leslie Cummings was ill-pleased with this ruling, but he sat without further protest.

"'Confessed what, Lord Craden?' Sir Hillary repeated.

"'Miss Turner told Mrs. Steward that when Professor Moriarty traveled to the Continent in the spring, he meant to take the children with him – *only* the children – and leave Miss Turner behind. He even spoke of placing them in a school on the Continent where Miss Turner would lose all access to them. Miss Turner vowed that that she would see her children dead before she would see them taken from her. Mrs. Stewart was horrified by this declaration and took the first opportunity to flee. She came to me and unburdened herself and begged me for my counsel.'

"'And you counseled her to go to the police, surely?'

"Craden passed his handkerchief across his forehead.

"'What did you counsel her to do, Lord Craden?'

"Craden did not answer.

"'Did you hear the question, Lord Craden?'

"'I – offered her money to leave the country rather than disclose what Miss Turner had told her.'

"'And what was her response?'

"'She refused.'

"'And what did you do afterward?'

"'I drank. I walked the streets. I cannot account for all of my actions. It was even said that I turned up at the mortuary, though I have no recollection of it. I do not remember much of anything for the next day or so.'

"'When did you next see Miss Turner?'

"'The morning of her arrest.'

"'Where did you see her?'

"'At my flat at Rotherhithe.'

"'Was that the first time she had been to this flat?'

"'No.'

"'At what hour did she arrive?'

"'I cannot say – I was not there.'

"'Then how did she obtain access to your flat?'

"'She had a key.'

"'And it was in this flat that she was arrested?'

"'Yes.'

"'And why was she at your flat, Lord Craden?'

"'I had always told her – begged her – that if her situation ever came to be more than she could bear, she must come to me at once and we would leave England together.'

"Sir Hillary gave the jurymen a pointed glance. 'I have nothing further at this time, My Lord.'

"Cummings shot to his feet like a swift, avenging angel. 'Lord Craden, have you seen Miss Turner since the morning when she was arrested?'

"'No.'

"'Sent her a message or provisions at Newgate?'

"'No.'

"'Are you paying for her defense?'

"'No.'

"'Your love and devotion overwhelm me, Lord Craden.'

"'My Lord!' cried the prosecutor.

"'Mr. Cummings,' the judge reminded him. 'You are to elicit testimony, not to accuse or censure. Continue.'

"'Would it be fair to say that you furthered an acquaintance with Professor Moriarty solely to pursue Miss Turner?'

"'Not solely. Moriarty and I move in the same circles. He is a learned man, and I do not suffer fools.'

"'You did not scruple to profess friendship to his face while courting Miss Turner behind his back?'

"'I am not known for my scruples.'

"'What are you known for, Lord Craden?'

"Sir Hillary sprang to his feet once more, but Cummings held up a hand before he could object, and said, 'I will withdraw that remark, my Lord. Lord Craden,' Cummings resumed. 'You have told us that you recommended Mrs. Stewart to the Professor. I am quite certain that Mrs. Stewart is very well-qualified for the post, but there are many well-educated women in London. Is it your opinion that it was your recommendation or her qualifications which gave her an advantage?'

"Craden seemed to reflect upon the question for a moment, and then said, 'In my opinion, it was her situation in life that worked to her advantage.'

"'Please elaborate.'

"'Mrs. Stewart was a widow, without relations, as, I believe, her predecessor, Mrs. Allen had been. Mrs. Hudson, the housekeeper, was likewise a widow with no relations except for a brother-in-law who was Moriarty's man. Miss Moran was one of several penniless daughters of a shiftless father who had done nothing to provide for them. It seemed that Moriarty chose to employ women in straitened circumstances, women unencumbered by friends or relations who might come forward if they were wronged.'

"Sir Hillary had half risen to object when Craden added, 'In my *opinion.*'

"'Lord Craden, you have testified that you were with a friend on the evening of February third and that this gentleman left you at ten or eleven. Yet you did not arrive at your club until midnight or thereafter. So for, perhaps, two hours you did nothing but drink and smoke and take morphia? Is there anyone who can verify that this was how your time was occupied between ten or eleven in the evening and midnight?'

"'I don't believe so.'

"'Now, Lord Craden,' Cummings continued, 'you state that you wanted Miss Turner to leave Professor Moriarty and that she refused because she would not abandon her children to him.'

"'Yes.'

"'Miss Turner and the Professor were not married, and her claim to custody was certainly equal to his. Surely a gentleman in your situation would be well able to offer a home and protection to Miss Turner's children, as well as to herself?'

"There was a long and painful pause. 'I did not want them,' he said at last, his voice barely audible.

"'What was that, Lord Craden? I do not believe that the jury heard you.'

"Craden threw up his head and declared, almost defiantly. 'I did not want them. I told her I did not want Moriarty's children, I wanted only her.'

"'And,' said Cummings, 'she would not abandon them. How can you have placed a woman you loved in such a dilemma, Lord Craden? It would seem quite enough to drive one mad.'

"Sir Hillary jumped up to make an objection, and Cummings coldly declared, 'I will withdraw that last. I want nothing more from Lord Craden.'

"It seemed to take Craden a moment to realize that he had been dismissed. Slowly, he took up his hat and stick, then abruptly turned toward the dock and uttered, 'Violet – forgive me!' and fled the courtroom."

CHAPTER TWENTY-NINE

"'Hanging is far too good for a cold one like her,' declared one of the two stout ladies seated in front of me, when the session ended for the day. 'Aye,' nodded her companion. 'She is the sort, no doubt, who has always used her pretty face and her coaxing ways to wheedle her way out of trouble. Well, there is no coaxing the hangman.'

"Outside, reporters were scrambling for the cab ranks, eager to hurry their copy to print.

"'It is past the visiting hour,' Gregson said to me, 'but I know one or two of the warders. I will see that your friend Brodie has something better than prison fare and a tattered blanket.'

"I thanked Gregson and made my way to Brodie's shop. The windows had been wiped, the brass knob polished and a neat path swept from the door to the curb. The interior had also been put in order, with the coal scuttle filled and a fire lit. Wiggins and little Bob were putting the shelves in order.

"I did not want to alarm the lad. I merely said, 'Mr. Brodie has been detained on a matter of business and may not return until tomorrow morning. Were there many customers?'

"Wiggins took off his apron and hung it on a peg. 'Yessir, wrote 'em down in the ledger book, just's Mr. Brodie showed me. You've no notion what some folks'll pay for books. Why one was three quid six, for a book no bigger than me 'and, an' it was nothin' but poems an' drawings.'

"Wiggins showed me the ledger, proudly. I saw that he had recorded the transactions diligently in a rude but legible hand. 'Ah, I see that you sold Sir Charles Bell's *System of Dissections*. I did not know that Mr. Brodie had set a price for it.'

"'Bloke said they'd settled on a pound.'

"'Tall fellow with a whining sort of voice?'

"Wiggins nodded. 'Did I do wrong?'

"'No, you have managed admirably.' I spoke calmly, but I was angry that Ernest had taken advantage of Brodie's plight and the boy's ignorance. 'Were there any callers?'

"Wiggins shook his head. 'I fink I saw t'Guv'nor pass not long ago. I called to 'im, but 'e went straight by.'

"'In which the direction?'

"'Th' Aglon.'

"'Well, take these shillings for a fare, so that you and your brother do not have to walk. I will lock up the shop and see that it is opened in the morning. Can you come tomorrow at your usual hour?'

"'Yessir.'

"When the lad and his brother had departed, I drew the shades and locked the door. I then went down the street to the L'Aiglon, which, as you will recall, Watson, was the site of my ignominious bout with Ernest.

"The interior of this establishment was illuminated with pink and amber lanterns. The tables were covered with fringed shawls, and 'round one of them, a group of men were assembled before a half dozen empty wine bottles.

"Two others were attempting to fix the center of a target with six-inch daggers. Anything akin to success was celebrated with a draught of wine, which had a detrimental effect upon subsequent attempts and which placed the patron slumped upon a table between the men and their target in considerable jeopardy. That patron was Lord Craden.

"A knife flew an inch above his head. Craden shifted and began to sit up as the second knife grazed his earlobe. Blood streamed onto his collar and as his fingers probed the wound, he emitted a slurred curse.

"The player retrieved his blade and retorted with an oath of his own. Craden lurched to his feet, threw his dark hair away from his forehead, returning taunt for taunt, until the man lost control of his temper and, brandishing his dagger, lunged.

"In that brief second, I understood that Craden did not intend to retreat, but meant to stand fast and allow the man to plunge the knife into his heart.

"Instinctively, I sprang into the fray, and seizing Craden's stick, used it to strike the knife from the attacker's hand and knock him back against the wall. Then, I took Craden by the collar and dragged him into the street, where I threw him down upon the pavement. 'Crawl back to Rotherhithe,' I spat, and then raised my collar and turned on my heel.

"'I love her, Holmes!' he called after me.

"I continued walking, almost sorry that I had saved his life once more.

"'God forgive me, I love her!'

"I continued walking, and then he cried out something that froze me in my tracks.

"'She's my sister!'"

CHAPTER THIRTY

"His *sister*!" I cried.

Holmes took up the poker and prodded at the fire. I glanced out the window and saw that dusk was long passed, and it was quite dark.

"What did you say to that?" I asked.

"Well, I did not want to 'rouse the denizens of the L'Aiglon into the sort of *mêlée* that had brought my disagreement with Ernest to such an ignominious conclusion. I pulled Craden to his feet, threw him into a cab and took him to my room. I cannot imagine what my landlady thought when I half dragged and half carried his staggering form up the stairs.

"I rang the bell and gave the order for a pot of coffee and when it was sent up, I poured a cup, and practically forced it down his throat, then pulled up a chair opposite him. 'All right, Craden,' I demanded. 'What do you mean, she is your sister?'

"'She must be. She *has* to be. The rumors had all died away, of course, long before that cursed Turner sold her to Moriarty. There is no one to recall it now, only me! Only me!' He began to laugh and sob, hysterically.

"'Pull yourself together, man! You will have me thrown out of my lodgings! What the devil are you talking about?'

"'It was so long ago,' he said, his eyes red-rimmed and weary. 'I was but five or six years old. My mother engaged a governess. She was very young, no more than eighteen, but someone had seen to it that she had been given a better education than many a university man. She was more beautiful than she was brilliant, and I was enchanted in the way a child will be when he comes under the spell of such an extraordinary person. I was not alone in feeling the force of her beauty and personality. Wherever she went, she was an object of admiration but sadly, she was...'

"'Too beautiful for a convent and too poor for a count,' I said, recalling Miss Turner's words.

"Craden nodded, cynically. 'And far too good for the likes of Turner, but he was said to have the devil's own charm, and I believe there may have been some mild flirtation between them, but I don't know that she would ever have seriously considered him a suitor unless – well, unless, it became expedient for her to take a husband.'

"'Because your father had seduced her and she was with child.'

"'Yes. Of course, much of this I pieced together quite a bit later. All I knew at the time was that a coldness rose up between my father and mother and that my beautiful governess was gone and an elderly tutor in her place. I overheard the kitchen maid remark that the governess had married a Mr. Turner, and what good fortune it was, for at least her child would have a name. It was years before I understood her meaning.

"'My mother died a few years after, and I was sent away to school, and went on to university, and then was left to drift upon the Continent, where my caprices – intellectual and otherwise – might be pursued with impunity, and at last and made my way home once more. I'd heard of Moriarty at Oxford, and in town we were members of the same clubs, and ran in the sort of circles that are bound intersect. I found him to be a brilliant fellow, and the devil's own master at the card table. It was at the clubs that whispers went 'round about Moriarty's beautiful young mistress. It was said that Rossetti and his band had taken a fancy to the girl's mother, who was one of those ripe, red-headed beauties they worshipped, and that the girl herself had modeled for them when she was scarcely more than a child. They told me that the mother had married a scoundrel named Turner – a common enough name, but it called up the sad tale of my former governess, and 'roused my curiosity to see the Professor's young mistress. I dragged myself to every insufferable social occasion where I might get a look at her, and at last, we were introduced at Arthur Paget's. Holmes, I got the shock of my life. She was my governess to the hair, though even more beautiful if that is possible.' He looked at me, pleadingly. 'They say you are a solver of problems. Have you ever come across a problem that had no solution?'

"'No.'

"'No. Because you confine your problem-solving to the laboratory where, if you follow the formula, work out the variables and provide against them, there is only one possible outcome. That is what Violet says. Have you ever played chess with her, Holmes?'

"'No.'

"'I don't recommend it. It is not conducive to one's vanity.'

"'Continue, Craden.'

"'I do not make excuses for my feelings or the manner in which I acted upon them. I made only one error. I believed that I had Mrs. Stewart's loyalty. But Moriarty paid her wage, and she was clever – clever enough to see what a fiend he was, and that if she must make an enemy of one of us, she would fare better if that enemy was not Moriarty. Monster!' Craden downed the last of his coffee. 'Oh, I know it is hard for the world to believe that such a brilliant scholar could be a monster, but that is how monsters get by, Holmes – they take on the form of those around them. And yet,' he sighed, 'I would have let it be if Violet had been happy, but he made Violet's life miserable, and no longer cared if that life came to a premature end. She was with child again last year – she lost the child and very nearly died, herself, and when she recovered, she told Moriarty that she would bear no more of his children, and his reply to was to say that he would take their children away from her, that she would never see them again, unless she agreed to marriage.'

"'And so, Moriarty threatened to take away her children if she did not yield, and she would not yield. A wretched stalemate, Craden, and one that could have been avoided if you had offered your protection to her children as well as herself.'

"'I know it,' he said, his voice choking. 'Well, they will be together in the grave at least.'

"'That will not happen, Craden. She will not hang.'

"'I don't see that it can be avoided.'

"'My brother, Mycroft, has some influence with the Home Secretary. If it should come down to the worst sentence, he has promised that he will persuade the Home Secretary to commute it to imprisonment.'

"Craden leapt to his feet. 'Are you mad!' he cried. 'What have you done! What have you *done*!' Then, to my utter amazement, he seized his things and ran from the room.

"Many months would pass before I saw him again."

CHAPTER THIRTY-ONE

"The first matter of business on the next day of the trial was to have Brodie brought into the courtroom, where he was asked whether he had experienced a change of heart.

"'My heart is what it was yesterday, and what it will be tomorrow and what it will be a year hence!' he declared.

"'We none of us know what a year will bring,' the judge replied, gravely. 'Something you may wish to reflect upon during another night's inconvenience.'

"'He is an obstinate old fellow,' Gregson muttered, as Brodie was removed. 'It will take more than another night in a cell to loosen his tongue, for when I went by yesterday, he had made himself quite at home in the place.'

"We then turned our attention to the first witness of the day: Veronica Stewart.

"I had not seen her since the morning following the fire and I do not know what I expected, Watson; perhaps I hoped to see some hint of grief or self-reproach, but she was a perfect study in dignified composure.

"'Mrs. Stewart,' Sir Hillary began, 'you had been the headmistress of a school, and most recently had been employed to supervise the children of Professor James Moriarty. As one who has had experience in the field, how would you characterize the Professor's system of education for his children?'

"'It was ambitious, to be sure, and quite dependent upon continuous encouragement, but the children always appeared very willing and able.'

"'You were recommended to the post by Lord Craden, who testified that he expected you to act as liaison between him and the accused.'

"'That expectation was not mentioned when he offered his recommendation.'

"'But you did, in fact, carry communications back and forth between Lord Craden and Miss Turner?'

"'Yes. I was grateful to Lord Craden for securing me an excellent position. But I came to have an appreciation for the Professor. He is a brilliant man, and as my employer, he was entitled to loyalty. This caused me some conflict.'

"'How did you resolve this conflict?'

"'I notified Lord Craden that I intended to resign my post.'

"'And what was his response?'

"'He called upon me at Paradise Walk one evening when he knew that the Professor would not be at home. He urged me to remain in the Professor's employ. The Professor meant to travel abroad in the spring and I agreed to remain until then.'

"'This exchange occurred on the evening of February third?'

"'Yes.'

"'And what occurred the next day when you arrived at the Professor's home?'

"'The unhappy news was given to me by a constable, who informed me that the coroner's officer had already begun an investigation.'

"'And it was during the investigation that a situation arose which prompted Miss Turner to leave the house.'

"'Yes.'

"'The coroner's officer asked you to chaperone Miss Turner to the shop of a friend, Mr. Aiden Brodie?'

"'Yes.'

"'And sometime after you were settled at Mr. Brodie's, you had a private conversation with Miss Turner?'

"The woman nodded. 'Yes,' she said, quietly.

"'And what did Miss Turner say to you?'

"'She said that she had killed her children.'

"Sir Hillary allowed the gasps of shock to be followed by a silence of many seconds. 'Please tell us what you can recall of this conversation.'

"'Miss Turner said that she would never have allowed the children to be taken away from her, as the Professor had meant to do, that it was for the best that they had died. I rebuked her for speaking so, when the children had suffered such a terrible death only hours before. She replied that I need have no concern for their suffering, that they had gone quite peacefully, and that they were dead well before the fire had consumed them. I asked her how she could know this, and she admitted that she had herself given them poison in a sweet drink. She said that they expired quickly and painlessly, and when they were dead, she

243

covered their bed clothes with pulverized coal and ignited the fire.'

"For a moment, it seemed that Cummings meant to make some objection, but he only shook his head and dropped back into his chair.

"Sir Hillary treated the court to another pause, in which only the frenzied scratching of the reporters' pencils could be heard. 'And what did you do then, Mrs. Stewart?'

"'I cannot describe my shock. I made some excuse to leave, I do not know what I said. Perhaps something about retrieving some of my belongings from my lodgings. I left.'

"'And where did you go?'

"'I went first to Lord Craden and appealed to him for his advice. He implored me to keep silent, and even offered me funds to leave the country. I was horrified by this proposal and told him that I could not behave so treacherously toward the Professor and then I left.'

"'Where did you go?'

"'To Paradise Walk to speak to the Professor. I was told by Mrs. Hudson that the Professor had gone to a hotel.'

"'And then you went to the hotel and told him all?'

"'Yes.'

"'And how did Professor Moriarty respond?'

"'With great kindness and generosity under the circumstances. He said that he had only himself to blame for allowing his judgment to be biased so by Miss Turner, and that he shared responsibility for the children's death.'

"'Thank you, Mrs. Stewart, nothing further.'

"Cummings stepped forward and stood silent for a few moments, as if allowing himself to come to terms with the information he had just heard.

"'Mrs. Stewart, after this confession which you allege the accused made, you went immediately to Lord Craden?'

"'I wanted advice.'

"'So rather than going first to a man who was entitled to your loyalty, you went to the man who had sought your participation in a clandestine arrangement, and who is, by his own account, not known for his scruples?'

"'I cannot say that I acted in the wisest fashion.'

"'You were not wise to act as Lord Craden's go-between, or you were not wise to seek his counsel?'

"'In retrospect, neither was wise.'

"'In the course of this – relationship – which Lord Craden pursued, did you ever have any indication that Miss Turner reciprocated his feelings?'

"'No.'

"'Very well. Mrs. Stewart, just now you referred to the Professor's kindness and generosity. Within the bounds of discretion, can you give the court some particular examples of kindness and generosity you saw the Professor display toward Miss Turner?'

"'I was not a witness to their private behavior.'

"'But certainly, there were some endearments, some tokens of affection that you can recall?'

"'Miss Turner was given the very best of clothing, jewelry, books, music. She was taken everywhere. There was nothing that was withheld from her so far as I could see.'

"'Her gowns were ordered by the Professor, is that not correct?'

"'I believe so.'

"'And her jewelry was chosen by the Professor, as well?'

"'Yes.'

"'And it was the Professor who decided which social engagements they accepted, and when they stayed home, and whether callers were admitted or turned away, is that not correct?'

"'The Professor is a scholar, who worked at his home during much of the day. It was necessary to maintain a certain amount of orderliness and quiet.'

"'And was it necessary to this orderliness to regulate the access Miss Turner had to her children?'

"'The Professor determined how the children's day was spent, that is correct.'

"'Mrs. Stewart, you lodged in St. Thomas Street?'

"'Yes.'

"'In fact, neither you nor the Hudsons resided in the Professor's home. What were your hours of employment?'

"'I arrived shortly after seven in the morning, and departed after the children were put to bed, just after seven in the evening.'

"'Your lodgings in St Thomas Street, they were decent, comfortable lodgings?'

"'Yes.'

"'And your fellow lodgers were primarily nurses who worked at St. Thomas Hospital, is that not correct?'

"'Yes.'

'So they would not be ladies whose habits or dispositions or schedules would be disruptive or disagreeable to you?'

"'No, not at all,' she replied, with a puzzled look upon her face.

"'But you have not returned to those lodgings in the wake of this tragedy, have you? In fact, Professor Moriarty arranged for you to move into a suite at Claridge's, where he has also taken up residence, isn't that correct?

"'The Professor asked me to assist with the funeral arrangements and with preparations for travel to the Continent.'

"'You need not have given up your lodgings to do that, Mrs. Stewart. You were still in London.'

"'I did as the Professor asked.'

"'You did as the Professor asked because you always did as the Professor asked, correct?'

"'Yes.'

"'And in the time you have resided together at the hotel...'

"'My Lord!' Sir Hillary cried out. 'I implore you!'

"'Mr. Cummings. You may wish to rephrase.'

"Cummings offered a deferential nod to the bench. 'Mrs. Stewart, after the fire, you left the house with Miss

Turner and then left her to speak to Lord Craden and finally returned to Paradise Walk, is that correct?'

"'Yes.'

"'What time did you return there?'

"'It was noon, or shortly thereafter.'

"'And when you returned, Mrs. Hudson and Miss Moran had been boxing up and preparing to dispose of Miss Turner's possessions.'

"'Yes.'

"'Thank you, Mrs. Stewart.'

"'Will you direct any further questions to the witness?' the judge asked Baen.

"'No, My Lord.' He remained standing while the lady was dismissed and walked out of the court.

"'My Lord,' Sir Hillary said, 'I will call one more witness, and before I conclude the case for the Crown. However, I will reserve the right to recall any witness, or to call forward another witness if testimony given in the defense's case warrants a rebuttal.'

"'I am certain that Mr. Cummings has no objection to that, do you, sir?'

"It was then that Cummings uttered the words that he would come to bitterly regret. 'I have no objection, My Lord.'

"'Who is your last witness, Sir Hillary?'

"'Professor James Moriarty.'"

CHAPTER THIRTY-TWO

"Moriarty stepped from the waiting room, head bowed, garbed in black, the embodiment of a man worn down with sorrow.

"'Professor Moriarty,' Sir Hillary began, 'the accused is your companion, is that not correct?'

"'She was.'

"'How long has she has lived under your protection?'

"'For almost seven years.'

"'You were engaged in scholarly pursuits and living in Oxfordshire at the time you met, is that not correct?'

"'Yes, it is.'

"'And how did people from such different backgrounds happen to come together?'

"Moriarty's expression seemed to take on a quiet nostalgia. 'Miss Turner's father was an art forger. Hearing, somehow, of my keen love of painting, he visited me and attempted to pass off one of his copies as an authentic Rossetti. I was not deceived, of course, and so I also doubted his assertion that the model for the original was his own daughter. To prove his claim, he brought the girl to my home. She was much younger than she appeared on the canvas and far more beautiful. I asked her several questions and was surprised to find that she was articulate, intelligent, quite well-read. More so than many of my own students at the time. At this point, Turner named a price which I mistakenly thought was his price for the work when, in fact, it was the girl he was offering to sell. I believed that if I declined, he would take his depraved proposal to another party, so I accepted his offer.'

"'And at some point, in the course of providing for her, your relationship became intimate?'

"'It did. I am sorry to say it, but the nature of her upbringing led her to believe that there was only one way to express gratitude – and I suppose I was weak.'

"'Of course, you may be vindicated somewhat as the girl had reached the legal age of consent."

"'Yes. Nonetheless, I should have exercised more restraint. I can only defend my actions by adding that from the first, I told her I wished to marry her, but she refused me. When we learned that she was with child, I had hoped that she would have a change of heart, and consent to marriage for the child's sake.'

"'But she did not?'

"'No.'

"'And after, in the course of time, when she gave birth to twin boys, did she reconsider?'

"'She was adamant. She would not marry me.'

"'Let us come to the evening of Monday, February third. Do you recall how you and Miss Turner spent the day?'

"'I gave the children their lessons, and then spent the afternoon in my study. Miss Turner went out to perform some small errands. We were to attend a reception that evening.'

"'And did you attend this reception?'

"'We did.'

"'But you did not return together?'

"'No. Miss Turner complained of a headache and expressed a desire to leave. I arranged for her to be taken home and remained for another hour or so, and then went on to my club, where I played cards...it seems a callous and trivial thing to have done in light of what came after. If I had gone home with Miss Turner...'

"'And,' Sir Hillary asked, softly, 'you were at your club when a constable came to summon you to Paradise Walk?'

"'I was.'

"'And when you returned, where was Miss Turner?'

"'She was in her sitting room.'

"'Did the two of you speak?'

"Moriarty nodded, sorrowfully. 'Yes. I, though I cannot recall all of my words, nor Miss Turner's responses. I do remember that I was shocked and angered by her unnatural composure. She even smiled and I am afraid that I was not able to govern my temper as well as I ought to have.'

"'Did you order her to leave the house?'

"'I did not. She informed me that she meant to leave as soon as she might gather a few possessions.'

"'What did you do, then?'

"'You must understand, I was overwhelmed. I was not myself. I left the house and walked the streets for some time. When I returned, it was with a cooler head, and with every intention to reconcile. We do not all express our grief

251

in the same way, and I realized that what I had taken for indifference might indeed be a state of shock. But, of course, she was gone when I returned, and as the house was...' he sighed, gravely, 'I had no reason or wish to remain there, and so I took a suite at a hotel.'

"'And it was here that you were visited by Mrs. Stewart?'

"'Yes. She had returned to Paradise Walk and was told that I'd gone to Claridge's, so she came to me there and told me of Miss Turner's confession – that she had admitted to poisoning the children and then igniting the blaze with the intention of making their deaths appear to be accidental.'

"'Professor Moriarty, I am certain that this question is an excessively painful one, but I must ask you to look back upon the sort of life which you provided for Miss Turner. Can you think of any incident which would account for the references to cruelty or oppression on your part?'

"Moriarty shook his head, sorrowfully. 'I can only think that once we left Oxford for London, Miss Turner was – seduced, I suppose you would say – by the sort of diversions in town that had not been available to her formerly. I made every attempt to provide her with entertainment and society, but perhaps I did not do enough and she came to resent...' He put the handkerchief to his eyes.

"'My Lord,' Sir Hillary declared. 'I will not prolong the pain of this witness by questioning him further. Thank you, Professor.'

"'Mr. Cummings?' the judge prompted.

"Cummings appeared unmoved by Moriarty's show of emotion. 'Professor Moriarty, when you were introduced to Miss Turner, she was fourteen years of age?'

"'Yes.'

"'And you were, what was it? Twenty-one?'

"Moriarty paused. 'I was twenty-eight.'

"'Yes, forgive me, I have mixed up my notes. It was at age twenty-one that you published a treatise on the binomial theorem which brought you the offer of university post and that, in turn allowed you to secure a more prestigious situation in Oxfordshire.'

"Sir Hillary rose. 'My Lord, I don't think that our purpose here is to review the Professor's credentials.'

"'I will give Mr. Cummings a bit of latitude,' the judge replied. '*Very* little, Mr. Cummings.'

"'Yes, My Lord. Professor, in this post, you earned a good salary?'

"'Yes, I did.'

"'Youth, income, education. All of this would have made you an eligible prospect. Why did you never marry?

"'A university town can be somewhat limited in the society it offers.'

"'Did it not offer you the opportunity to meet women of your own station?'

"Moriarty's head began to vacillate slowly, like a serpent fixing its prey. 'I was not seeking out opportunities, sir, I was too preoccupied with my studies at the time. It was Miss Turner's father who brought the girl to my attention, and when I knew her situation, my initial feeling was the desire to save her from a life of depravity – from a father who would put a price on his own child.'

"'And what was that price, Professor?'

"Moriarty's fingers closed over the hat in his hands, crushing the brim. 'Five pounds.'

"Cummings nodded, thoughtfully. 'And did the girl's mother agree upon this price for her child?'

"'I never met her. I understood that she was a mental deficient.'

"'Indeed? Was Mr. Turner a man of education?'

"'No. He was cunning man, but he had no formal education.'

"'When he sold his daughter to you for five pounds, did he mention what schools she had attended?'

"'She had never been to school.'

"'A fourteen-year-old girl who has not been to school, and yet is intelligent and well-read? Did she come by this learning from a father who had no education or a mother who was a mental deficient?'

"'I do not know how she came by her learning.'

"'Most men would doubt the wisdom of fathering children by the daughter of a lunatic and a criminal.'

"'A question, Mr. Cummings,' the judge reminded him.

"'Did Miss Turner's friends ever confide to you conduct on her part which might have given you some alarm?'

"'There were none.'

"'None of what, Professor? Incidents, or friends?'

"'Miss Turner was devoted to her own pursuits and education. She had no need for commonplace friendships.'

"'But you testified that when you came to London, she was very eager for society.'

"'I object to this hectoring of the witness, My Lord,' Sir Hillary protested.

"'I beg your pardon, Professor,' Cummings apologized, evenly. 'Professor, it has been stated that you provided Miss Turner with a great many material possessions.'

"'I gave her everything she could want.'

"'Now, following a quarrel with Miss Turner on the morning of the tragedy, you left the house, walked 'round for some time, returned to your home, found her gone and told your staff that you intended to move to a hotel. Is that correct?'

"'Yes.'

"'I say 'your staff' but Mrs. Stewart was not there at the time.'

"'No. Understood that she had returned to the house some time after I had left.'

"'Left with the intention of taking a suite at a hotel. Now, Mrs. Stewart stated that when she arrived, Mrs. Hudson and Miss Moran were boxing up Miss Turner's possessions, that they were to be disposed of.'

"'I could not bear to keep them when I knew what she had done.'

"'Can you tell the court when this order was given?'

"'When?'

"'Was it given before you left the house in anger, or when you returned with a cooler head?'

"Moriarty's thin lips pressed together for a moment. 'After my return.'

"'After – and yet, it could not have been long after, since Mrs. Hudson testified that she and Miss Moran were well into the task when they stopped for luncheon. Could you help the court, sir, by recalling the time that this order was given?'

"'Perhaps between ten and eleven.'

"'I don't understand, Professor. You say that you ordered Miss Turner's possessions disposed of because you *knew* what she had done. But how *could* you know it, sir, between ten and eleven that morning when Mrs. Stewart has testified that she did not disclose Miss Turner's alleged confession to you until after noon?'

"Sir Hillary sprang to his feet. 'My Lord, I implore my learned colleague to abandon this hostile – this adversarial – conduct. Professor Moriarty is not on trial.'

"Fury hardened Moriarty's gaze. 'The life I had enjoyed for seven years had ended in an instant. I hope that I can be forgiven if my memory is imprecise as to the details.'

"'Did you love your children, Professor?'

"'My Lord!" cried Sir Hillary.

"Cummings shrugged. 'I withdraw the question, My Lord, Nothing more.'

"'Sir Hillary?'

"The prosecutor rose. 'Did you love Miss Turner, Professor?'

"Moriarty looked up at the lady in the dock. There was a long pause, and then he replied with a quiet, 'Yes.'

"It provoked a strange sensation in me Watson, for I never felt a moment's sympathy for the man, not before and not since, but I felt pity for him then."

CHAPTER THIRTY-THREE

"There was to be an interval before Cummings would present his case. Gregson and I went outside to smoke a cigarette and found that a bazaar had formed in the area 'round the Old Bailey. Newspaper-boys hawked penny editions and halfpenny broadsides, flower girls hawked nosegays and dried lavender, street vendors hawked meat pies and ginger beer. I spied one of the latter who was peddling ham and onion pies, a favorite of Brodie's.

"'Keep a place for me. I want to see if there is time for me to visit Mr. Brodie.'

"I bought a few hot pies from a vendor, and carried them to the keeper's lodge, where a few shillings more were spent to keep the pies from being confiscated.

"The inch or so of wet snow which had covered the exercise yard of the male inmates. I saw Brodie in a corner of the yard, apparently entertaining a few lads, who could not have been more than eleven or twelve years of age.

"I raised one hand, and Brodie looked up with a wink, and excusing himself, shambled across the muddy yard.

"'Ah, what have you got there! Ham and onion pies!' I passed them through the bars and Brodie held them up to inhale their aroma, then shook his head, regretfully. He turned and crossed the yard to the lads, and handed them the pies, charging them to share with the younger ones, and then returned to me.

"'What passed in court this morning?'

"'Mrs. Stewart and Moriarty presented a united front.'

"'How does Cummings do?'

"'He is very skilled, but the testimony against Miss Turner is damning. The best Cummings can hope for, I fear, is to make a case against premeditation. There is enough precedent to draw upon – Martha Brixey, Esther Griggs, Emma Lewis, Amelia Snoswell – the Borley case, as well.'

"'What grim diversions you indulge in, Sherlock! I daresay you would not want *your* reading material divulged in open court!'

"These ladies, Watson, were child-killers, though they did not all kill children of their own, and all had escaped the gallows. Lewis was detained for a few years in Bedlam, I believe. Brixey was acquitted in the killing of her master's child, even after she had freely admitted her guilt and Amelia Snoswell was acquitted in the killing of a niece. Griggs maintained that she had been in the throes of a sleep-walking nightmare when she tossed her child from a window and she was not even brought to trial. Maria Borley had drowned her child, and her acquittal was largely secured through the argument that her husband's brutal treatment had driven her to a temporary state of insanity.

"'Go now,' Brodie urged, 'for you will not get a place in the afternoon session if you delay.'

"'Very well. But you must keep up your strength, sir.'

"I drew from my pocket an apple tart wrapped in paper, which I had held back when I had given him the pies.

"'What a clever lad you are. Doesn't that crust look like it would melt like butter on the tongue! Perhaps just a nibble,' he said, breaking off a bit of the crust. 'But the warders tell me that one of the women inmates was just delivered of a child, and women in her state must keep up their strength. I know just how to get it to her – what skills one learns in a prison, Sherlock! And we must care for the young ones when they need us most, else we will live to regret it.'"

CHAPTER THIRTY-FOUR

"The first witness for the defense was a Doctor John Batty Winslow. His bull-dog face and thick hands were more suited to a dock-worker than a doctor, but he was, in fact, a well-regarded specialist in the treatment of female disease.

"'Dr. Winslow,' Cummings began. 'You attended the accused at the time her sons were born?'

"'Yes.'

"'And after the birth,' Cummings was asking, 'did Miss Turner's recovery proceed in the normal fashion?'

"'A bit slower, perhaps, owing to the fact that the delivery of twins is always more difficult.'

"'And you were called upon last year, to attend to Miss Turner again?'

"'Yes, she was once again in a delicate state. Unfortunately, her situation ended in a miscarriage after only a few months.'

"Cummings paused for a moment. 'Doctor, are you familiar with the term puerperal mania?'

"'Yes.'

"'Would you define this for the benefit of the jury?'

"Winslow shifted his position so that he could address the jury more directly. 'It is sometimes called puerperal insanity. Many years ago, it was referred to as childbed melancholia, and the term applies to an aberrant mental state which may have its onset while a woman is expecting, but which more frequently follows after the lying-in.'

"'And how does this aberrant mental state manifest itself?'

"'Generally, there is either an extreme agitation, in which she may experience episodes of uncontrollable violence, or she may experience an overwhelming despondency. In the latter case, the mother may sink to such a profound despair that she may attempt to take her own life, or even the life of her child.'

"'And how soon after the birth of a child does this aberrant state manifest itself.'

"'The medical community has not always been in agreement on this point. It becomes evident most often within days or weeks of the birth, but many believe that symptoms may not appear for months, or even years.'

"'Is it a state which might also follow the loss of a child to a miscarriage?'

"'Yes.'

"'Would it be possible for a woman afflicted with this condition to conceal it from her husband, friends and servants?'

"'It could not escape the observation of anyone who saw her on a regular basis.'

"'And what if there were no people to observe the woman on a regular basis? If, for example, her physician or midwife did not visit her after the birth, or if there were no servants or friends close at hand?'

"'Then it is likely that the first indication that a problem existed would be – well, it would be as I have said: the infliction of injury or even the murder of the child, often followed by the mother's suicide.'

"I heard a strange murmur, Watson, and looking 'round, I saw that many of the women in the courtroom were nodding unconsciously in agreement with the doctor's remarks.

"'Now you visited Miss Turner during her confinement. At her home in Paradise Walk, I presume?'

"'Yes.'

"'Were these visits private, or was there a nurse or lady's maid or relative in attendance?'

"'Only the Professor was present.'

"Cummings raised his brows, affecting a look of surprise. 'Did Miss Turner ask him to be there?'

"'I do not know.'

"'Did you ever see Miss Turner alone?'

"'No.'

"'Never spoke to her privately?'

"'No.'

"'So there was no opportunity for Miss Turner to discuss with you the sort of matters that a patient might wish to discuss confidentially with her physician?'

"'No. The Professor was always there.'

"'But surely not when you delivered the twins?'

"'Yes, he was there then.'

"'Indeed? That is rather unusual, is it not?'

"'This would require an opinion,' Sir Hillary objected.

"'I will rephrase my question,' Cummings said. 'Doctor, in your practice, how common was it for a prospective father to be present during medical examinations?'

"'In my experience, it did not occur.'

"'How many prospective fathers were present at the time of the child's birth?'

"'Why...none, in my practice.'

"'And in Miss Turner's case, was the delivery a usual one – apart from the fact that it resulted in twins?'

"'Well, when there is more than one child, the mother's life is always at additional risk and the duration of the labor can be quite long and excessively painful.'

"'Is there anything a physician might do to alleviate the pain?'

"'Yes, there is anesthesia available.'

"'What sort was used in Miss Turner's case?'

"'None.'

"'She declined it?'

"'No, the Professor did. He was concerned that any form of sedation might injure the children.'

"'Did he express any concern for the mother's discomfort?'

"'No.'

"'And did her recovery proceed normally?'

"'She lost a good deal of blood and I was concerned that she might not survive, but she rallied at last.'

"'How long did it take for her to recover fully?'

"'Two or three months.'

"'And in those two or three months, how often did you visit Miss Turner?'

"'Only once during the week after the lying-in. The Professor was of the opinion that with proper rest, she would recover and as he worked at his home, for the most part, he was willing to see to her care. I inquired after her for several weeks, and was always informed that she was recovering favorably.'

"'Informed by the Professor?'

"'Yes.'

"'Doctor, after the birth of the twins, what recommendations did you make for Miss Turner's future health?'

"'I recommended that Miss Turner have no more children, and that if she should find herself in that condition, it would place her health, and perhaps her life, in jeopardy.'

"'She would not have survived another lying-in, you mean?'

"'Very likely not.'

"'And were you, therefore, concerned when you learned last year that she was once again with child?'

"'Yes, of course.'

"Cummings addressed the judge. 'My Lord, I have no further questions at this time, though I will reserve the right to re-address after my learned colleague.'

"'Very well, Mr. Cummings. Sir Hillary?'

"Sir Hillary rose and strode slowly toward the witness, his hands clasped behind his back. 'Now, Doctor Winslow, your specialty is female disease, is that not correct?'

"'Yes.'

"'You are not a specialist in mental disease?'

"'No.'

"'So any observations you may give on a patient's mental state would not be from the point of view of a specialist in mental disease? For example, when you testified that you had observed – what was it called – melancholia? – in your patients, you speak as a gynecologist, not as an alienist or psychologist?'

"'No, I am not an alienist or psychologist, but I have treated female disease for twenty-four years, and that has given me a great deal of opportunity to observe the mental abnormalities which appear to be associated with childbirth.'

"Sir Hillary hesitated, as if considering how far he could afford to irritate the witness. 'In your twenty-four years of practice, Doctor, how would you compare Professor Moriarty's attention to Miss Turner? Would you say it was greater or less than what you generally observed?'

"'He was very solicitous, very scrupulous about her welfare,' Winslow responded. 'Indeed, I have seen married men who are not so attentive.'

"This produced a ripple of laughter.

"'And in all the time you visited with Miss Turner, did she ever seem susceptible to morbid thoughts, or make any sort of declaration that suggested mental disease?'

"'No, she seemed a healthy woman of sound mind.'

"'Did she ever demonstrate a state of depression?'

"'No.'

"'Emotional instability or aberrant behavior of any sort?'

"'No.'

"'A tendency toward uncontrollable impulses?'

"'Not that I observed, no. But as I have said, the onset of this condition is often delayed.'

"'But you stated that you attended Miss Turner three years ago, and again last year. Did you observe that her mental state had deteriorated in the interim?'

"'No.'

"'And have you personal knowledge of cases where women kill their own children, Doctor?'

"'Sadly, yes.'

"'How many of these cases resulted in a coroner's inquest, or a police investigation?'

"'Why, none of them. There was no question as to what had occurred, nor who committed the act.'

"'There was no attempt upon the culprit's part to conceal or minimize the evidence, or to escape detection?'

"'No.'

"'That is peculiar, would you not say?'

"'Premeditation and concealment suggest a mind that is capable of reason and design. With puerperal mania or melancholia, there is an absence of premeditation. The patient is incapable of calculation.'

"'So, if a woman had been charged with killing her children, one factor that might be looked to, one factor that might be of use in determining whether she were sane or deranged, would be the presence or absence of premeditation?'

"'Well,' replied the doctor, 'certainly, if a loving mother, quite without warning and acting upon impulse, stabbed her child, or drowned it in a basin or tossed it into the Thames, the lack of premeditation would suggest that she had not been of sound mind.'

"'What of a woman who poisons her children?'

"'Well, poison must be obtained and administered...'

"'And that,' Sir Hillary concluded, 'might suggest that the act was planned rather than an impulse?'

"'I suppose that it would, yes.'

"'And if that woman then disposed of the body – or bodies,' he added, pointedly, 'in an attempt to make the death seem accidental, would that also argue against mental derangement?'

"Winslow nodded. 'A woman who is deranged does not have the presence of mind to conceal her act.'

"'Thank you doctor.'

"The judge looked toward Cummings, who rose. 'Doctor Winslow, would not all of the examples you raised have some degree of premeditation? A woman who tosses her child into the Thames must carry it there, and one who drowns her child in a basin must first fill the basin, and one who stabs her infant must first get 'hold of the knife?'

"'Yes, I see your point.'

"'Now, Doctor, you have said that you have observed childbed melancholia in some of your patients. What factors, in your opinion, might predispose a woman toward such a condition?'

"'Certainly, a family history of mental disease. A prior injury to the brain, or a bout of brain fever or seizures.'

"'What of poison? If a woman had been poisoned, even if she had recovered, might there be residual damage to the brain?'

"'Yes, it is quite possible.'

"'Thank you, Doctor, I have nothing further.'

"Cummings had only one more witness, and the name 'Ross Patterson' was called out.

"'Who the devil is that?' Gregson whispered in my ear.

"'I do not know,' I whispered back.

"Ross Patterson was young, perhaps twenty-eight or twenty-nine, with the coarse and ruddy complexion of a man who had spent a great deal of time out of doors. He looked about the unfamiliar milieu of the courtroom with some wariness, though his steely gaze was suggestive of a man who was not easily cowed.

"'Sir,' Cummings began, 'would you state your occupation for the court?'

"'I have been a Constable in Oxfordshire, in the village of Abingdon, for eight years, though I will leave my post next month to move to London.'

"'And do you know the accused?'

269

"'I have seen her, though not for seven years.'

"'On what occasion did you see the lady?'

"'I was called to the rooms where she was living with her father and mother, Mr. and Mrs. Victor Turner. The young lady and her mother were unconscious and the father was in a state of extreme agitation. The doctor arrived and tended to them as best he could, and then they were moved to Hanwell Private Hospital.'

"'What was the nature of their illness?'

"'Mrs. Turner had attempted to kill both herself and her child with poison.'

"All eyes turned toward the accused. There was not the slightest sign of emotion in her. Her attitude remained one of patient indifference to the proceedings.

"'What was the outcome of the situation?'

"'Miss Turner recovered and was returned to her father's care. Her mother was moved to Hanwell Mercy Asylum. It was an institution for the insane.'

"'And why was she placed there?'

"'Her mind never recovered. I attempted to interview her in order to make my report of the situation complete, but she would only weep and scream her child's name and cry out that her child would not be sold like a common...' The man broke off and glanced toward the public in embarrassment. 'Well, like common baggage.'

"I looked up at Miss Turner and saw her hands clutch at her skirt. This was the extent of her reaction to the man's remarks.

"'Mr. Patterson, you said that Mrs. Turner wept and cried out for her child. Had she been told that her child survived?'

"'I do not know – I supposed only that as Mrs. Turner had survived, she must believe that her daughter had recovered as well.'

"'What became of Mr. Turner and the daughter?'

"'Turner abandoned the girl and she was taken in by a university professor, a gentleman named Moriarty.'

"'Did you ever meet this gentleman?'

"'Only once, sir. I took the liberty of bringing his attention to Mrs. Turner's state and made so bold as to suggest that if he might allow the girl to visit her mother, it might give some comfort to the woman to see that her daughter was well and cared for.'

"'And what was Professor Moriarty's response?'

"'He said it was best to keep them apart as he feared that it might have an ill effect upon the girl, as her mind was in a fragile way.'

"'A fragile way,' Cummings repeated, with a glance toward the jurymen. 'And what became of Mrs. Turner?'

"'Hanwell Mercy closed its doors, and as there was no family to provide for her, she was sent off to the Priory.'

"'An institution for the insane.'

"'Yes, sir.'

'And do you know what became of her?'

"'I heard that she died within the year.'

"'I have nothing further, My Lord,' Cummings said.

"The judge looked to Sir Hillary, who said, 'I have nothing for this witness, My Lord.'

"When the man had left the courtroom, Cummings declared. 'My Lord, the defense will call no further witnesses.'

"'Sir Hillary?'

"'My Lord, considering the nature of the defense testimony, I will claim the right to call a witness in rebuttal. I realize that my learned colleague will want to prepare for his examination of this witness, so may I venture to suggest that we adjourn until tomorrow morning?'

"'Who is your witness, Sir Hillary?'

"I had supposed that Baen meant to call back Mrs. Stewart or Moriarty, perhaps, but he replied, 'Mr. Abel Norcross of Christopher and Klein, an insurance firm in Leadenhall Street.'

"'Mr. Cummings?' the judge asked.

"Cummings was clearly puzzled, but he made no objection and the proceedings were ended for the day.

"'How does Sir Hillary mean to refute the testimony of the doctor and the constable with an insurance clerk?' I whispered to Gregson.

"'Perhaps the Professor accuses Miss Turner of making off with some items of value. She would need something to live on if she had resolved on ending her relationship with the Professor. Or,' Gregson hazarded, dismissing the subject with a shrug, 'it may simply be Sir Hillary's way of having the final word by ensuring that his witness is the last that the jury hears. If it had truly been something that would advance his case, he would have introduced it before this.'

Gregson could not have been more wrong."

CHAPTER THIRTY-FIVE

"As the jurymen filed out of the room, I could see that the statements of Doctor Winslow and Constable Patterson had 'roused their compassion. Perhaps the testimony had called to mind suffering that they had witnessed in a mother or sister or sweetheart. Their accounts and the jury's sympathy might not be enough to secure Miss Turner's acquittal – I would not allow myself to hope for that – but a verdict of guilty but insane would allow for the possibility that she might, in time, recover her liberty.

"The prospect of that outcome was short-lived. On the following morning, Sir Hillary strode into the court-room, his piercing eyes alight with triumph, while Cummings was so white that I thought he was ill, and his bowed shoulders seemed to be weighted down by defeat. Something terrible had come to pass.

"The session began with the same little ceremony as on the previous day, with Brodie being escorted into the courtroom and to be asked if he had experienced a change of heart. Before he could be addressed, however, Sir Hillary rose and declared. 'We are quite willing to forgive the contempt which Mr. Brodie directed at these proceedings and ask My Lord to order his release.'

"The judge acceded and ordered Brodie to pay a fine, and allowed him to be set free. The old man turned and made his way toward the public seats. I nodded to him and made room for him in the pew next to me.

"'What has happened?' I whispered to him.

"Brodie shook his head. 'Look, here she comes! How well she bears it all – oh, how relieved I shall be when it is all done! If only I had not been so unyielding from the first – how we might all have been spared!'

"The public were called to order and Sir Hillary's witness stepped to the witness box.

"Mr. Abel Norcross was a small, primly dressed man with an open, honest face, though he clutched nervously at the hat in his hands, and his gaze darted about as though he did not understand if he were to direct his remarks toward the judge, the jury, the questioner or the public.

"'Mr. Norcross, do you know Professor James Moriarty?'

"'No, sir.'

"'Do you know the accused, Miss Violet Turner?'

"'Yes, sir.'

"'Is your acquaintance a social one?'

"'No, sir, Miss Turner is a client. I prepared insurance policies for her.'

"'She insured property with Christopher and Klein?'

"'No. It was life insurance.'

"'Life insurance,' Sir Hillary intoned, significantly. 'She took out a policy on her own life?'

"'No, sir, on her children.'

"'On her children? Is that not unusual?'

"'It is not often seen. And, as with many in our trade, Christopher and Klein will not write policies on children below three years of age.'

"'And the reason for that?'

"'Well...'" Norcross cleared his throat. 'as the mortality of infants and young children, such as it is ...'

"'It would not be sound business.'

"'No, sir.'

"'So, when these policies were written, the twin boys had reached their third birthday. That would have been some time near the end of last year?'

"Norcross nodded, and wiped his forehead with his handkerchief. 'Yes.'

"'And you are quite certain that these were insurance policies and not shares in a burial club of some sort?'

"Norcross jutted his chin forward. 'I have been in this trade for twenty-two years! I know the difference between a life insurance policy and a funeral club!'

"'Yes, but of course, they both end in the grave, do they not? And what expense was Miss Turner put to in securing these policies?'

"'Ten pounds a year for each one.'

"'Thirty pounds, all together' Sir Hillary remarked. 'Now, Mr. Norcross,' he resumed quickly before Cummings could object. '- who was the beneficiary?'

"'Miss Turner herself.'

"Sir Hillary stood with his head bowed, the personification of the shock that rippled through the courtroom. At last ,he raised his head and asked, 'And should this court rule that Miss Turner is not guilty, these benefits will be paid?'

"'Yes.'

"'And what would be the amount of that payment?'

"'Thirty thousand pounds.'

"'Thirty thousand pounds,' Sir Hillary repeated, gravely. 'For an investment of thirty pounds. That is an excellent rate of return, would you not say, Mr. Norcross?'

"Cummings looked too staggered even to object.

"'It is a good sum,' Norcross replied, awkwardly.

"'And when the matter of arranging these policies took place, I imagine that you needed to take a great deal of time to explain the particulars to Miss Turner?'

"'Oh, no, sir. She had taken the trouble to learn a great deal about the subject of policies and benefits and how they were to be paid. I would have put her to work as one of our clerks if she had been a man.'

"'So would you say that she made a calculated and rational study of the subject?'

"'Yes.'

"'And now, all that stands between her and thirty thousand pounds is the matter of the verdict.'

"'Yes, that is correct.'

"'And, if she is convicted, I expect that the children's father will be the beneficiary?'

"'No, sir Miss Turner stipulated that if both the children and she were to die, the money should go to a Mr. Aiden Brodie.'

"Beside me, I heard Brodie gasp. He sprang to his feet and called out her name.

"She turned and looked down at him, her lips curving in a smile of quiet triumph.

"'Checkmate!' he cried. 'Ah, clever girl! Clever girl! It is checkmate!'

"Then he exploded into a fit of sobs alternated with uncontrollable laughter, and the session was called to an abrupt end as Brodie was carried from the courtroom."

CHAPTER THIRTY-SIX

"I managed to get the poor man into a cab. By the time we reached Old Compton Street he was feverish and babbling incoherently.

"Wiggins, little Bob and I got the old man into his bed, and then I sent the boys off to fetch a doctor.

"I covered the old man with a blanket and stirred up a small fire in the grate. 'How cold, how cold!' the old man babbled. 'How coldly she plays. She said nothing of *that* move – Ha ha, how she plays the game! It is checkmate!'

"I paced helplessly for nearly an hour while he continued in this vein. Wiggins returned at last with the frail and disheveled-looking practitioner whom I had seen crossing the yard at Newgate in the company of MacInnes, the hangman. Wiggins introduced him as Dr. John Knowles, and taking me aside, whispered, 'I went to Mrs. Skinner first, but she's hoccupied with Mrs. Tanner's little 'un an' cannot get away. I don't fink 'e'll do much 'arm, for 'e's quite near sober.'

"I waited while Dr. Knowles examined the patient and administered a dose of medicine, which seemed to make the old man more comfortable. The doctor stated that Brodie's heart was sound enough for a man of his age, but that he had received a terrible blow, and must remain in bed for several days at complete rest. 'The sedative I administered will get him through the night. I will return in the morning, though you must not hesitate to summon me or Mrs. Skinner if his fever does not drop.'

"I thanked the doctor and left his fee at the door, then took a book from the shop, preparing to sit up with the old man. When I returned to the chamber, I saw that Wiggins had already pushed a chair up to the man's bed and was adjusting the blankets with a practiced efficiency.

"'You and Bob may go, Wiggins, I will not leave him.'

"'We cannot go, sir. Ma would not want us to leave one oo's been so good to Bob an' me.'

"'Well, I will tell you what, then. If you will run out for one of the evening editions, I will get something in the way of tea.'

"Brodie's living quarters had a bit of kitchen and larder where I found a half loaf of bread, peach preserves, bacon and tea. I threw together a simple meal and had it ready when Wiggins and his little brother returned.

"'You can read your paper at table if you like, t'won't hoffend me an' Bob. Saturdays, Pa'll make us wait our tea 'til Mr. Brock 'as done with 'is Pink 'Un an' sends it up, so's Pa can read it at table.'

"'Well, you and Bob will not have to wait your tea, it's quite ready. I will look the paper over though.'

"We pulled chairs up to the little table, and while Wiggins filled up his little brother's plate, I opened the edition of the *Evening Standard*. The headline read 'Paradise Walk Child Killing Goes to Jury. Final Testimony Suggests Murder For Profit. Conviction All But Certain.'

"I was staggered. I had not expected that, while I sat tending to poor Brodie, the matter had been given over to the jury. And when it comes to the law, Watson, haste and delay are equally ominous.

"I put the paper aside and saw that though little Bob was tackling his food with energy, Wiggins was not.

"'What's the matter, Wiggins?'

"'Mr. Brodie hain't gonna die, is 'e?'

"I was touched that the lad, who must be quite inured to death, was so concerned for the old man. 'No, he is under a great strain, but his constitution is strong.'

"'I'd not want t' see such a kind old gent go. 'E's as kind as the Guv'nor. 'Course, the Guv'nor cannot do much as 'e'd like, for Ma would not 'ave it. Ma says if you get to taking too much in the way of charity, you're hinclined to go soft.'

"'I am sure that it has been a winter when a great many people have had to accept a little charity. And I know that it has not been easy on your mother, for she has had the trial of burying a child. That is very hard on a mother.'

"'Yes, sir, not to mention the hexpense of it. T'was all we could do to find money for the box, an' not a penny over, so Ma wrapped 'im in 'er best shawl an' cut a piece for 'erself to remember 'im by. Some kind folk 'ave laid down a stone for 'im. I hexpect it's the Guv'nor's doing – the Guv'nor or some of the ladies oo come 'round when they're in a charitable 'umor.'

"'He was laid to rest at the Tower Hamlets cemetery?'

"Wiggins nodded, as his munched on his toast. 'Ma didn't like to – there's too much shufflin' habout, for they must sometimes bring 'em up an' move 'em 'round so's to make room, an' if a lid 'appens to pop off, some folks'll 'elp themselves. Ma says it's hawful bad luck to crack a box, that it puts the curse o' the grave 'pon you, an' dooms you to a solhitary life. 'Course, there was nothin' to pinch from the Little 'Un's box save for 'is kit an' Ma's shawl 'e was wrapped in.'

"I did not smile upon the lad's superstitious talk for I could see that he took it most seriously. 'I heard of a Mrs. Radley who claimed that her daughter's grave had been tampered with. Why would she say that, do you know? Surely there was nothing of value to take from the poor girl's coffin.'

"'Not a lock of 'air, for it was shorn when she was in a fever. Mrs. Radley declares 'er Etta's pinched for *hexperimental* doings, but Pa says it's likely she sold Etta to the medical men 'erself an' then forgot she struck the bargain, for Mrs. Radley's been known to tip a few. 'Ow else would she come by that fine stone she laid 'pon Etta's grave, Pa says, when Mrs. Radley spent all carin' for Etta, an' 'ad't two pennies left for 'er eyes? Which *I* say, why not sell 'er to the medical men right off? Why pay for the box an' 'ave 'er put in the ground if she's just to be brought up again? It seems a backward way to go about y'r business, in *my* opinion.'

"'Your mother has not noticed anything amiss when she visits your brother's burial place, has she?'

"'Oh, she does not visit. Pa will not 'llow it. 'E says she'd only come back more sorrowful than when she went an' it's bad 'nough she carries 'round the bit she saved from 'er old shawl an' cries at the sound of the Little 'Un's name. Pa says 'ow can she take on so when Mrs. Vye's got quite over losing *'er* boy who went right hafter the Little 'Un. An' the Guv'nor says our tears are wasted on the dead, for they're quite at peace, an' if we must cry, we'd best do it for the ones what's left be'ind. *I* cannot see the point in that myself, for's long as you've got breath, there's the chance fings might turn to your favor, an' then your tears 'ave all been wasted.'

"I confess I was entertained by Wiggins's straightforward philosophy. I have spent many hours, before and since, discussing the weighty matters of life and death, but never with one who had such a singular command of the subject.

"Brodie slept soundly through the night, and I managed a few hours of sleep in a chair. In the morning, I took the liberty of using Brodie's razor and basin to make myself as presentable as possible, and left for the court after giving instructions to Wiggins that Mr. Brodie was to be kept quiet, and that the shop ought to remain closed.

"The weather seemed a harbinger of ill, for the gray sky was thick with ink-blue clouds, and a powerful wind spun 'round the corners and barreled down the streets, knocking off bonnets and snatching morning editions from the grasp of the early newsboys.

"The crowd at the entrance to the Criminal Court was backed up to the middle of the street, a faceless mass of flapping skirts and flailing mufflers and billowing bonnet strings. I abandoned all civility and thrust my way through the crowd toward the entrance and when the doors were opened to the public, I found myself carried into the courtroom by a current of tightly packed bodies, with no more ability to navigate than a scrap of driftwood in a gale. This current swept me into the third pew, while the bailiffs at last had to pile themselves against the doors to stem the oncoming tide, which sent a backwash of humanity streaming upward to the gallery.

"As the spectators jostled and shifted, I looked 'round and saw the tall, somber form of Moriarty, sitting in the front row. He appeared defeated and sorrowful, and I found myself wondering if this melancholy aspect was a mere façade, an attempt to persuade the reporters and the public of his profound grief and erase any taint of his cruelty toward the accused that had been raised in Cummings' defense.

"Silence descended upon the crowd as Miss Turner was ushered to her place. She faced the jurymen, her head held high so that her white throat was visible above the collar of her dress. When I saw how their eyes avoided that slender neck, I knew the verdict even before I heard the words 'guilty as charged' and the gasp that followed it.

"The judge looked down at the accused, one hand laid over the blooms meant to sweeten a noxious air. 'Miss Violet Rose Turner, you have been found guilty of the most heinous and deliberate murder of Rose Moriarty, James

Moriarty and Amon Moriarty. Have you anything to say before this court pronounces sentence upon you?'

"'Only to ask that the sentence be carried out as swiftly as possible. I want to be with my children.'

"'A brazen wench to the end!' hissed a familiar voice. I turned and saw Ernest sitting in the pew behind me. Only my promise to Mycroft prevented me from laying him out right there in the courtroom.

"'Miss Violet Rose Turner, in due consideration of the verdict, the wanton nature of the crime and your own unrepentant conduct, and your own declaration, I charge that upon Monday next, the tenth day of March, you will be hanged by the neck until you are dead in full accordance with the law, and may God have mercy upon your soul.'

"On that grave note, the session was to have ended, but before the adjournment could be ordered, there was a most bizarre occurrence. A gust of wind rushed through the open window, stirring the magistrate's wig and lifting the square of black silk that he had laid upon it as he prepared to read the verdict of guilty.

"The silken square floated aloft, and all eyes in the courtroom followed it. A second gust flung it directly at Moriarty, and it landed flat against his waistcoat. Impatiently, he tried to flick the object away, as though some parasite had attached itself to him. For a few moments, the square held fast, then finally dropped to the floor at his feet.

"And then Miss Turner began to laugh. The laugh echoed, lilting as a bell, throughout the courtroom. She continued to laugh as the order was given for her removal, and when she was escorted down, and through the passage beneath us, her laughter could be heard, drifting upward, like the mocking of a demon."

CHAPTER THIRTY-SEVEN

"It was still morning when I left the court-room. In the street, I saw Moriarty shoulder through the knot of reporters and spring into a waiting carriage. The frustrated press scanned the crowd for another subject, and I watched with disgust as Ernest sidled into their midst. I overheard the fellow, all sham humility and smug conceit, invite their queries." Holmes mimicked a whining and unpleasant voice. "'And I believe I may have been the first to put the scenario together when I examined the remains at the mortuary. Some in surgical training find this aspect of our education to be distasteful, but you come to see its advantage when it aids the law in a matter such as this.'

"A disgusting creature, Watson.

"I would have gone straight to Mycroft to remind him of his pledge to me, but I felt that it was my duty to return first to Old Compton Street, as I would not wish for Brodie to hear the unhappy verdict from anyone but myself.

"I found little Wiggins and his brother dusting the shelves of books. 'Is Mr. Brodie still sleeping?' I asked.

"'Oh, no, sir, 'e woke an' took a bite, though 'e's still too low to leave 'is bed.'

"I found the old man sitting propped in his bed when I went up to his rooms. 'You needn't say anything, lad. I see in your face how it has gone. Who was there to hear the verdict? Moriarty, I expect. And how did dear Violet bear up?'

"'She faced it bravely. Yes, Moriarty was there. And Ernest.'

"'The little weasel. He cheated Wiggins out of Bell's *Dissection* for a pound, and the dear lad believes he struck quite a bargain! Well, that cowardly scoundrel will get his comeuppance, mark my words. His sort always does. You must not give him another thought Sherlock. Dwelling upon such people poisons the soul, and will shrivel up your heart like a rose in the desert. What a lovely thing a rose is. So much goes into cultivating it, but in the end, its beauty is a thing above nature. Though I think it is even surpassed by the violet. There is a tenacity about the violet; it will spring up from beneath the snow, and through a crack in the cobblestones. You can pluck it from its roots and bind it into a nosegay and still it will hold its bloom and not wither. Ah, me, I am rambling again. I hope that you will forgive *me*, Sherlock.'

"'For what, sir?'

"'Dear me – I cannot say – say I am forgiven anyway and I will give you cause when I am myself again. We should never withhold our forgiveness, Sherlock – we cannot count on having a second chance to bestow it.'

"I left him with the promise that I would try to get a bit of rest, but before I returned to Montague Street, I felt I must remind Mycroft of his promise to intercede with the Home Secretary. I went first to his Whitehall office, where I was informed by his clerk that he had not been seen for two days. I hurried 'round to his lodgings at Pall Mall, thinking that he had fallen ill, but his landlady informed me that Mycroft had left two days ago and told her that he would likely not return until Saturday night or Sunday at the earliest. This caused me a bit of anxiety, Watson, for Miss Turner's time was short, but I reassured myself with the knowledge that Mycroft had never disappointed me.

"I returned to my lodgings, where I had not spent more than a few hours at a time for the past week, at least. I found my room neatly swept and dusted. Fresh towels were hanging on the washstand bar, my shoes and boots polished, my coats cleaned and brushed and hanging in the wardrobe, the newspapers laid beside the grate and the mail in a neat stack upon the nightstand. The landlady had come to look upon any absences as her opportunity to engage in a campaign of organization that would require a week's effort for me to undo.

"I rang for hot water and took a fresh change of clothing from the wardrobe. When the girl brought up the basin, she handed me an envelope. 'This has just come for you, sir. The lad said there was no reply.'

"The envelope contained a sheet of official stationery from Leslie Cummings, Esq. 13 King's Bench Walk. It was a brief, handwritten note which read,

'Dear Mr. Sherlock Holmes,

My client, Miss Violet Turner has asked that you be permitted to visit her at your leisure. I have arranged for this dispensation, though I would like for you to call at my offices before you go to Newgate. Yours, etc.'

"This curious message drove away any fatigue I might have felt, and as soon as I put the hot water and soap to use and donned a fresh change of clothing, I was out the door once again, and in a cab directed to King's Bench Walk.

"I presented my card to the clerk and was immediately shown into the office of Leslie Cummings, who appeared warmer and more human in his brown suit, with his wig and robes laid aside.

"'I will get right to business, Mr. Holmes. Miss Turner has made two requests of me regarding you. One is that, upon Monday morning, after her sentence has been carried out, I turn over to you an envelope that she has entrusted to me. I do not know what the contents are, though it is quite a thick packet. I will be at Newgate that morning, but my business there should be concluded by ten o'clock.'

"'What is the other request?'

"'The policy for visiting the condemned is not a liberal one. It is always thought that they mean to escape or to commit suicide, so they are segregated and their visitors must have their clothing searched for weapons or poisons. Moreover, she has two matrons who must watch her, lest she attempt to harm herself. Because those conditions are so stringent and unpleasant for a visitor, Miss Turner wishes you to know that she will quite understand if you do not care to visit, but she hopes that you will.'

"'I will go, certainly, though I cannot imagine how I can be of service to Miss Turner.'

"'None of us can now, I am afraid, but I don't think that she means to ask for your help.'

"'What does she want, then?'

"'She said that she wants to challenge you to a game of chess.'"

CHAPTER THIRTY-EIGHT

"What a bizarre request!" I exclaimed.

"Yes, Watson. I wondered if she might be mad, after all.

"I walked the streets until twilight and then returned to my rooms, hoping that there might be some word from Mycroft. There was not so much as a line, and in great frustration I left my dinner tray untouched and smoked cigarette after cigarette while I read the evening editions, and then laid back upon my bed. My intention had been to close my eyes for a few minutes, but the next thing I was aware of was the maid's timid knock upon my door.

"I jumped out of my bed and saw that it was full daylight. I took my tray from the girl and bolted my breakfast while I tended to my toilet. I then hurried to a shop where I purchased a small chess set and took a cab to Newgate.

"I presented myself at the Keeper's Lodge and was instructed to wait until the warden and a male searcher could be summoned, and after it was determined that I was not carrying a weapon or poisons, I was conducted through a series of gates and corridors to the condemned cells.

"Two wardresses sat upon stools at the open door to Miss Turner's cell. They rose to allow me to pass and then resumed their chairs, where they would have a full view of all that transpired within the cell. The cell itself was a small apartment with one high, barred window overlooking the shed where the scaffold would be erected. Within, there was a rude table upon which rested a basin and folded towel, and a long wide bench. A rolled-up blanket lay at one end, and I concluded that this bench also served as a cot.

"When I entered the cell, Miss Turner rose to greet me with a quiet, 'Good morning, brother.' She was dressed in the shapeless, thin serge of a female prisoner. Her hair was tied back with a single ribbon but hung loose as she was not permitted to have combs or hairpins of any sort.

"'How are you?' I asked.

"Her gently mocking smile told me how absurd a question I had asked. 'We must take the bench, with the chessboard between us,' she said in a low voice. 'I am sorry there is no better accommodation. If we speak quietly, we will not be overheard, for the good matrons are not inclined to eavesdrop.'

"We settled ourselves on the bench and I laid out the chess set between us.

"'White or black?' she asked.

"'Your pleasure, Madam.'

"She chose black, and we played silently at first. Within a half hour, I was already at a disadvantage. 'You should value your knight better,' she said, as she claimed it. 'How is Mr. Brodie?'

"'Well. He is kept in his bed, and his young assistant tends to him faithfully.'

"We were silent for several more minutes, and she spoke again. 'Conversation does not distract me from my game.'

"What subject could I raise under the circumstances, Watson?

"'Perhaps, then, you will allow me to ask a question or two,' she said as she slid a rook with her finger.

"'Ask whatever you like,' I said.

"'What was your father like?'

"The question took me aback, but I answered it readily. 'Stern, and unaffectionate, though it was always made clear to my brother and me when we pleased him.'

"'And what did you do to please him?'

"'Attended to my studies.'

"'And what did you do to *dis*please him?'

"'Exhibit affection for my mother.'

"'Checkmate,' she said, quietly.

"So it was. 'What was your father like?' I asked, as she set up the pieces for another match.

"'I do not recall the earliest times, before he went off to prison. I was ten years of age when he was released, quite expecting to have my mother regard him with the same gratitude and submission she had shown when she threw herself away on him. He did not like to see that a deeper love had taken its place. I think that the devotion of a mother for her child will cause a bit of jealousy in even the best of men. And my father was not the best of men.'

"'What became of him?'

"She smiled. 'I have no idea, Mr. Holmes, but justice can be rather perverse. He may be happily plying his trade somewhere in the world.'

"We played silently for a time. Her moves were swift and appeared to be impulsive, their premeditation well-concealed.

"At last she asked, 'Why did your father not want you to demonstrate affection for your mother?'

"'He thought of it as weakness.'

"'And your mother was expected to refrain from instilling weakness in you and to curb her own displays of affection. But she could not, not always, though her life would have been easier if she could.'

"'Her life was not a hard one.'

"She waited until she had made her next move before she answered. 'I don't believe any man knows what makes a woman's life hard. And the few who do, too often use that knowledge to make her life harder. It is check, Mr. Holmes.'

"Three more moves, and the game was done and she was the victor once more." Holmes smiled ruefully. "I had not taken Brodie's praise of her game lightly, but her play had reached a mastery that I have seldom seen in a man, and never in a woman. Nothing kept her from her object, not her grim surroundings, nor the presence of the matrons, nor a sentence of death. I do not recall how many matches we played that day but I remember that I did not win one of them.

"I looked up and saw that the two matrons who sat at the entrance to the cell were not the same ladies that I had seen upon my arrival.

"'They work in shifts of four hours, save for the ones who remain overnight.'

"'How long have we been playing?'

"'Several hours,' she smiled. 'Will you come tomorrow? Do come. After all, the probability of winning a game must increase with the number of games played, would you not agree?'

"'I am not sure that I would, Miss Turner. I have not been able to decipher your game.'

"'There is no secret. I begin by envisioning victory, and make every move as if my life depended upon it.'

"I rose and pocketed the chess set.

"'I think we will be permitted to shake hands. Yes,' she said, with a look to the matrons. 'We may shake hands.' She took my hand in hers and turned my palm up and studied it. 'Have you given up your studies? I see that you have not been inside a laboratory for many weeks.'

"She dropped my hand and smiled. 'Well, I hope I have not been responsible for your delinquency. Shall we say *au revoir*? We will not say good-bye until Sunday.'"

CHAPTER THIRTY-NINE

"I returned to Brodie's shop and sent Wiggins home, then pulled a chair up to Brodie's bed and sat dozing at the old man's bedside until Wiggins came to relieve me on Saturday morning. When I left, I went straight to Mycroft's lodgings, where I presented quite a disheveled spectacle, for I had neither shaved nor changed my clothing.

"'I received a telegram from Mr. Holmes,' she informed me. 'He returns this evening.'

"'At what hour?'

"'I do not know, sir.'

"I thanked the landlady and returned to Montague Street in considerable anxiety. Mycroft had many concerns, far more important to the state of the world than a criminal trial, and I began to wonder whether he might have forgotten his promise to me.

"Within the hour, I presented myself, in a much more tidy state, at the Keeper's Lodge and submitted to the tedious procedure of being admitted to Miss Turner's cell.

"I was kept waiting for several minutes, and at last Marwood MacInnes, emerged from the cell. He bade the matrons a good-morning in his formal manner and spying me, he greeted me by name. It was an awkward moment, Watson, for I did not know if propriety required me to shake the hand that meant to fashion a noose around Miss Turner's throat. The man seemed to feel my discomfort and after an awkward word or two, he hurried on his way.

"Miss Turner had been given a shawl, which she wrapped tightly over her loose serge dress and she favored me with a smile as I sat opposite her and laid the chess set upon the bench between us.

"'How is Mr. Brodie?' she asked, immediately.

"'He passed the night comfortably.'

"'I do not think the same can be said for you.' She regarded me with a sympathetic smile. 'I suspect that he blames himself for introducing us, for the distress it has caused you. You must do everything in your power to persuade him that he must blame himself for nothing.'

"We played silently for half an hour before I could bring myself to ask, 'What was Mr. MacInnes doing here?'

"The lady answered readily. 'He must always visit the condemned to make some measurements and assess their weight so that he may adjust the rope and the knot properly.' I looked across the board at her and she returned my gaze. I have never seen such a pair of eyes so penetrating and yet so utterly unrevealing; they reflected a deep well of human understanding and a searing scrutiny that were almost inhuman in a woman so young. 'Check. And mate in three more moves, if you are not careful.'

"I turned my attention to the board. My king was indeed vulnerable.

"'I think,' she said, softly, 'had circumstances been different we might almost have been friends.'

"'Almost?'

"'I have every reason to look upon your sex with misgiving, and I think I have done away with any liking you may have had for mine. But we might have found each other's company just entertaining enough to forget our mutual distrust from time to time.'

"I moved a piece. 'It was raised in court that you had no schooling, no tutors. How did you come by your education?'

"'My mother. Check, again. She was an educated woman, and she was determined that I would not be raised in ignorance. She was not the sort of woman who did anything in half measures. That is the best and the worst I can say of her.'

"'She tried to kill you.'

"She looked at me, her eyes sparkling with a sort of reproachful amusement, as though I had attempted to gain advantage in the game by unnerving her. 'Checkmate,' she said.

"We set up the board again, and after several opening moves, the lady paused to study the arrangement of the pieces. 'My mother realized that she could not protect me.'

"'You must have hated your father a great deal.'

"'Not at all. As strange as it may sound, I have always been oddly grateful to him. He knew the rules of survival, you see. That was his contribution to my education.'

"'It does not appear to have served you, madam.'

"Her response was to smile, and it was that smile that did me in again, Watson. How could she smile so, two days before she was to die? She could not have devised a better strategy for undermining my game.

"When it was time for me to leave, the lady offered her hand, and said, 'You will come tomorrow? You must not come until noon, for we are obliged to go to chapel.'

"'Yes, I will come.'

"'It is a pity we cannot play for any sort of stake. Unless you value some sort of banal token, such as a lock of my hair. One of the matrons will cut it, if you like.'

"'How many games must I win to claim it?'

"She shrugged. 'A single one.'

"'I honor your confidence, Madam. But there is something that I would value more than a lock of hair.'

"'What?'

"'The truth. You are not mad. I want you to tell me why you did it.'

"'Very well. Come tomorrow, and if you win a single game, I will tell you the entire truth. But if you do not win, you must offer me a pledge in return.'

"'Anything you like.'

"'I want you to be present on Monday.'"

§

CHAPTER FORTY

"She asked you to be present at her execution!"

"Yes, Watson, and I was quite as shocked by the prospect as you appear to be. I gave my word, which I would never have done if I thought there was the least chance that I would have to keep it, but I was confident in the intervention of the Home Secretary.

"It was late afternoon when I emerged and immediately made my way to Mycroft's lodgings. His landlady informed me that he had returned only to leave his baggage and had gone out again, but that he had left instructions that I was to wait in his rooms until he returned.

"I was provided with a crackling fire and a pot of tea and after an hour I heard his heavy tread on the stairs.

"'Mycroft, where have you been!' I demanded, as he entered the door.

"'Sit down, my boy.'

"'I cannot sit. Where have you been? What news?'

"Mycroft sank into his chair and pushed aside his tea and muffin. 'I must say it right off, Sherlock. The Home Secretary has refused me. He will not commute her sentence.'

"I froze for a second as his words took hold. 'Mycroft, you gave me your promise. Your solemn word! You told me to stand down! I might have done something more for her if you had only told me that there was any doubt of your success!'

"'I had no doubt. And there is nothing you could have done that would have helped her in the least. You must think of those children, Sherlock, and reconcile yourself that justice must have its way.'

"'The law, you mean. Not justice.'

"'You would not make such a distinction had Moriarty not been involved. If they were another man's children, you would see that, here, the rule of law is just.'

"'If they were another man's children, she would not have thought that death was a better lot than living. If the Home Secretary will not commute her sentence, go higher.'

"'I cannot.'

"'You *will* not! I am not so naïve that I am blind to the *world's* treachery, Mycroft, but I never doubted *you*. I never believed that your word was not to be trusted.'

"'I am sorry to disappoint you.'

"'You won't be given the opportunity to disappoint me again!' I cried, in a tone I had never used toward him, before or since. 'I want nothing more to do with you. You are nothing to me! I have no brother!'

"Oh, you need not look so, Watson. I know how terrible those words were, and they were not nearly as atrocious as the ones which followed. A lesser man would never have forgiven me for what I said in that room.

"I stormed out and strode to Whitehall, for in my state, I thought of confronting the Home Secretary myself. The brisk air cooled my head, however and I realized that if

Mycroft could not persuade him, I could not. I had no power or political connections, and I did not know one influential person who might be persuaded to take her part. And then I thought of Lord Warrington. He was known to be on good terms with the Home Secretary. If Craden's story was to be believed – that there was a blood connection and Miss Turner was, indeed, his lordship's daughter – surely, he would use his influence on her behalf.

"I was thwarted once more. The staid butler, to whom I had entrusted Craden on the morning of Miss Turner's arrest, answered the door and informed me that the earl was at the family estate in Oxfordshire.

"'Lord Craden?' I enquired, with little optimism.

"'I have heard nothing from young Lord Craden for many days.'

"Now I was struck by his appearance, Watson. His manner was that of a retainer of long standing, and his face was lined with advanced age, yet his hair was glossy and of an artificial black that came from a dye bottle rather than nature. Vanity, I have often observed, is the trait most easily worked upon.

"'I am making inquiries on behalf of a lady who was acquainted with an employee of Lord Warrington's household almost twenty years ago,' I lied. 'Of course, I see that you are far too young to have been in his lordship's service so long, but perhaps you might direct me toward one of the elder staff?'

"The man smiled. 'I have been in Lord Warrington's service from the time Lord Craden was a year old.'

"'I cannot believe it! If you don't mind my saying so, you must have begun when you were a child yourself!'

"He did *not* mind my saying so, and asked who the lady might be.

"'She had been a governess to Lord Craden, a handsome young woman who left Lord Craden's service to marry. To marry quite beneath her – a fellow named Turner, I was told. At any rate, a friend of the lady's wishes to renew the acquaintance and asked for my assistance.'

"The servant shook his head, grimly. 'I know who you mean, sir. She was a comely thing, it is true, for all the good it did her. I heard that her marriage was a very unhappy one, and that it did not go well with her, but after she left us, I was often with His Lordship in town, and saw nothing of her. It was rumored that a flock of artists who set up around Oxfordshire had taken a liking to her, so you might enquire of them, perhaps, as I believe several of them have settled in town. They will remember her, to be sure. Even a fellow without the eye of an artist would not forget a face like Violet Brodie's.'"

CHAPTER FORTY-ONE

"What!" I cried. "Brodie?"

"Holmes nodded and his gaze drifted toward the pockmarked mantle with V.R. once more. 'I see in the twitch of your fingers, Watson, that you are eager for your pen and notebook. From this point, the events may be somewhat muddled. I will keep to the chronology as well as I can. But some details, I fear, will elude my memory."

"*Brodie?*" I repeated, astounded.

"Yes."

"And what did you say to that?"

"What could I say, Watson? I felt as though I were the weaker in a boxing match, who takes blow upon blow until he is numb to pain, and can only manage to keep his knees from collapsing. I stammered some thanks to the man and went straight to Brodie's shop.

"I found Wiggins and little Bob hobbling up from the cellar, carrying the coal scuttle between them.

"'How is Mr. Brodie?' I asked.

"Wiggins set the scuttle down. 'Olding 'is own. Mrs. Skinner's been by, as Doctor Knowles is needed at Newgate. She left some tea an' a spare dose of tonic. She says 'e'll mend nicely if 'e's kept quiet.'

"I found Brodie propped up upon his pillows, wearing a fresh bed jacket. 'Ah, lad, anyone who saw the two of us together would think that you were the invalid.

Come, pull up a chair and tell me what weighs upon your mind, for I have quite enough energy for conversation.'

"I drew a chair up to the old man's bed. 'I had extracted a promise from my brother that he would use his influence to have Miss Turner's sentence commuted if it went against her. He gave me his word, and now he has gone back on it.'

"Brodie looked upon me with grave sympathy. 'Has he ever gone back on his word before, or given you reason to distrust him?'

"'No, never.'

"'Well, we are all allotted one grave mistake in life.'

"'His mistake is unpardonable.'

"'I do not speak of his mistake, Sherlock. I mean yours.'

"'Mine!'

"'Yes, for I have no doubt there were some rash words on your part, vowing never to forgive him and so on, am I right?'

"'I never *will* forgive him, and I am surprised, sir, that you take his part.'

"'No one knows better than I of the consequences of an unforgiving nature.'

"'Because you have not forgiven yourself for your conduct toward your daughter. Miss Turner's mother.'

"He gave a sigh that was both sorrowful and resigned. 'Ah, Sherlock. It is a rare secret that can stay hidden forever. I should have told you the truth of it when this wretched business began.'

"'Then tell me now.'

"The old man nodded. 'Very well. I am an old curiosity, and fair looks did not come my way, even when I was a lad as young as you. But I found favor with as kind and lovely a young girl as ever walked the earth, and I was surprised as all the world when she agreed to marry me. In time, we had a daughter, who was named for her mother and mine, Violet Rose. She was bonny, headstrong, clever as she was beautiful, but of a wayward and ungovernable temper. In looks, she resembled her mother, far more than her younger sister did, and perhaps that is why I loved her the more. Or perhaps it is because we *will* love the troublesome child more than the tranquil one, God knows why. If I had had a title or fortune, there is not a duke or an earl who would not beg me for her hand, but the only dowry I could afford was education. She took a post in a nobleman's household, where she fell prey to his seduction. I was angry when I learned of it, and when she appealed to us for aid, I would not help her nor allow her mother to help her. This 'roused her pride, and she asked no more. Time passed, and ten years ago, my dear wife died, and upon her deathbed, she begged me to seek out our daughter and to reconcile with her.'

"'Why didn't you?'

"'I could not find her, try as I might. I knew nothing of her marriage, nor that her name was now Turner, nor that she had borne a daughter, and when Turner was released from prison, I'll warrant he made certain that she saw none of the advertisements I'd placed nor heard anything of the enquiry agents I'd engaged – clever fiend! And when he made his devil's pact with Moriarty, I daresay he made no mention of my existence. He would not want Moriarty to know that his wife had relations who might come forward on her behalf, or that of her child. I assure you, the day that Violet walked into this shop, two years ago – three – oh, dear, I forget – I had only to look at her face to know who she was. It was as if my own dear daughter had come back to me.'

"'You knew what Moriarty was,' I said, bitterly. 'How can you and Craden, her grandfather and brother, have allowed it to come to this? I would never have stood by and allowed a sister of mine to be abused so shamefully!'

"'And yet, just this day, you have cut yourself off from your only brother,' Brodie reminded me. 'Sherlock, I am far older than you and I know that sometimes the truth will set you free, and sometimes it must be taken to the grave.'"

CHAPTER FORTY-TWO

"There was rumor of a curious ceremony that was held at Newgate on the Sunday before a hanging. An empty coffin was set in the middle of the chapel, and the condemned was made to sit before it, and contemplate his – or her – miserable fate while the chaplain spoke of forgiveness and salvation.

"Miss Turner greeted me with a brilliant smile that was more disconcerting than terror would have been. My own wretchedness was ill-concealed for as we took our places at the rude bench, she turned my face to the light and studied me for some moments. Then she leaned forward, with a lock of hair lifted between two fingers. 'If you want your token, you will have to lay aside your troubles and concentrate on victory, Mr. Holmes.'

"We played silently, match after match. I would like to say that the tumult of my own thoughts was responsible for my succession of losses, but the truth was, she was a better player than I.

"In my sorry attempt to sabotage her concentration, I remarked, 'The evening of the Stokers' reception, I saw you walking upon the Embankment. I thought you were going to throw yourself into the river. Now, I realize that you would never have done it. You would not have left your children to Moriarty.'

"She lifted her brows, her eyes on the board.

"'Or, you might have poisoned yourself and died with your children, but you wanted to see the tragedy through, even if it meant that you would hang – you hated Moriarty that much. The children were everything to him and you wanted to witness the suffering you inflicted upon him.'

"'Check,' was her only reply. She smiled as she said it, and threw her hair over her shoulder. 'You will have to do better than that, Mr. Holmes. It is close to being mate as well.'

"I have never seen a woman so unfeeling, Watson. She was calculating, brilliant and utterly heartless. I was no longer surprised that she had killed her children. I was surprised that she had allowed herself to be caught.

"We played a few more games, silently, her eyes often drifting from the chessboard to study my expression. At last she said, 'How is my grandfather?'

"'Does Moriarty know of the relationship?'

"She moved her knight with assurance. 'We will not have occasion to speak again, so I will give you the truth, for it does not appear that you are going to win it from me. No, James does not know of the relationship. My mother had been thrown off by her relations, and as a child I knew nothing of them. If my father were aware of their existence, I'm certain that he'd thwarted any attempts at communication, and to James, he represented my mother and me as being quite unencumbered by friends or relations who might come forward if we were wronged.'

"I thought of what Craden had said in the witness box. 'Then how did you learn that your mother had family?'

"'You say that I hated James, Mr. Holmes? 'Hate' seems too weak a word. I had cause enough, God knows, and yet I might have forgiven him almost anything if he had been merciful. It would have cost him nothing, and may well have earned him my loyalty, which I flatter myself is worth a great deal.'

"'How should he have been merciful?'

"She was silent for a long time. 'After my mother attempted to kill herself and me, I was given to James. Sold. James told me that my mother had died. My own health was weak, and he had engaged a nurse to care for me. One night, when she supposed that I was sleeping, she and one of the servants began to gossip about my situation. From them, I learned that my mother had not died, but had been taken to an asylum. She was alive – and I persuaded myself that if she could only see me, she would rally and we would be reunited and all might be as it had been, and so, I made up my mind to go to her. A feat,' she added, with a reminiscent smile, 'that involved climbing out a window, scrambling down a drain-pipe and covering a distance of some five miles on foot.

"'The asylum was a small, two-story building, and there were only twenty or thirty inmates. I got into it easily enough, and as I made my way toward the patients' wing, I was able to single out, through the inmates' curses and sobs and wailing, the sound of my mother's voice. She was raving, Mr. Holmes, addressing a man as 'Father' as if he were in the room, begging him to forgive her. Something in her mad utterances rang true, and persuaded me that this father she spoke of was not the fabrication of an unstable mind, but a real person. I followed her voice to a door. It was locked, but there was a sort of small grille, and I peered through and saw my poor mother, pacing back and forth, raving. I whispered, 'Mother! Mother!' until some chord of recognition struck, and she ran to me, and with our hands clasped between the bars, she poured out her tale with a mad urgency, repeating the name 'Aiden Brodie' again and again, insisting that I must make my way to London and seek him out. Then I felt the grip of a matron's hand upon my shoulder and saw such a look in my mother's eyes as I have never seen and never wish to see again.

"'I will not describe how I pleaded and fought and attempted to flee. I was returned to James.' She paused. 'I never saw my mother again, and within the year, I was a mother myself. When I heard that Hanwell Mercy was to close, I begged James to provide a home for my mother so that she would not be sent to a mad-house, but he would not. It was the last time I begged for anything, Mr. Holmes, and I would not do it again, not to save my own life. Checkmate.'"

CHAPTER FORTY-THREE

"At the Keeper's Lodge, I was informed in a quite businesslike manner of when I was to report the following day and that after all was concluded, and after she was taken from the scaffold, the official pronouncement of death declared and the death mask made, she would be removed to a private burial site, as funds had been provided so that she would not be buried among the condemned of Newgate. I wondered, idly, whether it had been Brodie or Craden who had made these arrangements.

"I walked out into a dark sky and billowing rain and began to ramble aimlessly. What do you do on the evening before you are to watch someone die, Watson? Is it better to let the mind indulge in morbid dread, or to attempt a diversion? I began to feel a grudging tolerance for Craden and his morphia.

"I made my way to Brodie's, where I saw the light of a single lamp within. I looked through the glass and saw Wiggins perched on the arm of a chair turning the pages of a book, while little Bob slumbered in the seat, his head resting on his older brother's knee.

"I tapped on the glass and Wiggins looked up and laid aside the book, easing his brother's head from his lap.

"'How is your charge, Wiggins?' I asked.

"'Tolerable, sir. 'E's sleeping now, for I made 'im take a dose of tonic, though he did not like it. There's a kettle on, if you'd like some tea.'

"'I'll get it.'

"I removed my damp coat and laid it over the back of a chair by the fire. 'Wiggins, you have taken a lot on your shoulders, looking after your brother and Mr. Brodie and his shop as well.'

"Wiggins sat beside his brother and laid a hand on his hair, gently. 'Mr. Brodie's no trouble. 'E says it does 'im good to see young 'uns habout. An' I mus' tend to Bob, 'e's all the brother I've got now the Little 'Un's gone, an' brothers mus' stick together, you know.'

"'Sometimes brothers have differences between them.'

"'An' so'll friends, from time to time,' he said with a nod. 'But if you lose a friend or two, you'll likely pick up a few more, but once family is lost, they cannot be got back.'

"I poured a cup of tea and rose from my chair. 'I will go up sit with Mr. Brodie.'

"I pulled up a chair to the bed and found a bottle of brandy and poured far too much of its contents into my tea. The weight of sleeplessness, irregular meals and strong brandy sent me off into a slumber which produced dark dreams wherein I was one of the party erecting the scaffold, and when it was raised, I was sent up to test the drop. I began an endless climb, taking step upon step and yet getting no closer to the rope, as though I were a convict on a treadmill.

"I woke with a start and looked at the clock. It was seven, and I was to report to the Keeper's Lodge at eight.

"I availed myself of Brodie's razor and basin once more, shaving with a hand that shook so badly it is a wonder

I didn't cut my own throat. I hurried downstairs and seized my coat and ran into the streets and jumped into a cab.

"The ominous tolling of St. Sepulchre's was audible many streets from the destination, and as the cab approached, I saw that even at this early hour, the streets were bustling with activity. The vast, prying public mingled with swells and wastrels and pickpockets and the penny press, and above people leaned from upper windows or even stood upon rooftops in the futile attempt to get a peek within the walls of the prison.

"There was a small group at the Keeper's Lodge, waiting for admittance. Several of them were reporters, and the remainder were those who had been given access to the event by the sheriff or the Commissioner of Prisons. None were familiar to me save for two: Frederick Hudson, who had been dispatched by his master to witness the event, and Ernest, who came out of a morbid satisfaction of his own.

"The former gave a brief glance in my direction, but the latter was preoccupied in currying favor with the reporters, making mention of Sir Joshua's lecture tour and expressing the opinion – in the hope that his words might make their way to Sir Joshua by way of Fleet Street – that so extensive an engagement would be much to manage without an assistant or colleague.

"I felt a tap on my shoulder, and turned to face a pale, somber Cummings. 'Mr. Holmes,' he greeted with a look of sad resignation upon his face. 'I am glad – if one can be glad upon such a day – to see someone who is not here out of vulgar curiosity or profit. Though I am sure that Miss Turner would have forgiven you if you had stayed away.'

"'I gave her my word to be here, and I must keep it.'

"'I have made this unhappy visit more than once. I am sure it is of no comfort, but MacInnes is very good at his trade, and there is no suffering, save what takes place in the mind as it contemplates the event. The event itself will be over very quickly.'

"We were ushered through the yard by an under-sheriff and warder. The gallows shed was outside of the prison kitchen, and we were directed to a sort of box where we would observe the hanging only. Immediately afterward, we would be escorted out, for the deceased would remain on the rope for an hour afterward, and the medical officer's declaration was made privately, in the presence of the sheriff or under-sheriff.

"Of the next half hour, Watson, I can only say what memory has retained of the event, for I believe that when witnessing or experiencing some unimaginable horror, the mind makes a valiant effort to survive by wiping away the more sordid particulars.

"The door below the scaffold opened and there appeared the tall form of Marwood MacInnes who proceeded up the wooden stairs. He was followed by the chaplain and then Miss Turner emerged with a wardress on either side of her. She wore a shapeless, shroud-like dress of some heavy white fabric and her hair had been wound into a loose knot at the nape of her neck. MacInnes would have pinioned her arms in her cell before she was led into the yard.

These pinions made walking the scaffold steps an awkward business, for she could not take the rail to balance herself and had to depend upon the two matrons, one who lifted the trailing hem of her skirts the other who guided her by the arm.

"I did not see her face until she had reached the platform. Her complexion was white and her eyes glazed like a cornered creature who has only just realized its plight. All was silent except for the faint drone of the chaplain's prayer and the more immediate scratching of the reporters' pencils.

"The chaplain closed his book and spoke a few words to Miss Turner, to which she replied with a shake of her head. She then turned and spoke to the two ladies, evidently dismissing them, for they retreated down the stairs and disappeared through the kitchen door.

"MacInnes then approached the lady and spoke in her ear, while he gently adjusted the neck of her gown, and guided her up to the chalk line that had been drawn across the drop. My gaze involuntarily rose to the beam above her head, from which the noose hung, and through the oppressive silence I could hear the beating of my own heart, that living rhythm which will declare, 'There are two minutes yet for a reprieve, there are ninety seconds yet for a reprieve, eighty seconds, seventy seconds, one minute.'"

Holmes paused for a moment, his hand passing over his brow, and then he shook his head, gloomily. "It would have been a challenge to your literary talents, Watson, to render the sight which was at once so bizarre and yet so businesslike so that your readers would be neither fascinated nor revolted. While she stood with her dazed, unfocused eyes, MacInnes knelt and strapped her ankles. She seemed to sway feebly, either from the loss of balance or courage, and then he rose and mercifully placed the white hood over her face, covering the haunted eyes. He spent several seconds arranging the rope about her neck, lifting and then lowering the hem of the hood, adjusting the knot below the hair gathered at her neck.

"From there, it was so very quick that I believed it was done so in order to put a merciful end to any lingering hope for a pardon. He stepped to the lever and pulled it and the drop fell from beneath her feet and she was suspended by the rope.

"There was no convulsion of a life that was ebbing in agony, there was simply stillness, save for one unintended incident. The sudden jolt, as her weight pulled the rope taut, dislodged the knot of hair and the tendrils fell from beneath the hood, twisting and entwining themselves around her motionless form like living things."

THE TRUTH

CHAPTER FORTY-FOUR

The distant chiming of the landlady's clock told me that midnight had passed into morning. I made a move to rise, but Holmes shook his head and got out of his chair to retrieve the wrapped object he had taken from Newgate that afternoon.

He held it before me and threw back the covering to reveal a plaster cast of a woman's face. Even the rude execution of the cast could not disguise the refinement in the lines of the face, the fullness of the mouth and the graceful arch to the brows. "This is nothing like her, of course. But I could not let it go for five shillings to be hung upon the wall of a tavern, or worse." He paused. "I don't suppose it would have mattered in the greater scheme."

He covered it once more and laid it upon a shelf. I made a move to rise once more, but I recalled the incident at Newgate, and the beautiful companion whom I had spied with my friend. "But the lady!" I exclaimed. "Miss Eden Holmes? What is her connection to these events?"

Holmes smiled. "Ah, Watson – you were ready to bring my narrative to a close with when it is but two-thirds done! There is still a final act to be told, one which, I assure you, is well worth the loss of a few hours' sleep."

I settled in my chair once more, and Holmes prodded at the waning fire with the poker. "As soon as the body had been dropped, we were ushered out by the wardens, and in a matter of moments, I found myself on the pavement with Cummings.

"'I have been through this before, Mr. Holmes,' Cummings said, gently. 'What it often takes to hold onto one's reason is the belief that whatever violence has occurred, justly or unjustly, all are at peace now.'

"'Not all the living,' I replied, bitterly.

"Cummings removed an envelope from his pocket and placed it in my hands. 'Not long before her arrest, Miss Turner gave this to Lord Craden with instructions that it be entrusted to me with a sealed note from the lady that I was to surrender its contents to you when all was done. I am very sorry if I have failed her or her friends.' Then, with a tip of his hat, he made his way past the queue of prospective visitors who were lining up against the wall, waiting only for the body on the scaffold to be taken down, before they were permitted to visit a loved one."

Holmes settled back in his chair. "I turned away from the wretched place, tearing into the envelope as I walked. There were three items inside: a pawnbroker's ticket; an address in Tottenham Court Road; and a packet of coins, fifty-five shillings. It was evident to me that she had consigned something to a pawnbroker which I was to redeem with the ticket and the money.

"I hailed a cab and made my way to the Tottenham Court Road address. It was a narrow shop with diamond-paned windows, and three gold balls set above the door.

"I stepped inside and saw that, in addition to the silver and gold, the peddler traded in musical instruments. There were a number of decent violins, flutes, some eighteenth-century cornetti and a harmonium. The merchant was a wizened fellow, no more than five feet tall, with a graying beard that fell to his breast. When I gave him the ticket, a smile spread over his face. 'Yes, yes, such a beauty. Fifty-five shillings is what she asked for it and fifty-five shillings is what I gave. And it was to go only to you, for she gave me a description of you, sir.'

"I laid the packet of shillings upon the counter and the man tallied them quickly and swept them into a drawer. He motioned for me to wait and disappeared into the back of his shop. After a moment, he returned with the violin case bundled in a woman's shawl and laid it on the counter.

"I opened the case and lifted the instrument. Inside, laying upon the violin that I had seen in her sitting room, was a sheet of folded paper. I opened it, and read:

'My dear Mr. Holmes,

I am content that everything James ever bestowed upon me should be disposed of as he pleased, but there is one possession that I should not like to see fall to the great, unobservant public who would not know a Stradivari from a spike fiddle. I trust that you will not be as careless with it as I have been.

V R Turner'

"The note was dated February third, the date of Sir Joshua's reception. She had lied when she told Mrs. Hudson that she had taken her violin for new strings. She had been settling the last few matters of business before she murdered her children.

"I settled the instrument at my chin and laid the bow to the strings, and trying a chord or two. Then I attempted a bit of that haunting piece that Miss Turner had played at the Stokers' reception, calling up from memory the melody's mounting complexity. I do not know how long I played, so lost was I in the music and in the wonderment of my ability to, at last, play a piece that had eluded all of my former attempts. And then I saw the old man looking up at me with rapt astonishment, a tear running along his cheeks.

"He opened the drawer and took out the fifty-five shillings, pushing them across the counter to me. 'For the pleasure,' was all he could say. 'For the pleasure of hearing you.'

"I saw that it would be an insult to dispute the man, so I put the shillings in my pocket and carefully returned the instrument to its case. It had just begun to rain, so I wrapped the case tightly in the shawl, and left the shop. It was the busiest part of the morning, now, and cabs were few, so I began to walk, drawing shillings from my pocket and dispensing them to the beggars as I went."

CHAPTER FORTY-FIVE

"When I left the pawnbroker's, I took off my overcoat coat and wrapped it around the shrouded instrument case to further protect it against the rain as I made my way to my flat on foot. I was wet to the skin when I arrived at Montague Street, but once in my room, I did not take time to change, so eager was I to try the instrument once more.

"It was a bonny object, Watson, worth five hundred guineas if it was worth a pound. I examined it under the light and saw no markings upon it, no sign that the old peddler had scratched the ticket number onto the surface. With no attention to the passing of the hours, with no consideration for my fellow boarders, I played afternoon and into the night, longing only for the extraordinary sounds that the instrument produced to drown out the awful events of the morning.

"At last, I succumbed to sheer exhaustion and laid the instrument in its case. I fell onto the bed in a deep slumber and woke to the scrape of the coal scuttle upon the hearth. I opened my eyes to see the scullery maid kneeling at the hearth, attempting to sweep it out and place down fresh coal without walking me.

"'I am sorry, sir,' she whispered, and I saw in her timid expression that I must present an intimidating sight. 'I did try not to wake you.'

"I sprang out of bed, crying, 'Where is it? You did not touch it, did you?' in such a sharp fashion that the poor girl flinched.

"I saw the violin case lying where I had left it, quite untouched, and mumbled an apology.

"'Will you breakfast, sir?'

"'What time is it?'

"'Just past eleven.'

Eleven. She had been dead a day, longer. 'Just coffee,' I replied. 'And some hot water.'

"When she returned, she had my dark pea coat over her arm. She set down the tray and the basin of water, and then hung it in the wardrobe. I saw that some object had been pinned to its lapel.

"'What is that?' I enquired.

"'Mrs. Harker took the liberty of having your coat cleaned and brushed, sir. She found that bit of woolen in your pocket, and thought it was a keepsake of sorts, and so did not want to throw it away.'

"I dismissed the girl, and poured myself a cup of coffee, hoping that it would drive off the chills and a blinding headache. Days of irregular hours and infrequent meals were taking their toll, though I believed, with the carelessness of youth, that such neglect would do me no lasting harm.

"I removed the bit of fabric from the lapel and took out my lens to examine it. It was a sort of open weave, too light for a blanket, but it may have been torn from a shawl or muffler. One side had the clean, unfrayed edge as though part of it had been cut away with long-bladed shears, and a few splinters were fixed within the fragment's loose weave. I had seen this fabric elsewhere, I was certain, and yet try as I might, I could not recall why it struck such a chord.

"I puzzled over it all the way to Brodie's shop – then, when Wiggins answered my knock and unlocked the door, it came upon me in an instant. I had seen Mrs. Wiggins clutching a remnant of the identical fabric, a relic she had cut from the shawl that she had laid in the Little Un's coffin.

"'Wiggins,' I said, drawing the scrap out of my pocket, 'does this not look like a bit of your mother's shawl?'

"'Why that it does!' replied the lad. 'But it cannot be, for Ma only snipped a bit for a keepsake an' the rest was put in the box with the Little Un – an' Ma still 'as 'er bit, though she keeps it in 'er pocket when Pa's around.'

"How then, I wondered, had this bit got from the East End to the area railing of Paradise Walk?

"'How is Mr. Brodie today?'

"'A gent called Cummings was by an' Mr. Brodie spoke to 'im for a good long time an' hafterward a tall older gent an' Doctor Knowles come by. Doctor Knowles stayed just to content himself that Mr. Brodie was on the mend, but 'is friend stayed 'bove an hour. Mr. Brodie gave 'im some books, quite old ones, but the gent took on as if they was new.'

"'What was this gentleman's name?'

"'Doctor Knowles called 'im MacHinnes.'

"What an odd gesture of courtesy, Watson – for the hangman to call upon the bereaved! Yet odder still was the sight of Brodie, sitting up in his bed with his color restored and something of the old spark in his eye.

"'How ill you look!' he cried when I entered the room.

"'I have been through an experience that I should not like to repeat as long as I live.'

"'I know, lad,' he said, kindly. 'Cummings has been here to give me an account. He has quite the right philosophy about it – you must content yourself with the fact that time will mend all. She and the little ones are out of Moriarty's power, and for the part he played in driving her to her actions, the Professor has very likely driven himself into a life of bitter solitude.' He leaned forward and patted me on the hand. 'That is no consolation for you, now, is it?'

"'No, sir, it is not.'

"'Well, time will teach you to be reconciled to a great deal that is incomprehensible and unpardonable.'

"'I hope not.'

"Brodie nodded. 'Spoken like a man who is yet in his twenties. Go home, lad, and get some rest, or I shall be the one sitting at your bedside.'

"I bade the man good-morning with a promise to come on the next day, and stepped outside into the bustling street. Wiggins and little Bob were sponging the shop windows.

"'I give you credit for Mr. Brodie's improvement, Wiggins, for you have taken up most of the responsibility for his care.'

"'I hexpect it's Mr. Brodie's constitution what pulled 'im through. Ma says she prays that we 'ave a strong constitution to pull us though sickness. But *I* b'lieve it was a good gossip what brought Mr. Brodie 'round – the gent,

326

MacHinnes, an' Mr. Brodie had a good long spout, an' now Mr. Brodie's in good spirits.'

"'Gossip to do with the courts, or Newgate Prison?'

"Wiggins shook his head. 'Somethin' to do with the nobs. An hearl, I 'eard 'em say. The Hearl o' Granville, it was. I cannot fink why such talk hentertains folks so, for *I* say the rich are no more lively than the folk at Rother'ithe.'

"I set off on an aimless stroll, preoccupied with what Wiggins had said. This entire drama had begun back in December, when I had first met Miss Turner – no, earlier, when I had gone to Bart's where the porter had mentioned Craden and Marwood MacInnes talking about the Earl of Granville. Both the porter and Wiggins misheard, of course, as the present Lord Granville was styled Earl Granville, and not the Earl *of* Granville. He was, as you well know, a quite prominent figure at this time, and yet I could think of nothing, save for the possibility of some slight acquaintance between Lord Granville and Craden's family – or that he was known to Moriarty, perhaps – which would account for his name cropping up among those who had been closely connected with Miss Turner. The name Earl Granville had not been linked to Miss Turner's plight by the press, nor had it been introduced at the inquest or the trial. It may have been mere coincidence that his name should be on the lips of Craden and Brodie and the hangman, but I am not inclined to rely upon coincidence where there is the possibility of a plausible explanation. I could, of course, have confronted Brodie or MacInnes, but I decided to proceed in a more clandestine fashion. I took myself to Madam Sun.

"It was a bleak, wet, blustery day, one that ought to have driven everyone indoors, and yet there were a great many idle, ruffianly-looking types hanging about. Their appearance called up the tale of Mrs. Radley's daughter, for they did, indeed, look like the sort who might take to drink and dig up a coffin.

"The blue lanterns of Madam Sun's glowed through the dirty mist that rose from the water, and the interior of the place had the same sort of netherworld gloom, and the sweet aroma of the drug mingled with the foul scent of the river, which rose from the plank floor. Several men sat about, drinking, Orientals, Lascars, Scandinavians. I asked to speak with Madam Sun, and the lady's own voice emerged from behind a brocade curtain. 'Allow him to pass.'

"I passed through the curtain into a sort of sitting room, with numerous lamps, all shaded with pink gauze, and their glow was reflected in the black lacquered surfaces of the table tops.

"The lady was reclining on a sort of settee, wearing a Chinese robe of dark silk, stroking the sleek, green-eyed cat in her lap. 'What is it you want?' she asked.

"'Information.'

"'Information has a price. A sovereign will do.'"

"I took a sovereign from my pocket and laid it onto the table beside her. 'We will start with Lord Craden,' I said.

"She ran her fingertip over the coin. 'He has not returned since the night you carried him out of here. It is said that he has left London. You have cost me a very good client, you see. Do sit down, sir.'

"'Another name, then. The Earl Granville.'

"The arched brows raised in surprise. 'He had been the Foreign Secretary.'

"'I know that.'

"'He will be again. If the question is whether Lord Granville is a patron of mine, the answer is no.' The lady scrutinized my puzzled expression. 'I don't believe you have got your sovereign's worth. Is there something else?'

"I recalled my conversation with the porter at Bart's that December afternoon when Lord Granville's name had been raised. The porter had regretted that he could not admit me to the dissecting rooms where a young girl, *the sort of odd 'un that the medical students have a taste for*, was locked away.

"'Would like to try a pipe? Or Lord Craden's preference, morphia?'

"'No, I will try another question. There was some talk around these parts, about a woman named Radley who claimed that her daughter's burial site had been tampered with.'

"The woman stroked the feline, and shrugged. 'Well, a coffin is not unlike a house or a pocket book. People will plunder it for what it contains. A trinket, a garment, even a fine crop of hair. And then there are the medical men.'

"'The medical institutions are provided with subjects.'

"'Not enough. Certainly not of the rarer specimens. And Etta Radley was something of a curiosity.'

"'Some say that it was Mrs. Radley, in a state of drunkenness, who sold her daughter's corpse and then had no memory of the transaction.'

"The woman shook her head. 'If Fanny Radley wanted to profit from her daughter, she could have made a fine sum while the girl was living. I myself offered her two pounds a week, as I had clients who would have paid dearly for the use of her, but the mother refused me.'"

"Good God, Holmes!" I cried.

Holmes shrugged. "It is as Brodie said, Watson. There is no shortage of people who entertain themselves in unspeakable ways, and there will always be those willing to provide them with the opportunity.

"'You do not believe that Mrs. Radley sold the girl's cadaver, then?' I asked Madam Sun.

"'No.'

"'But you believe that it was taken?'

"'What is your name, sir?'

"'Sherlock Holmes.'

"'You are a determined questioner, Mr. Holmes. You must be an inconvenient adversary.' Her fingers raked through the feline's fur as she spoke. 'The paupers' graves are not dug very deep. And the skilled resurrection men do not need to take up the entire coffin, they only need to clear a corner of it to do their work. And Etta Radley? Well, there wasn't much of her to give them trouble. She was a stunted thing, far smaller than a child of ten. Yes, I believe she was taken.'

"'Then why did the mother abandon her appeal for justice.'

"'Perhaps, as it was *fait accompli*. Perhaps the remains were in no condition to be returned. Perhaps, as her child could not be brought back from the dead, Fanny was appeased by the handsome stone laid down to mark the girl's grave.'

"'Do you say that the gift of a grave stone was made to compensate for violating the grave?'

"'I say only that a certain stone mason took an order for three headstones, and the carter who was paid to carry them to the graveyard and lay them down has done some carting for me as well.'

"'Not headstones, I suspect.'

"The lady smiled. 'Well, there are many things which need to be taken from here to there. The man who paid for the stones gave his name to the mason, and the mason to the carter, and the carter whispered it to me.'

"'Lord Craden?'

"The woman rose. 'Come, it is getting to be the hour when my time becomes more than you can afford.'

"She escorted me to the door, where I secured my hat firmly, for the wind was driving hard off the river.

"'Do you not think that you have got your sovereign's worth?' the lady asked. 'Well, I will give you a bit of information, the only information that you can be assured is eternally true. There is nothing in the world as powerful as the love of a mother for a child. Etta Radley was blind and lame and stunted and nothing but a trial and an expense, who cost Fanny Radley money, friends, a husband, and her own youth and yet Fanny could not be persuaded to allow Catherine Skinner to put the poor girl out of her misery. The more difficult the girl became, the stronger grew Fanny's love. Imagine what it must be, to have your heart owned in such a fashion. It is much better to have no heart at all, I think. What is your opinion?'

"'Who paid for the girl's gravestone?' I persisted. 'Was it Lord Craden?

"'No. It was one of my lesser clients. Sir Joshua Reade's little toady, the one they call Heep.'"

CHAPTER FORTY-SIX

"What? That fellow Ernest?"

"So she said, Watson. And I had no reason to disbelieve her. The scrap of cloth, the puzzling allusions to Granville all faded before this astonishing pronouncement. Why should Ernest pay for the Radley girl's headstone? Was it a bribe to silence a troublesome mother because he had violated her daughter's grave?

"I decided to examine the burial site myself, and so walked along the riverside until I came upon a man making ready to push off in his wherry. I offered him a few shillings to take me across the Lower Pool, and from there, I made my way on foot.

"The cemetery at Tower Hamlets was not as bleak as one might think, for there were many superb stone figures, and the sort of handsome trees and thick foliage that might bloom into pleasing greenery in spring. Now, however, bare twigs littered the muddy ground, and the steady rain was turning the ground covered with melting snows into a dank and uneven morass. There were the common graves that were dug, it was said, as deep as forty feet, but the solitary pauper graves were shallow indeed; in fact, I could see portions of coffin lids jutting above the earth. If a person wished to bring one of them up, it would not be a difficult task. I searched among rows of graves, anonymous or marked with rude wooden crosses, until I came upon a broad,

333

polished stone set into the earth. I swept aside the coating of mud and read:

Henrietta Frances Radley

March 1, 1869 – December 26, 1878

"The date of her death suggested that she might indeed have been the wretched subject who had died at Bart's nearly three months earlier."

"But did you really believe that this Ernest was so vile that he would despoil the poor girl's grave?"

"A cadaver like the Radley girl's had tempted more high-minded students of medicine and surgery than Ernest. Of course," he added, gravely. "there was only one way to be certain. Now, now Watson. You have often agreed with me that there are crimes which have eluded the law and so merit some private justice. It was illegal, certainly, and wicked, possibly, but I was determined to know the truth.

"I searched the graveyard until I came upon the superintendent's lodge, and beside it was a tool shed. The door was locked, but there was a window that was easily pried open and I clambered in and helped myself to a trowel and a pick.

"I then returned to the site of the Radley girl's coffin and began to work up the earth with the pick until one end of the coffin surfaced, which I cleared 'round with the trowel. The coffin lid was no more than some badly fitted wooden slats and it was an easy thing to pry one loose. I took out a match and struck it, sheltering it from the wind and wet with some difficulty. The guttering flame gave off enough light for me to see that the box was empty."

"Then the Radley woman was right – her daughter's grave had been violated!"

"Yes, she was right – to some extent."

"Why, what do you mean?"

"I mean, Watson, that she was right as to *what* had been done, but not as to the *why*."

"I don't understand."

"Well, a comfortable chair and a warm fire will often blunt the senses, but standing in the cold and the dark, lashed by a driving rain and having endured weeks of strain and privation, my brain experienced one of those moments of clarity that will peel away every irrelevancy, leaving only the naked truth. I recalled Madam Sun's words. 'A certain stone mason took an order for *three* headstones.' Had there been two other graves plundered as well? I was determined to find out.

"It was a dark and dirty task, Watson, and nearly an hour passed before I found two markers of identical workmanship to the Radley grave stone. On the first, was engraved.

Timothy Vye

December 5, 1875 – January 30, 1879

And on the second:

Henry Wiggins

November 10, 1875 – January 28, 1879

Henry Wiggins was, of course, the Little 'Un for whom Mrs. Wiggins continued to grieve, and Wiggins had mentioned a Mrs. Vye who had also lost a child.

"The two little coffins were no more difficult to crack than the Radley girl's had been, and I was certain that I would find them empty even before I pulled back the lids. And it was there, as I closed the lids upon them and set them to rights, that I felt the horror of what had transpired settle upon me. The coffins before me had been ordered for two little boys not yet four years, while the Radley girl's had been for a girl of ten but one who was quite small - 'stunted,' was the term used – for a girl of her age. Do you begin to understand me, Watson? Two boys, both little more than three, a ten-year-old girl who might be taken for a child of six."

"Holmes!" I cried, horrified.

"What if, on the night of the fire, Moriarty's children were spirited away, and the remains of Etta Radley, Timothy Vye and Henry Wiggins were laid in their beds, and reduced to skeleton and ash."

"Then, that scrap you found snagged upon the railing? It was a bit of the shawl used for the little Wiggins' boy's shroud."

Holmes nodded. "Caught on the railing when the child's remains were carried into Moriarty's home."

"Good God, Holmes! It is diabolical!"

"Diabolical, indeed, and it had the stamp of the devil himself upon it."

"Moriarty," I said. "But the trial! Miss Turner hanged! The children – is it possible they were still living? What was the motive behind such a vile deception?"

"I didn't know. I could only speculate. Miss Turner could no longer produce, in the words of Mrs. Hudson, that more splendid strain. What further use could Moriarty have for her? It was the children he wanted – his little human laboratories. It may be that Miss Turner was not intended to survive the blaze, and was only through some blunder of the Professor's confederate – Miss Moran or Mrs. Stewart, for such a scheme could not be carried out without collaboration – that she escaped. What, then, could Moriarty do but apply himself to assuring her conviction?"

"But why did she not defend herself? Why did she do everything to support a conviction?"

"Here, Watson, I was compelled to enter the realm of probability. The most likely theory was that Moriarty got word to her that her children were alive and that he would not hesitate to do the unthinkable to them if she did not play her part. He made her the devil's bargain – she must go to the gallows or the children would go to their graves. And as she once said to me, one did not defy Moriarty, one stood down or was annihilated. What else could explain her wanton display at the inquest, her aloofness at the trial, even her confession to Mrs. Stewart? It had all been a brilliantly executed performance to spare her children. It is no wonder she was provoked by my attempts to acquit her – had I succeeded, I may well have cost her children their lives.

"To all that I had endured in the past weeks was now added shock, anger and a bitter desire for vengeance. I would not rest until the entire conspiracy was exposed and Moriarty and everyone who had acted as his accomplice hunted down and hanged for their part in it. You smile in spite of yourself, Watson. Ah well, I was younger then.

"The sky had gone black, and rain and wind drove in with the force of a gale. Mud welled up and flowed into the open coffins, and, insensible to the wet and the dirt, I hastily laid the lids upon the empty coffins and eased them back into the ground.

"I left the graveyard and found a bit of shelter in the doorway of a boarded-up warehouse. There I huddled for more than an hour, but the deluge did not abate, and I did not want to spend the night in a doorway, so at last I struck out for my quarters, walking some miles before I could wave down a cab that would take such a disreputable-looking fare.

"I was feverish and exhausted when I got to my rooms, but driving myself to action, I snatched up a sheet of paper and wrote a long, rambling missive, asking how three stone markers had come to be laid upon the despoiled graves of three pauper children, and suggesting what the fate of the purchaser might be – that party said to be Mr. Rayleigh John Ernest – if it came to light that he had been the despoiler. Perhaps he would find himself in the dock, or perhaps he would be left to the less tender mercies of a pack of Rotherhithe bludgers. I concluded with a threat to pass copies of this letter to all of Fleet Street if Ernest did not quit London within the week. Then pulling on my soaking coat and hat, I went back into the rain and carried it to his quarters. I handed it to the girl who had answered the door, instructing her to carry it up to Mr. Ernest at once."

Holmes sighed, ruefully. "Had I been possessed of a clearer head, I might have allowed myself time to consider the rationality of such conduct, but my nerves had been strained nearly to the breaking point. Ernest had rooms in a high, narrow house on Praed Street, his windows overlooking the street. I slipped away from the light of a street lamp and watched his silhouette pass behind the shade as he went to answer the door. He tore into the letter, pacing back and forth in agitation, and then throwing the letter aside, he pulled back the shade and peered into the street. I took in one glimpse of his white, weasel's face contorted in panic and confusion and then I made my way home. I stumbled up to my room, cold and hot, stiff and shivering and fell upon the bed.

"The next fortnight was lost to delirium."

CHAPTER FORTY-SEVEN

"When I returned to consciousness, I was lying in my bed, with the massive figure of Mycroft sitting in an unfamiliar armchair. I tried to pronounce his name, but my throat and tongue were parched.

"'Let me help you to some water.' Mycroft poured from a carafe at my bedside, and raised my head while I drank. 'There, I haven't spilled it, have I? I am a clumsy nurse.'

"'What day is it?'

"'It is Wednesday, dear boy, the second of April. How do you feel? I will ring for the landlady to send up some beef broth, and if it sits well, we can bring up something more nutritious.'

"'Am I in my own room?'

"'Yes. What, oh, you do not recognize the armchair? Well, I could not be expected to sit with you if I had to put up with those wobbling, splintered objects you call 'chairs.' I must have something a bit more substantial. Do not fear, I have not let them tidy up too much, save for your clothing which needed a good cleaning.'

"Mycroft laid his fat flipper of a hand over mine. 'You must not think of anything except your health, dear boy.'

"'What happened?'

"'The doctor says that you have had a complete breakdown. You were taken with a terrible fever and have been in and out of delirium. We all quite despaired of your life, Sherlock.'

"'Did I say anything when I was delirious?'

"'Oh, the usual drivel. I have heard worse from my associates in the government, and they haven't the excuse of delirium, nor the claims of fraternity to excuse them.'

"'I daresay I said much worse before I could claim illness as an excuse.'

"'My boy, it is the nature of brothers to have a few rough words exchanged between them from time to time. If you should find a friend or a wife to take my place, I will step aside and let them suffer your eccentricities.'

"'I don't foresee that, Mycroft.'

"'Ah, well. Stranger things have happened.'

"It is one certainty in life, Watson, that stranger events will always come along to wipe away all memory of what had gone before. The press might have wrung some more copy from the case, had not the sensational matter of Kate Webster's crime, trial and hanging eclipsed Miss Turner's tale, or had the principals remained on the scene to keep up interest in the scandal. But Moriarty, Mrs. Stewart, Hudson, Craden, Sir Joshua were all gone. Even Ernest, as Mycroft informed me during my slow recovery, had abruptly withdrawn from his course of study and decamped from London.

"'He will make a bad end of it,' Mycroft declared. 'He will sink to quackery or vice and come to the end he deserves. Justice is slow, but it is inevitable, Sherlock.'

"I remained in bed for many weeks, faithfully visited by Mycroft, Brodie and even little Wiggins. One or two old acquaintances also found their way to my rooms, bringing quite trivial problems and making a good show of seeking my advice. I saw Mycroft's hand in it, but I allowed them to believe that I was deceived and these little puzzles, if they did not raise my spirits, did at least keep them from sinking further into despair.

"It was very early in October of that year, when another of these old friends found his way to my door. You will recall many of the particulars from your account of the Musgrave Ritual, Watson. I heard Mycroft's coaching in poor Musgrave's attempt to convey his problem in a manner that might lure my out of my doldrums, and out of London as well. I consented to investigate my college chum's dilemma, not so much for the problem it presented, but because there was just such an echo in the tale of the handsome and callous Brunton and the wronged woman that he drove to madness, which called back the sad tale of Violet Brodie's fate at the hands of Victor Turner. I felt that if I could succeed in this matter, it would help to atone for one where, had I employed greater energy, I might have spared an innocent woman from the gallows – and to do the matter justice, it did prove to be a remarkable case on its own merit.

"Musgrave urged me to extend my visit, but I had not recovered my spirits enough to be a fit house guest, and the publicity which had followed the discovery of the ancient diadem made me anxious to retreat to the solitude of my room. In vain did Mycroft throw small cases my way, or attempt to coax me out to the theatre or a dinner party. I had suspended my studies and dropped what few friends I had, left my correspondence unattended, and was in a fair way to becoming a perfect recluse.

"It was the third week in November, when I declined another of Mycroft's invitations that I heard the lumbering steps upon the stair once more. I set down my violin and admitted him.

"The expression on Mycroft's face was one of patient surrender. I did not understand it. 'I would like for you to come to dinner tomorrow night, Sherlock. Just a nice, congenial, gentlemen's gathering. I am entertaining a fellow who has been 'round the world, and he means to set off in a week once more. He's a pleasant, conversational sort, and he heard some little account of your success in the Musgrave matter and I offered to make an introduction.'

"'I don't have patience for company, Mycroft. You had much better entertain him on your own.'

"'I will strike a bargain with you, brother.'

"I saw in his sad smile that he knew how the phrase pained me, for it called up the last time he had given me his word. 'I will not disappoint you, Sherlock,' he said with a sigh of resignation. 'If you will be so good as to be one of the party tomorrow night, I promise that I will ask no more.'

"'All right.'

"Dr. Charlton Fox was an intelligent gentleman of middle age, with the ruddy complexion of a man who had made his living in the open air. He was a learned and interesting fellow who had traveled throughout the world, and his tales of his adventures were rendered in such a witty and engaging manner that I did not once regret having accepted Mycroft's invitation.

It was when Mycroft rose to hunt up a bottle of port that Dr. Fox remarked, 'I am so grateful to your brother for assisting me in some small matters of business, as I must leave London the day after tomorrow, and in less than a week, I leave England for a year.'

"'Where do you go?'

"'New Zealand. I am to be superintending surgeon upon a fine barque that sails from Plymouth on the twenty-ninth. I been a ship's surgeon for so long that I do not believe I could perform an operation if the floor were steady under my feet.'

"'Is it a cargo vessel?'

"'No. Government emigrants. I will have to review the certificates for bodily health, as these excursions can be quite arduous, particularly on the women and children. Those who are fortunate as to have a state cabin fare better, but steerage can be rough for those who are used to even the modest quarters of a cottage.'

"'They are paupers, I imagine?'

"'Only a very few. Most are laboring or farming families, or merchants and tradesmen who may be on the decline into poverty and want to make a clean break and get a fresh start. A few are young rogues who mean to escape their creditors, or gentlemen who have been given a government appointment. And there are the women who go as teachers or governesses or who are to be reunited with husbands and fathers who have already settled.'

"'And have you sailed this vessel before?'

"'No, but I have heard that she is a fine, iron barque, nine hundred tons, and it is said that there is not a vessel more fit for such a difficult voyage as the Earl Granville.'

"'I beg your pardon? Did you say the *Earl Granville*?'

"'Yes. Have you heard of her?'

"I could only shake my head.

"Mycroft returned with the port and filled our glasses. 'Now, what shall we drink a toast to? To your journey, Fox? What is that old saying, 'Journeys end in lovers' meeting?' Shall we drink to that?'"

CHAPTER FORTY-EIGHT

"As the night was a cold one, the good doctor and I shared a cab, stopping first at his hotel. I took this brief opportunity to discuss his proposed journey.

'There is a great deal of business to be concluded before one embarks,' he said. 'Emigrants must provide certificates of birth and baptism and letters of good character, and pledges to abide by the rules of the ship. It is no simple matter to leave one's homeland and go halfway 'round the world.'

"'It must be difficult for people who have lived their lives as farmers and tradesmen to be confined to a ship for so many months.'

"'Yes, it is hard, but for the women, I think it is harder to bear those days in town before they sail, for Plymouth is a rambunctious sort of place, and the decent woman who ventures out to buy some additional provisions before embarking may wish that she had done without, and she may have trouble finding lodgings, for there are many available, but very few where you would like to see a sister of yours spend her days.'

"'The local parishes assist them, I suppose?'

"'Yes, and the shipping offices will post the addresses where a berth may be found, but you know how it is, when there is something desirable and in short supply, the price will be driven up.'

"The doctor offered his hand as the hansom drew up to his hotel, and I was never to see him again. It is a sad footnote to this narrative that there was an outbreak of fever on the voyage, and the doctor perished before they reached their destination.

"I was on the train from Paddington the following afternoon, and within a matter of hours, I was in Plymouth. From the railway station at Plymouth, I emerged into a labyrinth of narrow and crowded streets. It is an irony that while there is no more hale and hearty life than that of a British seaman, the communities devoted to his provisioning and leisure are drab and often unwholesome places.

"Though dreary in appearance, the streets were teeming with activity, for the local population had swelled in the past decade, and was busily provisioning some four hundred emigrants and crew who were preparing to sail. One could not avoid noticing that there were two or three women to a man, for most husbands and sweethearts were at sea.

"I asked the porter to direct me to a comfortable inn, and a rambling tram ride got me to the Rose and Crown, where a little chamber on the ground floor behind the tavern was made available, the rooms above having all been taken by those awaiting embarkation, or for other purposes which do not bear mentioning.

"A tour of the shipping offices was next, and this made for a lively afternoon. There is a great deal of last-minute provisioning to be done when some four hundred people are to be taken halfway 'round the world, goods to be assembled, papers to be put in order, small comforts such as an additional blanket or waterproof or a tin of biscuits for the children to be purchased. As I recall, some noted agitators were in town at the time, lecturing on indecency or intemperance or one of the other ills that befalls a seaman's retreat. Directing all good folk to where these rations or comforts or discourses were to be found was not solely left to the thriving daily papers. Public surfaces, from the railway station to the docks, were posted over with bills advertising merchandise, cheap lodgings, entertainment and directions to the various warehouses, shipping companies, public baths and recreation grounds.

"I perused these bills and then the passenger lists, searching for familiar names, whether Craden or MacInnes, Ernest or Moriarty, yet there was only one surname that I recognized: my own.

"'Holmes,' of course, is not an uncommon name, but there was an additional peculiarity about this Holmes, for it was a matron traveling with children. There was no male heading up the family party – it consisted of a Mrs. Mary Holmes, age thirty-five, and her four children, William, age eighteen; Henrietta, age seven; and twin sons, Henry and Timothy, age four. The lady, I concluded, was Mrs. Stewart and the lad posing as her elder son was some poor emigrant who had been paid to give them the look of a family group, and to help tend the children until they arranged to rendezvous with Moriarty.

"I felt all the thrill of discovery, Watson, yet none of the joy of success – I had come upon the conspiracy too late for that.

"My immediate thought, of course, was to call in the magistrate. Yet what had I, but an instinct, a theory and a preposterous tale? I must find proof. If I saw that Henrietta, Henry and Timothy Holmes were indeed Rose, Amon and James Moriarty, I could tell a tale that would be persuasive enough to have their party detained and their identities confirmed.

"Orders had been posted that Mary Holmes's mail should be forwarded to The Wards at Stoke Damerel. I asked of the young lady at the counter – for many of the businesses were tended by women in a place where most of the men were engaged in seafaring occupations – for directions to this place.

"'Aye, the Stokes,' she nodded, 'it was a fine piece of property, though the title has gone, and the lands have been used for public buildings and grounds. The Wards had been the old lunatic asylum, though now its rooms were let to the pilgrims what pass through and cannot bear the commotion of Union Street.'

"I followed the girl's directions to a manor that dated back some centuries. There was a stone carriage house up against the road and the remains of an ornate wrought-iron gate. The manor house appeared to be unoccupied, but there were a number of refurbished out buildings which served as workhouses, stables and dairy, with a low-eaved, stone structure which had evidently been the asylum and now supplied much-needed temporary lodgings. On the far side of this building was an area of greenery and a flat-roofed structure that I concluded was a boathouse, as I could hear the lapping of water beyond.

"The Wards provided clean, if Spartan, accommodations. Corridors extended outward from a sunny sitting area at the center. Its windows overlooked a sort of courtyard, and this arrangement allowed several rustic, ruddy-cheeked matrons to knit and mend in good light while watching the children at play. There were about a dozen of the little ones, frolicking around a decaying fountain, with an energy that seemed to anticipate a confinement of three or four months.

"I nodded to these ladies and passed out of the room into the courtyard and immediately spied a little girl who sat at the base of the fountain, reading from the book on her lap to the two little boys who sat at her feet.

"Watson, there could be no mistaking them. They were the children I had seen in Miss Turner's sitting room many months ago. I was struck with both an overwhelming sense of relief that they were alive and horror at the depravity of the plot against Miss Turner. With the wonderful resilience of children, they seemed completely oblivious to the loss of their mother, and the changes that had been wrought. As I paused to consider what would become of them after their situation was communicated to the police, I heard a gentle voice call out, 'Children, you must come in and have your tea.' Watson, it was Mrs. Stewart.

"The girl tucked her book under her arm and took each brother by the hand.

"'Auntie, see how that strange man looks at us,' the girl declared. Evidently, she had her mother's keen powers of observation, for she had seen me, though I had kept well to the shadows.

"The lady looked up and her eyes met mine. I saw only a momentary shock, which she quickly mastered. 'Children, go in, I shall come directly,' she said, and waited for them to go into the building before she approached me.

"Before I could speak, she said, 'Who knows that you are here?'

"'No one.'

"'Swear to it.'

"'No one. You have my word.'

"'Wait here, then. I will be only a moment. I beg you, sir, do as I ask, for the children's sake.'

"She hurried back into the building and I laid my hand upon the revolver in the pocket of my overcoat, and waited for Moriarty to appear.

"After a few moments, I heard a light footfall upon the path, and a slender youth in a tweed suit and cloth cap passed under the lintel. 'I must compliment you. Your game has improved considerably since our last match.'

"It was Violet Turner."

CHAPTER FORTY-NINE

Holmes surveyed my stunned expression with a twinkling eye. "I daresay, my expression was quite as dumbfounded as your own, Watson. In her suit of clothes and cloth cap, with her magnificent hair cut quite short, she might be taken for a lad in his teens.

"'Come,' she said, slipping her arm through mine. 'There is a secluded little path which leads down to the boathouse. We can talk there.'

"We began to walk along a narrow and overgrown foot-path that ended in a dilapidated wooden structure.

"'I don't know whether I ought to feel angry or humiliated that I was so ill-used,'

"'If you would prefer that I had been hanged, at least be glad that my children are alive.'

"'I *saw* you hanged.'

"'It doesn't matter what you saw, Mr. Holmes, or what you only thought you saw. All that matters is what you intend to do about it.'

"'You obviously perpetrated a monstrous deception on all of London. Tell me how it was done, and I will decide what I mean to do about it.'

"The lady was silent for a few minutes. 'You said once, Mr. Holmes, that you always knew when you had pleased your father. It is an instinct of dogs and children, to please those upon whom their survival depends. I was

James' prize dog, I would have performed in any way that pleased him, and seven years, I asked only one favor in return.'

"'That he take care of your mother.'

"'Yes. That one kindness would have earned him my loyalty, a loyalty that he could not have purchased at any price. When he refused, and then had her sent away to die a broken woman, my heart was hardened beyond all possibility of reconciliation. Oh, I suffered his tutelage and his gifts and his odious affection, but not a day passed when escape – and revenge – was not uppermost in my thoughts, and even my dreams. And then,' she sighed, 'barely fifteen, I was a mother myself, with an infant girl whose survival was entirely dependent upon me, and with no friend or ally or confidante in all the world. I had only one possession that had not been given to me by James, and that was not known to him: a name. Aiden Brodie. If my mother's ravings had any truth to them, he was my grandfather. And yet, even so, she'd said he lived in London. He may as well have lived on the moon.'

"'But then Moriarty left Oxford for London.'

"'Yes. When Rose was born, there were some unpleasant whispers about our situation, and when I was again *enciente*, James's reputation began to suffer, and he decided to settle in London. Attitudes are different in town, you see. There, impropriety is nothing, so long as you are not uncouth, boring or poor, where the *haute monde* is always ready to make a place at the table for brilliance and culture – so few of them have either, and James has both and to a degree not often seen. Never seen, I daresay. My sons were born in town and my convalescence was a prolonged one. When my strength began to return, I asked James' leave to take some exercise, to visit museums, attend lectures, to return to my music and studies, and he gave his permission because he believed that such activities would hasten my return to health – he hoped for more children, you see. Of course, I was to give a strict account of how I had passed my time.'

"'And, of course, he had your children as hostages should you ever take your liberty too far.'

"'Yes.'

"'And when you believed that it was safe to do so, you sought out Mr. Brodie.

"She nodded. 'I wanted nothing from him, I wanted only to satisfy my curiosity, to see what sort of man he was. He had cut my mother out of his life, his own daughter, and I had expected him to be like my own father, or like James, and was prepared to hate him. But when I walked into his shop that day...' She stopped and turned her face away, nearer tears than I had ever seen her. After a moment, she composed herself. 'He knew me at once, of course – poor man, what a shock I gave him. He spoke of the many attempts he had made to find my mother some years earlier, and I told him that my mother had known nothing of them.'

"'Mr. Brodie believes that they were thwarted by Turner.'

"'I daresay they were, and I know that my father had sworn to James that I had no relations at all. When I told Mr.

354

Brodie this, he was angry, but he was also shrewd enough to see that, if we were patient and alert, we might find some way to use James' ignorance of our connection to my advantage. For the present, it was enough to know that we – my children and I – were not alone in the world, that we had a relative and an ally. I went home with a few rare scientific volumes and some excellent sheet music, and told James that I'd found them at a curious old book shop on Old Compton Road, and what luck it was to have happened upon the place just when I'd begun to feel well enough to resume studies that had lagged during my convalescence. Of course, James made a point of visiting the shop, but I later learned that Mr. Brodie treated him to a wonderful performance, played the addled old eccentric to the hilt.'

"'And so, Moriarty encouraged the return to your studies, but not solely for your sake, I think. I daresay, he took great pride in parading before the *haute monde*, what his brilliance and intellect had produced.'

"'One cannot make bricks without clay,' she said, with a smile.

"'Yet, the *haute monde* didn't see the clay, did they? They didn't see the block of marble, only the Galatea, exhibited at theatres and supper parties. At the Stokers, for example, when I rather inconveniently interrupted your *tête-à-tête* with Craden. How did he come into the picture? Was there any truth to his testimony?'

"'Just enough,' she replied. 'In town, one could not avoid tales of the infamous Lord Craden, and on the strength of their Oxford connection and membership in the same clubs and mutual intolerance of fools, James and Henry became acquainted, and as we moved in the same circuit, it was inevitable that we should meet. When we were introduced, he was clearly taken with my appearance. Shocked.'

"'Because you so strongly resembled your mother.'

"'Yes.'

"'He began to pursue you.'

"'Yes, though not entirely as you think, Mr. Holmes. Oh, he did love me, I cannot deny that, but his pursuit might more accurately be called a crusade. Henry has a chivalrous streak, a passionate drive to stand up for the weak and make right what has been wronged. It is the sort of drive that will be the death of him, I am afraid.'

"I thought of Wiggins and Mrs. Skinner and the scarred girl, Laurel. 'And he embarked upon a crusade to rescue you from Moriarty.'

"'And my children. I know what he said in the courtroom, but he never asked me to abandon my children. But his crusade had a serious drawback.'

"'His vices.'

"'His hubris. Henry believed that if we left James, and accepted his protection, that a mere army tutor could do nothing to retaliate against the son and heir of Lord Warrington. He persisted in thinking of James as a mere hindrance, but never a threat, and nothing I said could convince him otherwise.'

"'Mr. Brodie once said that you only know what a man is when you know what he will not do, and that Moriarty would stop at nothing.'

"'He assumed that I must change my mind when James said he was taking the children away to the Continent. At our customary rendezvous...'

"'Mr. Brodie's.

"'Yes. We had a bitter argument. Again, I told Henry that the children and I were James' prisoners, and would be so until he chose to set us free, and that if we attempted to escape him, he would hunt us down even to the grave! Mr. Brodie overheard that remark and came into the room with a light in his eye, that wily, calculating light that I had often seen across his chessboard, and said, "But he could not hunt you beyond the grave, now, can he?"'

'I understood him immediately. It was one of those moments of utter clarity, when you see the endgame.'

"'And then it is only a matter of calculating each move, every variable toward that endgame as though your life depended upon it.'

"She nodded. 'We could be free of him if he believed that we were dead. But, of course, there would need to be remains, remains that might be taken for us, to convince James, and a public inquiry, of our death. What manner of death would offer that? Fire or water. One is lost at sea, only to wash ashore some time after, or one is burnt beyond recognition. The sea was not possible. James would not allow me to take the children rowing on the Serpentine, let alone a sea voyage, and so we must die by fire.'

"'A very fragile plan, Miss Turner.'

"'Say, rather, that there were a great many details necessary to its success.'

"'Principal among them would be securing those remains that were to be taken for your children. I daresay Craden enlisted Mrs. Skinner, who nursed the poor, to inform him when there were eligible candidates, and Evans, the carter, got them to Paradise Walk, and carried your children away, and his young forger produced the papers you would need for travel. And those errands that you performed before the fire. The violin did reach its destination – I thank you very much! – and as for the children's clothing, it was not taken to a rag fair, but set aside for the journey. And then there was the matter of Craden's bizarre conduct at the morgue – he did not go there to purchase some morbid keepsakes, but to remove evidence of anatomical dissimilarities that might have raised questions about the true identity of the deceased.'

"'The Radley girl had a misshapen jawbone and the Vye boy's ankle had been broken and badly set.'

"'But Craden and his minions were not the only collaborators. You had the advantage of a more rational accomplice in Mrs. Stewart. Your daughter addresses her as 'Auntie.' She is Mr. Brodie's younger daughter.'

"'Yes. Mr. Brodie wondered whether I might cultivate an ally in the household, but I knew that wasn't possible. Hudson, Moran, Miss Allen, were entirely loyal to James, and Mrs. Hudson was a decent, honorable sort, but intrigue was not in her nature. "Then we must install one," he said, and offered to approach his widowed daughter to replace either the housekeeper or the nurse. I did not want to let go of Mrs. Hudson – she was the only one of the household who showed me any kindness – but I thought Miss Allen might give notice for a price. Henry managed that, and congratulated himself that it had cost him only two hundred pounds, less than he was known to lose at cards.'

"'I imagine that it was no easy task to act the go-between while persuading Moriarty of her loyalty. And on the night of the fire, it was she who saw to it that Moran was so exhausted – drugged, I have no doubt – that she fell asleep in her chair, and did not wake until you rang for her – well after your children had been carried away and the remains of three surrogates had been placed in their beds. But, tell me, Miss Turner, when you spoke just now of your plans, you implied that all of you would be taken for dead, 'there would need to be remains, remains that might be taken for us' were your very words. Yet, you did not have Craden's accomplices hunt up the remains of a young woman who might be taken for you. Instead, you chose to suffer the indignity and perils of a trial? Why not escape immediately? Why prolong the charade? You would have had far fewer variables to account for and provide against.'

"'*You*, Mr. Holmes,' were the only variable that I did not account for and needed to provide against,' she continued, with a look of mock sternness, 'Our scheme would not bear a postponement, for James meant to take the children out of the country in a matter of weeks. And yet, only hours before the fire, Henry found you lurking 'round

Paradise Walk, and hours after, you appear with the coroner's investigator. And then, to go so far as to persuade your brother to have my sentence commuted, after I had gone to such lengths to lay down incriminating evidence and conduct myself in such a shocking and heartless fashion so that I would hang. What a great mercy that you told Henry what you had done. He went straight to your brother and confided all, and your brother – dear man! – threw in his lot with us, and at the cost of some discord with you, I understand.'

"'And Cummings – was he also party to the scheme?'

"'No. A conviction was certain – we wanted only someone who would offer up a persuasive defense. And he was an honorable man. He would never have agreed to take part in a scheme that required witnesses – Mrs. Stewart and Henry – to perjure themselves.'

"'But MacInnes did agree to take part in the scheme, and he was also an honorable man.'

"She nodded. 'Mr. Brodie told me that you had a taste for the annals of crime. Do you recall the matter of Priscilla Biggadike?'

"'She was hanged as a poisoner ten years ago. There was some question, I believe, as to whether she was truly guilty.'

"'Considerable question. It was Mr. MacInnes' predecessor who carried out the hanging, but Mr. MacInnes was there as his apprentice. The poor woman had refused all pleas from her family and the chaplain to make her confession and protested her innocence until the end and.

The hanging was badly done, and her death was a prolonged and gruesome spectacle. Afterward, evidence came forth that might have saved her had it been discovered sooner. Mr. MacInnes never forgot it. It has preyed upon his mind for the last ten years.'

"'And so, he saw an opportunity to make amends by allowing one whom he knew had been wrongly convicted to go free. And yet, Miss Turner – I saw you hanged.'

"'You saw an illusion, Mr. Holmes. Mr. MacInnes had adapted a harness he had developed for lifting livestock – you smile, Mr. Holmes! – which might be concealed under my dress. The hangman is entirely trusted, and never searched as he passes in and out of the prison, and he is the only one permitted some privacy with the condemned, whom he must visit beforehand to calculate height and weight in order to determine the drop. When he came to my cell, he brought this harness with him. The device was no worse than a corset, and well camouflaged by the fullness of my gown and the bulk of the pinions. The harness had a pair of metal rings just below the neck of my gown, and these were concealed by my hair and the collar, and by the fold of the hood.'

"I recalled MacInnes' words. *The apparatus has been fitted up and should be ready within a week – no more than two – but there are some small adjustments which cannot be made until the last.'*

"'And so, the rope was anchored to these rings, and when you were dropped, the harness supported your weight – still, there must have been some discomfort in the process.'

"'Mr. MacInnes had brought me a strong dose of valerian when he came to my cell to fasten the pinions and I felt its effects even as I was being walked up to the scaffold. I felt the jolt of the harness when he pulled the lever, but well before I was taken down, I was quite senseless. Mr. MacInnes also saw to it that Doctor Knowles and the plasterer had been treated to some excellent brandy before their services were required; the one pronounced me dead, and the other took me for dead when he made up the death mask. I woke up in a coffin rattling its way to a private burial ground, where I was liberated by Henry and spirited off to a hideaway he had prepared in Gravesend. There I was reunited with my children, and there we laid low these many months. That was the hardest, the waiting. I believed we had anticipated every variable, yet even though James had left England, I could never know whether we were truly free...'

"'Or only feeling the full measure of agonized suspense before the Professor exacted his revenge. And you felt no scruple about plundering the graves of three pauper children?'

"'None. Their souls were in heaven, while on earth, my children faced a life as James' little human laboratories. It may have been criminal, Mr. Holmes, but I am convinced that it was morally justifiable. There only remained the question of risk, and *that* is nothing to a mother when her children's lives are at stake.'

"I thought of the words of Madam Sun's words: *'There is nothing in the world as powerful as the love of a mother for a child.'* 'And the insurance policies – Mr. Brodie did not know that you named him as the beneficiary – *that* bit of larceny cannot be morally justifiable.'

"'Perhaps not. But it is a very distinct touch all the same,' she said with a smile and a shrug. 'And I think that Mr. Brodie will make better use of it than the insurance company would.'

"'But you did still have not answered one question, Miss Turner. Since you had no scruples in robbing a grave, why not secure remains which might be taken for you, so that you and your children might escape together?'

'What is your theory?'

'I think it is as you said before – you hated him. You had cause enough, to be sure, and you wanted to witness the utter despair he must feel upon losing all that was most precious to him. To make him suffer as he had done to you.'

"She looked at me with a cold determination that one does not often see in the eyes of a woman. 'That, I could never accomplish, Mr. Holmes. What I did could not avenge all that I had endured in seven years of living with James. But it will have to suffice. And I have my freedom and my children. Now, Mr. Holmes,' she said, gravely, 'you must tell me what you mean to do.'

"We heard the patter of steps and turned to see the little girl, who confronted me with bold suspicion. 'Are you coming in to tea?'

"She did not address Miss Turner as a daughter would a mother. She had been well coached in how they were to conduct themselves under the aliases they had assumed.

"'Come here,' her mother said.

"The little girl approached, warily.

"'This is Mr. Holmes. He is a very good friend of mine and has come to bid me farewell.'

"'That is our name,' the girl said, extending her hand to me. 'I am Henrietta Holmes.'

"'And I am Sherlock Holmes,' I replied.

"She grimaced. "'Sherlock' is quite as bad as 'Henrietta.'"

"'Yes,' I agreed, 'But I am too old to change it. In your case, however, there is still time for an alteration. If you could choose any name for your own, what would it be?'

"She had her answer ready. 'Eden,' she replied. 'It is said to be the most beautiful place that ever was.'

"'Then I cannot think of a more fitting name for you, Miss Holmes, than Eden Henrietta.'"

CHAPTER FIFTY

"And that is how the striking young woman with me today came by her name.

"I remained in Plymouth for three more days until the Earl Granville sailed. And I am afraid, my good Boswell, that what occurred over the course of those three days must be held back from your commendable accounts of my career.

"After I saw the party off on their journey, I went back to the Rose and Crown to gather my belongings and prepare my return to London. When I arrived at the inn, I was informed that a man was waiting for me in my room.

"You can imagine my anxiety, Watson. If I had been tracked to Plymouth, I might well have delivered Miss Turner to the enemy. I approached the door to my room with some caution, and opened it soundlessly.

"The disheveled and wretched creature sitting in the one chair was Lord Craden. He was a sorry sight, Watson. In the time since our last meeting, a great deal of gray had lightened his black hair and his eyes were set deeply in dark sockets. He had aged two decades in six months.

"'So, she's gone now, I expect,' he said to me. 'I ought to have killed Moriarty. It's a mistake, Holmes, leaving him alive.'

"'You would have faced a death sentence.'

"'I am facing one now.' His haunted eyes confronted me. 'She told you all, I expect. How it was managed with the children. It was why I went to Paradise Walk that night, to tell Mrs. Stewart that she needed to see to it that Moran was put out of the way for a few hours, because we had got the three – Damn you, Holmes! You nearly ruined everything. You need not mourn for those little ones who were used. Moriarty saw to it that they were given fine burials.'

"'And the stones placed upon the burial sites at the Bow?'

"'My conscience would not allow me to do less, after plundering their graves like a resurrectionist.'

"'And, of course, there is a lot of shifting around of burial sites because there is never enough room for the dead. It is likely that one day, those crude coffins will be brought up to be moved. And if they should fall open and found to be empty, questions will be asked. The only clue will be those fine stone markers, and so those questions will be put to the stone mason, who will recall that they had been ordered by a fellow named Ernest.'

"'You are wrong, Holmes! There is always room for the dead! Ha ha!'

"'Craden, you're ill. Let me take you back to London and get you to someone who can help you.'

"'You want to help me, Holmes? You'll take that revolver that you carry in your coat pocket and you'll put it to my head.'

"I will dwell on the state of his misery no further, Watson. I did get him to London, where he was placed in a sanatorium, but he did not stay there, and a month later, when he could find no one to put a gun to his head, he did it himself and so ended his unhappy life."

"And what became of the other principals?" I asked, after many moment's silence.

"Miss Turner and her party arrived safely in New Zealand and a regular, if covert correspondence began. Living by my wits began to produce a bit of income, and as my needs were few, and I was fortunate enough to find a good fellow to share the expense of my lodgings, I was able to arrange for something to go toward the children's maintenance and education. They remained in New Zealand for seven years, until circumstances compelled them to re-settle in the eastern United States."

"Why?"

"After the trial, Moriarty had asked Mrs. Stewart to accompany him to the Continent as his secretary. She had agreed to take the post, but asked if she might remain in town to settle some affairs, and then join him in a few months. She did not join him, of course, and he made some attempts to find her, but Craden had the whole party well-hidden. I daresay, Moriarty would have let the matter pass, but as Craden had observed, pauper graves are always shifted 'round, and some years later, when three small coffins were brought up and found to be empty, the press gave considerable ink to the matter. Well, scandal does sell pulp. Perhaps Moriarty began to think of the funeral arrangements that had been made for the three charred cadavers of his children, and who had aided him, and whether the remains had indeed been his children, or if some 'shifting about' had taken place. Moriarty began to wonder whether she might have played a role in some sort of deception."

"What did he do?"

"I have few facts, and as much speculation, but it seems he sought out the woman – Mrs. Allen – whose abrupt resignation had brought Mrs. Stewart into his household. It was no difficult task to find her whereabouts, as she had placed her name with several agencies. I daresay it cost Moriarty little more to have a peek at their ledgers than it had cost me to bribe my way into the mortuary. Within her files, he no doubt came upon an excellent letter of reference from Lord Craden. This, Moriarty would have found peculiar, since Craden hadn't known Mrs. Allen at all, and naturally the Professor might begin to wonder whether Craden had deliberately brought about Mrs. Allen's resignation in order to install a collaborator in his household.

"Moriarty immediately set out to find Mrs. Stewart. He had no idea where she might be found, and assumed that she must be living under an alias. Recalling that she had once been employed at St. Andrew's Collegiate School, he arranged to have a report published about the crippling accident suffered by the headmistress of a school for young ladies at Lauder, giving her name as one of Mrs. Stewart's former colleagues at St. Andrew's. The false report stated that the accident had placed the unhappy lady in danger of losing her establishment – they laid it on thick, Watson – and it was just the sort of report that finds its way into all of the papers at home and abroad, those most widely read and therefore most likely to fall into Mrs. Stewart's hands."

Holmes sighed, grimly. "I believe I may have read the report, but the subject's name meant nothing to me, and I made no connection between her and Mrs. Stewart. The report must have reached that lady, and I daresay she resolved to come to her dear friend's aid. For my part, I learned nothing of the matter until I read of the shocking murder of Mrs. Veronica Stewart at Lauder. Immediately, I got word to Miss Turner – we had carried on a very judicious and clandestine correspondence – insisting that she take herself and her children away immediately, and arranged for her to emigrate once more, this time to the eastern part of the United States, where an old associate of mine, Hargreave of the New York Police Department, saw to her protection."

"And what became of her?"

"I think you know what became of her, Watson. Are you not an avid reader of the detective novels of Henry Escott?"

"What? You do not mean that Henry Escott is a woman!"

"As this occupation left her without need for any financial assistance, my role gradually became that of correspondent and distant friend."

For some moments, I reflected upon Holmes' strange tale. "Not so distant, I think."

Holmes raised his brows. "Why, Watson, what do you mean?"

"I mean that after Moriarty's death, there is a period of your life that you were three years in anonymity and exile – an exile that you have accounted for in a most implausible manner. I mean that ten years ago, Persia would have been an inhospitable place for an Englishman, and I have never heard of a Norwegian explorer named Sigerson. I mean that if you wanted to elude Moriarty's surviving associates, you would not have gone East, a region with which Moran and his agents were quite familiar, you would have gone West."

Holmes leaned back in his chair, his gaze drifting toward the pock-marked V R once again. "Good old Watson," he said.

EPILOGUE

And so, what ought I to do with this remarkable tale? Three times I have held these papers to the fire and three times I have drawn them back again. Shall I preserve the past, or shall I destroy it forever?

The fire has gone out now, and I will have to kindle it once more if I want to destroy this testament.

I will do it tomorrow.

THE END

NOTES ON THE TEXT

PROLOGUE:

Pg 1: "*...in the vicinity of Charing Cross...*" In *The Problem of Thor Bridge*, Watson tells us: "Somewhere in the vaults of Cox and Co., at Charing Cross, there is a travel-worn and battered tin dispatch-box with my name, John H. Watson, M.D., Late Indian Army, painted upon the lid. It is crammed with papers, nearly all of which are records of cases to illustrate the curious problems which Mr. Sherlock Holmes had at various times to examine."

CHAPTER ONE:

1. "*...a first class passage to Aix-les-Bains..*" A spa resort in eastern France, renowned for its thermal baths and water cures, frequented by sufferers of rheumatism, arthritis, dyspepsia, gout and the like.

2. "*I am lost without the old Horatio.*" Holmes alludes to the intimate friend and confidante of Hamlet.

3. "*whistled sharply...four wheeler...*" This was one of two types of cabs; the four-wheeler, or "growler, and the two-wheeled vehicle, the *hansom*. The fact that the lady whistled once suggests that she summoned a four-wheeler; the custom was to whistle once (often pedestrians carried cab whistles for this purpose) for a four-wheeler and twice for a hansom.

CHAPTER TWO:

1. *"Stamford...Bart's"*. Stamford, the mutual acquaintance who introduced Watson to Holmes. St. Bartholomew's Hospital was commonly called "Bart's".

2. '*...Montague Street...*" In *The Musgrave Ritual*, Holmes tells Watson, "When I first came up to London I had rooms in Montague Street, just round the corner from the British Museum."

3. *King's College*. Likely Holmes means King's College Hospital. During the Victorian era, King's College made higher education available to the under-classes and to women.

4. *...she goes only to the carrion hunter...*' 'Carrion hunter' was slang for an undertaker.

5. "Christison's *Treatise on Poisons* and a very rare volume of Nicholas Culpeper's *The English Physitian*": Sir Robert Christison's *A Treatise on Poisons* was published in 1829; he argued for the application of toxicology to jurisprudence as well as medicine. Culpeper, whose book was published in the mid-1600s was an early proponent of herbal medicine.

6, '*The story of the Roman officer who does not need to see his commands carried out. "Do it," he says, and it's done.*' See Matthew 8:5-13.

7. *Executioner*. Does Watson deliberately misidentify "Marwood Laird MacInnes? "MacInnes does bear some striking similarities to William Marwood, who served as executioner from 1874 until 1883. Marwood, like MacInnes, was a cobbler. He was the developer of the "long drop".

CHAPTER THREE:

1. *"One cannot make bricks without clay."* Compare this to Holmes' "I can't make bricks without clay!" in the course of another "Violet" case, that of Violet Hunter and *The Copper Beeches.*

2. *"Lady Lilith...Rossetti".* Holmes refers to an early work of Rossetti. In mythology, Lilith is Adam's first wife, banished from Eden; also, a temptress, a she-demon and killer of children.

3. *Grosvenor '77.* The Grosvenor Gallery, London, which opened in May, 1877.

4. *"Stradivari di Cremona"* – Antonio Stradivari, who designed and produced musical instruments, principally violins, from his shop in Cremona, Italy in the late 17th and early 18th century.

5. *"Miss Violet Turner..."* This may have been the first of Holmes' "Violets"; he appears to take a particular interest in cases that involved a lady with that name.

6. *"I saw you, Mr. Holmes at the Wagner Festival last year."* A series of concerts given at the Royal Albert Hall in May, 1877.

7. *"...army tutor..."* An army tutor, or army coach, prepared students for military examinations.

CHAPTER FOUR:

1. *He bought her. Paid five pounds for her...* At this time, the age of consent in England was 13. It was raised to 16 in 1885 following the exploits of sensational journalist William T. Stead, who, as part of his exposé of the sex trafficking of

young girls, bought 13-year-old Eliza Armstrong for five pounds.

2. Violet Rose...V R...In *The Musgrave Ritual*, Watson writes: "Holmes in one of his queer humors would sit in an armchair, with his hair-trigger and a hundred Boxer cartridges, and proceed to adorn the opposite wall with a patriotic V.R. done in bullet-pocks..."

3. *She had attracted the notice of Rossetti and his set...* The Pre-Raphaelites, a loose confederation of painters and poets, formed in 1848. A number of the paintings were red-haired women.

4. *Rumors of the manner in which Moriarty acquired the girl...made it uncomfortable for him to remain in Oxfordshire.* In *The Final Problem,* Holmes relates: "Dark rumours gathered round [Moriarty] in the university town, and eventually he was compelled to resign his Chair and to come down to London..."

CHAPTER FIVE:

1. *"I left Brodie's with a copy of Winwood Reade's The Martyrdom of Man."* Was it Brodie who introduced Reade to Holmes? In *The Sign of Four*, Holmes recommends Winwood Reade's *Martyrdom of Man* to Watson.

2. *"Hamlet! Henry Irving! A box!"* This establishes the date as 30 Dec. 1878, when Henry Irving and Ellen Terry performed in *Hamlet* at the Lyceum. Irving was also the theatre manager.

3. *The Stokers...The one who had a flirtation with that fellow Wilde some time ago.* Bram Stoker, author of *Dracula*, was

the Lyceum's business manager. His new wife, Florence, *nee* Balcombe, had indeed, been courted by Oscar Wilde.

4. *Whistler, Alfred Kempe, The Hunts and their daughter, Francis Buckland, who is said to be an interesting fellow.'*

'Until the household pets disappear."

"Whistler" was, of course, James Whistler; Alfred Kempe was a gifted mathematician, musician and barrister; Alfred Hunt was a painter, and his wife Mary, a novelist; the daughter was likely the elder, Isobel Violet, who also became a novelist, and who was also courted by Oscar Wilde. Francis Buckland was a surgeon-turned-naturalist whose dietary ambition was to eat his way through every animal species.

5. *"Sarasate... the Swedish Nightingale"*. Pablo Sarasate was a violinist; Holmes goes to hear Sarasate in the course of *The Red-Headed League*. The Swedish Nightengale was 19th century soprano, Jenny Lind.

6. "Moriarty thinks like an American... If you see something you want, set your price from the outset." In *The Valley of Fear*, Holmes comments on Moriarty's strategy for hiring criminal talent as "...paying for brains...the American business principle."

7. *"...I am sure you have some fond remembrance of the place."* Watson accompanies Mary Morstan and Holmes to a rendezvous at the Lyceum in *The Sign of Four*.

8. *"You may have heard the rumor, Watson, that Miss Terry, overwhelmed by the passionate adulation of the audience, suffered a fit of nerves and fled to the solitude of the Embankment.* It has been reported that Ellen Terry, either

drained by her emotional performance or overwhelmed by a feeling that she had performed badly, fled to the Embankment without taking her curtain call.

9. *Amati*: The Amatis were a family of Italian violin-makers; Nicolo Amati taught his craft to Stradivari, among others.

CHAPTER SIX:

1. "....*colorful custom of the public house inquest*...' Dickens gives a colorful portrait of a coroner's inquest at the Sol's Arms Public House in *Bleak House*, noting that "The coroner frequents more public-houses than any man alive."

2. *Resurrection Reade...*" A "resurrection man" was a body-snatcher, one who stole corpses to sell to medical researchers. The allusion to "dark episodes" suggests that Reade may have been a "resurrectionist" in his youth.

3. "Not the young doctor, Ray Ernest, who seduced the wife of that miserable fellow Josiah Amberley!" An account of Ernest's fate may be found in *The Retired Colourman*.

4. *Heep...*"Heep" alludes to Dickens' Uriah Heep, the toadying antagonist in *David Copperfield*.

CHAPTER SEVEN:

1. "...*Admiral Sinclair.*" An Admiral Sinclair of Barclay Square is mentioned in *The Bruce-Partington Plans.*

2. 'Claude Bernard's *Lecons sur les Effets des Substances Toxiques.*' The complete title was: *Leçons sur les effects des substances toxiques et médicamenteuses,* which discussed the effects of toxins. Bernard was a French playwright and

physician, considered one of the founders of medical research.

3. *"It is an occasion for some good wishes, if I have my dates right."* The date would then be on or near January 6, 1879, Holmes's birthday.

CHAPTER NINE:

1 ... *crawlers* – The most abject, destitute of beggars.

CHAPTER TEN:

1. *"Those were bitter vigils, Watson, for the weather was not my friend..."* Records indicate that the winter of late 1878/early 1879 was among the coldest and snowiest recorded.

2. *"Mary Reade from New York City. She comes with a clear half million dollars, and Sir Joshua has agreed to help her to a title. I think Falkland will take her."* One of many American heiresses who married British nobles, exchanging sizeable dowries for a title in in the mid-19th into the early 20th century. Falkland did, in fact, take her.

CHAPTER ELEVEN:

1. *"Do you know what I see? I see that these stone façades and velvet curtains can muffle a scream as effectively as if it rang out in the middle of a desert."* Contrast Craden's view with Holmes' in *The Copper Beeches:*" ...look at these lonely houses, each in its own fields, filled for the most part with poor ignorant folk who know little of the law. Think of the deeds of hellish cruelty, the hidden wickedness which

may go on, year in, year out, in such places, and none the wiser."

2. The poem Craden quotes is *The Bridge of Sighs*, by Thomas Hood; it describes the body of a woman whom suicide has put "past all dishonor." The bridge is Waterloo Bridge.

3. *...four-in-hand...* His necktie; also the type of knot.

4. *"She is a fair chemist..."* A sort of amateur compounding pharmacist, who concocted medicinals.

CHAPTER FOURTEEN:

1. *"The sottish manservant...Frederick Hudson"* The male Hudsons that appear in the Canon are not a particularly sterling bunch. The most innocuous of the three is Morse Hudson, the shopkeeper who sells the coveted busts in *The Six Napoleons*; there is the Hudson who survives the Gloria Scott explosion and returns to blackmail two escaped convicts and the "Hudson" whose name is recorded in the case of *The Five Orange Pips*, presumably a member of the KKK.

2e. *Frederick and I each are paid a hundred twenty pounds a year'...'above five hundred pounds per annum...'* This was two or three times what a competent manservant and housekeeper would normally command.

3. Miss Serenity Moran..."my uncle is a friend of the Professor's..." No doubt this is Colonel Sebastian Moran.

CHAPTER FIFTEEN:

1. *'...governess to the Merryweather girls. Their father is the chairman of directors of one of th*e principal London banks.' This bank that was the object of John Clay in *The Red-Headed League.'*

CHAPTER SIXTEEN:

1."*It's enough to make a fellow take to burking.*" In the 1820s, William Burke and William Hare suffocated several people in Edinburgh and sold their corpses, primarily to a lecturer in anatomy, Robert Knox. While "burking" refers specifically to the manner in which the victims were killed – smothering and chest compression – it more loosely is used to mean any murder commtted in order to sell cadavers to anatomists, or even grave-robbing.

2. '*...Physic Gardens...*' The Chelsea Physic Garden, a large botanical garden.

3. '*...Wardian cases...*' The precursor of the terrarium, these were enclosed glass cases, named for their inventor, physician and botanist, Dr. Nathaniel Ward.

4. '*Valeriana officinalis.* A flowering herbal plant, the source of valerian. Not to be confused with the other garden heliotrope, or common heliotrope which is a flower.

5. '*...soporific properties. They are often dried and ground and brewed into a sort of tea – valerian tea...*' Valerian, its extracts and its essential oils, have long been used for headaches, insomnia, and sedation.

CHAPTER SEVENTEEN:

1. '...*two gold sovereigns*...' A gold coin with a value of 20 shillings.

2. '...*Claridge's*...'A London hotel. Neil Gibson, the Gold King stayed there in the course of *The Problem of Thor Bridge*, and Holmes was to go there in *His Last Bow*.

CHAPTER EIGHTEEN:

1. "*Captain Shaw of the Metropolitan Fire Brigade*' This would be Captain Eyre Massey Shaw. He served for 30 years with the fire brigade, championed modern fire-fighting innovations, wrote a book on the subject and was a friend of royalty.

CHAPTER TWENTY:

1. "...No better'n a crocus." "Crocus," is slang term for a quack. One has to wonder whether Holmes was giving Dr. Grimsby Roylott a jab when he quips, "I have heard that the crocuses promise well," in *The Speckled Band.*

CHAPTER TWENTY-ONE:

1.'...*theobroma*....' An alkaloid found in tea leaves, coffee and cocoa beans that has stimulant properties.

CHAPTER TWENTY-TWO:

1. '...*Isandlwana and Eshowe*...' The battle of Isandlwana and the siege at Eshowe occurred in early 1879 during the Anglo-Zulu War.

2.'...*the household of Lady Morcar...*' The Countess of Morcar was the possessor of *the* precious stone, the blue carbuncle.

CHAPTER TWENTY FOUR:

1.'...*Robert Hooke's Micrographia, printed two centuries ago....Kircher...Lessing's Laokoon...*' Hooke was a scientist, philosopher and architect whose primary field was microscopy; Kircher was a Jesuit scholar, a "Renaissance man" who was a mathematician, scientist, linguist and historian; Lessing was a literary critic and poet.

2.'...*Leslie Cummings...*' Perhaps the father of the "rising barrister" Joyce Cummings, who appears in *The Problem of Thor Bridge*.

3. "...jail fever..." Epidemic typhus.

4. Charles Bell's *System of Dissections* – Bell was a physician, scientist and illustrator.

CHAPTER TWENTY-FIVE:

1. '...*van Eyck or van der Goes...*' Flemish artists; their subjects often appear pale and elongated.

CHAPTER TWENTY-SIX:

1. '*What say you to The Cheese?...The Cheshire Cheese* public house on Fleet Street. Popular with writers and journalists.

2.'...*Tower Hamlets cemetery...* An East End cemetery, called Bow Cemetery by locals, a large number of the burials were of the poor, who were often buried in communal graves.

3. *'They take a page from Rossetti's book...'* Brodie exaggerates. It was seven years before Rossetti obtained an order of exhumation to retrieve the poems. He was egged on by the art world parasite Charles Augustus Howell, a Machiavellian character who was the inspiration for Conan Doyle's merciless blackmailer Charles Augustus Milverton.

CHAPTER TWENTY-EIGHT:

1. '*...Marlborough and Brooks...*' Brooks was the older of the two, founded in the mid-1700s; it had a reputation for high-stakes card games; the Marlborough was founded in 1869 by the Prince of Wales. All of its original members were personally acquainted with the Prince. It later merged with two other clubs and closed in the mid 20th century.

CHAPTER THIRTY:

1. '...introduced at Arthur Paget's...' Sir Arthur Paget was a military officer, novelist and racehorse owner.

CHAPTER THIRTY-THREE:

1. '*Martha Brixey, Esther Griggs, Emma Lewis, Amelia Snoswell – the Borley case, as well.*' Martha Brixey was not convicted; Emma Lewis was sentenced to Bedlam for killing her newborn; Esther Griggs's child survived and no indictment was brought; Amelia Snoswell slit the throat of her 18-month-old niece, saying afterward, "Now she is happy"; Maria Borley, suffering gross mistreatment by her

husband, drowned her child, and was judged insane and acquitted.

CHAPTER THIRTY-FOUR:

1. '*...puerperal mania...puerperal insanity...childbed melancholia...*' What is now called post-partum depression.
2. '*...alienist...*' A physician who diagnoses and treats insanity, or a physician who was sanctioned by the court to determine mental competence.
3. *Ross Patterson.* Many years later, in *The Final Problem*, Holmes consigns his file on Moriarty to an Inspector Patterson.

CHAPTER THIRTY-FIVE:

1. '*burial club*...funeral club' A form of "friendly society", whereby members paid money into a common fund, and then drew upon it to cover funeral expenses.

CHAPTER THIRTY-SIX:

1. '*...Pink 'Un...*' *The Sporting Times*, a weekly sports periodical, known primarily for its coverage of horse racing. It was printed on pink paper.

CHAPTER THIRTY-NINE:

1. '*He must always visit the condemned to make some measurements and assess their weight so that he may adjust the rope and the knot properly.*' William Marwood made several improvements in his grim profession; there were innovations to the pinions, the type of rope used, the

configuration of the noose and a chart that coordinated the weight of the subject with the length of the drop.

CHAPTER FORTY-THREE:

1. '*...ominous tolling of St. Sepulchre's...*' The Church of the Holy Sepulchre, in the vicinity of Newgate. The bell tolled before an execution.

CHAPTER FORTY-FOUR:

1. '*...Tottenham Court Road...fifty-five shillings...the violin...*' In *The Cardboard Box*, Holmes prevaricates, telling Watson "...how he had purchased his own Stradivarius, which was worth at least five hundred guineas, at a Jew broker's in Tottenham Court Road for fifty-five shillings."

2. '*...the great, unobservant public, who would not know a Stradivari from a spike fiddle...*' Holmes may have recalled this when, in *The Copper Beeches*, he decries '... the great unobservant public, who could hardly tell a weaver by his tooth or a compositor by his left thumb".

CHAPTER FORTY-SIX:

1. '*...there are crimes which have eluded the law and so merit some private justice...*' To disturb a grave or remove a body, other than on the order of a legal authority, was a misdemeanor.

2. '*...bludgers...*' A bludger was a thief armed with a bludgeon; later came to mean a pimp or a slacker.

CHAPTER FORTY-SEVEN:

1. '...the sensational matter of Kate *Webster's crime...*' Webster was a career criminal who brutally murdered and dismembered her employer.

2. '*Dr. Charlton Fox...the Earl Granville...*' Dr. Charlton Fox was the medical officer on the Earl Granville, which sailed from Plymouth on November 29, 1879.

3. '"*Journeys end in lovers' meeting,*'" Holmes delivers (approximately) the same quote – from *Twelfth Night* – upon the apprehension of Colonel Moran (*The Empty House*).

CHAPTER FORTY-EIGHT:

1. "*It was a sad footnote to this narrative that there was an outbreak of fever on the voyage, and the doctor perished...*' Fever, measles and whooping cough broke out in the course of the three-month voyage.

CHAPTER FORTY-NINE:

1. '...the matter of Priscilla Biggadike...' She was hanged for poisoning her husband, the first private hanging of a woman.

2 '*... but I am convinced that it was morally justifiable – to there only remained the question of risk...*' In *Charles Augustus Milverton*, Holmes similarly rationalizes his intention to burgle Milverton's house: "I suppose that you will admit that the action is morally justifiable, though technically criminal...Since it is morally justifiable, I have only to consider the question of personal risk. Surely a

gentleman should not lay much stress upon this when a lady is in most desperate need of his help

CHAPTER FIFTY:

1. '*…I read of the shocking murder of Mrs. Veronica Stewart at Lauder.*' In *The Empty House*, upon apprehending Colonel Moran, Holmes remarks: "You may have some recollection of the death of Mrs. Stewart, of Lauder, in 1887. No? Well, I am sure Moran was at the bottom of it." As Moriarty's agent, perhaps.

2. "*Hargreave of the New York Police Department.*" In *The Dancing Men,* Holmes tells Watson, "I therefore cabled to my friend, Wilson Hargreave, of the New York Police Bureau, who has more than once made use of my knowledge of London crime.

3. *Escott.* When Holmes disguises himself as a plumber to romance Milverton's housemaid in *Charles Augustus Milverton*, he calls himself "Escott". Some theorize that this is derived from his full name William (or Thomas) *Sherlock Scott* Holmes.

.

Milton Keynes UK
Ingram Content Group UK Ltd.
UKHW022142230823
427374UK00011B/761

9 781804 240922